WENDY PERCIVAL's interest in
the time honoured 'box of old d(
became the inspiration behind h
novels: *Blood-Tied*, *The Indelibl*
*Angels*, as well as her novella *Dea*
by SilverWood's "Short Reads" imprint, sBooks) and prequel
novella, *Legacy of Guilt*.

Wendy shares the intriguing, sometimes shocking, discoveries in her own family history on her website blog and has had several articles published in *Shropshire Family History Society's* quarterly journal and in *Family Tree* magazine.

She lives in South West England, in a thatched cottage beside a thirteenth-century church, with her husband and their particularly talkative cat.

You can find out more on her website: wendypercival.co.uk

# The Esme Quentin Mysteries

*Blood-Tied*
*The Indelible Stain*
*The Malice of Angels*

Novellas

*Death of a Cuckoo*
(A SilverWood sBooks "short read")
*Legacy of Guilt*
(An Esme Quentin prequel – FREE to subscribers)

# The Fear of Ravens

## WENDY PERCIVAL

OLD KEY PRESS

Published in 2020 by Old Key Press

Old Key Press
Worlington, Devon, England
www.wendypercival.co.uk/old-key-press

ISBN 978-1-83808-600-8 (paperback)

Page design and typesetting by SilverWood Books
www.silverwoodbooks.co.uk

# THE FEAR OF RAVENS

# Acknowledgements

Thank you to all the people who have helped me during the writing of this novel. My thanks go to Lynn Heiden for allowing me to pick her brains for the Photos Reunited idea in the book and to Lorna Manton for her valuable feedback on the final draft. Thanks also, to Alison Jack on her comprehensive editing and for her eagle-eye on dates and consistency, and to Kath Middleton for another meticulous proofread. And, a big thank you to Helen Hart, Alice van Raalte and the SilverWood team for their expertise and assistance in preparing the print edition.

I must also give huge thanks to all those readers who've got in touch with me to share their enthusiasm for the Esme Quentin books or who've posted reviews. Such small things keep writers motivated when the going gets tough!

And last, but never least, my love and huge appreciation to Brian, both for his fabulous cover design and, as always, for his enduring support throughout the plotting, agonising and writing process.

# 31st October 1995

The chanting began earlier than usual.

She jolted upright, sloshing water over the edge of the bath, dousing candles and drenching the bathroom floor. Three nights of torrential rain had brought her respite and she'd dared to believe they wouldn't come again. How naïve. They'd relish tonight of all nights.

She scrambled out of the tub, grabbing a towel to wrap around her, and glared towards the window. No use in peering out into the darkness trying to see them. She wouldn't give them the satisfaction. Besides, they never came close enough.

Until now.

She swapped the towel for her dressing gown, and stormed out of the bathroom, through the kitchen and into the living room. She'd had enough. This time they'd not have it all their own way. This time she'd go out there and confront the little tykes. She seized the CD player on the shelf beside the fireplace and pressed play, turning up the volume to its maximum setting. Then she ran up to the bedroom.

Upstairs even Black Sabbath wasn't loud enough to deaden the escalating cat-calls from outside. *Witch, witch, witch.* She grabbed her clothes and raced back downstairs, suppressing the fear that was in danger of triumphing if she allowed it a chink of opportunity. Kids, she kept telling herself. Bored kids. Don't let them rile you. Don't let them win.

As she reached the hall, she heard the clatter of the letterbox and she faltered. She laid a finger on the kitchen door and pushed it open. A folded piece of white paper lay menacingly on the mat. What now? More religious ranting? There was something about this that implied more than kids and their warped kicks. She moved towards the door, snatched up the note and retreated.

It had gone quiet outside. She held her breath and listened. Only the sound of the blood pumping in her ears and the hissing of the tall oak behind the cottage, as the wind breathed in and out through its gale-scorched leaves. If they'd finished for the night, she'd got off lightly this time. Perhaps they were getting tired of their perverted games.

She drew herself back against the wall, steeling herself to unfold the paper and wincing as she read the spidery writing.

"*Hate the whore...burn her with fire.*"

What tormented person was this? What had she ever done to them?

Hammer blows began pounding on the door and she clamped her hands over her ears. She backed away, sliding along the wall, her eyes staring; terrified the door would give way under the force. When the letterbox rattled, she screamed.

The acrid stench of burnt flesh polluted the kitchen as a tangle of smouldering fur and feather dropped on to the door mat.

# 1

Esme Quentin first met Sean Carlton three days before his fatal visit to The Kings Arms.

She'd driven into the car park of Torridge Reclamation salvage yard and was climbing out of her Peugeot when a yellow Fiat Coupé sped through the gate and pulled up beside her. The driver unfolded his long limbs and got out of the car, pulling up the collar of his inadequate jacket against the rain. Late thirties, she reckoned. Cropped blond hair emphasised the neatness of his appearance: smart black trousers and fresh white shirt.

'Excuse me,' he called over the roof of his car. 'I'm looking for Temperance Mill. You don't happen to know where it is, by any chance? I was told it was out this way.'

Esme grabbed her duffel coat hood as a gust of wind threatened to snatch it off her head. 'Yes, it is around here, but I'm not sure exactly where.' She glanced across the yard towards the outbuildings on the opposite side. 'My friend will know. I'm just on my way over to see her. You might as well come with me and get out of the rain.'

He nodded. 'OK. Thanks. That'd be good.'

They picked their way past neat rows of bricks, old wooden beams and reclaimed roof tiles lying on the ground towards the stone building on the end of the row. Above the entrance hung a small wooden sign saying, *Ted Henderson, furniture restoration*. Esme pushed at the half-open door and went inside.

The workshop smelled of sawdust and resin. A workbench stood in the centre and woodworking tools of all descriptions hung on a rack above. A small pot-bellied stove squatted in one corner, its black flue towering up through the roof of the corrugated iron building, beside a battered leather armchair.

Maddy Henderson stood by the workbench, her hands on her hips, staring into the distance. She was dressed in jade-green running gear with a white headband, her copper hair gathered tightly in a ponytail.

'Maddy?' Esme said.

Maddy looked up as though she'd just been shaken out of a trance. 'Esme,' she said, shaking her head. 'Sorry. I didn't hear you come in.'

Esme pulled down her hood, rescuing her dislodged hair clasp. She gestured to the man behind her as she fixed the clasp back in place on the top of her head. 'Maddy, this guy's looking for Temperance Mill. That's the name of Anna's place, isn't it?'

'Anna?' the man said, stepping forward. 'Is that Anna Brannock, who owns the reclamation yard?'

Esme shot a cautious glance at Maddy. He seemed very well informed.

Maddy walked towards him. 'Sorry? And you are?'

The man reached inside the pocket of his shirt and pulled out a card which he handed to Maddy. 'Sean Carlton. Private Investigator.' He cocked his head over his shoulder. 'Erm… couldn't help noticing the sign out there. If this is Ted's workshop, I'm guessing you must be his daughter.'

'Yes, that's right, I am.' Maddy swallowed. 'Was.'

Carlton frowned and slowly shook his head. 'Hey, listen. I was gutted to hear about the accident. Sorry I couldn't make the funeral.'

She peered at him. 'You knew Dad?'

'Sure. Have done for years. We were in the force together for a while before I went freelance. In fact, I only saw him recently… I couldn't believe it when I heard. Terrible. Especially knowing how much he loved being in his boat…' He shifted his weight. 'Sorry. I'm not being very tactful. It must still be a bit raw.'

Maddy gave him a weak smile. 'Yes, it is. But that's OK.' She glanced over at Esme. 'I'm still trying to…well, you know…I haven't quite got used to it.'

He nodded. 'Sure. I understand.'

Maddy cleared her throat. 'So what's your interest in Temperance Mill, then?' she asked.

'To be honest, it's Temperance Cottage my enquiry relates to, rather than the mill,' Carlton said, scratching his cheek. 'The name intrigues me, though. Temperance. One of the infamous Bideford Witches, who were executed in the 17th century, was called Temperance, wasn't she? Is that how it got its name? Someone even suggested it was haunted.'

Maddy gave him a sardonic smile. 'I think someone's been having you on. The cottage assumed to be theirs burned down in the 19th century. But that was up in Old Town, not down here near the river. More likely the name's associated with the pledge to stay off the evil drink. You know, The Temperance Movement. There was a Temperance Hotel in Bideford once, I think.'

'Weren't they the last women in England to be hanged for witchcraft?' Esme said.

'Pretty much. There's another woman, Anne Molland, they think was executed 3 years later, in 1685.'

'I really need to get up to speed with the story,' Esme said. 'It's fascinating.' She turned back to the private investigator. 'You were saying it was the cottage you were interested in?'

'Yeah, that's right. Temperance Cottage. I'm trying to trace a Miss Ellen Tucker. She lived there about 24 years ago?'

'Really?' Maddy said. 'I didn't know it was lived in that recently. I always assumed it'd been derelict for years. Like, for ever.'

'So you've never heard of Ellen Tucker?'

'No, sorry.'

Carlton looked at Esme, who shook her head. 'Don't look at me. Can't help you, I'm afraid. I've only recently moved to the area.'

He turned back to Maddy. 'Ever aware of unpleasant things going on down there?'

'What sort of unpleasant things?'

'Strange goings on? Trouble from the locals? Talk of witchcraft?'

She frowned and shook her head. 'No. Nothing like that.' She cleared her throat. 'Look, you're probably right about talking to Anna. She's lived here all her life and would know the mill's history. And the cottage, too. She's out demolishing a wall at the moment, but she should be back in an hour or so. Why don't you call back then?'

'But if this was 24 years ago,' Esme said, 'Anna would have only been about 7 or 8 back then, wouldn't she? Isn't she younger than you, Maddy?'

Maddy nodded. 'Yes, you're right. Of course she would. So she may be no more help than me. But her parents would know. If this...what's her name again?'

'Ellen Tucker.'

'If Ellen Tucker lived in Temperance Cottage, she'd have rented it off them. They live at Hill Farm.' Maddy gestured towards the door. 'I'll show you.' The three of them stood at the threshold as Maddy pointed to the area of rising land beyond the yard. 'It's up that way. Go back up the main road towards Bideford, then first left up the lane there, about a mile or so. Farm's on the right hand side. Can't miss it. Daniel or Marianne Meddon is who you need to speak to.'

'OK. Great. Thanks.'

The sound of an engine eclipsed his reply. They all turned to see a Torridge Reclamation van screech into the car park below and skid to a halt.

'Or you could have a word with Drew,' said Maddy, nodding towards the new arrival. 'Anna's husband. He's local. He might remember. He's a bit older than Anna.'

Carlton nodded. 'OK. Will do.' He inclined his head. 'You've been very helpful, both of you. Appreciate it.'

'No worries,' Maddy said.

Esme smiled. 'Good luck.'

They both watched as Carlton headed back across the yard towards the car park. 'That's if Drew Brannock deigns to talk to him, of course,' said Maddy, under her breath.

'Not the friendly type?' Esme said. 'Ah, see what you mean,' she added, as Carlton approached Drew only to receive a cursory glance, before Drew muttered something and turned away. Carlton shrugged philosophically and walked back to his Fiat before getting in and driving off.

'I assumed he'd be out helping Anna,' Esme said, watching as Drew picked his way across the yard, dressed in clean jeans and a white tee-shirt, clearly having been nowhere near a building site.

'You're joking, of course. He's supposed to be a partner in the business, but I've never seen him contribute anything. It's Anna who does all the hard graft.'

'And she puts up with that?'

Maddy rolled her eyes. 'He has contacts, she says. Which means he doesn't have to get his precious little hands dirty.'

Drew reached them. A fringe of dark, dishevelled hair lay flat against his forehead, damp from the rain. His piercing blue eyes skimmed Esme before he addressed Maddy.

'That guy,' he said, tossing his head back towards the car park. 'What did he want?'

'Hello, Drew,' Maddy said. 'How lovely to see you. May I introduce my friend, Esme Quentin?' Esme found it hard to hide her smile at the sarcasm in Maddy's voice, but Drew didn't seem to notice.

'Hi, Drew,' Esme said.

Drew grunted and cocked his chin briefly at Esme before turning back to Maddy. 'So? What did he want?'

'Why didn't you ask him yourself?'

'Cos I'm asking you,' Drew said.

Maddy rolled her eyes and folded her arms. 'He's a private

eye, if you must know. Not that I could tell him anything. I told him to talk to Daniel or Marianne.'

'About what?'

'Oh, some woman who used to live at Temperance Mill Cottage.'

'Ellen Turner or Tucker or something, wasn't it, Maddy?' Esme added. 'Lived there twenty-odd...'

But Drew had already turned away, heading back to the car park.

'Charming,' Maddy said with a shrug. They watched him jump inside his van and squeal out of the entrance, narrowly missing a milk tanker coming down the road.

# 2

Maddy Henderson was a photographer by trade with a passion for the restoration of old photographs, which is how she and Esme had met. Maddy's expertise had been crucial in unravelling a mystery linked back to the history of convict transportation, in which Esme had become involved.

But Maddy's interest in history wasn't limited to photographs. She'd recently become more involved in her father's restoration business, only to have the potential of their joint venture cruelly snuffed out by Ted's untimely death.

Ted had sold the pieces he restored at antique fairs or from his stall at Bideford's Pannier Market, along with an assortment of kitchen and garden paraphernalia, and Esme had been helping Maddy at the market on a temporary basis, while Maddy worked out the future viability of the business.

'You've obviously been having a good sort through your dad's stock,' Esme said, looking around. An eclectic collection of wooden boxes and small items of furniture filled the wide shelf which ran across the end of the building. 'Come to any conclusions?'

Maddy shoved her hands into the pockets of her sweatshirt. 'I've always loved helping with his restoration work. Particularly the small-scale stuff - boxes, writing slopes, that sort of thing.' She gave Esme a sad smile. 'And he was a good teacher. I'd like to think it was a tribute to him, to carry on with his work.'

'You don't need to convince me, Maddy,' Esme said. 'You go for it. You've got the skills, why not use them? A fitting legacy to carry on with your dad's work. He'd built up a nice little business here since his retirement and it'd be a shame to let it slip away. And you can still keep your photography going.'

Maddy folded her arms and gave Esme a quizzical look. 'But I can only do it with your continuing help on the market stall, though, Esme. It might be too much of a juggle to do everything, otherwise. Would you be up for that?'

'Yes, of course I would,' Esme said, smiling. 'I think it'd be fun. Hard work, yes. But fun.'

'I know it's not particularly lucrative coming into the winter, but that'll improve when we get to the summer season.'

'You don't need to worry, Maddy. I'm up for it. And I'm really enjoying it. It's good to have another string to my bow.' She stretched. 'I love my research work, but it's good to be a bit more active now and again. Why don't we give it a try for a while and see how it goes?'

Maddy nodded, and for the first time in weeks, Esme saw her face lift a little from the dark shadow of bereavement.

'And of course, with our extra little idea, too,' Esme said. 'I'm quite excited to see what happens with that side of things.'

Maddy's smile widened into a grin. 'I've always wanted to do it, but never really had the time. It's great we might manage that as well.' Her face fell a little. 'You don't think we're trying to run before we can walk, though, do you?'

Esme laughed. 'Probably. But we've made a start, haven't we? And we can just go with the flow.' She glanced up at the old school clock displayed on the wall. 'So when's Anna due back?' Anna had arranged to meet Maddy and Esme, saying she had a proposition to put to them. Esme was intrigued.

'Any time soon, I should think.' Maddy wandered over to the window and peered out. 'Think that's her pick-up now.' She turned back into the workshop. 'I told you she was pregnant, didn't I?'

'Yes, you did. A little girl.'

Maddy pulled a face. 'Can't imagine what sort of dad Drew's going to make, though.'

'Might be the making of him,' Esme said, with a wink. 'Stranger things have happened.' She looked round as the door clattered open and Anna came inside.

Maddy let out a shriek. 'Oh my God, what the hell have you got there?'

'It's grotesque, isn't it?' said Anna, wrinkling her freckled nose and flicking a thick chestnut plait of hair over her shoulder. They stared down at the grinning skeletal remains of a cat as Anna laid it down on the workbench. Any fur had long ago disintegrated. What covering remained was fragile and leather-like, sucked in against the contours of its bones. 'The builders came across it on the site where we took down that wall. You can imagine the expression on the face of the poor guy who dug it up. Anyway, as I was so fascinated by it, the owners offered it to me. I think they were glad to get rid of it.'

'I'm not surprised, gruesome old thing,' Esme said. 'To ward off evil spirits, I assume.' She wondered if the cat had died of natural causes or whether it had been sacrificed for the express purpose. She shuddered, the thought provoking a childhood memory of a local farmer admitting to drowning unwanted kittens in a rainwater tank.

'I guess so,' Anna said. She slipped off her dust encrusted work gloves and dropped them on the workbench. 'Well, I hope it did the trick for whoever put it there.'

'You better not let Gypsy see it,' Maddy said, 'or she'll think she's next.'

'Gypsy?' Esme asked.

'Anna's cat,' Maddy said. 'You might see her around the yard. She's jet black and very friendly.'

'She's my office cat,' Anna said. 'Can't have one at home because Drew's allergic to them. Oh, nearly forgot.' She pulled out a small sealed bottle from her jacket pocket and displayed it in the palm of her hand. 'I saw it lying on the floor. I rescued it before someone trod on it.'

Esme took the phial and held it up to the light. 'It's a witch's bottle, isn't it?' she said, giving it a tentative shake. Grime obscured the contents, though the jingling against the glass sounded like something metal inside; pins, perhaps, or nails. 'We could take it to show Cerys at the market?' she said, looking at Maddy.

'Is she into all this sort of stuff, then?' Anna asked.

Esme nodded. 'She runs the Mystic Gifts stall opposite Maddy's. Quite an authority, so I understand.'

Anna shrugged. 'Be my guest. I'd be interested to hear what she has to say. Anyway, I thought I'd donate them both to Barnstaple Museum. Do you think they'd be interested?'

'I'm sure they would,' Esme said. She saw Maddy give an involuntary shudder. 'You OK?' she asked.

'Yeah, it's all this talk about witches,' Maddy said. 'And the second time today.'

'Really?' Anna said. 'What else's been said?'

They told Anna about Sean Carlton's visit and his interest in Temperance Cottage. 'He seemed to be under the impression it was haunted,' Esme said.

Anna chuckled. 'Someone's having a laugh. It's the first I've heard of it.'

Maddy nodded. 'That's what I said, too. Someone's winding him up.'

'He didn't say where he'd got that from, did he?' Esme said. 'Pity we didn't think to ask him.'

'He probably wouldn't have revealed his sources, even if we had. Don't private investigators work on the same principle as journalists?'

Esme grinned. 'You may have a point.'

Anna chewed her lower lip. 'Can't say I've ever heard any stories about witchcraft. And the name Ellen Tucker doesn't ring any bells with me either. I'm not sure I even remember anyone living in the cottage. Apart from Gypsy, of course.' She grinned at Esme. 'She likes it down there. Plenty of mice.'

'Anyway, I sent him to talk to your parents,' Maddy said. 'I figured they'd be able to answer his questions.'

'Yes, I'm sure they will.' Anna scanned around the workshop. 'So, any decisions, then? Are you going ahead, d'you think?'

Maddy looked at Esme and grinned. 'We're certainly going to give it a go.'

Anna clapped her hands. 'Well, that's brilliant, guys. I can now tell you about my proposition.'

Maddy folded her arms. 'Yes, we've been dying to hear about this. Do tell.'

'Funnily enough, it involves the mill.' She turned to Esme. 'Maddy may have told you, Esme. I'm the proud new owner of all the land above the yard, which includes the mill.'

Esme smiled. 'Congratulations!'

Anna gave a little bow. 'Thank you. It was Mum's idea. She knows I've always loved it so she wanted me to have it. As you'll see shortly, it's a dilapidated old place that's going to waste, in my opinion. Why Mum and Dad have never thought about harnessing it for better use, I'll never know.'

'Lack of funds?' suggested Maddy.

Anna rolled her eyes. 'Now you sound like Drew. He says it's all too expensive.'

'What is?' asked Maddy.

'Refurbishing the mill. Create workshops with better facilities than in here,' she swept her arm around the room. 'We could even generate electricity, making it not only economically viable, but sustainable, too. And you, Maddy, could be the first business to take advantage.'

'Wow, Anna. That's a great idea,' Maddy said, her eyes bright.

'And it's perfectly feasible?' Esme asked.

21

Anna nodded. 'I've done my research and I'm arranging for an expert in these things to take a look.' She put her hand flat against her chest. '*I* think it's doable. I just need to convince Drew.'

Maddy grinned. 'We'll all have to work on him, then, won't we?' she said, winking at Esme.

Anna checked her watch. 'Dad should be there by now.' She cocked her head towards the door. 'So shall we go and take a look?'

'Sounds good to me,' Maddy said. 'Lead on!'

# 3

Temperance Mill stood on an area of land behind the reclamation yard, on the opposite side of a narrow lane which ran along the valley. The persistent rain from earlier had eased off and they trooped along a stony footpath from the yard in watery sunshine. Anna led them through the access gate, taking them left over a humpback bridge. Esme could see the mill ahead of them. A tall stone building with a slate roof, it loomed above them as they got closer, its boarded-up openings giving the impression of a beast sleeping. Esme wondered how it felt about being woken up.

A stocky man with thinning black hair and dressed in navy blue farm overalls was pacing up and down in front of the building. When he saw the party approach, he came forward to meet them.

'Hi, Dad,' Anna said. She turned to Esme. 'Dad, meet Esme.'

The man smiled. 'Hello, Esme,' he said as they shook hands. 'Daniel.'

Esme nodded. 'Hi, Daniel. Nice to meet you.'

'Maddy's new business partner, I hear,' he said, with a teasing nod to Maddy standing behind her.

Esme laughed. 'Well, we'll see. I'm really just helping out, for now,' she said, glancing over her shoulder and grinning at Maddy. 'While she gets things back up and running.'

'Though we do have a new venture in mind, don't we, Esme?' Maddy said, with a wink. 'But it's early days, yet. All will be revealed in due course.'

'Ah, big secret, eh? So, will you be dropping your photography work?'

Maddy shook her head. 'No, not completely. But it might go on to the back-burner while we get the project off the ground.'

Daniel nodded. 'Talking of projects…' He turned to Anna. 'I'm still not convinced the one you've got in mind is a good idea, love,' he said. 'I've told you about the state of the place. I'm not so sure it's not going to come tumbling down on your head.'

Anna laughed. 'Well, Mum seemed to think it was OK, so it can't be that dangerous.'

Daniel regarded her sceptically. 'Yeah, well. I'm not sure she's taken a look inside for years.'

Anna smiled and walked over to the building. 'Well, let's take a look inside ourselves now, shall we?'

Daniel sighed and pulled out a bunch of keys from the pocket of his overalls. He unlocked a heavy duty padlock on the low, wide door at the front of the mill and pulled it open. 'Hang on,' he said, holding up his hand. 'Better just check it's OK first.' He disappeared inside.

Anna rolled her eyes and went in after him. Esme exchanged an amused glance with Maddy before they followed on, pausing at the threshold to peer inside.

The interior looked a lot better than Esme had expected. From Daniel's comments, she'd imagined something much worse. The huge beams above looked solid enough, unless their true state was masked by the feeble light of the bare bulb, shrouded as it was by a filthy mat of cobwebs. At least there was a viable electricity supply.

As her eyes adjusted to the light, she could make out a few openings in the stone walls which had once been windows perhaps, but now had planks nailed across them. The light from outside seeped in through the gaps. The floor had been concreted over at some point in the past. It was cracked and worn now. She wondered when it was last used. Obviously the project would need a lot of work, both physically and mentally. She wondered whether Anna appreciated what she was taking on, especially with a baby on the way.

But according to Maddy, it was Anna's hard work and determination which had created Torridge Reclamation and turned it into the viable business it was, so perhaps she had what it took to make things work out.

A narrow wooden stair to their right-hand side climbed to the floor above and the height of the building suggested there was another floor beyond that. The ground floor access to the stair, though, was blocked by a thick plank of wood, wedged at an angle across the first step.

Daniel gestured towards it. 'Don't go up there,' he said. 'I'm not sure of the state of the floorboards on the level above. Could be pretty rotten. Don't want anyone falling through.'

Anna wandered further into the large ground floor space. 'First things first,' she said, looking round, 'we need to get a survey done to know exactly what we're playing with.' She turned to them all, her eyes shining with anticipation. 'A friend told me that, depending how I go about this, I may be eligible for a lottery grant.'

Daniel scoffed. 'Not for commercial projects, you won't be. Which means you'd have to fund the whole thing yourself.' He shook his head. 'Face it, Anna. It's way out of your league. You know Drew thinks the same.'

Anna tapped her father's arm. 'Oh, ye of little faith,' she said, with a laugh. 'Well, I'm not giving up until I've researched thoroughly. I'm sure there'll be some sort of route. And there's one route where I'd need to glean something of the history of the mill and the cottage. It will help with any application, apparently. Which is where you come in, Esme. I wondered if I could engage you to do the research? Your usual rates, obviously. Perhaps you could give me an estimate of what it might cost.'

Esme nodded. 'Of course. I'd be delighted to. I always love an assignment associated with an old building. What do you already know about its history?'

Anna wrinkled her nose. 'Not much, to be honest. Dad?'

Daniel shrugged. 'Don't ask me. Ask your mother.'

'I did. She said she thought the building on the side had once been where the miller lived and had burned down at some point in the 19th century. But nothing much other than that. She said it has been in the family for so many years, she's taken it a bit for granted. So we'd all be interested in understanding how the mill and our family are connected.'

'Well, that shouldn't be a problem,' Esme said. 'The census records will tell us who lived there over the years. And Devon has recently made its tithe maps available online, so I should be able to establish ownership from back to the mid-1800s, at least. Any idea how long there's been a mill on this site?'

'Not exactly, though someone once said it had been mentioned in the Doomsday Book.'

'If that's true, the name Temperance Mill is relatively new, assuming you're right, Maddy, and it was named after The Temperance Movement, as it didn't come to the area until the 1850s. So if you can find out its original name, that would be helpful. But don't worry too much. It should be reasonably easy to establish through old maps and other records. I'll get digging.'

With Daniel's cautious ban on looking further than the ground floor, there was little else to see, so they went back outside and Daniel locked up behind them. Esme got the sense he was relieved to have the visit over and done with, either because he had genuine concerns over the safety of the building or because of his antipathy towards Anna's ambitious plans.

'Do you mind if I have a look around?' Esme said, as they walked away from the mill. 'Get my bearings.'

'Of course,' Anna said, nodding. 'Go right ahead. See you later.'

# 4

Esme wandered away from the mill and out on to the narrow lane in front of it. She walked over to the field opposite and leaned on the top bar of the gate, gazing out across the rough grass to the River Torridge in the distance to watch the chocolaty water spiralling back and forth upstream.

Talk of the mill's renovation chimed with her own future plans for where she might make her permanent home. Her cottage near Warren Quay was rented and her long-term aim was to sell her property in Shropshire and buy locally. Perhaps it was time to put her plan into action. The idea of a renovation project interested her, but how easy would it be to find somewhere suitable? And would it be taking on too much, especially now, with helping out Maddy and the new project?

Her desire to live by the sea – the reason she'd moved to North Devon in the first place – was as strong as ever, but she suspected she'd been spoiled by the privilege of living in such a stunning location as she currently did. She doubted she'd find anywhere to match it, let alone a place with the necessary potential that she could afford.

But even assuming she could, was an isolated property on the coast a sensible choice? While she had no problem with isolation as such – she was happy in her own company – it did mean being a greater distance away from local archives and her travel time was much longer when she needed to go further afield for research. And now, with her offer to help Maddy on the market stall, being closer to Bideford would be an advantage. Of course, she might still find somewhere near the sea – not quite as wild and bracing a location as currently, perhaps, but nevertheless, it might still hold the necessary appeal.

She sighed and straightened up. No point in mithering about it, as they said in these parts. She had plenty of time to think about it. For now, though, she'd concentrate on Anna's request to research Temperance Mill.

She turned and walked back down past the mill, over the humpback bridge they'd crossed earlier and along the lane. The gable end of a small building came into view and she wondered if this was the cottage the private investigator had mentioned which Maddy had said had been derelict for many years. Beyond, Esme could see a fork in the road, which must lead to Hill Farm where Anna's parents lived and to where Maddy had directed Sean Carlton earlier.

When she reached the building, its condition, and that of the concrete apron in front of it, told its own story. This indeed must be Temperance Cottage, abandoned and uninhabited. Large tufts of grass and oversized dandelions ruptured the concrete, depositing bulges of green across the otherwise featureless yard. Not boarded up like the mill, it didn't have the same somnolent appearance, but instead seemed forbidding and watchful. She stood for a moment, wondering at the implications of Carlton's questions. Had something menacing happened down here? Surely he didn't seriously believe ghosts had caused its abandonment?

She tried to imagine the cottage in happier times when it was someone's home, loved and cared for. Anna hadn't mentioned any plans for the cottage and she wondered why. It would make someone a wonderful home, and might even have the potential to help finance Anna's ambitious mill scheme. If it had been closer to the sea, Esme might have been interested in it herself.

She opened the gate and made her way across the courtyard for a closer inspection. The scarlet paint on the front door was now faded and peeling. The lower panel had been modified to incorporate an opening with a flap. Of course. Anna had joked about her cat taking up residence, drawn by the mice population.

She moved over to a window and peered inside, shading out the light with her hand to try and see between the ragged print curtains hanging in shreds on either side of the casement. Grime rendered the glass all but opaque, but she could see feeding bowls at the far end and a pet bed. She pulled away and walked across to the window on the other side of the door, giving her a view of a second downstairs room.

Faded linoleum covered the floor, and against the end wall was an old-fashioned mottled brown tiled fire surround and hearth. Here the linoleum had been torn up, huge holes showing the dirty concrete floor underneath. She imagined how it might have once been furnished, a high-backed settle beside the fireplace, perhaps a rocking chair and a rag rug at the sitter's feet. Why hadn't Anna's parents ever re-let the cottage? Had there been structural defects which they couldn't afford to repair? Perhaps that had been the reason for the previous tenant moving out.

She stepped back and glanced down at her watch. Time was moving on and the weak sunshine had long since disappeared behind gathering clouds. She ought to get back.

As she turned, she saw Anna's cat stroll out from the opposite gable end of the cottage, tail erect, nose in the air. She walked towards her, calling her name. The cat paused and looked up at her with amber yellow eyes as Esme bent down to pet her.

'Hello, Gypsy.' She stroked the sleek black coat, the velvet fur silky smooth beneath her fingers. 'Nice to meet you.'

She turned at the sound of footsteps from behind the cottage, jerking backwards as something flew through the air close to her ear. Gypsy yowled and shot off across the yard.

Esme scrambled to her feet just in time to get out of the way of a second missile, which skidded across the concrete next to her.

She spun round. A dark figure, leaning on a stick, stood in the shadow of the cottage. A gruff voice bellowed out of the gloom.

'What you'm be doing on my land?'

# 5

Esme stared into the shadows as an elderly man, walking stick in hand, shuffled towards her. He had a full head of grey hair, parted on one side and brushed back, revealing a pronounced widow's peak.

She scowled at him, still shaking from the onslaught. 'I don't take kindly to having stones thrown at me,' she told him.

'Worn't aiming it you, maid,' he said, resting on his stick, his dark eyes watching her from under thick eyebrows.

'Well, you shouldn't be throwing stones at animals, either.'

'I dun't hold with vermin.'

'That's not vermin, that's Anna's cat,' Esme protested.

'Shouldn't be on my land.'

'Your land?'

'Been Brannock land for generations.'

'Ah,' Esme said, realising what he was implying. 'So, you're also a Brannock, are you?' He clearly didn't regard Anna as one, despite Brannock being her married name. She wondered where the grouchy old man sat on the family tree.

'You can tell that Anna that her'd better not be getting ideas 'bout the mill,' he said, ignoring her question. 'Us don't need no clever schemes. Tis fine as it is.'

He must be a fairly close member of the family to be aware that something was being planned. 'There's been a mill on this site for hundreds of years, I understand?' she said, trying to distract him.

'Aye. And what be that to you?'

'Oh, I'm always interested in the history of old buildings. It's part of my day job. My guess is that it wasn't always called Temperance Mill.'

'Is it now.'

'Do you happen to know what it was called before?' she went on, more in hope than anticipation. Clearly, the old man preferred confrontation to sharing information.

'Like I says, what's it to you?'

'It's no bother. I can always look it up in the records.' She made to move away. 'Well, I'd better be getting back. Anna will wonder where I've got to.'

The old man reached out and grabbed her arm with a grip that belied his years. 'You'm better not be coming here again, you hear, maid?'

Esme pulled her arm out of his grasp. 'Look, I'm leaving now, all right?' While she had no intention of being told what to do by a belligerent old man, she didn't plan to challenge him here, now, and provoke him further – not if he was capable of wielding his stick with the same surprising strength as he'd grabbed her arm.

She turned on her heel, anxious to get out of range as quickly as possible. In her haste to get away, she failed to check her exit, almost running into someone on the path. She stumbled backwards with a cry, looking up, hoping to see Anna or Maddy. It was neither. It was a man she didn't know, though his face looked familiar.

He gave Esme a cursory look, irritation showing on his face, before looking over her shoulder. 'Granddad,' he barked. 'What the bloody hell are you doing down here, you 'ckin' idiot?'

'You watch your language, bay,' chastised the old man. 'I never brought you up to cuss.'

Esme realised why the newcomer looked familiar. He could have been Drew Brannock, except his hair wasn't as dark and he was stockier than the man she'd met in the reclamation yard earlier. His brother?

The newcomer pushed past Esme and took the old man by the elbow. 'Wondered where the hell you'd gone,' he told him.

For the first time, the older man's face broke into a smile. 'Just passing the time of day, weren't we, maid?' he said, turning to Esme. 'Er's been having a look round the place.' He elbowed his grandson in the ribs. 'Friend of Anna's, you know.'

Esme cast a wary eye at the old man. What was he playing at? Was he now regretting his taciturn behaviour? She addressed the younger man. 'Are you Drew's brother?' she said.

He scowled and regarded her suspiciously. 'How come you know Drew?'

Esme gestured over her shoulder. 'I met him earlier. In the reclamation yard.'

He grunted and steered his grandfather away from the cottage. 'Now let's get you home. Mother will be fretting.'

The two of them shuffled off across the yard. Esme followed. There was a silver pick-up truck parked in the lane. The passenger door opened and a thin woman with grey hair hanging in rat's tails about her face and dressed in a lightweight cotton skirt and a fawn-coloured fleece climbed out of the vehicle and helped the old man inside. The woman glanced nervously at Esme before getting back into the truck beside the old man.

The pick-up truck did a U-turn in the lane and roared away up the hill. Esme slipped out of the gate and made her way back to the mill to find the others.

# 6

'He's a sullen old bugger, that Joseph Brannock,' said Maddy as they walked back to the car park, each carrying a box of old photographs. 'Sounds to me like he's losing it, too, from what you say.'

'Well, it *was* a bit odd. One minute lording it over me, and then the next making out we'd been engaged in cosy social chit-chat. Putting on a show for his grandson, d'you think?'

Maddy scoffed. 'Hardly. Alec Brannock is just as crabby as his granddad.'

'You know Alec then?'

Maddy pulled a face. 'Went to school with him. Well, that's only half true. He was a couple of years above me. But everyone in the school knew his reputation and avoided him wherever possible.'

'Reputation for what?'

'Unpredictability. Bit of a wild child. Graduating to turbulent adolescent. Always in trouble for something. Assault, arson, GBH.'

'He seemed quite caring towards his granddad,' Esme said, recalling Alec's apparent concern at the old man wandering off.

'Peas in a pod,' was Maddy's curt response.

'And Drew?' Esme said. 'Cut from the same cloth?'

'Well, you've met him. Not exactly a charmer, is he? But not in Alec's league as far as unpredictability goes. Sometimes it's difficult to know where you are with Drew. He can be pretty erratic.' Maddy laughed. 'If I was a nicer person, I'd be more forgiving. It can't have been easy for either of them, after their

34

dad died.' She glanced at Esme and raised her eyebrows. 'Drank himself to death. Don't think Alec and Drew's mother ever got over it. Withdrew into herself.'

'Would it be their mother I saw in the pick-up? Painfully thin, straggly hair?'

Maddy inclined her head. 'That sounds like Ria. Don't see her about a lot. She keeps a low profile. Doesn't often stray from the farmhouse, by all accounts.' She jerked a thumb over her shoulder. 'They live in a rambling old place at the top of the valley.'

'Alec said something about his mother fretting because Joseph had gone missing.'

'Sounds like the boot's on the other foot now, then.'

'How d'you mean?'

'Well, after the boys' father died and Ria was in no fit state, Joseph took on the boys' upbringing himself. And ruled with an iron fist, too. A great advocate of *spare the rod and spoil the child*, and all that sort of stuff.'

'I can quite imagine,' Esme said, conjuring up the image of the old man wielding his stick at her. 'So now Ria's taken over as carer. That can't be easy.'

'No. And poor old Anna's married into it all,' Maddy continued. 'Though it doesn't seem to bother her. Even Drew's moods are water off a duck's back.'

'A coping strategy, perhaps?'

'Maybe. I've never really understood why she got hooked up with him in the first place. Perhaps she felt sorry for him. It certainly wasn't his business prowess. Can't say I've seen him put much effort into the running of Torridge Reclamation. It's always been Anna's passion, not Drew's. In fact, I can't say I've seen Drew Brannock put much into anything, ever.'

'Maybe it was a simple love at first sight,' Esme said. 'He's very good looking.'

Maddy screwed up her face. 'If you like the silent, broody type. Though I take your point. He always had at least one girl draped over his arm at school.'

They arrived at Esme's car. Esme rested her box on her hip while she fished the car keys out of her pocket and unlocked the boot. When their two boxes were safely stored inside, Esme slammed down the lid. 'I'll try and make a start tomorrow, even if only to begin uploading them on to the website. I'll probably not get to any research for a while, though, what with Anna's to do.'

'No, of course not. We know it'll be a slow build, as and when you're able to spare the time.' She grinned. 'You do need to eat, after all!'

'What I will do, though,' Esme said, 'is choose a few photographs which have local connections for a display on the stall in time for Saturday's market.'

'That'd be fab,' Maddy said. 'We might strike lucky and have someone recognise one. Get the ball rolling.' She gestured towards Esme's car. 'Local photos are in red folders. It's all marked up.'

'It doesn't sound as though Drew's particularly taken on Anna's grand plan for the mill,' Esme said, over the roof of her car. 'D'you think he's got a point about the expense of it all? Daniel, too, for that matter.'

'If Anna goes down the lottery grant route, they won't have that as an argument.'

'Be nice if it works out for her,' Esme said. 'Though, I've heard it's not as straightforward as she might think. You need to know your way around the system, and the bureaucracy is a nightmare, apparently.'

'Well, let's hope the friend who's advising her knows his stuff. Mind you, I think Drew's antipathy is more to do with what it'll mean for him. He's gonna have to take on more at the yard, if she's tied up project managing.'

'He's going to have to do that anyway, isn't he?' Esme said. 'With the baby coming and Anna taking time off?'

Maddy nodded. 'Sure is.' She grinned. 'That'll test him. He might actually have to get his hands dirty. Literally.'

*

Esme drove down the bumpy track and pulled up on the grav-elled parking bay alongside her cottage. She turned off the engine and climbed out of the car, pausing to fill her lungs with the sea air as it whipped off the water. Perhaps she'd take a walk down to the shoreline once she'd unloaded, while there was still some light left in the day.

She carried the boxes of Maddy's photographs into the cottage and put them on the kitchen table. This was just the start. Maddy had collected hundreds of photographs over the years from junk shops, flea markets and car boot sales, even out of skips. Where necessary, she'd used her photography skills to restore them before filing them away.

Recently, Maddy had dug out her collection, looking for clues to the photographs' origins – a scribbled name, a date, a place, a photographer's mark – and Esme had occasionally helped out, taking the information and using research skills to compile a family tree of the sitter. Sometimes their efforts had been rewarded by locating an enthusiastic family member to whom a precious photo could be returned.

Now, their plan was to develop this ad hoc arrangement into something more sustained in the form of their new venture, *Photos Reunited* – its mission, to reunite as many of Maddy's collection as possible with the families to which they belonged. If there were no clues to follow, they planned to display the images on their new website so family historians could visit and check for any lost treasures.

Esme was itching to get started, though she'd have to make sure she kept her eagerness for this unpaid task in check so she had time for her paid research work. Anna's assignment intrigued her. The history of a building always added an extra fascination for her. Who'd lived there? What changes had the mill seen over the years? What secrets did it hold? It was disappointing that there was no link between Temperance Mill, its cottage and the Bideford Witches. She'd have loved the excuse to learn more about the story.

With the boxes unloaded, Esme slammed the back door and headed off down the track towards the beach. The tide was on its way in and she sat on the bench on the grass overlooking the cobbles below, watching the waves break on the rocks, throwing spray into the air.

She'd been lucky to find such a fabulous location to live, the sea barely fifty yards from her back door for whenever she wanted to lose herself in the beauty of the North Devon coast. When her friend Ruth Gibson had called her excitedly to say the cottage was available to rent, she hadn't hesitated. After her sabbatical, staying in the holiday accommodation on Ruth's family farm a couple of miles away, she'd yearned to come back on a more permanent basis, despite the traumatic incident that had occurred on the day she'd arrived. With the matter resolved, her desire to live by the sea hadn't diminished, and before she'd had time to question the wisdom of her decision, she'd signed the rental agreement.

Ruth's husband, Pete, found it hard to believe that Esme wasn't ready to scuttle back to Shropshire the moment the distressing incident reached its conclusion but, as she'd told him, her childhood memories of Ravens Farm, and the holidays she and her family had spent there, more than compensated for the difficulties of those weeks following the discovery of poor Bella Shaw's battered body.

Esme took a deep breath and gave her head a shake. No point in dwelling on that now. Life had moved on. She should give Ruth a call and find out how she was. And Ruth's mother, Bea, too. Both she and Ruth had been forced to confront personal ordeals after Esme had helped them discover the truth about Bea's sister's wartime disappearance.

Esme found herself fingering the scar on her cheek as she recalled how Ruth had been more concerned for Esme's state of mind than her own, when what was revealed proved as explosive for Esme as it was for Ruth and Bea.

Lately she'd been less conscious of her scarred face. Although it represented a traumatic period in her life, it no longer rankled her in the way it once did. Perhaps she'd reached the point where she'd learned, finally, to accept the disfigurement, to acknowledge that it would always be a part of her.

The light was fading now. The sound of the surf penetrated the dusk, the air filled with the smell of salt-spray. Esme dropped her hands into her lap, luxuriating in the pleasure of the atmosphere, her mind drifting to her suggestion to Maddy: setting up a display of locally taken photographs in time for Saturday's market day. As her thoughts filled with the prospect ahead, she realised that the unresolved issue of whether it was time to sell her cottage in Shropshire and invest in a permanent home in Devon had shifted from indecision to certainty. She imagined Ruth's excited response to Esme's intention to put down roots into the local soil, allowing herself a wry smile as she stood up and made her way back to the cottage.

# 7

Esme helped Maddy unload her campervan of the items she had selected from her father's stock for the market stall. It was still dark, with an early morning chill in the air. The lights of Bideford's historic Pannier Market seemed overly bright as they came in from the gloom outside, illuminating the beautifully restored interior, its principal roof trusses supported on elegant iron columns, dividing the space into bays in which stood the individual market stalls, sporting cheery red and white striped canopies.

As they carried their stock over to their stall, Esme scanned around at the other traders. There was a wide range of goods on offer from homemade food to handcrafted jewellery, local pottery to knitwear and everything in between. Cerys Evans was sorting out her Mystic Gifts and gave them a wave as they arrived.

Maddy went to park the van leaving Esme to arrange their stock for sale. There were a number of wooden boxes and a collection of kitchen and garden paraphernalia, including an assortment of old clay flower pots, several enamel jugs and a set of copper jelly moulds. At the end of the stall, Esme placed the display she'd created using the old photographs taken by photographers who had operated in the local area.

With everything set up, Esme fetched coffees for herself and Maddy from the market cafe. As she waited to be served, the tempting smell of hot pasties wafted out from the cafe kitchen. She forced herself to look around for a distraction and noticed a poster on the wall advertising a Halloween painting competition organised by the Pannier Market committee. First prize was a portfolio case, along with a comprehensive list of art supplies and equipment.

Someone came up beside her and she turned to see Cerys had joined her, pulling her oversized woolly cardigan around her body, her hands encased in knitted fingerless gloves.

'Bit chilly 'smorning, is'n it?' Cerys said, in her gentle Welsh lilt. Her long greying hair flowed out from under a woollen bobble hat and lay thick on her shoulders.

'Yes,' Esme agreed. 'I thought a coffee would warm us up.'

'My way of thinking, too.' Cerys rubbed one eye, heavy with black eyeliner, and yawned. Esme imagined she'd been a child of the sixties, dressing now in exactly the same long floral skirts as she had done in her teens.

Cerys nodded towards the poster about the painting competition. 'Been trying to persuade my granddaughter to go in for that.'

'She should,' Esme said. 'Great prize.'

'Thing is, she doesn't think she can paint,' said Cerys, shaking her head. 'But her pictures are beautiful. I don't think schools give artistic talent enough recognition any more. She's got no confidence in her ability. I keep telling her she's good, but I'm only her granny so naturally I'm biased, according to her.'

'It's probably just her age,' said Esme. 'How old is she?'

'Eight.'

'There you are, then. Younger children draw and paint from the heart and don't care what it looks like, but soon as they get to about 8 or 9, they get critical. I suppose they get more conscious of the world around them, and think their painting doesn't look like it should.'

'I thought if she entered and won a prize, it'd convince her that her granny knows what she's talking about and it might boost her confidence. What do you think?'

'It's a great idea. Do you think you can convince her to have a go?'

Cerys tucked a strand of hair under her woollen hat. 'I'll have to use the in-it-to-win-it argument.'

Esme reached the front of the queue and ordered coffees for herself and Maddy. 'We've got something to show you, when you've got a minute,' she told Cerys over her shoulder as she picked up the two steaming mugs from the counter. 'I'll just take these back and come and find you.'

Esme made her way back to the stall and set their drinks down on the table as Maddy arrived.

'Oh, just what I need,' Maddy said. 'Thanks.' She picked up a mug and wrapped her hands around it.

'I've just seen Cerys,' Esme said, taking her own coffee and blowing on it to cool it down. 'I told her we'd got something to show her. I'll take it across when she gets back.'

But it seemed Cerys's interest had been piqued. She headed across the aisle towards them, dunking a fruit teabag up and down in the mug she was carrying. 'So what you got for me, then?'

Esme put down her coffee and reached over to pull out Anna's little bottle from a box behind the stall.

'It's a witch's bottle, isn't it?' she said, handing it to Cerys.

Cerys let go of the teabag and took the bottle, holding it up to the light. 'So it is. Where d'you get it?'

'Anna Brannock,' Maddy said. 'You know, Torridge Reclamation. They were dismantling a wall over Torrington way. They found a dead cat, too. That was to ward off evil spirits, wasn't it?'

Cerys nodded. 'To create a barrier to stop witches entering the house. Which is why you find them over door lintels, under roof rafters, in the chimney stack or under floorboards.'

'Does the witch's bottle do the same thing?' Esme asked.

'It can be for protection, yes. But it could've been made for a specific purpose. Bit of Earth Magic to repel troublemakers. Get rid of unwanted guests.'

'A spell, you mean?' Maddy said.

Cerys chuckled. 'I know it sounds strange to you. But there was a time when belief in witches was deep-rooted. People thought witches prowled amongst them inflicting harm with their evil magic.' She handed the bottle back to Esme and picked up her fruit tea.

'So what's the significance of the pins?' Esme asked, shaking the bottle. 'I assume that's what they are? The glass is too stained to see inside properly.'

'More than likely,' Cerys agreed. 'Nails, thorns, spikes... anything sharp was used. Think of how a hedgehog turns his spines against a threat. If there was a liquid in it – usually wine – that was back-up. The evil either got impaled on the spikes or drowned in the wine.' She flinched. 'Oh, so sorry, Maddy. I didn't mean that to sound...'

Maddy waved a hand. 'That's OK, Cerys. I can't go around expecting people not to mention the word drowned because of what happened to Dad. I'd have to avoid talk about water and boats, too, and that'd be impossible living round here.'

Cerys inclined her head. 'That doesn't mean it won't touch a nerve.'

Maddy gave Cerys a wan smile and nodded.

'So what date would this bottle be?' Esme asked. '17th century, d'you think, during the height of witchcraft mania?'

Cerys shook her head. 'Not necessarily. Been found in buildings dating from as late as the early 20th century.'

'We had some guy round at the yard the other day asking about witchcraft,' Maddy said.

Esme nodded. 'He was on about *strange goings on* and seemed to be under the impression that Anna Brannock's mill was haunted by the Bideford Witches. Maddy put him straight.'

'He was some sort of private eye,' Maddy continued. 'He was looking for someone who'd lived over at Temperance Cottage years ago. Ellen Tucker, wasn't it, Ez?'

'Heavens,' Cerys said. 'There's a blast from the past.'

'You knew her?' Esme said.

'Oh, I wouldn't go that far, exactly. But, yes, I remember her.'

'He was right, then,' Maddy said. 'We thought he'd got his wires crossed. So what do you know about her, Cerys?'

Cerys cradled her mug, considering. 'Bit of a looker, she was. Long black hair, legs up to her armpits. You know the sort. Wore long black skirts and Doc Martins.'

'Bit of a Goth, then?' Esme suggested.

Cerys gave Esme a brief nod. 'You got it. Had the men's tongues hanging out. Women didn't take to her much, for that reason, more than likely.' She frowned and looked pensive for a moment. 'Always got the sense she was more vulnerable than everyone made out.'

'What d'you mean, *than everyone made out?*' Esme asked.

'Seemed pretty sure of herself and some didn't like her for it, see. But didn't ring true for me. Like it was all an act.' Cerys flapped a hand in the air. 'Oh, take no notice. I don't know what made me say that. It was a very long time ago. I'm probably thinking of someone else.'

'So what happened to her?' Maddy asked.

Cerys shrugged. 'Went back to where she came from, I assume.'

'Which was where?'

'Search me. Can't say I wasn't surprised when she upped sticks, though. Don't think she was happy here. Didn't settle, you know? Like she was out of place.' She looked across to her stall. 'Ah. Customers. Better go.'

'Carlton wasn't on a wild goose chase, then,' Esme said, when Cerys had left. 'I wonder if he's found out anything about her. Perhaps we should suggest Cerys get in touch with him and pass on what she remembers.'

Maddy rubbed her hands together and blew on them. 'Not sure what she told us is going to be any use to Carlton.'

'No, you're probably right. He might have cracked the

case by now, anyway.' Esme picked up the empty mugs. 'I'll get rid of these.'

She took the mugs back to the stallholders' cafe, mulling over what Cerys had said about Ellen Tucker being popular with the men but not the women and thinking back to Drew's reaction when they'd mentioned her name. She did a quick calculation. He'd have been in his teens when Ellen Tucker had rented the cottage, so old enough to remember someone living in his neighbourhood, surely? Unless he was going through the teenage phase of being oblivious to everything going on around him. Even so, it had been a strange way to behave, whether he'd remembered her or whether he hadn't.

But, as Maddy had said, you never can tell with Drew.

# 8

'Shall we grab a bite of lunch?' Maddy said, as they packed up their market stall. 'The Kings Arms should be still serving, just about.'

'Yes, please,' Esme said. 'I'm starving.'

'Good. Cos I've got something to show you.'

'Sounds intriguing.'

Maddy laughed. 'Cringeworthy, more like. You'll see what I mean later.'

They dropped off the stock at the workshop, leaving Maddy's campervan in the car park at the yard and taking Esme's car back into Bideford. They parked on the quay and crossed over the road to The Kings Arms. The early lunchtime punters had eaten and moved on, leaving behind a tang of garlic and fried food.

'You remember Harry, don't you, Esme?' Maddy said, as they reached the bar.

Harry was pulling a pint, a tea towel thrown over his shoulder. He seemed to take up all the space behind the bar, the quiff of his brown hair almost brushing the low ceiling. He looked up when he heard Maddy's voice and grinned, showing a row of even white teeth. 'Sure she does,' he called. 'Once met, never forgotten, me.'

Esme laughed and gave him a wave. 'Hi, Harry.'

Harry served the customer at the end of the bar and came over to Esme and Maddy. 'OK, guys. What can I get you?'

'Orange juice and soda for me,' Maddy said. 'I'm going for a run later. I don't need beer legs.'

'Same for me,' Esme said. 'I'm driving.'

Harry grabbed two glasses from the shelf and stood them on the bar before tapping his watch. 'You two eating?' he said. 'Cos the kitchen's closing in about five.'

They studied the bar menu while Harry dealt with their drinks, then placed their orders and took their glasses over to a table by the window.

'Didn't you and Harry go to school together?' Esme said, as they sat down.

Maddy dropped down on to the chair opposite Esme. 'Yeah, we did. We've always been on the same wavelength.' She tightened her pony tail in its hairband. 'Been seeing quite a lot of each other lately.' She flushed and gave Esme a crooked smile. 'It's good.'

Esme returned her smile and nodded. She looked round at the pub's interior, taking in the low beams and the old Bideford photographs hanging on the walls.

'Nice atmosphere in here,' she said. 'Been here a long time, I'd guess.'

'Sixteenth century, I think. Yeah, I like it. It's handy for me.' Maddy took a sip of her drink. 'Only downside is that it's Drew's local, too. But he's more an evening drinker so we should be safe today.'

Esme nodded. 'I wonder if Anna's made any progress on persuading him about the viability of the mill conversion.'

Maddy pulled a face. 'Don't hold your breath. I can't see it happening.'

'That's a shame. It would make a great workshop for you. Your dad's place isn't exactly in the best condition.'

'No, you're right there.' Maddy fiddled with her glass on the mat and gave Esme a weak smile. 'The corrugated iron is bloody noisy in the wind. You wouldn't believe it. I was always telling him that the next south westerly gale would blow it down.' She let out a lengthy sigh, her head bowed, her eyes fixed on the table top.

'You OK?' Esme asked.

Maddy looked up and blinked, a flush of red on her cheeks. 'Yeah, sure. Just thinking about Dad's place. His house, I mean. Not the workshop. I really need to get on with sorting through his home stuff. I keep putting it off.'

'D'you need a hand?' Esme said. 'Happy to keep you company, if it would help. I remember when I did my parents' house. It was no minor task. And I had my sister helping. It would have been pretty daunting doing it on my own.'

'That's kind of you, Esme. But I couldn't. It'd be a huge imposition.'

'No, it wouldn't. But you might prefer to be on your own doing it, anyway. It's going to be pretty emotional, whichever way you look at it.' Esme tapped Maddy's arm. 'Think about it. The offer's there if you want it. Don't need to decide now.'

'Thanks. And I might just take you up on it, so be warned,' Maddy added, with a watery smile.

'So,' Esme said, sitting back in her seat. 'You said you had something to show me.'

'Oh, so I did.' Maddy dragged her backpack on to her lap and delved inside. 'Came across this last night,' she said, pulling out a narrow, tightly wound roll of paper. She pushed their drinks aside and unrolled it to reveal a long school photograph.

'Oh, that's brilliant,' Esme said, holding down the end closest to her and scanning the tiny faces. 'I assume you're on here somewhere?'

'I am. See if you can spot me.' Maddy giggled. 'I'll give you a clue. It was definitely a bad-hair day.'

Esme searched the rows, finally tapping her finger on one girl with wild, messy hair. 'Don't tell me that's you,' she said, laughing.

'Spot on.' Maddy chuckled. 'I suppose I thought "unkempt" made me look cool.'

'It was always a laugh having those photos taken,' Esme said, remembering her own school photo sessions, some standing on benches at the back, others sitting at the front. 'The photographers must have hated it, trying to organise everyone to get into their places.'

'Yeah, and then the jokers running around the back so they could be on both ends of the picture.'

'Is that what I think it is?' Harry said, arriving with their plates of sandwiches.

'You must be on here somewhere?' Maddy said.

Harry put the plates down on the adjoining table and bent over to take a look. 'There's me. The handsome one on the back row.'

'Handsome?' Maddy said, elbowing Harry in the side. 'You're joking? You look like a scared rabbit.'

'Oh, uncalled for, you cruel woman. Oh, look,' he said, stabbing his finger on one of the staff at the end of a row. 'Remember him, Dodgy Denham?'

Maddy peered at where he'd indicated. 'Oh him, yes. We always reckoned he was a Russian spy.'

Esme laughed. 'Why?'

'No real reason, other than he spoke Russian,' Harry told her. 'Though, he was a bit of an odd ball. And to be honest, he did have the look of a Cossack about him.'

Maddy slid her finger up to the back row. 'Mmm, guess who? And scowling, as usual.'

'Yeah, nothing changes much.'

'Who is it?' Esme asked, studying the face. 'Oh, I get it. Drew Brannock? Or is it his brother?'

'No, right first time. It's Drew.' Maddy frowned. 'And look at that lot next to him. Drew's little bunch of low-life vermin.'

Esme stared at the boys on the row beside Drew, who were linking arms and, unlike Drew, wearing smug smiles.

'You remember them, don't you?' Maddy said, looking round at Harry. 'Stubby and...' she shook her head. 'Can't remember the other one's name.'

'Glen,' Harry said. 'Stuart 'Stubby' Boden and Glen Williams.'

'That's right. Wonder what they're up to now? Living a life of crime, probably.'

'Right then, clear the decks,' Harry said, turning back to the sandwiches. 'Or your food will get cold.'

'Oh very funny,' Maddy said, as he put the plates down on their table and left them to eat.

Esme tucked in readily, not realising how hungry she'd been. Perhaps she should have given in to the temptation of a pastie from the market kitchen. It was a long time between breakfast and lunch on market days.

'How big's your dad's house?' she asked after a while, brushing crumbs off her lap.

Maddy shrugged. 'Big enough. Could take a while to go through everything.'

'Was he a hoarder? My mum was. Though, at least it was orderly hoarding.'

'Not so much,' Maddy said, wiping her fingers on a napkin and pushing the plate away. 'His study will be the biggest challenge, I imagine. It's chocka.' She gave Esme a sheepish smile. 'If you're sure about your offer of help earlier, I think I'd like to take you up on it.'

Esme nodded and returned her smile. 'Of course I'm sure. When d'you want to start? Tomorrow?'

Maddy took a deep breath and chewed her bottom lip. After a moment, she let out a long sigh.

'Oh, OK, then. If you like. Best to hit it head on, I suppose.'

The outside door opened and Esme looked up to see a familiar figure sauntering into the bar.

'Uh-oh,' she said, shooting a glance at Maddy. 'So much for Drew only dropping in for the evenings.'

Maddy snatched a glance over her shoulder before turning back to Esme. She picked up her glass and downed the remainder of her drink.

'Our cue to leave, I think,' she said, standing up.

Drew was standing at the bar, his back to them. Maddy

glanced across at Harry who was on the other side, pulling a pint. She gestured towards the exit. Harry nodded, throwing her a sly wink, and began chatting to Drew, keeping him talking and allowing them to escape into the street.

'Thanks for the heads-up,' Maddy said, as they walked back along the quay. 'I wasn't in the mood to cope with Drew today.'

'How old would Drew have been when Ellen Tucker lived in Temperance Cottage?' Esme asked, revisiting her thoughts of earlier.

'Er, let me think,' Maddy said, mentally calculating. 'Fifteen, I think.'

'Old enough to remember her, then?'

Maddy frowned. 'What are you saying?'

'Nothing. Just thinking what Cerys said about Ellen being attractive. *Had men's tongues hanging out*, was the way she put it. You said Drew always had a girl draped on his arm at school and it's clear from the photo that he was good-looking as a teenager.'

'You're thinking he would have been aware of someone like Ellen? Yes, I see where you're coming from. Thinking about it, I reckon some of the younger women teachers were a bit taken with him.'

'So the fact that she was older than him…'

'Might have been half the attraction,' Maddy finished. 'It's a thought.' She grinned. 'Perhaps they had a bit of history? It explains why he hared off the other day when her name was mentioned - he was embarrassed.'

Esme nodded. 'Shame. He's another one who might have had something useful to tell Sean Carlton.'

# 9

Maddy's father had lived in the picturesque fishing village of Appledore, a short distance down the Bideford estuary. His house, originally built in the 18th century for a sea captain, was hidden away down an alleyway behind a row of cottages and looked out across a small cobbled courtyard.

Esme followed Maddy as they crossed the yard to the front door, over which projected a small but ornate cantilevered porch. Maddy slid the key into the lock and pushed open the door, bending down to pick up the post from the mat.

'More bills to sort out by the look of it,' she said, flicking through the envelopes. She moved to one side and gestured for Esme to come inside.

Esme stepped across the threshold into a tiny square entrance hall. Ahead was the tell-tale slope of the underside of a flight of stairs, and to the left a door led into the kitchen. She peered inside. The window above the sink looked back into the courtyard from where they'd just come. A Rayburn cooker nestled in the wide inglenook on the end wall of the house and a narrow scrubbed wooden table took centre stage. All the cupboards – under the sink, on the wall opposite and under the worktops below – were painted a muted spring green, giving it a satisfyingly old-fashioned appearance.

Maddy had turned right off the hall and Esme caught up with her in a large dining room. A huge table stood against the back wall, dressed in a tartan patterned vinyl cloth which was almost obscured by piles of papers, folders, magazines, books and a large disorderly heap of envelopes.

'This is a good sized room,' Esme said, looking round.

'Yes, not bad, is it?' Maddy pointed towards a door in the far corner. 'Stairs there. Two floors above.'

'Two?' Esme said, surprised. 'It's bigger than I thought. How many bedrooms?'

'An estate agent would have you believe it was 5, but the top two are just small attic rooms with low ceilings. Useful for storage, as long as you don't mind humping stuff up the two flights of stairs, that is.' Maddy added the post from the mat on to a teetering pile of correspondence sitting on the table. 'Come on through to the lounge. It's my favourite room.'

She opened a pair of glass folding doors on the far right-hand side of the room and they walked through into the space beyond.

'Oh, I can see why you like it,' Esme said, noticing the large squashy sofa draped in a woollen throw. A traditional leather armchair stood beside a fireplace dominated by a substantial cast iron wood-burning stove, a deep-pile wool rug in front of the hearth. The appealing clutter of framed photographs on the mantlepiece added to the room's homely character. 'It must be lovely and cosy. I bet you can get quite a fug going in here.'

'Yes, you can,' Maddy said. She settled her gaze on the fireplace, apparently lost in her memories. Esme guessed her emotions weren't far from the surface.

'Maddy, are you absolutely sure about this?' Esme said. 'I feel a bit mean. I rather bullied you into getting started today, but if it's all too soon...'

Maddy held up her hand. 'No, no, it's absolutely fine. And, it's nice you being here. I've not liked coming into an empty house. So you're doing me a favour.'

'Well, if it all gets too much and you want to kick me out, I won't take it personally.'

Maddy nodded and gave Esme a faint smile. 'OK.'

'So, where do you want to start?'

'I thought we'd clear the table in there of all Dad's junk, to start with,' Maddy said, wandering back into the dining room. 'It's doing my head in.'

'Yes,' Esme agreed, following her. 'Having a clear surface will make you feel more in control.'

'The kitchen can stay as it is for now. Gives us somewhere to make a cuppa and rustle up something to eat, if we want.'

Esme pointed to the table. 'That's not your dad's study you were talking about, is it?'

Maddy shook her head. 'No, that's a whole 'nother room upstairs. This is just the overflow. Well, you'll see in a minute. There's no room to move in his office. He must have been using the dining table instead.' She shivered. 'Not particularly warm in here, is it? I'll fire up the boiler. It's out of the ark, but it's usually fairly reliable. Why don't you go and have a look upstairs? See the rest of the place.'

Esme climbed the steep stair on to the landing and peeped into one of the bedrooms, recalling another occasion when she'd helped clear a house which she'd not known beforehand, packing up someone's life into boxes. How long ago that seemed now. So much had happened since, it felt as though it had taken place in another existence.

She wandered into the bedroom and over to the tall multi-paned sash window on the far side. Down below was a large garden, stretching away from the house, planted with shrubs around a scruffy lawn.

She heard Maddy come up the stairs. 'The garden's huge,' she said, as Maddy came into the room.

'Yes, I know,' Maddy agreed. 'Far more than Dad really needed, to be honest. In the summer he'd always prefer to be out on the water when he wasn't in his workshop, rather than gardening. Bit of a waste, in a way.'

They walked out on to the landing. 'Dad's office is one of the attic rooms up here,' Maddy said. She led Esme up a narrow flight of stairs on to a tiny landing on the floor above and pushed open a narrow door.

Esme ducked her head and peered inside. All of the wall space was shelved, loaded with books and filing boxes. A small desk nestled in the corner, on which sat a computer monitor and tower. A printer stood on the floor.

'See what you mean about it not being suitable as a bedroom,' she said. 'You'd never even get a bed in here, let alone any other furniture.'

Maddy sighed. 'We're not going to get all the stuff from the dining room table in here, though, are we?'

'Perhaps we need a bit of a tidy up first,' Esme said, stepping into the room. 'Just stacking up a few things. We should be able to free up some space on the floor.'

'Yes, OK,' Maddy said, walking over to the desk. 'It'd help if we could find somewhere else for the printer.' She began heaping the books lying on the desk top into a pile. Esme went over to the printer and put it on the desk, as Maddy made space.

'Good, that's better already,' Esme said, looking around for what to organise next.

Maddy was staring at the pile of books. She picked one up and opened it.

'What is it?' Esme asked.

Maddy shook her head. 'Oh, nothing, really. Just noticed this bible...well, it was the bookmark inside which caught my eye.' She looked up with a sad smile. 'I gave this to Dad for a birthday present years ago.' She handed it to Esme. 'I saved up my pocket money for weeks, I remember.'

Esme took the piece of faded red leather and read out loud the words embossed on it. '*Outside of a dog, a book is man's best friend. Inside of a dog it's too dark to read.*' She chuckled. 'Groucho Marx. One of my all-time favourite quotes.'

Maddy nodded, tears filling her eyes. 'Dad's too.'

Esme handed Maddy back the book mark. 'It's never easy, this job,' she said. 'Always gets you. No way round it, I'm afraid.' She reached out and squeezed Maddy's arm.

Maddy blinked away her tears and returned the bookmark to its place. She closed the book and put it back on the pile.

'Right. That's better. OK, we're on. Come on.' She sniffed. 'Let's get started on the rest, and then we can tackle that table.'

They spent most of the morning clearing as much floor space as possible before going back downstairs to ferry the piles of paperwork from the table up to the attic.

'We've earned some lunch after this,' Maddy said, picking up one of the last two loads and climbing the stairs.

Esme followed behind. 'We certainly have.' She arrived on the first landing and turned the corner for the next flight. 'My treat, though.'

'No, that's not fair,' Maddy said, from above. 'You paid last…arhhh…oh no!'

Esme laughed and ducked as a heap of envelopes came fluttering down from above. 'I'll get it,' she said. She dumped her pile on the top landing and hurried back down to pick up the fallen items. As she gathered them up, she noticed a post-it sticker attached to a simple Manilla folder, on which were written the words, "*You didn't get this from me*".

'Sorry about that,' Maddy said with a laugh, running back down the stairs. 'Hope I didn't brain you.' She stopped. 'What?'

Esme handed her the folder. 'What do you make of that?' she said. 'On the post-it.'

Maddy shook her head. 'No idea. Could mean anything.' She opened up the folded piece of card and shrugged. 'It's just an empty file.'

'Yes, but,' Esme said, taking the folder from Maddy and turning it round the other way. 'You haven't seen what's written on the front of it.' She pointed to the name, scrawled in untidy capital letters in black felt pen at the top. Ellen Tucker.

# 10

Esme and Maddy stood in the doorway of Ted's cluttered office. They'd searched all through the papers which had spilled down the stairs but found nothing that could have come from the folder with Ellen Tucker's name on it.

'I was sure it was going to be in this lot somewhere,' Maddy said, with a frustrated sigh.

Esme folded her arms and propped herself against the door jamb. 'Perhaps it was never there,' she said. 'Given what it said on the post-it, he could have got rid of what had been in the file once he'd read it. It was obviously against the rules. I assume it was one of his former police colleagues who'd given it him?'

'So why keep the folder?'

'Maybe he just forgot. Or planned to reuse it.'

'I guess so.' Maddy chewed her lip. 'But it was Dad's writing so I'm sure it's not an official police file.'

'Could it have been a *copy* of an official police file? Though the question is, why would there *be* a police file on Ellen Tucker?'

Maddy shook her head. 'No. The question is, why was my dad interested in Ellen Tucker in the first place?'

'Hang on,' Esme said, standing upright. 'Didn't Sean Carlton say he'd seen your dad recently?'

'Yes! Yes, he did.' Maddy strode over to the desk and opened the top drawer. 'His diary should be here somewhere. He never got the hang of using his phone to make... Ah, yes, here it is.' She took it out and began flicking back through the pages, her face fixed in a concentrated frown. 'Here,' she said, after a few moments. 'Back in August. Look.' She thrust the open diary at Esme.

Esme took the book and held it away from her so she could bring it into focus. '*Sean. 1 pm.*' She handed it back. 'So who got in touch with who? I'm guessing Carlton. It was his investigation. Unless, of course, we're jumping to conclusions.'

Maddy looked up. 'What d'you mean?'

'Well they were friends, weren't they? How do we know they weren't just meeting up for a pint and to share old times?'

'Because,' Maddy said, 'as any TV detective will tell you, there's no such thing as coincidences when it comes to crime investigation.'

'What crime? We don't know there's a crime involved. Carlton could be making enquiries about Ellen Tucker for any number of reasons – an estranged family member wants to make amends, an old flame trying to track her down, or she could have come into money and Carlton's working for an heir hunter.'

'I thought they did that in-house?'

'If they're specialists, but I think executor solicitors might use a PI. Why don't you give Carlton a call and find out? He gave you his card, didn't he?'

Maddy pulled a face. 'Yes. But where the hell did I put it?'

'Jeans pocket, if I recall.'

'Which means it's been through a wash since. Cos I'm pretty sure I didn't take it out when I got home.'

'Google him, then. There can't be many Sean Carlton Private Investigators out there.'

Maddy pulled out her phone from her back pocket and began swiping at the screen. After a few minutes she nodded.

'Got him,' she said, stabbing at the screen and putting the phone to her ear. She listened for a moment, shaking her head. 'Voicemail,' she murmured, before leaving a message and cutting the call.

'Well, it is Sunday,' Esme said. 'He's probably taken the day off. He knows who you are, so he should get back to you pretty quick.'

Maddy returned the phone to her back pocket and looked at Esme with an anxious expression. 'Well, let's hope he does. Finding that folder has given me an uncomfortable feeling.'

Esme gave Maddy a reassuring smile. 'Don't worry. Carlton will be able to explain everything and put it into perspective. You'll see.'

\*

Esme sat down at her desk and sipped her cup of coffee, while her laptop booted ready for her to start on Anna's assignment into the history of Temperance Mill.

Sean Carlton had not responded to Maddy's voice-mail message by the time Esme and Maddy parted company the previous day, so they were still no wiser as to the nature of Ted's involvement in Carlton's investigation concerning Ellen Tucker. Maddy hoped to hear back from Carlton today and promised to get in touch as soon as she did.

Esme turned her attention to her first task: to discover the original name of the mill. She brought up the National Library of Scotland's website where she'd be able to access copies of the earliest 19th century Ordnance Survey maps of England. She negotiated to the relevant page and the screen filled with a mass of red rectangles covering the whole country. Zooming in on Devon, she clicked the rectangle covering the Bideford area to bring up the associated maps held by the library. The left hand section of the page, showed her two options: 1886 and 1904. She clicked on the earlier map and homed in on the approximate location of Anna's reclamation yard, finding the stream which ran alongside and following it until she reached the mill, clearly identified as Temperance Mill. So it had already been renamed by 1886.

She went back to the Internet search engine and called up the Devon Tithe map website. Created 44 years before the earliest Ordnance Survey map, a tithe map could be the simplest way to establish the mill's original name.

She found Bideford parish in the drop-down list and, again, homed in on the relevant map to find the location of the mill. The map itself didn't show any names, only numbers which she'd need to cross reference with the list of owners and occupiers, called the Tithe Apportionment. She noted the number and called up the scan of the original document.

The list had been transcribed, but Esme preferred to see the original wherever possible, albeit in this case the image of the original. Not only did she enjoy the greater connection with history, she avoided the risk of any errors made when the transcription process was carried out.

She scrolled down the scanned pages until she came across the relevant number and found what she was looking for. In 1842, the mill had been called Corvus Mill and, as Joseph Brannock had alluded to, was owned and occupied by a member of the Brannock family, in this case, Solomon Brannock.

She switched her search to the census returns, starting with 1841, the earliest census to record names of individuals. It was fairly straightforward to locate Corvus Mill and, as with the Tithe Apportionment, the occupier was listed as Solomon Brannock, his wife and two sons, the elder being Silas, aged 21. In the next census, in 1851, Solomon was 56 and a widower. His elder son Silas was still living at the mill, but he was now married to Bessie and they had a daughter, Sarah, aged 2 months. Ten years on and the mill had become Temperance Mill. Solomon had disappeared – presumably having died. Meanwhile, Silas and Bessie had had two further children, another daughter, Susannah, who was 6 and a son, Isaac aged 4.

By 1871 there had been a complete change to the household. Isaac, now 14, appeared to be the only member of the original family still living in Temperance Mill. The head of the household was Jacob Brannock, his occupation recorded as farmer. Isaac was listed as his nephew, occupation labourer. There was no sign of Isaac's parents or his sisters. Esme considered a possible explanation. The girls could have been working away from home, perhaps in service. Susannah would have been 16 by then and Sarah 20. Working as a domestic servant was the most common occupation for a female in 1871 England. Or Sarah may have married, living elsewhere with a family of her own. And the parents? Died? Moved in with their married daughter? Silas would have been 50 and ordinarily would have still been in work. Unless, he'd had an accident and was no longer fit. There were any number of scenarios. Should she follow up any of them?

But Anna's brief was to research the history of the mill itself, so perhaps for now Esme should focus on that and not get sidetracked. She could always follow that line of enquiry another time.

She turned back to the censuses, steering her way through those of 1881, 1891, 1901 and 1911. She established that Isaac remained at the mill for the rest of his life. He married, had two sons, Abraham and Jared, and the elder son, Abraham, was still living there in 1911 with his wife and daughter Grace, aged 6.

With no further census records to consult, Esme looked at the 1939 Register, taken at the outbreak of the Second World War. Abraham, now a widower, was still living in the mill, meaning it remained at this time in the ownership of the Brannock family. Grace was also listed, aged 34, unmarried, occupation shop assistant. But in red ink, above her entry was noted her married name, added to the records at a later date, indicating that at some point in the future, Grace had married into the Meddon family. If Grace had been an only child, she may have inherited the mill and this could have been when it passed from the Brannock family name to the Meddon's.

Esme's thoughts returned to the mystery of what had happened to Isaac's parents, Silas and Bessie. She searched the death indexes for the couple and found they'd both died in the third quarter of 1868. She placed an order for a copy of their respective death certificates and, blinking her now gritty eyes, closed down the laptop lid. She needed a break from all this screen work.

# 11

Maddy's daily run took her along the Tarka Trail, a cycle and footpath following the route of the old railway line which had once run between Bideford and Barnstaple. She enjoyed Monday mornings when it was generally quiet and the regular dog walkers were the main users of the trail. At the height of the tourist season, the number of bicycle riders increased, many of whom had never thought to invest in a bell to alert other path users. Not that she put herself at risk by wearing earphones and cocooning herself in another world. She liked the thinking time and preferred the sounds of the natural world around her, often hearing curlews which inhabited the marshy nature reserves along the route.

As she arrived back into Bideford, she diverted off the trail and jogged on to the old Bideford Bridge. She stopped to pause the tracking device on her watch before crossing to the other side. On the opposite quay there seemed to be an unusual number of people milling around. She wasn't aware that the *SS Oldenburg* was sailing today, the boat which ferried visitors to Lundy Island on day trips. The wild and beautiful island was a walker's joy and a haven for birds and wildlife. With a tally of inhabitants fewer than twenty, clustered together around the island's pub, The Marisco, Lundy was the place for those who enjoyed solitude and making their own entertainment - the antithesis of most tourist attractions. Maddy had made the trip herself on several occasions.

She gazed down the Torridge towards the new bridge at the calm and deceptive waters of the estuary, and beyond to the notorious Bideford Bar, a ridge of sand at the point at which the rivers Torridge and Taw collided. The bar had a lethal history, responsible for a great many wrecks over the centuries with hundreds of lives lost. Amongst them, her father's.

She took a deep breath to try and dispel the heaviness in her chest cruelly reminding her of her loss and the tragedy of his drowning. Ted had been an RNLI volunteer crew member. Maddy had always assumed him to be in most danger when out on a shout, in atrocious weather, saving the life of someone else, not at leisure in his own boat.

But as any sailor knows, an engine failure exposes you to the mercy of the sea. And it can happen to anyone, as it had to Ted Henderson. Sometimes Maddy tortured herself with the image of her father desperately trying to restart the engine as the tide, slowly and heartlessly, pushed his boat towards the bar. Inevitably, the vessel was picked up by the surf and washed broadside to the waves. And over it went.

By the time his empty tender was spotted and the coastguard alerted, it was too late. Appledore Inshore Lifeboat found one of their own floating face down in the estuary, having succumbed to hypothermia. Misadventure, was the anticipated outcome of the forthcoming maritime investigation.

Maddy took a deep breath and tried to focus on what she knew she should – that it had been her father's dream to own a boat and explore the north Devon coast. Retirement from the police force had given him the luxury of enough spare time to indulge both his passions – sailing and working with his hands. *He died doing what he loved*, was a mantra several friends had expressed and suggested she use to console herself.

She tried, even though it gave little comfort. But she knew there was no point in fretting. She just had to get on with it. At least with Esme's help, she'd be able to face up to sorting out his things and tackle the inevitable selling of the house. Except now, stumbling on that empty file amongst her dad's things had given her more to fret over. What had been her dad's interest in the mysterious Ellen Tucker? Sean Carlton must surely get in touch today and put her out of her misery. She'd hardly been able to stop thinking about it since the puzzling discovery.

She slowed as she reached the opposite side of the bridge to look down on the quay. Whatever it was attracting so much interest, it appeared to be centred on the car park which ran alongside the river, where she and Esme had parked to go to the pub on Saturday lunchtime. People were pointing into the water, where a scuba diver was gesticulating to a colleague on the quayside.

Below her a man in a high visibility jacket climbed up into the cab of the crane, normally used for loading and unloading ships' cargo. She looked up at the sound of an engine on the water and saw in the distance Appledore's RNLI inshore lifeboat speeding up river towards her.

She hurried along the bridge. At the opposite end, a girl with blue hair and a nose stud intercepted her and handed her a leaflet. Maddy stuffed it into her fleece pocket and dodged around her, stopping beside a group of onlookers on the corner of the street.

'What's going on?' she said. She had to shout to be heard above the drone of the crane and the clanging of its beam as it swung over the water.

A woman in a turquoise alpine jacket responded. 'Not sure, dear,' she said. 'A car over the edge, someone said.'

The man in a bobble hat standing in front of the woman turned to look at her over his shoulder. 'Must have been down there a while,' he said. 'We never saw anything.'

Blue flashing lights flickered across the quay and a police officer urged everyone back to allow an ambulance through. It pulled up close to the edge and the crew jumped out, opening the rear doors before standing in readiness. Had the scuba diver seen someone inside the car?

The ambulance obscured Maddy's view of the water. She jogged around the group of people on the pavement and down towards the quay, hearing a shout from one of the men directing the action at the far end. She stopped and looked up as the tail of the crane's chain came into view, revealing its quarry. The crumpled body of a car gently swayed from the crane's giant hook, water gushing over the quayside. There were cries and muted shrieks from the crowd as they backed away to avoid getting their feet wet.

For a moment, Maddy couldn't process what she was seeing. Something about the sight registered familiarity. Then it struck her. She was staring at a yellow Fiat Coupé. Sean Carlton's car.

# 12

Esme's landline phone was ringing when she returned to the cottage after a restorative walk on the headland. She snatched up the handset.

'Esme Quentin. Hello?'

Maddy's voice greeted her at the other end of the line.

'Hang on, slow up,' Esme said, dropping down on to a kitchen chair to listen, as Maddy began a garbled explanation of Carlton's accident. 'He was in the car?' Esme asked, trying to make sense of it. 'Not that he'd left the handbrake off or something and it rolled away?'

'No,' Maddy said, a little breathless. 'The police are being a bit tight-lipped about it all, but from what I hear he'd been drinking and must have forgotten he'd parked close to the edge of a ten-foot drop.'

'Oh my God. Poor man. How horrible. Are you OK? Must have been a shock.'

Esme heard Maddy take a deep breath. 'You're telling me. If he'd driven something very ordinary, I might not have realised, but...' She cleared her throat. 'Now we know why he wasn't picking up my calls.'

Esme shuddered. In a way, she hoped he'd been too drunk to realise what was happening to him. Then again, if he'd been sober, he'd have been able to get himself out of the car.

'Did no one see it go in?' she asked. 'When did it happen, anyway?'

'Nobody seems to be sure. But no one could have seen it or they'd have raised the alarm at the time.'

'Yes, I suppose so.'

'So what are we going to do now? How are we going to find out why Dad had that file?'

Esme closed her eyes and pinched the bridge of her nose. 'Who else might know? Your dad's secretive former colleague, presumably?'

Maddy huffed down the phone. 'Well, they're not going to put their hand up, are they?'

'If you had an idea who it was, you might be able to have a discreet word.'

'If. But I don't.' Maddy sighed, her frustration obvious.

'I wonder why there was file on Ellen Tucker in the first place?' Esme said, her mind picking away at a number of scenarios in her head.

'Missing person?' Maddy suggested.

'Possibly,' Esme said. 'Carlton was trying to track her down, after all.'

'But if a family member engaged him, which we're assuming they would have, they'd be able to tell him everything he needed to know, wouldn't they? Why would he need to get his hands on anything the police had? Unless she was a hardened criminal, of course,' she added, dryly.

'Now, that's a thought,' Esme said, an idea forming in her mind.

Maddy laughed. 'I was joking, Esme.'

'Yes, I know, but you might have hit on something. Was she arrested for something? I don't know...a protest, drink driving? Was she caught up in an incident of some kind?'

'Well, it's all a bit academic if she did,' Maddy said, sounding unconvinced. 'We're not going to know now, are we?'

'Unless her name appears in the press,' Esme said. 'Tell you what, I'll have a search and see what I can come up with.'

'Search? Where?'

'*British Newspaper Archives* database online. And if nothing comes up, I'll pay a visit to the records office in

Barnstaple. They'll have past copies of *The North Devon Journal* on microfilm.'

Esme cut the call, realising she'd not had a chance to tell Maddy what she'd discovered about the residents of Temperance Mill. That could wait for now. The focus had shifted.

*

A quick drill-down of the British Newspaper Archives search engine told Esme that the latest date for copies of *The North Devon Journal* available online currently was only up to the 1950s. So it wasn't going to be as easy as putting Ellen Tucker's name into a search engine and have something magically pop up.

As she'd intimated to Maddy, she would need to make a trip to the North Devon Record office if they wanted to establish whether Ellen Tucker had made it into the pages of the local press. And a slow search awaited her when she got there, as everything would be on microfilm, through which she'd have to trawl by eye, in the traditional way.

Neither was it going to happen immediately. The record office was closed until Wednesday. They'd just have to be patient.

# 13

Gossip was rife at Tuesday's market the following day about the recovery of Carlton's car from the Torridge. Everyone was speculating on the circumstances, asking why no one had seen anything and wondering whether the police would classify it as a suspicious death.

'I suppose there's no point in giving the police our two penn'orth?' Esme asked Maddy.

Maddy, propped against the iron column at the end of their stall, folded her arms and gave Esme a sceptical look. 'What would we say? *Are you aware that one of your officers is passing police files to the general public?*'

'No, of course not. I mean mentioning the case Carlton was working on, saying how he'd come round asking questions and about who.'

'Won't they establish that as part of their enquiries into his death?'

'Yes, I suppose so. I wonder if whoever gave your dad that file had their own suspicions and will flag it up.'

'Why would they?' Maddy said, frowning. 'They'd already have done that, wouldn't they, if they thought a case worth flagging?'

'Perhaps they didn't have enough to go on before. Carlton's accident might change that.' Esme shook her head. 'Oh, I don't know, I'm sure. Let's see what happens. And we don't know what I'll dig up in the newspaper archives. Ah, looks like we've got a customer heading our way,' she added, seeing a woman dressed in a well-worn Barbour jacket and Wellington boots aiming purposefully towards their stall, a canvas shopping bag hanging from her arm.

Maddy looked round. 'Oh, that's Marianne,' she said, standing up to greet her before introducing her to Esme. The likeness to Anna was striking – the central peak in the hairline, the same green eyes.

'Good to meet you, Esme,' Marianne said, as they shook hands. 'You're helping Anna with this mad-capped idea of getting lottery money for the mill.'

'Well, I'm gathering some history on the place which she might use in her bid. I believe someone else is advising her on the application. You sympathise with your husband's view, then? He's obviously not convinced the project's viable.'

Marianne flapped her hand in the air. 'Oh, I don't know, I'm sure. Personally, I quite like the idea, but I'm worried that Anna might overstretch herself. I think she's underestimating the juggling act she's lining up for herself.'

'You mean becoming a mother?' Esme said.

'Oh, don't get me wrong, I'm thrilled to bits at the arrival of my first grandchild and I'm happy to help where I can, but still think it could be one project too far. But we'll see.' She turned to Maddy. 'Talking of projects, Maddy, did Daniel mention the writing slope?'

'Yes, he did. Needs a lot of TLC, apparently.'

'I'll say. Been in the loft of one of our barns for goodness knows how many years. We thought you might be able to bring it back to full health, so to speak.'

'Oh, that's brilliant, Marianne. Thank you. You'll be my first proper client! I'll take a look at it, shall I, and give you a quote?'

Marianne nodded. 'Perfect. That's exactly what I thought. So we've brought it in.' She scanned around the market. 'Daniel's got it with him. Can't imagine where he's got to.'

Esme looked around and spotted him standing just outside the entrance, something bulky under his arm. He was deep in conversation with someone on the pavement out of her sightline.

'Isn't that him?' she said.

Marianne looked over to where Esme was pointing. 'Oh good. He's on his way.' She turned back, tipping her head to one side. 'Terrible about that man going over the edge in his car, wasn't it?'

'Did you know he'd been to the yard?' Esme said.

'No?' Marianne's eyes widened. 'He was a customer?'

'Did Anna not say?' Maddy said. 'He was a private investigator. I sent him up to talk to you.'

'Me? Whatever for?'

'He was after someone who used to rent Temperance Cottage.'

'He's a bit late,' Marianne said, stiffly. 'The place hasn't been rented out for years.'

'So he never made it up to your place then?' Esme said. 'We got the impression he was on his way to you after he'd left us, weren't we, Maddy?'

'You'd have laughed, Marianne,' Maddy said, chuckling. 'Someone'd told him the mill was haunted by one of the Bideford witches.'

'How silly,' Marianne said, adjusting the shopping bag on her arm. 'What could have given him that idea?'

'He was asking about someone called Ellen Tucker,' Esme said. 'Do you remember her? About 20 odd years ago, he said.'

For a moment, Marianne looked startled, before giving a brief shrug of her shoulders and turning away. 'I don't think so. It's such a long time ago.' She stared over towards the entrance, her chin cocked. 'Now where's Daniel got to? He's taking for ever. Excuse me, I must go and jigger him along.' She left them and walked away.

'So did Carlton go there or not?' Maddy said. 'She seemed a bit evasive, don't you think?'

Esme thought back to what Cerys had told her about Ellen. *Bit of a looker*, Cerys had called her and talked about men's tongues hanging out, suggesting Ellen had found few allies amongst the women in the town, for that reason. Perhaps Daniel had been one of the men mesmerised by Ellen's looks and Marianne had been jealous. It would explain why she didn't want to talk about her.

'Maybe Marianne wasn't in when Carlton called,' Esme said, 'and he spoke to Daniel?'

'We can ask him. He's coming over.'

Esme watched as Marianne said something to Daniel before striding out of the market hall. Daniel shifted the box up under his arm and weaved his way between the shoppers to their stall.

'Morning, you two,' he said. He tossed his head back the way he'd come. 'Marianne says sorry to dash, but she's got to get something in the high street she'd forgotten.'

'That's OK,' Maddy said.

'Here it is. I'm afraid it's seen better days,' Daniel said, putting down the wooden box. The inlaid decoration on the lid was damaged and pieces of the veneer were missing. 'We should have taken more care of it, I suppose. It's got damp being out in the barn.'

'Oh don't worry about that, it's beautiful,' Maddy said, reaching out and rubbing her hand across the lid. 'Or, at least, it will be.' She opened it up to reveal the inside. At either end of the slope were narrow compartments for pens and at the deeper end two glass inkwells were slotted in the corners.

'Do you know its history?' asked Esme.

'Not really,' Daniel admitted. 'Only that was my late mother's. A birthday present from my father a few months before he died. So naturally it was very special for her. She always used it to write letters to friends or pay her bills.'

'The laptop of its day,' Esme said.

Daniel laughed. 'Yes, you're right there. Mother often let Anna do her drawings on it. In fact it was that memory which gave me the idea to get it restored.' He rubbed his thumb along his jaw. 'I thought, Maddy, whether there's any chance you could have it done in time for us to give it to Anna for her birthday on the 26th. She was fond of Mother. If it's not pushing it. It only gives you a little over two weeks.'

Maddy smiled. 'That's not a problem. I'll look it over and give you a price, shall I?'

Daniel's shoulders relaxed and his face broke into a broad grin. 'Ideal. Thanks, Maddy.'

Esme cleared her throat. 'You heard about the guy they fished out of the river, did you?'

'Yeah, tragic.' Daniel gave his head a shake. 'Bloody idiot. Fancy thinking he could drive. From all accounts he'd had a skinful.'

'Yes, all too easy to forget about the quay edge if you're not local and it's dark. Did he ever get to have a word with you?'

Daniel's face puckered into a frown. 'Have a word? Sorry, I don't...'

'It's just that Maddy sent him up to speak to you,' Esme said, disappointed in Daniel's response. It didn't sound as though Carlton had got as far as Hill Farm, after all. 'He was asking about a tenant of yours from years back. Ellen Tucker.'

'Ellen?' He flushed.

'Oh, you remember her, then?' Maddy said. 'Marianne wasn't sure.'

Daniel shuffled from one foot to the other. 'Yeah, I remember her.' He rammed his hands into the pockets of his jacket and shrugged. 'She rented the cottage for a few months. Then she left.'

Esme nodded. She wondered what havoc Ellen had caused in the short time she'd lived in Bideford. Daniel's embarrassed reaction suggested that her earlier supposition that he'd been one of Ellen's admirers was correct.

'Right then,' Daniel said, backing away. 'I'll leave the box with you, Maddy, and wait to hear from you. Nice to see you again, Esme,' he added with a nod. 'I'd better go and catch up with the boss.' He hurried away.

Maddy gave Esme a wry grin. 'One of Ellen's conquests, d'you think?'

'My thoughts exactly,' Esme said, watching Daniel head across the market hall. 'So, did he see Carlton or was he also avoiding the subject?'

Maddy raised her eyebrows. 'Good question. At least he acknowledged Ellen had been a tenant. Which is more than Marianne did.'

Daniel had reached the entrance to the market and stopped to talk to someone. An elderly man, leaning on a walking stick, jabbing in the air with his finger. Joseph Brannock. And the body language suggested it wasn't a friendly exchange.

# 14

Esme climbed the stairs at the back of Barnstaple library's ground floor, past the reference section on the first floor and up to the North Devon Record Office. She signed in at the reception desk and claimed a microfilm reading machine at the tables on the opposite side of the room. Hanging her bag over the back of the chair, she wandered across to the window while she waited for the archivist to locate the relevant film for the *North Devon Journal*'s editions for 1995.

She peered out at the green space, watching the shrubs below blowing in the wind, depositing the remainder of their leaves over the grass, and contemplated the scene she'd observed at the market - Daniel's odd exchange with Joseph Brannock. Was there antagonism between them? Or was this merely another manifestation of Joseph's advancing dementia? When she'd encountered Joseph at Temperance Cottage, his grievance seemed to focus on the Brannocks' ownership of the mill. Did that suggest he was a descendant of the family who'd lived there during the mid-1800s? But it would have passed out of the Brannocks' hands long before Joseph had been born. And whatever land disputes had occurred between the Meddons and the Brannocks in the past were now irrelevant since Drew and Anna's marriage. Everything had come full circle. The mill was back under the Brannock name. Had Joseph not grasped that? Or was there something else between Daniel and Joseph which had nothing to do with long historical family feuds?

She felt someone at her elbow and turned to see the archivist beside her. He pushed his Clark Kent style glasses up on to the bridge of his nose and grinned.

'I've put the film by your machine,' he said, gesturing behind him.

Esme smiled. 'Great, thanks,' she said and hurried back to her table. She removed the reel from the box and threaded it on the spool, before switching on the machine and settling down in front of the screen. It was going to be a slow search. Her only comfort was that as Ellen had only been in Bideford a few months, any incident must have happened in 1995. At least she didn't have several years to trawl through.

She made herself comfortable on the chair and adjusted her reading glasses. Right. January.

*

Maddy sat down at the workbench and turned her attention to the wooden writing box which had belonged to Daniel's mother, Alice. She'd half expected Daniel to barter hard to get her to drop her restoration fee, but he'd seemed happy enough. Did that mean she was under-pricing herself? She guessed she'd get the hang of the business side of her work as time went on. For now, she was pleased to have her fist commission.

She ran her finger over the smooth surface of the box and appraised the work to be done. Made of walnut, it was decorated with an eye-catching zig-zag design, inlaid around the edge of the lid. A small piece of the veneer was lost and another section loose. No doubt dirt and dust had crept underneath and lifted it. Careful cleaning would be her first task.

She opened the lid and laid it down to form the slope on which the user would rest to write their correspondence. The condition was much better inside, although one corner of the leather was torn and would need patching. But the two glass inkwells, which slotted neatly in their corner partitions, remained intact.

She tipped the lid of the narrow pencil box and lifted it out. A flat woodworker's pencil was its only occupant. She allowed herself a wistful smile. No valuable Mordan dipping pens or pencils secreted away inside, then. British silversmith Sampson Mordan was the co-inventor of the world's first propelling pencil, patented in 1822, and Maddy knew that rare examples of the Georgian or Victorian writing implements could reach over £1,000 at auction.

The thought prompted an idea. She explored underneath the pencil box, sensing the twinge of anticipation as she felt the tell-tale false wall in the wood and realised it had a concealed drawer. Not all writing boxes had hidden compartments, but there were still some out there with their mysteries intact. She took out the ink bottles and pulled up on one of the wooden dividers. The panel clicked open to reveal two tiny secret drawers, a small piece of ribbon attached to allow for easy opening.

The first drawer was empty, but inside the second was a single folded scrap of paper. She pulled it out and unfolded it, amused by a child's drawing in smudged crayon, a series of wonky buildings and lollipop trees at either end. Perhaps it was Anna's? Daniel had mentioned that his mother had allowed Anna to use the writing slope on occasion. Most of the drawing had been scribbled over, heavily at one end. Perhaps she'd not been pleased with her efforts.

Maddy turned it over, looking for a name. On the reverse something had been written in crayon, but it was too faded to make out. Anna's initials? She must remember to show it to Anna and see if she recognised it. On the other hand, perhaps not. She'd have to say where she found it and that would spoil the surprise. She could ask Daniel and Marianne if they recognised it or, better still, wait until after Anna's birthday.

She put the drawing to one side and set out her tools ready to begin the renovation.

*

Esme had reached saturation point in the record office. Her concentration was beginning to drift and she risked missing something important. She knew it would be wise to take a break. But she didn't want to run out of time and come away without something to show for her afternoon's efforts. That's assuming there was something to find.

She should at least take a walk around the room to stretch her legs and free up her brain. She slid back her chair and stood up.

The archivist was pinning up a poster on the display board and she wandered over to read it. He looked round as she came up behind him.

'Should be an interesting talk,' he said, nodding towards the poster. 'And an appropriate subject, given the time of year.'

'Time of year?'

'Halloween.'

'Oh yes, of course,' Esme said, looking up at the poster. It depicted a woodcut image of an old woman in a pointed hat and advertised a forthcoming talk in a local bookshop. *Damned, Denied & Defended,* she read. *The changing attitudes to witchcraft in history.* 'Oh, I know Morris Beveridge,' she said, seeing the name of the author. Morris was a genealogist. His information had proved crucial in uncovering the truth behind the untimely death of Bella Shaw and the link with the mystery of a 19th century female convict who'd been transported to Australia.

'Yes, he's a regular in here, as you'd imagine,' the archivist said. 'I've heard his talk is very good.'

'Is it about the infamous Bideford Witches?' Esme asked. 'I've been meaning to find out more about them.'

'I think so. And some lesser known stories, I believe.' He handed Esme a leaflet. 'Might go along myself.'

Esme took the leaflet and returned to her microfiche reader. A glance at the clock told her she had another half an hour. She took a deep breath and began scanning.

Twenty minutes later Ellen Tucker's name leaped out at her. She froze and stopped the machine, aware of the increase in her heart rate. She scrolled back slowly to look for the place she'd seen it, hoping it hadn't merely been her desire to discover something playing tricks on her.

Whether by instinct or simple curiosity, her eye pounced on a headline. "*WOMAN HARASSED BY YOUTHS. Half-term holiday boredom has been blamed for a spate of anti-social behaviour in Bideford recently,*" the article began, and went on to describe various incidents reported in previous weeks, from late-night revelling to broken windows.

She skimmed the page as the report continued, "*More serious complaints have been reported to us by Miss Ellen Tucker of Temperance Cottage, Bideford.*"

Esme flopped against the back of her chair, took off her reading glasses and let out a deep sigh. Was that why there'd been a police file on Ellen? Had she made an official complaint to the police of what she'd told the newspaper?

She put her glasses back on and returned to the screen to look at the rest of the piece, her pulse quickening as she read the last sentence. "*Miss Tucker alleges that she has received death threats and accusations of being a witch.*"

# 15

Esme walked across the car park, mulling over her discovery, a printed copy of the report in her bag to show Maddy. It was obvious now why Sean Carlton had asked about *witchcraft and strange goings on*. He'd been aware of the newspaper report of Ellen's unwelcome visitors. It could also explain the empty file she and Maddy had found in Ted's house – a copy of the formal complaint Ellen had made to the police concerning the harassment, perhaps. There must have been more in the file than appeared in the newspaper, otherwise Carlton would already have all the information he needed, but it confirmed one thing, at least. Their theory that Ted had helped out his former colleague in obtaining information the police held on Ellen Tucker was correct. Hopefully it would put Maddy's mind at rest.

The newspaper report both intrigued and disturbed her. While taunting a woman for being a witch might be dismissed as merely the antics of bored schoolchildren acting out Halloween fantasies, Esme could easily imagine, having been to the cottage in its isolated location, how terrifying it would have been for Ellen Tucker alone, on a dark night, being bombarded by the catcalls of youths on a high.

She was puzzled, though, even in the context of an impending Halloween, as to what made a group of school kids target a woman like Ellen Tucker. From Cerys's description, Ellen was attractive, even glamorous in some eyes, and as far removed as anyone could be from the usual, ugly old hag image, of most fairy-tale witches.

Esme reached her car and climbed inside, taking out her phone from her bag and dialling Maddy's number. As she listened to it ring, Esme wondered at the reaction at Hill Farm to the newspaper report back in 1995. Perhaps it was the reason why Daniel and Marianne had been evasive about Ellen Tucker. Maybe they'd been embarrassed by their tenant's being subjected to such taunts. Perhaps Ellen had complained to them and asked them to do something about it. It might have even created a dispute between them.

Maddy's phone switched to voicemail. She was probably busy with a client and couldn't take the call. Esme hesitated. Should she leave a message? She decided against it and cut the connection. She'd rather speak to Maddy directly. Perhaps she'd drop in to the workshop on her way home.

She started the car and set off for Bideford.

*

When Esme came through the workshop door, Maddy was putting on her coat.

'Oh, sorry,' Esme said. 'You're off out, aren't you? To see that band in Exeter. I forgot.'

'Yes, Harry's picking me up in a minute. How did you get on at the record office?'

'Good,' Esme said. 'Which is why I dropped by. Couldn't get you on the phone.'

Maddy shook her head. 'No, I'd put it on silent. It messes with my head when I'm working.'

Esme slipped the bag off her shoulder and put it on the workbench before delving inside and pulling out the print-out of the newspaper report. 'There you go,' she said, giving it to Maddy to read and watching for her reaction.

'A witch?' Maddy said, dropping her chin. 'So that's why Sean Carlton was so fixated on the witch thing.'

Esme nodded. 'Exactly.'

Maddy handed the copy back to Esme. 'Even though

Temperance Cottage is a bit out on a limb,' she said, 'it's not that far from habitation. Easy for kids with nothing better to do to have their bit of fun and still leg it home easily.'

'I wondered if it's the reason Daniel and Marianne were so evasive?' Esme said. 'It can't be much of a recommendation, having your tenant targeted like that. Maybe that's why they never re-let the cottage.'

'Seems an odd reason to turn down potential income. Most people wouldn't know.'

Esme slipped the paper back in her bag. 'So looks like Carlton called in a favour and your dad was able to help out,' she said.

Maddy sighed. 'Yes, it does, doesn't it? Shame the poor bugger never got the chance to finish his search. I wonder if whoever hired Carlton will send someone else. We could find ourselves answering the same questions all over again.'

'We'll be clued up next time. Might tease a bit out of them. Well, I won't hold you up, then,' Esme added, turning away.

'No, it's OK. He's not here yet. Come and see what I've been doing.' Maddy went across to the workbench where Daniel and Marianne's writing slope stood and indicated the components of the box laid out on the bench. 'I've made a start, but I'll need to get some leather for the interior. I don't have the right colour in my limited stock.'

'How's it going?' Esme asked.

'Good, thanks. I'm enjoying it.'

Maddy picked up a sheet of paper lying beside the box and handed it to Esme. 'Look,' she said. 'I found this in a drawer.'

'Oh, how sweet!' Esme said, smiling at the archetypal child's representation of a house: four windows, a central door and a pointed roof, with smoke coming out of the chimney. There was even a face at the window. Another building stood beside the house behind a ball-like bush. 'Shame about the scribble all over it. Is it Anna's?'

'I'd imagine so. The slope belonged to her grandmother, and Daniel said his mother used to let Anna rest on it to do her drawings. But I daren't ask her or I'll give away Daniel's birthday surprise. And saying that, I'd better hide this away before she comes in and sees it.'

Esme handed it back and Maddy slipped the drawing into a drawer of her desk. She threw a cloth over the partially dismantled writing box as the door opened and Harry came inside.

'Hi, Harry,' Esme said, snatching up her bag. 'I won't hold you up. I'm off home. Just called in to show something to Maddy.'

'Ellen Tucker was accused of being a witch,' Maddy told Harry.

'What, that woman Carlton was looking for?'

Maddy nodded. 'Bit creepy, isn't it?'

'Any more from the police on what happened to Carlton?' Esme asked. 'Or have they written it off as a drunken error?'

Harry shrugged. 'They've not been back to the pub, as far as I know. Not that I was working that night, so I've got nothing to tell them. Eddie was, though.'

'Has he said anything about it?' Maddy said.

'Well, he saw him, obviously. Wouldn't have been that busy, being a Sunday.'

'Odd that no one saw him go over,' Maddy said. 'Though it was a foul night, so people wouldn't have been out on the quay, I guess. When did he leave the pub?'

'Eddie didn't know,' Harry said, shaking his head. 'Didn't see the Brannocks leave either, for that matter.'

'The Brannocks?' Maddy frowned. 'They were there?'

'Drew and Alec were, yeah. But it's their local. You know that.'

'Yeah, but you said Eddie didn't see them leave, as though it was significant or something.'

'Only because they were all drinking together.'

'Sean Carlton was with Drew and Alec?' Harry nodded. Maddy and Esme exchanged glances. Esme recalled watching Carlton trying to talk to Drew when he'd visited the yard.

'Drew changed his tune, then,' she said. 'He wouldn't give Carlton the time of day when he called in here.'

'They were knocking it back, Eddie said,' Harry added. 'Which explains the state Carlton was in.'

'So why did he think he could drive?' Maddy asked, slowly shaking her head. 'What was he thinking of? Surely he'd have realised, wouldn't he? At least, by the time he got out to his car.'

'Maybe not. It happens.' Harry checked his watch. 'Look, this in-depth analysis is all very well, but...'

'Yes,' Esme said, striding to the door. 'You need to go.'

They parted in the car park. Harry and Maddy turned right towards Exeter and Esme turned left towards town. As she pulled out into the road, Drew's van flew past her, heading in the opposite direction.

She reflected on Drew's behaviour the day Carlton had called in at the yard, his odd reaction to the name Ellen Tucker and the way he'd brushed off Carlton's approach in the car park. She assumed that Carlton had gone into The Kings Arms on the night he'd died to ask the same questions he'd asked her and Maddy.

So why had Drew been so rudely dismissive of Carlton here in the yard and yet willing to sit and share a drink with him a couple of days later?

# 16

Morris Beveridge's talk on history's changing attitudes to witchcraft was well attended. When Esme arrived, people had all but filled the small bookshop on the high street and were already at the counter buying copies of *Damned, Denied & Defended* for Morris to sign later.

When the start of the event was announced, Esme found a seat next to a bald-headed man with heavy black-rimmed glasses who took notes throughout the presentation.

Morris got to his feet and straightened his snug waistcoat, its paisley pattern resplendent in black and gold. Adjusting his rimless spectacles, he cleared his throat in readiness and the audience hushed.

He began, inevitably perhaps, given the location, with the story of Temperance Lloyd, Susanna Edwards and Mary Trembles, the three women executed in 1682, whom Carlton had mentioned on his visit to the reclamation yard.

Temperance Lloyd was the first person to be arrested, after a local shopkeeper issued a complaint against her. It hadn't been the first time she'd faced such charges, having been accused a number of times over several years of causing sickness and even death to members of the community. On those occasions, she'd been tried and acquitted. This time, though, there would be no such benign outcome.

Mary Trembles was accused a week later. She had called at the house of one of the complainants, whose symptoms had worsened after Mary's visit. Mary was subsequently arrested, along with Susanna Edwards, who had the misfortune to be in Mary's company at the time.

As Cerys had explained when they'd shown her Anna's witch's bottle, the power of magic and the existence of witches was an accepted, feared and deeply held belief within society of the time. The people looked to the authorities to ensure that such evil was exposed and punished. Once word got out about the women's indictment, others joined the cry, adding stories of their own sufferings as a result of the women's witchcraft, all eager to blame someone for their illnesses and misfortunes.

Esme was horrified at not only how easily a falling-out between neighbours could result in accusations of witchcraft, but how flimsy the evidence could be for someone to be charged. Hearsay and general consensus were sufficient. Morris told them of one case in Leicestershire where nine women were executed for witchcraft, following an accusation by a 12-year-old boy who later admitted he'd made it up.

Given that those accused believed in witchcraft and the influence of the Devil in the same way as anyone else in society, Esme wasn't surprised that so many of them confessed to their so-called crimes, as did the Bideford three. Perhaps they genuinely believed that they had been possessed. When questioned at her trial, Temperance mentioned she'd sold an apple to a child, whose mother had taken it away. Temperance had been angry and later the child had died of smallpox. Had she held herself responsible, believing through her anger she'd "bewitched" him?

The Bideford three were shipped off to Exeter to face trial, waiting for over a month for the justices to arrive in the city and begin proceedings. Unfortunately for the three, the long wait allowed an unhealthy curiosity to develop in their case, and by the time the trial began, public hysteria was rife with tales of the women's supernatural powers. Such was the mood in the city, those in charge feared an uprising if the women were acquitted. Under pressure to keep the peace, they found all three guilty, and the women were hanged in Heavitree, near Exeter, on Friday 25 August 1682.

Tea and biscuits were served after the talk. Esme let the others join the queue and went over to congratulate Morris on his presentation.

'Mrs Quentin, thank you so much for coming,' Morris said, taking her hand and giving it a rigorous shake. 'How nice to see you again.'

Esme laughed. 'Oh, for goodness' sake, Morris,' she said. 'No need to be so formal. It's Esme.'

He flushed. 'Yes, of course. But it doesn't do to be presumptuous. Now, tell me. What are you up to these days?'

Esme smiled at his old-fashioned manner and told him about the new *Photos Reunited* project she'd started with Maddy. 'You must go and look on the website, Morris,' she said. 'You might recognise someone from one of your clients' families.'

'I shall do that, Esme,' he said. 'And I'll spread the word.'

'Thank you, that'd be really helpful. So what about you, Morris? Are you busy?'

He nodded. 'Oh, yes, particularly since the book came out. My time is more often than not spent giving talks, rather than in any client research.'

'Ah, what it is to be a famous author,' Esme said.

'Now you're teasing me,' he said, colouring once more. 'Did you enjoy the talk?'

'I did, yes. Fascinating. It's interesting, isn't it, that people still believed that witches were the cause of their misfortunes even in more so-called enlightened times? I was surprised by the case of the poor woman attacked by that couple in 1852 for being a witch, while she was on her way home minding her own business.'

'Yes, also note that the law was, effectively, on the side of the old woman assaulted, not the one making the accusation, as in earlier examples.'

'Yes, a complete turnaround, as the title of your book suggests. I'm guessing that was a slow process.'

Morris nodded. 'Oh indeed. When the Witchcraft Act was passed in 1736, the objective might have been to outlaw belief in the existence of witches, but you can't just expect superstition that's endured for millennia to suddenly evaporate in a puff of smoke,' he chuckled, 'if you'll pardon the pun.'

Esme smiled. 'I'll forgive you.'

'Of course, not everyone agreed with the act when it came out. John Wesley, the famous Methodist leader, saw it as a huge mistake that witchcraft – or the "invisible world", as he called it – should no longer be considered a crime, declaring that he'd stand by his certainty with his last breath.'

'Well, from the stories you told us, he wasn't the only one.' Esme glanced across the shop. 'Looks like you've got some book signing to do, so I'll leave you to your fans.'

Afterwards, when Esme was walking up the high street back to her car, the newspaper report about Ellen Tucker concerning the harassment and alleged accusation of being a witch, slipped into her mind. Esme suspected the youths who'd participated would see their behaviour as nothing more than innocent fun, unaware of the chilling and gruesome history which lay behind it.

# 17

Maddy stood in her workshop, looking at Esme with a worried frown. 'Now, you're sure about this, Esme? I feel I'm leaving you in the lurch.'

Esme laughed. 'Don't be silly! It's fine.'

Maddy continued to look concerned. 'I know it was one of Dad's best fairs. I'd rather not cancel. I might not get another opportunity. The pitches are hard to come by.'

'Maddy, will you stop fretting! This is precisely why I'm getting involved, for occasions like this.'

'Yes, but I didn't expect it to happen so quickly. You're still only just learning the ropes.'

'Oh, I expect I'll cope,' Esme said, with a teasing smile. 'I can do really hard sums in my head now, you know. And joined-up writing, too.'

'Oh, very funny.'

Esme giggled and waved her hand around the workshop. 'So what do you want me to take with me? If we put it in my car now, I can unload it at the market tomorrow morning without needing to come back here. Obviously I won't be able to get in as much as you can in your van, but if we concentrate on the smaller stuff, it'll be more than adequate, I'd have thought.'

They spent the next half hour going through a jumble of items that Maddy had assembled, packing the most appropriate into cardboard boxes ready to transfer to Esme's car. With that done, they turned their attention to what Maddy would take with her.

They were struggling to manhandle a wooden trunk with decorative metal strapping over to the entrance, ready for loading into Maddy's campervan, when the workshop door opened and Anna came in.

'Ah, Esme,' she said, 'I'm glad you're here.'

Maddy grunted and lowered her end of the trunk. Esme did likewise, breathing heavily.

Anna laughed. 'I'd give you a hand, guys, but I'm under strict orders not to lift heavy objects.'

'Should think not, too,' Maddy said. She sat down on the trunk and wiped the back of her hand across her forehead. 'I'm sticking to small portable boxes after I've sold all the big stuff. This is way too much hassle. And I thought I was fit.'

'Where's it going?' Anna asked.

'Big fair up near Bath,' Maddy told her. She nodded at Esme. 'Esme's standing in at the market.'

'How will you get it out of the van when you get there?' Anna said.

'Oh, don't worry about that. One of the other guys will give me a hand.'

'Well, be careful,' Anna said.

Maddy saluted. 'Yes, ma'am.'

'So,' Esme said, you wanted to see me?'

'Oh, yes,' Anna said. 'Mum's remembered there was an old plan of the mill somewhere which you might find useful. She's going to see if she can find it. I'll give you a call if she does.'

'OK, great,' Esme said. 'Oh, and thanks for those names, by the way. It helps tie everyone in with my initial research using the censuses.'

'Sorry it's not more,' Anna said. 'It's embarrassing I don't know beyond my grandparents. I keep asking Mum and she said she would scribble something down, but then she's busy and never gets to it...'

'Don't worry,' Esme said. 'I've enough to go on.'

Esme heard footsteps and the door was flung open. Anna stepped to one side as Drew came inside.

'You gone deaf or something?' he said, turning to his wife. 'Your office phone's being ringing out across the yard for the last 5 minutes.'

Anna flashed Drew an irritated look. 'So why didn't you answer it?' she said.

Drew shrugged. 'No point. They'd want to speak to you anyway.'

'Oh, go on, Drew, please,' Anna said, puckering her brow. 'It might be that weirdo again.'

Drew sighed and rolled his eyes. 'Pregnancy's making you paranoid,' he said. But he did as she asked and went back outside, letting the door bang behind him.

'Weirdo?' Maddy said.

Anna shrugged. 'Oh, you know the sort. You pick up the phone and there's no one there. It's no big deal, really.'

'Well, Drew might as well get in some practice at taking over the office responsibilities,' Maddy said.

'He hardly needs that, Maddy. He's been involved in the business from the start.'

Maddy flushed. 'Yes, I know that. I meant, you've always taken the lead on the administrative side.'

Anna pinched her lips together. 'I know you think he's not capable of running things when the baby arrives and I might not be around as much,' she began.

'Look, I didn't mean...'

'I know exactly what you meant, Maddy. You and Drew have always rubbed one another up the wrong way. Even when you were at school, from what I gather.'

Maddy shrugged. 'Yeah, well. That was a long time ago.'

'Exactly. So perhaps it's time for a truce? Especially now you've taken on the workshop and you'll be around more often.'

Maddy held up her hand. 'Point taken. I'll do my best.' She gave Anna a reassuring smile, but Esme sensed it lacked conviction.

'It'll be even more important when we get the go-ahead on the mill conversion,' Anna continued. 'Drew will be in charge of the yard, then. Keeping it ticking over while I'm busy project-managing everything.'

'So you've convinced him it's viable, then?' Maddy said.

Anna winked. 'Oh, he'll come round.' She patted her stomach. 'After all, we've got the future to think of, haven't we?' She turned towards the door. 'Well, I'll see you guys later. I must go and feed Gypsy. And I'll give you a call when I hear back from Mum about that plan, shall I, Esme?'

'That'd be great, Anna, thanks.' Anna nodded and disappeared out of the door. 'Well, that puts you in your place,' Esme said, grinning at Maddy.

Maddy sighed. 'Oh, I expect Drew's been strutting about, pretending to be the big I AM. I'm certainly not going to lose any sleep over it.'

'Except Anna's put you on notice to be nice to him. You'd better watch your step,' Esme teased, waving a finger at her.

Maddy laughed. 'Yeah, I'm quaking in my boots. Now, let's get this lot loaded up.'

*

Esme drove her car, fully-laden with the stock for the market stall the following day, back home with care, even more so when she reached the rough track down to the cottage. It was already getting dark, and by the time she'd fixed herself something to eat and cleared up, it was well into the evening. With a dawn start ahead the following morning, she decided to light the wood-burner, luxuriate on the sofa in front of the fire and read Morris's book before having an early night.

While the flames took hold, she checked the emails on her phone, noticing there was one from the General Registry Office, telling her that the death certificates she'd ordered for Bessie and Silas Brannock were available to view.

She booted her laptop, logging on to her account to bring up the list of ordered PDF files and clicking on the image for Bessie, noting that Bessie had died at Temperance Mill on 4 October 1868. She scanned across the screen to the cause of death column, wincing as she read it. One word, but chilling in its message - *burning*. She shuddered. She'd come across similar circumstances on many occasions. Open-fire cooking and the long skirts of the Victorian era often proved a lethal combination.

She turned to Silas's certificate. He'd also died at Temperance Mill, but on 26 November 1868. When she read the cause of death, she stared at it for a moment before flicking back to double-check the name. But no, it was correct. Silas had also died of *burning*.

Esme took off her reading glasses and sat back in her chair. Anna had said something about there once being a miller's cottage attached to the mill, which had burned down in the 19th century. Had the couple both died in that fire? But Silas had died over two months later than Bessie. Surely he hadn't lingered for that long from his injuries?

Esme slipped her glasses back on and returned to the screen. Perhaps she'd find some answers in the *British Newspaper Archive*. She found the website and logged in her subscriber details, entering Bessie's name in the archive search engine and limiting the dates to the years of Bessie's death and the area of interest to South West England. She clicked the button to activate the search.

As the results popped up on the screen, Esme's eye was drawn to the words of the first item on the list – *sad fatal accident*. She pulled up the newspaper article and read the report. Bessie's death, it appeared, had been as the result of her falling into the kitchen fire. Although she'd sought assistance from other family members in the house, it had been too late to save her and she'd died a few hours later from her injuries. Esme pressed her fist against her mouth and shuddered at the thought of such a horrific end to a life.

So what had befallen Silas? She bookmarked the piece about Bessie and changed the details for Silas. The search engine whirred for a few moments before displaying its findings. At the top of the screen, she read, "*MAN BURNED TO DEATH.*" She clicked on the heading and was taken to the image of the newspaper page where she read the remainder of the article.

A shocking fatality was discovered yesterday when a charred body was discovered in the remains of the miller's cottage at Temperance Mill, Bideford. The victim is believed to be Silas Brannock. The origins of the fire are unknown.

# 18

Saturday morning was quiet at the market and Cerys took the opportunity to show Esme her granddaughter's entry for the Halloween painting competition.

'I said I'd hand it in for her,' Cerys said proudly.

Esme studied the painting. It was clear the girl had talent. Her depiction of a witch with long black hair flowing behind her was striking.

'That's fabulous,' Esme said, handing it back to Cerys. 'She must be in with a good chance of a prize, I would have thought.'

Cerys grinned. 'I'm so glad you think so,' she said, slipping the painting back inside a large Manilla envelope. 'I was beginning to worry I was biased.'

'Talking of witches,' Esme said, 'I stumbled upon something interesting the other day.' She gave Cerys a brief summary of the newspaper report and how Ellen Tucker had been the target of abuse.

'Never,' Cerys said, wide-eyed horror on her face. 'Ellen?'

'And bad enough to put in a complaint to the police, according to the newspaper. You don't remember anything about it at the time?'

Cerys shook her head. 'No, I don't.'

'What I don't get,' Esme said, 'is why modern-day kids would accuse someone like that of being a witch. OK, it *was* Halloween, but it's not as though she looked like the archetypal weird old woman.' She shrugged. 'Then again, we are talking about back in the nineties. Perhaps the teenage witch thing hadn't got going down here then.'

'A positive witch image isn't that new. You must remember *Bewitched*, that American comedy? That was around back in the sixties or seventies, wasn't it?'

'Oh yes,' Esme said, laughing. 'I loved that. I was always trying to wriggle my nose like Samantha did when she cast a spell. Never did crack it.'

'Of course, not everyone's enamoured with the idea of witches.' Cerys tapped the envelope containing her granddaughter's painting. 'Someone on the committee was even against running the painting competition.'

'No. Really?'

Cerys nodded. 'Oh yes. Don't forget, some primary schools have always been anti-witch, especially church schools. The one I went to wouldn't allow stories about witches of any description on the premises.'

'What - even those lovely *Meg and Mog* picture books and *The Worst Witch* stories?'

Cerys grinned. 'Sounds far-fetched, doesn't it? Until you realise how many references there are in the bible about witchcraft being a sin and condemning sorcerers and mediums. It's created a tall order for the teachers, I've always thought. Think how often witches come up in fairy stories. I can't see how you could avoid them without slicing a big hole in children's literature. But it happened.'

'How do they cope with the *Harry Potter* phenomenon?' said Esme. 'They must have had to give in then, surely.'

'Not everywhere. *Harry Potter* books were actually burned in Poland.'

Esme shook her head. 'Goodness. I hadn't realised.' She recalled an episode of a TV drama she'd watched as a child, set during the height of the Second World War. A mob of angry villagers had discovered a collection of German books and set light to them in the street. A deeply religious community, they were mortified when they realised the books they'd torched were bibles.

They wandered back towards their stalls. Esme noticed a bearded man in a brown leather jacket standing at the far end of the aisle. A potential customer?

'I don't think,' Cerys said, 'that Ellen's experience has anything to do with children's perspective of witches.'

'No? How d'you mean?' Esme said, looking towards the man. He regarded her briefly before turning and marching out of the market hall.

'Like I told you,' Cerys was saying, 'Ellen had a bit of a reputation with men. Which brings us back to the church. In the church's eyes, women like Ellen use their wicked ways to lure men to immoral behaviour.'

Esme pulled a face of disgust. 'Oh, typical. All the woman's fault, then. Eve and the apple all over again.'

Cerys raised her eyebrows. 'You're getting the general idea. Now, think about the basic premise of most fairy stories.'

'The battle between good and evil?'

'Exactly. They reinforced the church's attitude towards women. Wicked stepmothers – they represent the evil witch, the bible's Jezebel, if you will, synonymous with depravity – ensnare men with their sexual magnetism. The father is led astray by the step-mother. She represents the evil of the woman, see, and so he's absolved of all responsibility.'

'Poor Ellen,' Esme said. 'You really think she was labelled a witch because she was an attractive woman? But not by kids, surely?'

'They may have picked up the idea subliminally from their parents, if it was something under discussion...' she flapped a hand.

'Yes, I take your point. But all this didn't apply to the Bideford witches, did it?' Esme said, recalling what Morris had said in his talk. 'They were accused of causing harm to their neighbours through witchcraft. And they were in their dotage, not the sexy young wench variety.'

'Didn't matter. Even though that wasn't where the accusations began, promiscuity got dragged in to the mix eventually.

Read the transcript of the trial. There are references all over the place. Cavorting with the devil was a common assumption. It was all in the How-to book of witch identification, of course.'

'The what?' Esme said. 'You're having me on.'

'No, I'm deadly serious. Published in 1486. Called *Malleus Maleficarum*, roughly translated as The Hammer of Witches, it became the reference de rigueur in spotting a witch back then: who might be a likely candidate – herbalists, independent women, anyone who was a bit different, who didn't fit in with society, that sort of thing – and how to punish them if you discovered one. And it pulled no punches.'

'So would this be the era of the Witchfinder General and dunking stools and all that?'

'That's right. Thousands of women – and some men, it has to be said – were executed as witches across Europe in the years following its publication. It had quite an impact.'

'The Bideford witches were much later, though, weren't they, when the trend for exposing witches was on the wane?'

'Yes, that's what made it unusual. And the fact that Bideford was such a cosmopolitan town. Rooting out witches was generally associated with rural areas.'

'So what's the explanation?'

'Ah, well, there you go. There's been speculation about that ever since. Oh, look. A customer. I'd better get back to my post.'

She headed across the aisle, calling to Esme over her shoulder.

'You should read *The Trial of the Bideford Witches*. There's a copy in the library. Fascinating stuff.'

# 19

Esme could tell by the buoyant way Maddy answered the door that her weekend trip had proved successful. She'd called in to collect another box of old photographs for uploading on to the *Photos Reunited* website and was heartened to see a renewed spark of excitement for the embryonic venture. Maddy invited Esme into the living room, her eyes shining as she told her how she'd secured funds for an auction she planned to attend in a couple of weeks' time.

'I've got my eye on an adorable little sewing box and a medicine cabinet,' Maddy enthused. 'They'd be perfect. Just the sort of thing I want to specialise in.' But her elated expression faded, giving way to a furrowed brow. 'Trouble is, I'm so new at this game, someone more experienced is bound to outbid me. So I'm trying not to get my hopes up.'

'Oh, you never know,' Esme said. 'You might be lucky. And this is all part of the learning curve. You win some, you lose some, I guess.'

'That's what I keep telling myself. Oh, almost forgot.' Maddy spun round and strode across to the table in front of the window. 'I got something for the project, too.' She picked up a large photograph album, bound in faded brown leather. She cleared a space amongst the files and set the album down, opening it up so Esme could see inside.

'Oh, fabulous,' Esme said, gazing at the Victorian images displayed in decorative frames on the first page of thick card: a serious gentleman with bushy side whiskers, the chain of his pocket watch hanging from his waistcoat pocket, and in the photograph next to his, an elderly woman, hair curled tightly at the side of her head, dressed in a taffeta dress, a series of buttons and elaborate tucks on the bodice echoed around the edge of the skirt. 'What a fantastic find.'

'It is, isn't it? There are some names on the backs of the early pictures.'

'What's going to happen to your photo archive when I've finished scanning everything?' Esme asked as she explored the rest of the book, smiling at the photograph of a little girl standing on a chair holding a bunch of flowers almost too big for her, hair in ringlets around her face. 'I assume you'll have them back here?'

'In the short term, yes.' Maddy's eyes shone. 'But if Anna's grand plan for the mill goes ahead, it might be the perfect place to create a depository of some sort, particularly for the local photos. And another criteria box to tick for her application for lottery funding.'

'That's brilliant. Have you told her about it?'

'Not yet. Thought I'd wait till after the meeting with the expert next week when we're sure it's viable.'

Esme closed the photo album. 'How are you getting on at your dad's house?' she asked. 'Let me know if you need a hand again.'

'I can't keep imposing on you,' Maddy said, bending down to pick up her ginger cat who was rubbing around her ankles.

'Nonsense. I know what it's like,' Esme said, tickling Ginger under his chin. 'I've been there, remember? I knew what I was signing up to when I offered my help.'

'Well, you don't have to think about it for a couple of weeks, anyway,' Maddy said. 'I'm pretty tied up one way or the other.' She gestured towards a number of boxes on the floor behind Esme. 'I cleared a few shelves of books, though. Thought it would be easier to load up boxes and bring them here to sort through. It was quite cathartic seeing some empty space, I must admit. Made me feel like I was getting somewhere.' She nodded towards the boxes and dropped Ginger down on to the floor. 'Go and have a rummage. There might be something in there you'd like. I'll go and get you another batch of photos.'

Maddy disappeared upstairs and Esme turned to the boxes behind her, crouching down beside the one closest to her and lifting the flap. The top two books concerned boating, the third an illustrative guide to tying knots. She laid them aside on the carpet and took out the next one, feeling a flutter of disquiet in the pit of her stomach as she read the title. A sheet of paper was sticking out of the top, torn from a spiral-bound notebook. She opened the book where it was marked, but the paper had been simply slipped inside the back cover and didn't appear to mark anything.

But as she put it back in, she realised there was something written on the paper. A name that made her stomach flip and two questions.

"*Ellen. Where did she come from? Where did she go?*" The second question was heavily underlined, as though it had been asked in frustration.

Esme tried to marshal her muddled thoughts into order as she heard Maddy's footsteps coming down the stairs.

'Mads?' she said, straightening up as Maddy came into the room.

'That's me,' Maddy said. She dropped the two boxes she was holding down on to the table and looked at Esme. 'What is it?' she said, frowning.

'I just found this in the box. Cerys mentioned it when I was telling her about Ellen Tucker and that piece in the newspaper. She told me there was a copy in the library. This is it.'

She handed the book to Maddy, who took it and read the title out loud. *The Trial of the Bideford Witches*, by Frank Gent.'

Esme cleared her throat. 'There's a note inside.'

Maddy glanced up at Esme before pulling out the note and reading it. She dragged her gaze away and stared up at Esme.

'Dad didn't just pass on that information to Carlton, and then forget it, did he?' she said, her voice barely a croak. 'He was way more involved than that.'

Esme bit her lower lip and gave a brief nod. 'I think you may be right.'

# 20

For a moment, neither of them said anything. Maddy sank on to a chair at the table, her face screwed up in an expression of angst, almost fear.

'Who the hell is Ellen Tucker, Esme?' she said. 'And what was she to my dad?'

Esme pulled up another chair and sat down beside Maddy, random thoughts beginning to line up in her head. 'Do you remember how we'd wondered whether your dad saw Carlton in August to discuss the case, or whether it was just old mates meeting up?'

'Yes,' Maddy said, her tone wary.

'And then we found the file with Ellen Tucker's name on, so we guessed they must have discussed it.'

Maddy frowned. 'Where are you going with this, Esme?'

'I'm trying to get my head around the chronology.' Esme leaned forward, resting her forearms on the table. 'I'm wondering, what came first?'

Maddy blinked. 'You've lost me.'

'OK,' Esme said, shifting in her seat. 'Think about this. Your dad's workshop is right at the centre of events, isn't it? The cottage where Ellen Tucker lived isn't far away. He pays his rent to the same landlord as Ellen did.'

'No, not the same landlord,' Maddy said. 'Anna was Dad's landlord and she was just a child back in Ellen's day. Dad only took on the workshop when he retired. He was still in the force when…oh.' Maddy sat upright. 'You're saying Dad already knew about Ellen Tucker when Carlton sought him out?'

'Exactly. Let's say he remembered there being a file on Ellen from back in the mid-nineties – whether a missing-person file or when she reported the harassment is immaterial.'

'So, go on,' Maddy said, 'something about chronology.'

Esme counted off on her fingers. 'Carlton looks up your dad. They go for a beer and Carlton tells him about his case. Whether he purposely sought out your dad to talk about the case or it came up in conversation, we don't know.'

'Could Carlton have known about it from before?' Maddy said, considering. 'No, he was probably too young to have been on the force then.'

'Whatever the truth of it,' Esme continued, 'your dad offered to dig around, call in a few favours, perhaps. For his own curiosity, as much as anything else.'

'Because it was unsolved, perhaps?'

'Maybe. For all we know, he'd been originally involved.'

'It would have bugged him, wouldn't it? A cold case. And now here he was, working in the location where it all kicked off.' Maddy stood up and went to the window. 'So presumably Dad says he'll be in touch, or whatever, when he's got something to report, but then...' she swallowed, 'there's the boat accident. And Carlton has to come back to pick up the threads himself.'

Esme nodded. 'Which is when we saw him at the yard.' She looked at Maddy's back as she gazed out towards the church opposite and wondered what was going through her head. 'Does it help?' she asked. 'Or does it make matters worse?'

Maddy turned back into the room. 'I'm not sure I can answer that one,' she said, giving Esme a sad smile. 'Did Dad solve it, d'you think?'

Esme shrugged. 'I don't see how we'll ever know, being as Carlton isn't here to tell us.'

'Maybe he had an associate,' Maddy said, sitting back down and perching on the edge of the chair. 'Or even a secretary? I could call his office. Speak to someone.'

'Even if you do,' Esme said, sighing, 'no secretary is going to break client confidentiality, are they, even if they have any information? They'd have already passed it to the police, anyway. Besides, they're hardly going to confirm what your dad's role was in the investigation, assuming he had one.'

Maddy scowled. 'You might be right, but I'm not giving up without trying,' she said, pulling out her phone.

*

A scour of Carlton's website and a phone call confirmed that he'd operated completely on his own. No partner and no associate, it seemed. And no one to explain where Ted fitted into the bigger picture.

'I'm sorry,' Esme said, as Maddy cut the call. 'I know how frustrating this must be.'

Maddy gave a snort of exasperation. 'Short of nicking his computer and hacking into it, I doubt we're ever going to find out.' She sat down again, tapping the phone against her chin.

As Esme had done before, she wondered who'd hired Carlton. A family member? Sister, brother, father, mother?

'I suppose the police would've established what Carlton had found out as part of their investigation into his death?' Maddy said.

'I'd have thought so.'

'Not that that helps us much. Unless...' Maddy's eyes glazed over, staring unfocused into the middle distance, '... I can work out who sent Dad the file and go and see them.'

'That's unlikely, isn't it, given the "*you didn't get this from me*" sticker on the cover?'

'I suppose I could have a look through his address book again. See if a name rings a bell,' Maddy said, almost to herself.

'Do you know any of your dad's police friends?'

Maddy blinked and looked at Esme as though she'd forgotten she was there. 'Not really. Dad tended to keep work and home separate. And to be honest, I went through his contacts to let everyone know after his accident. I don't remember registering any police colleagues.' She gave Esme a wistful smile. 'But then I was pretty much on automatic pilot. I probably wouldn't have been focused enough to notice.'

'Worth checking, then, perhaps?'

Maddy nodded. 'Yes, I will. And I'll check his computer files, too. Might have more luck there. Emails and such.'

'I was just thinking about what your dad had written,' Esme said, an idea coming to her. '*Where did she come from?* Perhaps it would be worth me researching Ellen Tucker herself. From a family history perspective, I mean. Getting her birth certificate might reveal a local connection. Which in turn might lead us to who hired Carlton. Got to be worth a try, anyway. I'll see what I can do.'

They parted, keen to pursue their respective agendas.

# 21

After Esme had left, Maddy grabbed the campervan keys and went out. A rosewood jewellery box awaiting its final polishing sat on her workbench at the yard and there were still a couple of useful hours left of the afternoon.

She pulled the front door behind her and walked down the hill and out into the street, crossing the road to where she parked her van. The heavy mist which had persisted all day sucked the light out of the afternoon, pressing against her face, depositing delicate droplets of moisture on her hair and eyelashes. She pulled up the hood of her jacket and hurried along the pavement, mulling over what she and Esme had discussed about her dad's police contact. Had she overlooked the name when she'd informed his friends after he died? Might there be something useful on her dad's computer? He'd been more pencil and paper than digital, so she thought it unlikely he'd set up a spread-sheet file of addresses of his personal contacts, but it wouldn't do any harm to double-check. And, as she'd said to Esme, his emails might throw up something. Perhaps she'd pop round to her dad's place later.

She pulled up at the mini-roundabout by the old bridge, but instead of turning right to go to the workshop, she turned left and headed to Appledore.

Without Esme's company the still, emptiness of his house hit her as she pushed open the front door. She wondered if, had her plan been to keep the house, the feeling would fade over time. But she guessed she'd never find out as she intended to sell. Which could be a while yet, she thought, scanning round at the half-packed boxes and cupboards yet to be emptied.

She took a breath and bounded up the stairs to her father's office, switching on the light against the gloomy afternoon. The piles of files, books and other paperwork remained neatly stacked as she and Esme had left them last time they'd been here but, as she'd commented to Esme, in this room at least, the empty bookshelves suggested progress and added to a sense of order.

She made her way over to the desk and switched on the computer. While it booted, she rummaged around in the drawers for her dad's traditional address book. When she couldn't find it, she remembered she'd taken it to the workshop as it contained contacts associated with her dad's business. She must remember to look for it when she went over there later.

The computer indicated it was ready for action and Maddy clicked on the mail icon, scrolling through the long list of unanswered emails which had landed in the inbox since she'd last logged on. She sighed. This was going to be far from a quick check. If she'd known her dad's log-in details, she could have accessed his account from home, but this was her only option at the moment.

She checked her watch and sat down on the office chair. Half an hour, and then she must go. She deleted the emails from commercial companies without reading them, and any obvious friend correspondence she forwarded to herself for appraising later. The half an hour came and went. After telling herself *just a couple more* on several occasions, she eventually forced herself to stop. Although she'd found nothing of note, she told herself that the exercise had been useful, anyway. She'd managed to get up to date with the most recent mail so she should be reasonably satisfied with her efforts.

She switched off the computer and hurried downstairs, turning off the lights as she went through the dining room and into the hall, plunging the house into thick darkness. As she pulled the front door behind her, she sensed someone in the courtyard. Her head shot round, homing in on the dark corner beside the entrance to the alleyway.

'Hello?' she called out, more assuredly than she felt. 'Who is it?'

No reply. She told herself she'd imagined it and, thrusting her hands into her jacket pockets, she strode towards the archway leading back to the main street where she'd parked the van. As she emerged out on to the pavement, a figure stepped out in front of her.

She shrieked. 'Jesus wept!' she said, stumbling back, her hand against her chest. 'What the hell...'

'Sorry, sorry.' The man who'd stepped out of the shadows was dressed in a padded jacket and jeans, a baseball cap rammed down on his head. He held up a hand. 'Didn't mean to freak you out,' he said.

'Well what the hell did you think was going to happen, jumping out on me like that?'

'Sorry,' he said again, shuffling from one foot to the other. 'Saw the light, you know? Thought there must be someone in.'

Maddy eyed him warily. 'So what's your game? Staking out the place or something?'

The man took a few steps backwards, again his hands up, palms out. 'Hey, look. Guess I messed up. Not great timing, hey? See you again, yeah?' And he turned and disappeared back up the alley away from her.

She let out a long sigh and shook her head. Bloody idiot.

*

It was completely dark by the time Maddy got back to the yard, and getting late. Any satisfaction she'd felt at the visit had evaporated and she cursed her impulsiveness at going to her dad's place without anything to show for it. Bumping into the creepy guy lingering around outside hadn't helped her mood, either. She should have gone straight home for a soak in the bath and written off the rest of the afternoon instead of kidding herself she'd be able to focus on her work. But she was here now. She might as well pick up the address book and call it a day.

She parked the van and scrambled out of the driver's seat. As she hurried across the yard to the workshop, she saw a light on in Anna's office. At least someone was getting some work done.

Maddy unlocked the workshop and threw the light switch, the fluorescent tube clicking and flickering before bathing everywhere in its stark white light. She trotted over to the desk and fumbled around in the drawers until she found the address book, giving it a cursory skim through before slamming the drawer closed and heading back to the door. As she paused on the threshold to reach in and turn out the lights, she heard footsteps approaching.

For a second, she was back in the courtyard at her dad's, moments before Mr Baseball Cap pounced out of the darkness. But when she turned, her shoulders relaxed. The shadowy figure was Anna, wearing her old wax jacket. As she stepped into the light pooling through the door, Maddy could see black circles under her eyes.

'Hi, Anna,' Maddy said. 'Still working, eh? I should've been really. Don't know where the day went.'

'Oh, just sorting the inevitable paperwork. You know how it is.' Anna buried her hands deep into her pockets and looked at Maddy with red-rimmed eyes. 'You haven't noticed anyone hanging around the yard, have you?'

'Just now, d'you mean? Or generally?' Maddy looked out into the dark, the wariness of a few moments earlier returning.

'Either.'

'Only Drew's granddad. But that's nothing new, as we both know. Why d'you ask?'

Anna shot a nervous glance over her shoulder. 'Someone's been throwing stones on the roof.' She forced a laugh. 'And you can imagine. With our corrugated roof, it's bloody loud.'

'Did you see anyone?'

Anna shook her head. 'No. By the time I'd got outside,

they'd scarpered. I expect it's kids with nothing better to do.' She shivered and pulled her coat closer. 'You arriving probably scared them off.'

Maddy looked into Anna's tired face. 'Hey, perhaps it's time to knock off, eh?' She switched off the inside lights and closed the door, blinking as the movement triggered the yard's security lamp into action. 'Why don't you do what I'm going to do? Have a long soak and pour myself a glass of wine. Oh, no, sorry. You can't do that, can you? But the first idea's got to be worth going for.'

Anna gave a half smile and nodded. 'You're probably right.' She turned and began walking back across the yard, giving Maddy a wave over her shoulder. 'See you tomorrow.'

Maddy watched her go, her mind drifting once more to the encounter with the strange guy outside her dad's house. She locked the door of the workshop and hurried back to the van. Must be something to do with the phase of the moon, she joked to herself.

*

Esme closed Frank Gent's book on the trial of the Bideford witches and let it drop into her lap. As she slumped back in the sofa, she tried to imagine living in that time period. Gent maintained that violence was an accepted and normal part of life in the 17th century, as society still reeled from the traumas of the Civil War. Despite the restoration of the monarchy in 1660, the whole country remained in the grip of political upheaval, plots and counter plots. The fragility of life continued in the toxic atmosphere of an uncertain world and the oscillation of persecution against whichever religious faction was out of favour at the time.

Cerys had been correct in her comments regarding promiscuity. Gent had noted regular references made during the trial to the women having *carnal knowledge of the devil*, that their bodies had *secret parts* and *witches' teats*.

Esme was fascinated that Temperance Lloyd had also been

accused of changing into a cat, but it had been the allegation that she'd practised magic by sticking pins into wax models or dolls which she'd denied so strenuously. Did that mean she'd believed in her cat transformation?

At the time the three wretched women were arrested for witchcraft in 1682, Bideford was going through an economic bad patch. Once a flourishing port, Bideford had seen its population dramatically increase as immigrants were attracted by the town's prosperity. As the population grew, so did its associated problems of poverty and disease, placing a strain on the town's resources. Jealousy, resentment and suspicion were rife amongst inhabitants of the town, distanced as they were from rural communities, and so devoid of family support and the neighbourliness of their villages. Victimisation of the poor and unfortunate became the norm as conditions deteriorated. A distraction. An outlet for the communal angst.

Esme sighed. While it explained why these three old women had suffered what was usually a rural indignation of being accused of witchcraft, it hardly explained the rationale behind the hounding of Ellen Tucker. The country might have been in recession in the early nineties, but it seemed far-fetched to believe that one promiscuous woman could be the focus for the disgruntled impoverished.

Esme's hope that finding out more about Ellen Tucker the individual might provide some useful information had proved short lived. Even approximating Ellen's age to narrow down her sweeping search had thrown up over 800 potential matches. She simply didn't have enough to go on to identify which one was their Ellen Tucker and order a birth certificate. It was impracticable to pursue everyone of that name on the list. If Daniel or Marianne hadn't been so evasive and so visibly uncomfortable on the subject, she might have learned more from them.

But assuming they did have information to pass on, Marianne's tactic of denying she even remembered the woman suggested Esme would have a hard job extracting it.

# 22

'I fetched Dad's address book last night,' Maddy told Esme as they set up their stall on the market the following morning.

'And?' Esme said, stopping and turning towards her.

Maddy pulled a face. 'Zilch. At least, no one I remembered, anyway. Doesn't mean there isn't a police colleague in his book but I don't relish the idea of phoning each one up and asking.'

'Well, even if you did identify someone,' Esme said, 'they're unlikely to hold up their hand to passing over confidential information.'

'Yeah. Depressingly, I thought the same. And with you getting nowhere on any sort of Ellen Tucker trail, tracking her down in the records doesn't look likely, either. So we're snookered unless we can find more to go on.'

Esme rubbed her finger along her scar. 'I could do with something to narrow the field a bit. Date of birth, mother's maiden name, that sort of thing.'

Maddy sighed. 'And who the hell's going to know that? It's hopeless.'

Esme glanced up and saw Cerys waving to them from the other side of the aisle.

'I thought I'd ask Cerys,' she said, returning the wave. 'She did know Ellen briefly, remember.'

Maddy gave a dry laugh. 'Oh, yes. We drop our mother's maiden name into conversations all the time.'

Esme grinned and gave her a dig in the ribs with her elbow. 'Stop being such a defeatist,' she teased. 'She might recall when Ellen's birthday is, mightn't she? That'd be a start.' Esme's grin turned to a frown as she saw the anxiety in Maddy's eyes. 'It's bothering you, all this, isn't it?'

Maddy looked down at her hands. 'I don't really understand why it should,' she said, fiddling with her thumbnail. 'Dad would've been involved with hundreds of investigations in his working life and I wouldn't have given it a minute's thought.' She looked up at Esme. 'So why does this one freak me out?'

'Perhaps because, as you've just implied, this wasn't part of his working life. Which suggests there was something about it that was important to him.'

'I keep thinking about what you said, about Dad being in the centre of things.'

Esme bit her lower lip. 'Sorry, I didn't mean to worry you. I was merely trying to work out why he...'

'No, no, don't apologise,' Maddy said, shaking her head. 'It makes perfect sense. And perhaps I'm being naive. If you've spent your working life as police detective, you can't simply turn off your curiosity, can you? Not if it's part of your psyche. I mean, look at *you*.'

Esme put her hands on her hips. 'Meaning?' she said, with mock indignation.

Maddy tapped the side of her nose. 'I'm saying nothing.' She nodded in the direction of the other side of the aisle, towards Cerys's stall. 'Go on, then,' she said. 'Test out your theory and see what Cerys recalls.'

As Esme crossed the aisle, a customer nodded her thanks to Cerys and hurried away from the stall. Esme watched her go.

'Wasn't that Ria Brannock?' she said to Cerys.

'You know Ria, then?' Cerys said.

'I only know *of* her. I know some of her family, but I've not met Ria, yet.'

'Ria's been a customer of mine for years,' Cerys said, tucking a £5 note into the money pouch around her waist. 'But don't let on to Joseph, for goodness' sake. He wouldn't approve.'

'Ah, now Joseph is someone I have met. And I get the impression he doesn't approve of very much.'

Cerys chuckled. 'Sounds like you've got the measure of the man.'

Esme scanned Cerys's stall. Packs of gemstones and crystals jostled with incense sticks, talisman pendants, Tarot cards and candles in a variety of colours.

'Interest you in anything?' Cerys said, straightening the display. 'Got a new stock of candles just in. White ones for healing, black for protection, green for prosperity, red for vitality.'

Esme smiled and shook her head. 'Not at the moment, Cerys, thanks. I wanted to ask you something.'

But when she asked the question, Cerys shook her head. 'No, sorry, Esme. I didn't really know her that well. We only spoke a few times.'

'That's OK. It was just a thought.'

'Actually, there is one thing, though.'

'Yes?' Esme felt a flutter in her stomach.

'Now you ask, I'm pretty sure Ellen grew up on Exmoor.' She flapped a hand, dismissively. 'Don't know why I think that. I just have a vague memory that she once said something which put the idea in my head. Sorry I can't be more specific than that.'

'No, that's really helpful, Cerys,' Esme said. 'Thanks.'

Maddy's eyes widened as Esme told her what Cerys had said. 'That should pin things down a bit, shouldn't it?'

'I'm sure it will,' Esme said. 'I'll check it out later.'

'When later?'

'After we've finished here?' Esme said. 'Just don't ask me to do it now using my phone.'

'No, that's cool,' Maddy said, jiggling from one foot to the other. 'After we're done here is good. And if we get a hit...'

'*If* we do,' Esme reminded her. 'We don't know for certain she was born on the moor.'

'But say we do find her, will you get the certificate as a priority order?'

'Yes, if you like.'

'Perfect,' Maddy said, moving towards a customer browsing the collection of wooden snuff boxes on the end of their stall. 'Then we can get this sewn up once and for all.'

Esme gave Maddy a reassuring smile. But she knew that making a promising start was no guarantee to reaching the end. Not for the first time, she wondered how far along the trail Ted had reached.

*

With Cerys's information on Ellen's background, it took Esme no time to locate her birth on the registration indexes. Her name appeared under Exmoor, Somerset, in the third quarter of 1968. There was a blank in the maiden name column, indicating that Ellen's mother had been unmarried at the time of Ellen's birth.

Esme completed the necessary information online, made the payment and set the application wheels in motion. After confirming the order, she picked up the phone and dialled Maddy's number.

'All done,' she said. 'Birth certificate should get to me by Thursday.'

'Thanks, Esme. You'll let me know when it comes, won't you?'

Esme laughed. 'What do you think?'

She cut the call and turned back to Anna's research project, wondering what answers Thursday's post would bring. Something tangible, she hoped. For Maddy's sake.

# 23

Anna phoned Esme to say Marianne had dug out the old plan of the mill which she'd mentioned a few days before and suggest Esme collect it from Hill Farm. Anna wouldn't be there, but her parents would.

Esme drove to the farm and parked beside a concrete building with a corrugated iron roof in the yard. The tinny sound of a radio greeted her as she climbed out of the car, accompanied by the clinking sound of metal on metal which echoed around the farmyard. It was coming from a large open-fronted barn across the other side of the yard.

She headed towards it, passing the redundant outbuildings which she guessed had once housed milking machinery and cattle stalls from when Hill Farm had a dairy herd. The Meddons now earned their living from Daniel's business maintaining and restoring farm vehicles. Anna said her father's preference would always be the restoration side of the business, though it was his skills as a peripatetic mechanic, visiting farms all over the district, which provided the more reliable income.

Inside the barn she spied two legs clad in dark blue overalls sticking out from underneath an old Massey Ferguson tractor parked inside. She called Daniel's name and he slid out from under the tractor on a small wheeled trolley, shading his eyes with his palm as he looked to see who wanted him, oil smeared on his cheek.

'Esme,' he said, sitting up. 'Anna said you'd be calling in.' He got to his feet, pulling an oily rag from his pocket to wipe his large hands.

Esme nodded at the tractor. 'Your passion, I understand,' she said, smiling.

'Ask me that another time,' he said, laughing. 'This one's being a right bugger this morning.'

'Well, I won't interrupt you,' Esme said, turning towards the farmhouse. 'Marianne in, is she?'

'She'll be around somewhere.' He threw down the rag on to a galvanised toolbox sitting on the concrete. 'I'll come with you. About time I had a break.'

'I hope Anna isn't wasting your time over this mill business,' Daniel said as they headed towards the farmhouse.

'I don't think so. I gather it's important to have information on the history of the mill if she's a chance of getting any sort of lottery grant.'

Daniel screwed up his face. 'It's a pipe dream. The place is a disaster area. Cost a small fortune to do what Anna has in mind.' He swept an arm around the yard. 'She'd be better off developing one of these old buildings.'

'Not as romantic, though, is it?' Esme said, with wry smile.

Daniel snorted. 'That just about sums it up. Never had Anna down as a romantic, though. She's always been so practical and down to earth. Perhaps it's something to do with the baby.' They arrived at the back door. Daniel pushed it open and gestured for Esme to go inside. 'I'm sure reality will dawn before too long.'

The back door opened into a wide kitchen with a long, narrow scrubbed pine table across the room. Marianne was at the sink with her back to them. She turned as the door opened.

'Esme. Nice to see you again,' she said, snatching a towel from the rail on the Rayburn cooker and drying her hands.

'I hope it was OK to drop in,' Esme said. 'Anna said you had some information on the mill for me.'

'Yes, that's right.' Marianne smiled. 'She's been nagging me to dig it out for the past few days.'

'Oh, sorry,' Esme said. 'I didn't mean to put you to any trouble.' She glanced at Daniel. 'I know not everyone is as keen as Anna is on the idea.'

Marianne raised an eyebrow and looked at her husband. Daniel rubbed a thumb along his jawbone.

'I was just saying to Esme that I think Anna's getting carried away with this plan of hers.'

'Well, you better get used to it,' Marianne said. 'It's her land now. She can do what she likes with it.' Esme recalled that it was Marianne's idea for passing over the land's ownership to Anna. It didn't sound as though Daniel had had any say in the matter.

Marianne threw the towel back on the rail and addressed Esme. 'I hope you're not expecting too much. It's only an old plan of the site. Nothing very exciting, but you're welcome to look at it. I'll go and fetch it.' She disappeared out into the hall beyond.

'Will you have a coffee or something, Esme?' Daniel said, crossing to the sink and filling the kettle.

'That's kind of you, but I won't hold you up. I'd like to have a wander around the mill again, if that's all right?'

Daniel shrugged. 'Fine by me. As long as you don't want to go inside. I don't want to be responsible for you falling through those rotten floorboards.'

Esme shook her head. 'No, it's not inside. I just want to remind myself how everything fits together. I've been researching into the occupants of the mill. From what I've found in the census records, the Brannock family used to live there in the early 19th century.'

'The mill's always been a bone of contention between the Brannocks and the Meddons, that much I do know. But as for the who's who, I've never given it much thought.'

Marianne reappeared, a roll of paper in her hands. 'This is all there is, I'm afraid. If there were others, I don't know where they are now.' She laid down the roll on the table and opened it out. 'See what I mean, though? It's just a glorified field boundary map, really.'

Esme leaned over to study the plan. The outline of the mill was marked, as well as the cottage further down the lane where she'd encountered Joseph Brannock. The only other markings were the thin lines denoting the surrounding fields and their corresponding numbers.

'It's very similar to the tithe map I saw online,' she said. 'Even so, it's nice to have something tangible, rather than just a screen image.' She looked up. 'Are you OK for me to borrow it?'

'Of course,' Marianne said. 'Keep it as long as you like. As I've just reminded Daniel, that part of the farm's Anna's now.'

Esme went to pick up the plan and noticed a cross marked in faded red ink in the field a short distance from the mill. She didn't recall seeing it on the Devon Archive version.

'Do you know what that is?' she said, pointing to the cross. Marianne peered down, joined by Daniel from across the room. Both shook their heads.

'No idea,' Marianne said, straightening up. 'You'll have to see if you can find it.' She laughed. 'Buried treasure would come in very handy, though, wouldn't it, Daniel?'

'Always,' Daniel said, with a chuckle.

'Well, if I find any,' Esme said, smiling at them both as she rolled up the plan, 'I promise you'll be the first to know!'

*

Dark clouds hung heavyily over the mill as Esme drove through the gate into the yard. She got out of her car and walked round to the rear to open the boot to get her raincoat and wellingtons, glancing up at the sky to appraise the weather. A chink of blue gave her hope that the rain would keep off long enough for her to survey the curtilage of the mill. She slipped the rolled plan into her bag, threw it over her shoulder and slammed down the lid.

She explored the outside of the main building first, noting the decayed wooden mill wheel, gently rotting away into the overgrown sump. The adjoining wing, at right angles to the mill itself, which had once been the miller's cottage was now reduced to a single-storey open barn, supported by huge oak posts. She peered inside, looking up at the roof, mindful of Daniel's warnings about the dangerous condition of the building. She could see the skittering clouds through the gaps opened up by missing slates and detected signs of charring on the beams. A shiver scuttled down her neck as she realised the fire which killed Silas Brannock had caused the charring she was gazing at now. And somewhere under this roof, his poor wife had fallen in the kitchen fire a few months before that. She withdrew back into the yard with a shudder.

She skirted around the front of the mill to the other side, pausing to gaze across the field, towards the cottage where Ellen Tucker had lived. It was a shame she couldn't ask Daniel and Marianne about the newspaper report, but after their reaction at the market, she didn't want to sour relations between them. If Daniel had indeed been one of Ellen's conquests, as she and Maddy had suspected, neither he or Marianne was likely to be very forthcoming with any information. They'd probably be dismayed that she and Maddy were interested in learning more about Ellen. Best to keep that fact to themselves for now.

Something moved in her peripheral vision and she turned her head. Had Anna come to join her? But she could see no one coming along the lane. It must have been a bird flying out of the trees.

She turned away from the cottage and wandered along the other wall of the mill. Behind the building, an uneven rock face formed the boundary, stretching high above her and as far to the right as she could see. Scrub, ferns and misshapen trees pushed between the strata and loose boulders. She slipped her bag off her shoulder and took out the plan, unrolling it and holding it out in front of her, her back towards the lane, the mill on her left. There was no scale marked on the plan, but Esme decided to assume it was drawn accurately. Using the mill itself as a reference, she calculated the approximate location of the faded red cross.

She rolled the map back up and began pacing the building from front to back. She was about halfway along when, once more, she sensed she was being watched. She stopped and scanned the area, but still there was nothing to be seen. She shook her head, telling herself it was the eerie recollection of the horrific fate of the Brannock pair making her jumpy. She took a deep breath and resumed her strides along the outer wall.

The building measured eight strides. She consulted the plan once more, estimating the distance of the cross from the rear wall as a little under twice its length along the outcrop of rock. She returned the plan to her bag and strode out along the boundary, following the mill leat and counting under her breath. When she reached sixteen, she stopped and looked around. But she couldn't see anything on the ground that warranted demarcation on a map. Maybe whatever it was didn't exist any more. Or it wasn't on the ground.

She looked over to the bank beyond, searching amongst the scrub. Her eye settled on an area of rock jutting out, a little further along, at knee height and half hidden in vegetation. She dropped her bag down on the grass and wandered over for a closer look. A branch of blackthorn partly obscured the rock and she crouched down to lift it out of the way, catching her finger on one of its brutal barbs. She recoiled and straightened up, cursing and sucking her bloodied finger.

She retreated to her bag to find a tissue, and as she picked it up, she caught sight of a figure in the distance, shuffling through the entrance gate to the mill. She narrowed her eyes. Joseph Brannock. He'd probably been watching her since she'd arrived. She let go of the bag and stood, hands on hips, staring back at him. Realising he'd been spotted, he turned away and hobbled back through the gate and up the lane out of sight.

Esme gave a snort of satisfaction at his departing back and, wrapping the tissue around her finger, she returned to the protruding lump of stone and dropped down on to her haunches. Taking more care this time to avoid the vicious thorns, she lifted the offending branch, her skin tingling as she revealed the rock's secret.

Something had been carved into the stone. She wriggled to one side to allow the sunlight to penetrate the vegetation, catching her breath as the light fell on the inscription, enabling her to read it.

In bold capital letters was the word: *MURDER*.

# 24

Esme stared at the rock. Whose murder? When? Who had put this here?

As she studied further, she saw that there was more lettering, smaller this time. She could make out the first few words before they faded into nothing. *Let future generations know...* Below that, there might have once been a name. Was that a letter E? But there appeared to have been a deliberate attempt to scratch it out. Marks had been gouged out across the inscription. Someone had done their very best to deface what had been written here.

Esme straightened up. Was this some kind of murder stone? She knew something about murder stones, though they were not like this. They were usually similar to headstones, often erected by the family of a murder victim. She'd seen one once on the South Downs, erected by the family of a murdered young woman a year after the crime, in frustration that the murderer had never been caught. The inscription on the stone itself left no reader in any doubt as to the fate which awaited the perpetrator in the next life, should he continue to evade justice on earth. Had a similar message been the intention of this stone? Or was it a warning to others – urging either care against being a victim or a potential offender to watch his behaviour?

She reached out and ran her fingers along the remains of the lettering. Was that a date on the bottom line? She dug out her phone from her pocket and turned on the flash-light, angling it so as to create a shadow on the surface. There were two numbers not as damaged as the others. A six and possibly an eight – 68? 66? 88? 86? Murder stones were common in the mid-1800s, so 1866 or 1868 seemed more likely than during the latter part of the 19th century.

Perhaps the date would be enough to find out what had happened here. The incident would surely have been reported in the press. And someone local must know the story – perhaps Marianne or Daniel? Though perhaps not, as they'd not mentioned it when Esme had pointed out the mark on the plan. Someone else, then – someone whose family had owned land here for generations.

Joseph Brannock, for instance. She spun round and peered across to the gate where she'd spied him a short while ago. Was he still out there, watching? Even if he wasn't, he couldn't be far away.

She picked up her bag from the ground, looped it over her shoulder and strode across the grass towards the gate. Perhaps he hadn't walked away, but had merely slipped out of sight. Did his curiosity imply he knew exactly what she was looking at?

She reached the gate, unlooped the knotted piece of binder twine which served as a fastening, and walked out into the lane, gazing up the hill in the direction she'd seen him go. And there he was, almost out of sight, shuffling at surprising speed up the valley and back to the Brannocks' farmhouse, she assumed.

She hesitated. Did she really want another encounter like last time when he'd rudely warned her off his land? Well, this wasn't his land. It was a public highway. It had to be worth a try. And there was always the chance there was an amiable side to the crusty old renegade.

Esme set off after him at a brisk walk, catching him up just after the gateway where she'd stood the other day, admiring the view across the River Torridge.

'Ah, Mr Brannock,' she called out and fell into step beside him, a little breathless from her exertion. She turned and gave him what she hoped was a disarming smile. 'I thought it was you I could see at the gate. Nice it's cleared up well enough for a walk, isn't it?'

Joseph Brannock scowled at her and grunted, before returning his focus to the road ahead.

'Interesting carving back there in the field, isn't it? I expect you guessed that's what I was looking at.'

Joseph gave no reply and Esme resumed her one-sided conversation. 'It seems to have something to do with a murder.'

Joseph flashed her an angry glare and carried on walking.

'It's quite spooky, isn't it?' Esme continued. 'And rather sad, too. Makes you feel for the family of the victim, don't you think?'

If Joseph had any sympathy for the victim or their family, he clearly wasn't about to share it with Esme. He plodded on.

'I couldn't make out the inscription, though,' Esme went on. 'But you probably know all about it, being as it's on your ancestors' land. I'd imagine it's one of those stories which gets passed down the generations. I don't think Marianne or Daniel know about it, though. They certainly didn't mention it.'

They reached a turning in the lane and Joseph stopped to catch his breath, resting on his stick before turning to glare at Esme.

'Will you stop your jabbering, maid. You'm doing my head in.'

'Oh, I'm sorry,' Esme said, not sure whether to feel amused or contrite. 'I didn't mean to annoy you. It's my curiosity, I'm afraid. Always gets the better of me, and it's not every day you come across a murder stone.'

The old man narrowed his dark eyes and glowered at her, his face flushing deep red. He jabbed a bony finger into Esme's shoulder.

'That wore no murder, maid. Her got what her deserved. And that's a fact.'

And he shuffled away, leaving Esme reeling from his words.

# 25

'A what?' Maddy said, looking up. Esme had been relieved to find her in the workshop. For some reason she needed to tell someone what had happened.

'A murder stone.' Esme sank down on to a stool next to the workbench where Maddy was working. 'Well, I say murder stone. Usually they look something like gravestones. This one was different. They'd used the rock outcrop for the inscription, rather than a headstone. But the principle's the same.'

'So who was murdered?'

'A woman, according to Joseph Brannock.'

Maddy's mouth fell open and she dropped her cloth on to the bench. 'You got some information out of Joseph Brannock?'

Esme grinned. 'In a moment of madness on his part, I'm guessing. He's probably already regretting saying anything.'

'Well, I'm impressed. How come you got talking to him?'

Esme gave an involuntary shiver. 'He was watching me from the edge of the field. I decided to go after him and challenge him.'

'Good for you. The creepy sod.' Maddy leaned forward and rested on her elbows. 'So what else did he say?'

'That was it. I don't think he'd have given away even that, if I hadn't gone on and on about it. I think I got to him.'

'So what about the rock? Was anything written there to give you any clues?'

Esme shook her head. 'I couldn't make out much of the text.'

'Don't you genealogists have some clever way of highlighting worn inscriptions to make them easier to read?'

'Not sure that'd be much help. Someone had tried to scratch it out at some point.'

Maddy frowned. 'Who'd do that?'

'Someone who didn't want the truth to come out, perhaps?' Esme said with a shrug. 'I could make out a date, though. Not all of it, but enough to take a stab at a guess. 1866, perhaps, or 1868.'

'Someone must know the story. The Meddons, for one. How can you have had a murder on your patch and not know about it? You'll have to ask Daniel and Marianne.'

'They didn't mention it when I pointed to the mark on the map. So the story may have got lost in the mists of time.'

'The three witches were hanged in 1682 and we still know about them,' Maddy said, sitting back in her chair.

Esme gave a rueful smile. 'It's surprising what things have been kept secret over generations. Perhaps this is one of them.'

'Well, given the public's thirst for the macabre, you might be doing Anna a favour if you find out. It will all help in generating interest in the mill for her restoration project.'

'There is that. I'll give it my best shot.'

'How do you even go about finding out something like that?'

'Searching the *British Newspaper Archives* is as good a start as any. It must have made the press.' Esme hesitated. 'Unless it never came to light.'

Maddy's eyes widened. 'Who'd keep something like that under wraps?'

'Perhaps someone went missing, someone else was under suspicion for being involved in their disappearance but no body was ever found.'

'And the accusers carved their allegations into the stone in frustration,' Maddy added.

'It would explain why it was defaced,' Esme said, 'if the alleged perpetrator was innocent.'

'Of even if he wasn't,' Maddy pointed out. 'Who'd want that in full view for anyone to stumble across? *Innocent until proven guilty* undermined by libellous rock carvings.'

'It wasn't uncommon in the 19th century for a death certificate to record the name of an alleged murderer if an inquest decided it was an open and shut case,' Esme said.

'What? Before the trial?'

'Yes. And in theory, even if the accused was acquitted, the death certificate remained with the damning indictment.'

'Perhaps that's what happened here?' Maddy suggested.

Esme stood up. 'Well, I plan to do some research when I get home. I'll let you know. But I need to do a food shop first, so don't expect a quick result.'

Maddy nodded and picked up her cloth. 'In the meantime, if I see any of the Meddons, I'll mention it. Oh, by the way,' she said, looking up and inclining her head, 'I don't suppose Ellen Tucker's birth certificate arrived early, did it?'

Esme smiled. 'You think I'd have kept it quiet if it had?'

'Well, no, it's just...'

'Yes, I know. Don't worry. I understand your impatience, but I haven't forgotten about it. It's due to come tomorrow and I'll phone as soon as it arrives.'

*

Esme headed off to the supermarket, intending to be as efficient as possible, eager to get home and settle down to browse the online newspaper archives. But with her head full of possible murder stone scenarios, while pushing her trolley at speed, she almost collided with Marianne in the dairy aisle.

'Oh, I'm so sorry, Marianne,' Esme said, pulling back her trolley. 'I wasn't concentrating. Are you OK?'

But Marianne was laughing. 'If you could have seen your face,' she said, adjusting her basket. 'It was a picture. You were obviously miles away.'

Esme rolled her eyes. 'I was trying to be really quick, but

I think it's a case of more haste, less speed. I don't think I've put a single thing in my trolley since I left fruit and veg.' She tapped her forehead. 'Much too much going on up here, I'm afraid.'

'So, how did you get on with the map?' Marianne said, resting her basket on Esme's trolley. 'Was it useful? Didn't look particularly informative, but then you historians can see things which we mere mortals are blind to.'

'That mark I pointed out was interesting. It seems to be some sort of memorial to a murder.'

'Murder? Goodness.'

'You've no idea what it's about, then?' Esme said. 'I was hoping you might know the story. It was carved into an outcrop of rock up behind the mill.'

Marianne shook her head. 'It's a new one on me,' she said. 'Are you sure that's what it's about?'

'Joseph Brannock knew what I was talking about.' Marianne raised a quizzical eyebrow. 'He happened to be walking past,' Esme explained. 'I saw him and went after him to ask. Something about a woman getting her just deserts, or words to that effect.'

Marianne scowled. 'I wouldn't put too much store on what Joseph Brannock says, Esme. He's a mischief maker. Always has been. He was probably winding you up.' She lifted her basket off Esme's trolley. 'Well, I'd better get on. Happy shopping. See you again, no doubt.'

Marianne's assessment of Joseph stayed with Esme as she weaved her way around the store, and was still bugging her on the journey home. So, had he been telling the truth about the stone? Or, as Marianne suggested, had he been winding her up? She thought back to her animated state as she'd caught him up in the lane. Perhaps she'd been an easy target.

*

Maddy stood back to assess her work on the writing box she'd been commissioned to restore for Anna's birthday. Overall she was pleased with her efforts, and she hoped Daniel and Marianne would be too.

She ran her fingers over the lid. Just the final polishing to do and it would be ready to be collected. As she picked up the cloth, the door to the workshop opened.

'Ah, Daniel,' she said, as she saw him step inside. 'I was just...'

'What's this rubbish about a murder?'

'Pardon?' Maddy peered up at him. 'What are you on about?'

Daniel jerked his thumb out behind him. 'Marianne's just told me about it. She bumped into Esme in Morrison's.'

'Oh, that,' Maddy said, reaching for the bottle of polish. 'Esme found some sort of memorial. As I'm sure she'll have explained to Marianne. It was marked on the map that you gave her. I said that if I saw you, I'd ask if you knew what it was. Do you?' She tipped her head to one side and looked quizzically at Daniel. 'What's the problem? You seem agitated.'

'Course I'm bloody agitated. It's this stupid so-called feud, isn't it?' He flung out an arm. 'You people seem to think it's all a laugh. Well I tell you, it's just a lot of hot air and it doesn't help, OK?' He scowled, his eyes boring into her, his face redder than she'd seen before.

'Doesn't help what?' Maddy said, returning the bottle to the bench.

'Uh?' Daniel seemed thrown by the question.

'You said it didn't help. Help what?'

'Help Anna.'

Maddy continued to gaze at him. 'Meaning?' she said, when he didn't elaborate.

Daniel picked up a metal rule from the workbench and fiddled with it, avoiding her gaze. 'I would have thought it was obvious. She was born a Meddon and married a Brannock. It's not healthy being reminded of aggravation between the two families. We don't need that sort of thing to kick off all over again, do we? Especially not now, with the baby on the way.' He glanced up then. His expression had softened a little and she got the sense that his bluster was forced; that really he wanted to plead with her, rather than throw his weight about.

Maddy folded her arms. 'Don't you think you're overreacting a tad, Daniel? This murder happened, what...150 years ago? What can it possibly have to do with the relationship between the two families now?' When he didn't answer, she shifted slightly and slid her hands into her jeans pockets. 'What do you know about the story, anyway? Surely it features somewhere in your family history?'

'Look, Anna's under a lot of pressure at the moment. I would have thought you'd have been keen to do your bit.'

'If Anna's under pressure, you not backing her on this mill project must be contributing, Daniel. You must see that.'

'I'm wasting my time, aren't I?' he said, throwing the rule back down on to the bench. He lifted a finger and pointed it at her. 'Stop digging things up from ancient history, OK? And you can tell that to Esme, too.'

And he stormed across the workshop and left, banging the door behind him.

# 26

Back at the cottage, Esme unloaded her groceries and put them away before cooking herself a meal. She decided on a mushroom omelette and salad for expediency. By the time she'd cleared up, her anticipation was building at what she'd find on the online newspaper archive.

She forced herself to pause long enough to set a match to the wood-burner so that the room didn't chill, before sitting down at her desk and booting up her laptop. She slipped on her reading glasses and logged into her account on the *British Newspaper Archives* website. As she opened up the search engine, she decided to start with the two possible dates she'd made out on the inscription.

She typed in the word *murder,* set the dates and the location as Bideford and clicked on search. The icon whirled on the screen for a moment and settled, displaying over 600 articles, the majority from the *Bideford Gazette,* a local newspaper first published in 1856.

The size of the list didn't mean there had been a murder spree in Bideford during the two-year time period. Local papers regularly reported on events wider afield as well as those within their local community. She winced as she read about a young mother, aged 21, accused of murdering her illegitimate child by cutting its throat. The sex of the child wasn't revealed, and the report appeared to surround the discovery of a newly born baby's body in a cellar. It was surmised that a servant girl of "*weak intellect*" had given birth to the baby and a bloodied kitchen knife found near the scene was the evidence against her. In the event, the mother was found guilty not of murder, but of concealing a birth. Esme wondered what happened to her. The report didn't say.

Esme gave herself a shake and reminded herself that she wouldn't make much progress if she got so easily distracted by every sad case which appeared in the Victorian press.

With so many clippings to check, she wondered if adding more keywords to her search might help reduce the number. If only she had a name! Perhaps the location might help. She went back to the search engine and added in *Temperance Mill* to the box labelled *exact phrase* and clicked again.

But her search only resulted in an apology. *Sorry, no results were found for "+murder +temperance mill"*. Perhaps her comment to Maddy about the crime not being known to the authorities would prove to be true. Maybe that was why she'd drawn a blank.

She got up from her desk and diverted her frustration by attending to the fire. Perhaps she'd simply misread the dates? Maybe the figures she'd seen on the rock hadn't been an 8 or a 6, but a 9 or a zero? She should widen the date search anyway. If, like the murder stone she'd seen on the South Downs, it was erected because no perpetrator had ever been found, time would have passed. The crime may have been committed in one year, but the memorial created some time later and what she'd read was the date of the inscription, rather than the event itself.

Of course, there were still many newspaper pages not yet digitised. Perhaps what she was looking for had fallen into one of the gaps yet to be filled. If so, she could be looking at many hours of brain-numbing searches on the microfiche film in the records office, as she'd done to find Ellen Tucker's name. The thought was dispiriting.

But she mustn't give up until she was sure she'd checked everywhere first. Only then would she adopt Plan B. While a gripping story might help Anna's grant application, Esme would be better engaged researching the mill's more tangible history, if it turned out she was merely chasing shadows.

She returned to her desk, put her glasses on and widened her search. When her eye caught the name Temperance Mill in the summary at the top of the page, she pounced on it.

But it concerned allegations of flour adulteration. Miller Silas Brannock was accused of adding alum to his flour, a not uncommon occurrence in Victorian England, where cheaper ingredients, often with dangerous health implications, were put in flour to maximise profit. It could have easily been chalk, bean flour or plaster of Paris. Despite a robust defence, the bench considered the case proved and Silas was fined 40 shillings, plus 18 shillings cost. The case had been thrown up by the search engine because the word *murder* appeared on the same page. This time, it referred to the discovery of a woman's body on a roadside in Kent. A labourer had been apprehended for the crime.

Esme clicked back to the list of results, wriggling herself into a more comfortable position in her chair, and turned her attention back to the screen.

Half way down the page, she saw it. *Frightful Murder.* The word *fire* jumped out at her from the summary. She clicked on the headline to be taken to the full newspaper page and zoomed in on the small blue box which highlighted her key words. *"The badly burned body of a man thought to be Silas Brannock, of Temperance Mill, was discovered in the ruins of the miller's cottage yesterday evening."*

Esme blinked at the screen, digesting the information. Murder? Nothing on Silas Brannock's death certificate or in the newspaper report she'd found had indicated that the burning which killed him had been murder. But perhaps it hadn't been known when the body was found, that the crime had only later come to light. So who was the perpetrator?

She returned to the main list of articles, looking for a later report which might reveal more information. Had there been an arrest? A trial?

Many of the extracts were from other publications, merely reiterating what she'd already read. But on the following page, she saw another damning headline. "*Frightful murder. Daughter charged.*"

Daughter? She brought up the full page on to the screen and scanned the details. Sarah Brannock, aged 17, was accused of arson and murder.

Esme frowned. This couldn't be the murder Joseph meant. His words of condemnation implied the victim was a woman. *That wore no murder. Her got what her deserved.* Had there been another murder?

Perhaps, Esme thought, taking off her glasses and sitting back in her chair, someone had killed Sarah in an act of revenge.

# 27

Questions and potential answers whirled around in Esme's head long after she dragged herself off to bed, causing her a fitful sleep.

She woke late to the sound of rain rattling against the bedroom window. The mysterious murder story immediately flooded into her conscious thought and the questions began again. Had Joseph Brannock been confused about his information? Had there really been more than one crime on Brannock land?

She threw back the duvet and wriggled to a sitting position on the edge of the bed, rubbing her eyes. While she itched to go and see what else she could dig up about the story, she knew she had other pressing matters to deal with first. There were more scanned photos to upload on to the *Photos Reunited* website and research to conduct on several names they'd identified. She stood up and padded off to the bathroom.

After breakfast, she booted her laptop and checked her emails. There was one from Morris Beveridge, saying he'd recognised one of the collections of photographs Esme had posted on the website as being from a family he was researching. She smiled as she replied. Maddy would be pleased. One more family reunited with its lost belongings. Their success rate was growing. She suggested Morris call in on a market day and pick up the collection from their stall.

After dealing with her correspondence, she took a break and was making herself a cup of coffee when the Royal Mail van pulled up in front of the cottage. She peered out of the window over the sink, spying at what the postman had in his hand. When she saw the tell-tale envelope, she put down the kettle and went to the door to intercept him.

'Been waiting for this one, then?' he said, with a grin, as she opened the door. He'd become accustomed to her orders from the General Register Office over the months.

She nodded. 'Priority order,' she said, smiling.

He handed over the envelope. 'I haven't brought you so many recently. Thought perhaps it had all gone online.'

'Not everything. There's still a few things to keep you in work.'

He winked. 'Glad to hear it,' he said. He turned back to his van as Esme heard the phone ringing out behind her. She gave the postman a wave and closed the door before going over to answer the call.

'Has it come yet?' Maddy's voice sounded anxious.

Esme laughed. 'Are you psychic or something? It's just this minute arrived. Hang on, I'll see what it says.' She tucked the phone under her ear and tore open the envelope. 'By the way,' she said as she unfolded the document inside and laid it out on the table, 'I found out something about a murder last night which I must tell you about.'

'Oh, that's a coincidence,' Maddy said. 'I've got something to tell you on that subject too.'

'Really?'

'Yes. But first things first. Birth certificate.'

'Yes, of course. Hang on.' Esme pulled up a chair and put the phone back to her ear. 'OK. Let's see. *"Ellen Hope Tucker, born 15 June 1968. Mother Arabella Tucker. No father's name recorded. Address, The Coach House, Bremleycott, Near Porlock, Somerset."'*

'Where's Bremleycott?' Maddy asked.

Esme got up and walked over to her laptop. 'I'll have a look, wait a sec.' She opened up Google Earth and typed the village name into the search engine. The image spiralled around on the screen and zoomed in on a location on the edge of moorland, not far from the Somerset coast. 'It's near the Doone Valley, from the looks of it,' Esme said. 'It's not very big.'

'So easy enough to find The Coach House, then?' Maddy asked.

Esme dropped down on to the sofa. 'Probably,' she said, folding an arm across her lap. 'Sounds like a conversion of an estate building, doesn't it? Not that finding it is any guarantee that the current resident has a connection with Ellen Tucker. We are talking 40 years plus. But worth giving it a go. Did you want to take a visit out there?'

'Oh, yes, let's. Tomorrow?'

'OK, why not? What time.'

'Oh, no, I can't,' Maddy groaned. 'I've got two potential clients calling in tomorrow. I wouldn't want to put them off. Don't want to get a reputation for being unreliable.'

'Day after? Oh, no, it's Saturday, isn't it. Market.'

Esme heard Maddy sigh down the phone. 'And then it's Sunday and I'm at a car boot sale. Oh, this is hopeless.'

'Would you like me to go tomorrow on my own?' Esme asked. 'Then it won't stretch into next week.'

'Oh, Esme are you sure? It's such a cheek.'

'No it isn't,' Esme said, leaning back into the sofa. 'By the time I've spent all day at the screen with these latest photos, I'll be in need of a break. I can update you on Saturday if I find something.'

'OK, it's a deal. Now, tell me about what you found out.'

Esme gave Maddy a brief summary of her discoveries the night before. 'The odd thing is, it doesn't fit with what Joseph Brannock said about it concerning a woman. So it can't be the same murder.'

'You mean there's another one?' Maddy gave a chuckle down the phone. 'Oh, Daniel's gonna just love that. He's already on the warpath.'

'About what?'

'Apparently we're a serious threat to Anna's health because of digging up ancient history. He said Marianne had seen you in Morrison's and you'd told her about the carving in the rock.'

'She didn't seem particularly bothered about it,' Esme said. 'In fact, she seemed to think it was all a hoax and that Joseph Brannock was having me on. Which he may well be, of course.'

'Well, Daniel seemed pretty freaked out by the whole thing. On about some family feud being reignited.'

'Yes, he did mention something about there being a bone of contention about the mill when I called in to get the map. Not that he made a big deal about it. Wonder what's changed his mind.'

'So, what d'you reckon?' Maddy said. 'Can you find out more about the murder of Silas Brannock?'

'I hope so,' Esme said, standing up at the sound of a car engine approaching the cottage. 'I'll get back to it as soon as I get the chance. Look, I must go. Got a visitor. See you on Saturday. Maybe by then I'll have something to update you on the mysterious Ellen Tucker.'

# 28

Esme put down the phone to Maddy and went over to the kitchen window. A Torridge Reclamation pick-up truck pulled up alongside her own car and stopped. Esme watched to see who alighted from the driver's door. Surely Daniel hadn't discussed his gripe about stirring up old family feuds with Drew and sent his son-in-law to take issue with her? She found herself holding her breath and was relieved when Anna emerged from the pick-up.

She went outside to meet her. 'Anna,' she said. 'This is a nice surprise. Don't often see you out in these parts.'

'I was delivering some roof slates in Hartland,' Anna said, nodding her head towards the track behind her, 'so I thought I'd come and see where you hang out.'

'Glad you did. It's good to see you.'

Anna turned and gazed out to sea. 'Wow,' she said, standing with her hands on her hips. 'I can see the appeal of living here. And your own beach, too.'

Esme smiled. 'Yes, it's spoiled me. I ought to start looking for a place of my own, but it's going to be difficult to drag myself away.'

'Yeah, I bet.' Anna turned to Esme and inclined her head. 'Actually, one of the reasons I dropped by was to apologise about Dad. I hope he's not been bending your ear too. Apparently he had a go at Maddy. Has she told you? Something about a murder back in the way back when.'

Esme nodded. 'Yes, she did. I've just been on the phone to her, actually. He's worried about reigniting old quarrels, I understand.'

Anna pulled a face. 'He had no right to take it out on Maddy, or you for that matter. It was me who asked you to do the history. He doesn't get it.'

'Ironically, I'm not sure I have found out about the murder he's talking about. There seems to be some confusion.' She gestured back towards the cottage. 'Come on in and I'll tell you about it.'

In the kitchen, Esme gestured for Anna to sit down. 'It all sounds very intriguing,' Anna said, taking off her jacket. 'That's if you've got time to bring me up to date?' She checked her watch. 'I don't have to be back in Bideford for another hour or so.'

'Sure,' Esme said. 'Hang on and I'll get the file. Do you want a coffee?'

'No, don't worry. I've just had one, thanks.'

Esme fetched her findings from the sitting room and they sat at the kitchen table where Esme laid out her notes. She took Anna through the census returns, pointing out her initial discoveries of the people who'd lived in the mill from 1851 and every ten years since, until 1911, and then in 1939 at the outbreak of the Second World War.

Esme explained how she'd wondered what happened to Silas and Bessie and the rest of the family between the 1861 and 1871 census, and the shock discovery of the murder.

'I've only read a brief summary in the *British Newspaper Archive* online,' she said. 'But if I find out any more, I'll let you know.'

'That's incredible, Esme,' Anna said. 'I can't believe anyone in the family didn't know about it.'

'I'd imagine that it wasn't something the family were proud of,' Esme said, sitting back in her chair. 'It's fine for us to be looking back to an event that happened over 150 years ago, but if you were directly affected by it, you might want to forget.'

'So how do *I* connect to this bit of the family tree?' Anna asked, pointing to herself. 'Through Dad or Mum?'

'Both, actually,' Esme said. 'Your maternal grandmother, Edna, was a Meddon. She was the great-granddaughter of George Meddon, who was a cousin of Sarah.'

'The same Sarah who murdered Silas?'

'That's right. Sarah's mother, Bessie, was a Meddon, the sister of George's father James. The Brannock link is on your dad's side, as his mother's maiden name was Brannock.'

'That'd be Granny Alice. I knew her quite well. She died a few years ago. I don't really remember Granddad Peter. He died when I was a baby. The bungalow where me and Drew live was originally built for them.'

'Well, Alice's great-grandfather was Sarah's younger brother, Isaac Brannock.'

Anna frowned. 'Hang on, if the mill was owned by the Brannocks, how come it was in Mum's family, when it's Dad's who were Brannocks?'

'That's because your mum's maternal grandfather, Henry Meddon, married Grace Brannock. As an only child, Grace inherited the mill from her father, Abraham, who in turn had inherited it from his father, Isaac Brannock.'

'Sarah's brother.'

'Yes. Who was Silas's son, of course. So through Grace marrying Henry, the mill passed into Meddon ownership.'

'And the mill and the farm came together and were eventually passed down to Mum.' Anna screwed up her face. 'It's hard to get your head round it all, isn't it?'

'It can be, yes. The interconnections between both families are numerous. The genes of Brannocks and Meddons must be well mixed up by now.'

'So Drew and I must be related way back on the family tree?'

Esme smiled. 'That's right. I'll check out his branch of the family. Find out where it all joins up.'

'Funny how you don't think about these things until you start a family of your own,' Anna said, laying a hand on the bump of her developing pregnancy. 'Makes old Joseph Brannock look a bit stupid with his "Us and Them" prejudices, doesn't it?'

'Yes, it certainly does,' Esme agreed. 'He seems to have a fixation about the mill being on Brannock land. I think he's just lost in a time warp.' Perhaps Joseph's confusion stemmed from the age-old dispute between the Meddons and Brannocks, currently vexing Daniel. Had it all started when Grace Brannock dared to marry into the Meddon family, meaning the mill no longer belonged to the Brannocks?

'I don't think he likes me,' Anna said, wrinkling her nose. And it seems to be only because I'm a Meddon. He even went for me the other day and called me a bitch, can you believe?' She rubbed the back of her hand and Esme noticed a reddened scratch on her skin. 'Drew said it's his dementia. Some days he's OK, and then others...' She shrugged.

'That seems to be the way of the disease, unfortunately,' Esme said. 'I wouldn't let it get to you.'

Anna got to her feet. 'Well, this isn't getting any work done, and I'm sure you've plenty of research to be getting on with.' She grabbed her jacket off the chair and slipped it on. 'Thanks, Esme. Keep me in the loop with anything else you find, won't you? I'm fascinated.'

Esme waved Anna off, reflecting on Joseph's attitude towards his granddaughter-in-law. It was ironic, and not a little sad, that given his obsession over land, he appeared unable to grasp that the mill was again in the ownership of the Brannock family. Perhaps having a new baby great-granddaughter would mellow him little.

# 29

The village of Bremleycott amounted to a cluster of stone outbuildings, a pub-cum-cafe and a shop. Esme parked her car in the deserted car park beside the outbuildings and walked across to the shop on the opposite side of the road. She wasn't surprised to see it closed. From the faded displays in the window, it clearly served the tourist trade. Not much custom on a Friday in mid-October. Perhaps it would reopen for the half-term break. But that didn't help her now, with no one to ask for information.

As she debated her next move, a Royal Mail van came round the corner and pulled up in front of her, alongside the entrance to the pub. The postman, wearing a black beanie hat with the Royal Mail logo on it, climbed out, a bunch of jangling keys in his hand. He noticed Esme and said good morning, before striding across to the small red post box embedded in the wall.

Esme walked over to him and asked him where she could find The Coach House. Her online check on the postcode search website had thrown up nothing. But the service wasn't infallible and she'd hoped local knowledge would be more informative.

The postman thought for a moment and shook his head. 'Sorry, can't help you, I'm afraid,' he said, bending down to unlock the little red door of the postbox and reach inside. 'Nowhere of that name around here. Maybe it's been changed. It happens.'

Esme agreed that it was a possible explanation. She looked around. 'Where's the church?' she asked.

He gestured towards a small humpbacked bridge ahead. 'Down that way about half a mile on the right,' he said. 'You can't miss it.'

She thanked him and he nodded, slamming the door of the box closed and climbing back in his van before driving away in the direction he'd just indicated. Esme pulled up the hood of her duffel coat against the chill of the breeze and set off across the bridge to find the church.

If the postman hadn't directed her, she might have doubted she was coming the right way. High hedges bordered the narrow lane, making it hard to see more than a few metres ahead. Either side, the valley rose steeply away, the green moorland grass punctuated by the rich ochre of areas of bracken. She was thankful that no traffic came along. Pressing herself into the bank would have been the only way to avoid being run down.

She was relieved when the road widened and she could see a T-junction ahead. As she reached it, the church appeared on her right-hand side, its unpretentious stone knave punctuated by a castellated tower beneath which stood a wide whitewashed porch. A stepped ramp led from the road up to a wooden gate between two stone pillars, forming the entrance to the churchyard accessed by a flagstone path beyond.

Esme could hear the muffled drone of organ music coming from inside. Not wishing to interrupt the organist's practice session, she stepped off the path and walked around the gable end of the church. The churchyard's grassy slope stretched out ahead of her and she wandered around, pausing occasionally to read the inscriptions on the gravestones, contemplating the stories behind the names and dates.

Sometimes a cluster of gravestones with similar dates told a story in themselves. A disease epidemic, perhaps, like the outbreak of scarlet fever which had struck down so many in a village near Bideford in 1871. Or a natural disaster of flood or famine. Not everyone would have a stone to mark their passing, of course. Many poor souls would have been buried in unmarked graves, with no physical evidence of their existence.

Most of those buried here in the rural community of Bremleycott appeared to have lived a long life, although one rustically carved stone made her wonder what had caused the death of Evelyn Cosway, who'd passed away in 1923, aged only 24. Had she died in childbirth? There was no clue on the stone - no reference to her being someone's wife or daughter. Merely the words *"In remembrance"*. Esme itched to look her up in the databases, follow the trail and unpick the story, but this wasn't the time to get distracted. She was here to unravel a different story.

She climbed further and walked along behind the back of the church and up to the top of the slope, where the gravestones were more recent. Her eye was caught by a plot in the corner. At first, she wasn't sure it was a plot, as only a small, slim piece of slate served as a headstone, peeping out from the tufts of spiky fescue grass threatening to overwhelm it.

Esme cut across to take a closer look at the curious memorial. She crouched down and parted the grass obscuring the words, which had been crudely written in white paint on the dark grey slate. Her stomach gave a jolt as she read the name: *Arabella Hope Tucker, 5th April 1946 - 24th August 1994*. Ellen's mother. And with the same middle name as Ellen had recorded on her birth certificate.

Esme re-read the date of Arabella's death. 1994. The year before the newspaper reports of youths harassing Ellen in Temperance Cottage. Ellen must have come to Bideford and rented the cottage shortly after her mother died. Was there any particular reason why she'd chosen Bideford?

As Esme sifted through the information, she became aware of someone behind her. And a hand touched her shoulder.

'Ellen? Is that you?'

# 30

Esme stood up and spun round, pulling the hood off her head. A man stood behind her, wispy grey hair dancing in the breeze, his cassock flapping about around his legs.

'Oh, I'm so sorry,' he said, backing away, palms up towards her. 'I thought for a minute…'

'That I was Arabella Tucker's daughter, Ellen,' Esme finished for him.

He stopped. 'Yes,' he said, pushing a strand of hair off his face. 'You know Ellen?'

Esme smiled. 'Not exactly, no. I'm…' She fumbled around in her pocket. 'I'm a researcher,' she said, pulling out a crumpled business card and handing it to him. 'I'm looking into Ellen's family history.'

The clergyman's face brightened. 'She's a client? Is she well? I haven't seen her in years.' He nodded towards the grave behind her. 'Not since her mother was buried, in fact. I hadn't been here long then, of course.' He flushed and Esme wondered whether, as a young clergyman, he'd been as awestruck as the other men whose lives Ellen had touched.

He held out his hand and introduced himself. 'James Willoughby, rector of St Mary's.'

Esme shook his hand. 'Esme Quentin.' She turned back to the grave. 'Did Arabella grow up in the parish too?' she asked.

He gazed down at the unconventional headstone. 'Before my time, I'm afraid. I only knew her for a short time before she passed.' He gave a sad half laugh. 'Though, long enough to know that being buried here wasn't something she'd ever have ever imagined happening, I'm sure of it.'

'Why was that?'

'Arabella was rather unorthodox. A free spirit. She didn't hold with religious convention.'

Esme looked up at the raw moorland landscape stretching out beyond the church. 'As a location for someone with a free spirit, it seems a pretty perfect solution.'

'Yes, you have a point,' he said, nodding. 'Though that wasn't Ellen's reason for insisting this should be her mother's last resting place.' He inclined his head. 'Where is Ellen now? You didn't say.'

Esme took a deep breath. 'I really *am* a researcher,' she said. 'And I really *am* researching Ellen's family history.'

He raised an eyebrow. 'But she's not a client?'

'I don't know where Ellen is, if that's what you were hoping I could tell you.'

'So if Ellen isn't your client, who is?' He shook his head. 'Sorry, that was a stupid question. That's confidential.'

'Yes, I'm afraid so. But what I can tell you is that when she left here, she ended up in Bideford for a while. Then the trail goes cold, as they say.' She frowned as a thought slipped into her head. 'Did someone come looking for Ellen recently? A private detective, called Sean Carlton?'

Willoughby pursed his lips. 'Not that I'm aware. But he could have spoken to someone else in the village, I suppose. Nothing's reached me on the jungle drums anyway.' He regarded her quizzically. 'Why would a private detective be looking for Ellen?'

'That's a very good question. And another I don't have the answer to, I'm afraid. It's not even possible to ask Mr Carlton, sadly, as he drowned in a tragic accident a little over a week ago.'

'Oh dear, poor man,' Willoughby said, a troubled expression on his face.

'If he did come, he may have spoken to Ellen's friends, I suppose, if anyone's still in touch with her?' Perhaps it had been a friend who'd pointed Carlton towards Bideford.

Willoughby frowned. 'I can't think of anyone still living here who I'd term a friend of Ellen's. She did have a boyfriend for a time, but he came here as a seasonal worker. He wasn't from the village.'

'Do you remember his name?'

He shook his head. 'No, I don't. And it was more of a summer romance than anything serious. Arabella made sure of that. She was set against it. Or set against him,' he added, rubbing his chin and looking pensive. He shrugged a shoulder. 'She probably felt Ellen was far too young to get trapped in a permanent relationship.' He gave Esme a wry smile. 'That free spirit philosophy coming into play again.'

'So what happened?'

'Oh it all fizzled out. Ellen went off to college - Bristol or Bath, I believe, one of the two - and then when she came back, life pretty much continued as before. The boyfriend wasn't on the scene by then, anyway.'

'Were they still living at The Coach House?' Esme asked. 'I haven't been able to find it. The postman didn't know it.'

Willoughby laughed. 'I'm not surprised. It's probably rotted away by now.' He gestured across the fields. 'It was *literally* a coach. One of those wonderful old vintage buses, to be precise. It sat in the corner of a copse down there by the stream. To give Arabella her due, she made quite a fist of it, turning it into a home. No running water or electricity, of course. But that didn't seem to bother her.'

'I can see why you described her as unorthodox,' Esme said.

Willoughby smiled. '*Alternative*, I believe is the modern term.' He glanced down at his watch. 'I'm so sorry, but I have a meeting I need to get ready for. So nice to have met you. The church is open if you want to go inside.'

'Thank you, I will.'

He hesitated for a moment. 'If you do catch up with Ellen, perhaps you'd let me know?'

Esme smiled. 'Of course.' Willoughby nodded before turning and walking away. 'Oh, just one more thing,' Esme called out after him.

He paused and looked back at her over his shoulder as she caught him up. 'Mm?'

'You said Ellen had insisted her mother was buried here. Do you know why she felt so strongly about it?'

Willoughby said nothing for a moment. Perhaps he was already regretting revealing so much. But after a few moments, his shoulders relaxed and he sighed.

'Given what I've told you, it won't come as a surprise that Arabella had very few resources. Certainly not enough to cover the cost of a funeral.'

'The local authority took on the responsibility, I assume?' Esme said.

'Yes, that's right. Ellen was desperate. So I did what I could to ensure Arabella remained here.'

'Desperate?' Esme said. 'What was Ellen so desperate about?'

'She worried that the local authority would arrange for her mother to be cremated. She was adamant that must never happen or it would be a complete betrayal.'

'A betrayal?'

'That's right,' Willoughby said, his face sombre. 'Ellen said her mother suffered an irrational life-long terror of being burned.'

# 31

After Willoughby left, Esme took up his invitation to explore inside the church. She stepped into the porch and through the door into the church itself, scanning the modest interior. The organ which she'd heard playing earlier was tucked into the corner by the door, its tall pipes towering up towards the ceiling. The bright whitewashed walls contrasted starkly with the rich dark wood of the 18th century box pews. Light from the simple mullion windows fell on wooden plaques hanging on the walls, displaying the text of the Ten Commandments.

She wandered down the aisle, assessing the new information about Ellen her visit to Bremleycott had given her, uncertain what to do next. From everything Willoughby had told her, it seemed Arabella had been an independent soul, no family with whom she was in contact. Esme wondered how many people had attended Arabella's funeral. What had the village made of the unorthodox resident? Had they come to pay their last respects or had the mourners been only Ellen, the vicar and the funeral director? The latter didn't bode well for finding anyone with information on Ellen.

Esme carried on past the polished pews to the chancel. High on the wall above the wooden panelling hung an ornate plaster plaque and she paused to read the inscription.

*In loving memory of Richard Slaney, son of Richard Arthur Slaney who departed this life 25th May 1844, aged 17 years.*

Richard. The name of both father and son. And possibly grandfather too. Sadly, the Richard for whom the memorial had been erected would never be able to continue the tradition, his life being cut short at such an early age.

Esme retraced her steps back down the aisle, and as she emerged into the autumn air, her thoughts turned to the name Ellen and Arabella shared. Hope. Such a poignant name. Had it been chosen by Arabella's parents for its intrinsic meaning, Arabella continuing the custom when naming her own daughter? Or had Hope been someone important in the family? Arabella's mother, perhaps? Or her grandmother? Could Hope be a name which had been passed down several generations?

Her curiosity piqued, Esme walked back to her car with renewed purpose.

*

As she walked along the lane, Esme pulled out her phone and called Maddy. After relaying what Willoughby had told her, she mooted her theory of the two women's middle name.

'It might help track back a family connection,' she said.

'But you found nothing to suggest why Dad was involved?' Maddy said. She sounded disappointed.

'I wasn't really expecting to, at this early stage,' Esme said. 'This is just the start of the trail.'

'Yes, of course it is.' Maddy sighed. 'Take no notice of me. It's obvious you're not gonna establish something like that after one brief visit. Sorry.'

'No need to apologise,' Esme said, anxious that Maddy didn't get disheartened. She knew full well how hard it was to have questions that a loved one wasn't able to answer. 'I did ask the vicar if Sean Carlton had been there. If he was trying to track Ellen down, he'd surely have visited where she grew up. It would be an obvious place to start.'

'That's assuming he knew where she came from.'

'If it was a family member who engaged him, they'd have

given him that information, wouldn't they?'

'And had he?' Maddy said. 'Carlton, I mean. Had he been there?'

'The vicar didn't think so. But that's not to say Carlton hadn't spoken to someone else. He's going to ask around.' Esme moved to one side as a horse and rider passed her in the lane. 'Look, I'm going to head back now. I'll do some more digging when I get home. I'll update you at tomorrow's market.'

*

That evening, Esme sat down on the sofa with her laptop on her knee and switched it on, mentally working out the route she would take to track back in Ellen's family tree, using Arabella's blood-line. She opened up her *Ancestry* account and typed in Arabella's full name along with her date of birth, which she now knew from the information on Arabella's unconventional gravestone. The search engine combed rapidly through the files at its disposal and Arabella's details appeared on the screen.

Her birth had been registered in Wellington, Somerset. Her mother's maiden name had been Bricknell. Esme made a note and returned to the main search engine to locate the marriage of Arabella's parents.

She entered Tucker into the surname field, selected *male* from the drop-down box and entered the name Bricknell as the surname of the spouse. As Arabella had been born in 1946, she entered an approximate date for the wedding as being 1944, plus or minus 5 years, and clicked the search button.

The screen refreshed and listed potential matches. One in particular looked promising. A marriage in Somerset in 1945 - Frank Tucker and Olive H Bricknell. Did the H stand for Hope?

Applying for Frank and Olive's marriage certificate would confirm whether Olive's middle name was Hope, but that would take a couple of days to arrive, even if she opted for a priority order. But if she was on the wrong track, she'd have wasted time and money. Perhaps there was another way of checking.

She returned to the main search page and put in Olive's full name, along with her approximate date of birth. On the drop-down menu she chose *Census & Electoral Rolls* and navigated her way to the 1939 Register, taken at the start of the Second World War.

When the page appeared before her, she could see an Olive H Bricknell on the list, living in Taunton, occupation: shorthand typist. Although her middle name was again only recorded as the initial H, Esme knew she had the correct Olive, as the records had been amended before release to include a woman's married name. Written in red in capital letters above Bricknell was TUCKER. As well as confirming Olive's date of birth, the record listed her as living with Emma H Bricknell, a widow, born in 1891, making her 48. Olive's mother, perhaps? And was Hope *her* middle name, too?

Esme repeated her strategy for establishing Emma's marriage to Olive's father. This time, their union appeared as a parish record and Emma's full name had been recorded. Esme felt a surge of exhilaration when she read it. In 1917, William Bricknell had married Emma Hope Davidson. The thread continued.

By now, Esme had traced far enough back to make use of the census records. She searched for Emma Hope Davidson in the 1911 census and found her living in the Somerset village of Stogumber, with her parents, 46-year-old Theo Davidson and her heart leapt as she read Emma's mother's name the screen – 41-year-old Hope.

Esme closed her eyes and leaned her head against the back of the sofa. She'd found her.

She put aside the laptop and went into the kitchen for a glass of water, her excitement building. Nearly there. Should she call Maddy and let her know? No, not yet. Not until she'd found out what this woman had done to inspire every generation to honour her name.

She downed her drink and swilled out the glass before putting it on the draining board. Now, the last piece of the jigsaw. She returned to the sofa and pulled the laptop back on to her knee. What next? Should she search for Hope Davidson in the newspaper archives? Not yet. Best to get back to the start of Hope's life.

She carried out a search for Hope's marriage in the same way she'd done for the others, quickly establishing that Hope's maiden name was Moss. Taking her birth information from the 1911 census, Esme returned to the main *Ancestry* search page and entered Hope's details. *Ancestry* generated a list of records it held in its vast databases which it considered relevant to Hope Moss. Esme scanned down it, looking for Hope Moss's birth, but there was nothing in the birth indexes or baptism records, as might have been expected.

But there *was* a listing for Hope Moss on the 1881 census. Esme clicked on the link and brought up the image of the page from the enumerator's book in which the information had been recorded. She found Hope, aged 11, living in Barnstaple with her parents Thomas and Susan Moss and three younger siblings.

As Esme stared at the page, she noticed something in the column which recorded the relationship of each person with the head of the household. It was partly obscured by the check marks made by transcribers as information was copied out from the enumerators' books. The relationship of Hope to Thomas had been recorded as stepdaughter. Hope, it seemed, had taken Thomas Moss's name. It explained why Hope Moss hadn't shown up in the birth records.

Questions buzzed around Esme's head. Was Hope Susan's daughter? Had Thomas agreed to take on another man's child? What was Hope's surname at birth?

The last question prompted her into action. She opened up the *FreeBMD* website and activated the search page. If she entered the information she'd gleaned from the census, the search engine should throw up any girls called Hope born in any chosen year. Could there really be many? It wasn't a common name, like Mary or Elizabeth.

She selected 'birth' as the type of record she sought and put Hope in the 'first name(s)' box and an asterisk in the surname. The 1881 census was taken in April of that year. If Hope had been 11, she would have been born in 1869 or 1870, depending when her birthday was. Esme set the search to cover the two-year range. She could have limited the search to Exeter, the place of Hope's birth, according to the census return, but that may not be accurate. Sometimes people gave misleading or false information as to where they were born, either because they had reason to be reticent or because they honestly didn't know. This could easily be the case for a child who was adopted.

With this in mind, Esme left the location as 'all counties', crossed her fingers and hit the 'Find' key. The website went into action and presented Esme with the births for 1869 and 1870 across England and Wales, divided into the four quarters, March, June, September and December.

Esme hurriedly cast her eyes over the list, noting the places where the different births were registered - Lincoln, Isle of Wight, Winchester, Islington. And Exeter. The only Devon entry on the page. She felt a lurch in the depths of her stomach as she saw the surname recorded beside the name Hope in the June quarter of 1869.

Brannock.

Esme stared at it, blinking. So where was Hope Brannock when the 1871 census was taken? Was she with her birth family? And on which branch of the Brannocks did her birth family sit?

Esme returned to the search page, selected *Census & Electoral Rolls* and narrowed her focus to the 1871 census. She entered Hope's details in the online form – name, year of birth, place of birth, female – and clicked search.

The page refreshed, filling the screen with a long list of

names, under the heading St Thomas's Union Workhouse. And half way down was the entry Esme was looking for. Hope Brannock, inmate.

A toddler of under two years old and Hope was growing up in the workhouse. No family members were listed alongside her. She was completely alone.

# 32

'So Ellen Tucker's related to the Brannocks?' Maddy said, when Esme filled her in the following morning at the market. 'Have you told Anna?'

'We don't know if it's the Brannocks associated with the mill, yet,' Esme cautioned. 'Ellen's ancestor, Hope Brannock, was born in Exeter. I've sent for her birth certificate. We'll know more then.'

Maddy rubbed her cheek. 'Poor little mite. What must life have been like for her, growing up in a workhouse?'

'Not a bed or roses, that's for sure. You do read of some heart-wrenching stories. Such as children of Hope's age cooped up in the Infant Nursery where they slept, never let out for any fresh air or exercise.'

'That's terrible.'

'Of course, we don't know that Hope suffered such abuses. It would be nice to think the matron in St Thomas's workhouse was sympathetic towards orphans in her care.'

'Even if she was, it's a heartening story that Hope found a family in the end. Are you sure she wasn't the daughter of the people who adopted her? What did you say their name was?'

'Moss. Susan and Thomas Moss. It's unlikely. From the age Susan gave on the 1881 census, she'd only have been fourteen when Hope was born.'

Maddy looked thoughtful for a moment. 'Not that any of this ancient history explains why Dad was so interested in Ellen Tucker. We still don't know if she was an official missing person. And with me coming up blank with who might be the police colleague he was in touch with, we're not likely to, either.'

Esme set up the display of old photos and stood back to check it was straight. 'You never know. You might yet have a flash of inspiration.'

'Do you think her being a Brannock is the reason why Ellen came to Bideford?' Maddy said, sliding a storage box out of sight under the stall table. 'She might have been searching for her family.'

'It's possible. Though the name could just be a coincidence.'

Maddy raised her eyebrows. 'I seem to remember pointing out the other day that the rule in any investigation is not to believe in coincidences.'

Esme grinned. 'In detective circles, maybe. But any genealogist will tell you that when it comes to matching families, coincidences happen. That's why so many people end up going down the wrong bloodline and create a family tree of fiction.'

'I'll take your word for it. By the way, are you coming to the mill next week when Anna's expert is visiting?'

'Yes, I am. You?'

Maddy nodded. 'Too right. If she gets this project up and running, I want to be her first tenant.'

Esme noticed a slip of paper lying on the floor and bent down to pick it up. It was a leaflet promoting a charity event. A banner across the top displayed the acronym LOST. 'What's this?' she said, reading it out loud. "*Loved Ones Search Team.*"

'Oh, it must have fallen out of one of the packing boxes,' Maddy said. 'They were collecting on the quay a couple of weeks ago and giving out fliers.' She hugged herself. 'Actually, it was the day I saw Carlton's car being pulled out of the river.'

'Ouch,' Esme said, squeezing Maddy's arm. 'You don't need to be reminded about that particular day, I'm sure.'

Maddy cleared her throat and nodded at the leaflet. 'What's it all about anyway? I don't think I've even read it.'

Esme scanned the information. 'Some sort of local missing persons charity,' she said. 'Connects families who've lost touch.' She looked up. 'It was founded back in the 70s. Do you think it's worth asking if Ellen Tucker's on their books?'

'Bit of a long shot,' Maddy said. 'But worth a punt, I suppose.'

Esme stuffed the leaflet in her back pocket. 'I'll give them a call later.'

*

Word had got around about their old photograph project and several people stopped by to study the images on display. Esme guessed the increased interest was due to Morris Beveridge making good with his offer of spreading the word. She must email him and thank him.

Some of the viewers offered suggestions as to families they thought the sitters resembled, often sharing their own memories, and occasionally someone identified the location where a photograph had been taken. Esme spent much of the morning jotting down notes which may help in her research and reunite the photographs with the family to whom they belonged, while Maddy dealt with buying customers.

As visitors to the stall eased, Esme wandered over to Maddy to fill her in with the information she'd gathered. As she did so, she noticed a man wearing dark glasses standing by the entrance, scanning the hall as though he was looking for someone. She was sure he'd been there earlier. He saw her watching him and turned away. Why did he seem familiar? Had she spoken to him? She didn't recall anyone stopping by wearing sunglasses. She'd have noticed, especially given it wasn't a sunny day. Perhaps he'd only just put them on.

'What are you looking at?' Maddy said.

Esme purposely turned away and began rearranging things on the stall. 'That guy over there by the exit. I'm sure he's been standing in the same place for the last half hour.'

'Where?'

'No, don't look.'

'Well, how can I see him if I don't look?'

'I mean, don't make it obvious you're looking.'

Maddy folded her arms and began a casual sweep of the hall. 'Where am I meant to be looking, again?'

'Over by the entrance. Dark hair, beard, brown leather jacket, wearing sunglasses.'

'Yep, got him.'

'Anyone you know?'

Maddy made a moue and shook her head. 'Don't recognise him, no. And you say he's been watching us?'

Esme shrugged. 'Not sure. I just caught his eye and he turned away, as though he'd been caught out.'

'He could be waiting for someone? And they've stood him up?'

'Well, yes. I could be just imagining things.'

'More than likely,' Maddy said, losing interest. 'It's probably cos he's wearing shades. Makes him look dodgy, even if he's not.'

Esme snatched another glance. 'Except, I think I've seen him before.'

'Where?'

'Ah, well. Now you're asking. He hasn't bought anything off the stall, has he?'

Maddy shook her head. 'Not today.'

'Perhaps Cerys knows who he is. I'll go and ask her.'

Esme crossed the aisle to Cerys's stall. She had started to tidy up and looked round as Esme came over.

'Hi, Esme. Had a good morning?'

'Yes, not bad at all, actually. You?'

'Can't complain.'

Esme cast another quick look at the man. His gaze seemed to be trained on Maddy. 'Cerys,' she said, lowering her voice, 'that man by the entrance, there. Anyone you know?'

Cerys peered round her stall's canopy and stared across the hall. 'Don't think so. Why?'

'Not a customer, then?'

'No, definitely not.' She straightened up. 'Something the matter?'

'Probably nothing. He just seems to have a fixation on our stall, that's all. Ah, that's it. That's where I've seen him before,' she added, as an image materialised in her head. She pointed to the end of the aisle. 'Over there. Same situation. Just staring our way, but not coming any closer. But he wasn't wearing sunglasses, I don't think. You and I were having a conversation about witches, I think.'

Cerys raised her eyebrows. 'Perhaps he's buying a present for someone but can't make a decision?'

'So why not come over and say so? It's all a bit odd, don't you think?' Esme turned back to the stranger, but he'd obviously decided his vigil, whatever it was, had come to an end. He peeled away and strode out of the market hall.

'I'm going to ask him,' Esme said, moving away.

'You're going to what?'

'Tell Maddy, will you, Cerys?'

Esme left Cerys staring after her, a bemused expression on her face, and hurried out of the hall. By the time she'd got outside, the man had crossed the road into Buttgarden Street, off the market square. She waited to see which direction he would take. He hesitated before turning into Tower Street, trotting down the steps past the odd little triangular building at the top of the pedestrian alleyway.

Esme checked for traffic and hurried after him, wondering whether she should call out to attract his attention. But what would she say? *Who are you? What do you want? Why are you staring?* The absurdity of her decision almost changed her mind but she imagined returning to Cerys and Maddy, and them asking, '*Well?*' It seemed a bit feeble to say she'd chickened out.

She decided she'd follow him, to start with. Perhaps she could engineer getting closer to him, as though she'd bumped into him in the street, and start a casual conversation. Though, if he'd been watching their stall, he'd recognise her, wouldn't he? Well, it would be interesting to see his reaction when she demanded to know why he found them so fascinating.

They passed down the narrow street between the row of cottages on the left and the taller terraced houses on the right, emerging out in front of the church green. Would he turn right behind the church or left down past Maddy's house and out of the close into Bridge Street? She was sure he'd go right, otherwise there was no reason to walk down Tower Street, as he could have gone straight down Bridge Street from the market exit.

But to Esme's surprise, he turned left. She held back, surprise turning to alarm when he slowed as he reached Maddy's house. For a few seconds, she became paralysed by indecision. Should she approach him? Ask him if he was lost? Walk past him to take a closer look?

To her relief, he moved on. Perhaps he'd just been taken by some aspect of the row of cottages, of which Maddy's was one. Perhaps he was interested in architecture. Maybe he'd merely been studying the roof structure of the Pannier Market. It was an interesting listed building to anyone with an eye for such things. She began to feel a little foolish.

But she wasn't ready to abandon her quest, just yet. Not until she was sure his apparent interest was completely innocent.

He'd got away from her a little now and she had to pause on the corner to find which way he'd gone. To the car park opposite, perhaps, back to his car? Had he headed up Bridge Street back towards the market? Or out towards the quay? Then she saw him, hurrying down Allhalland Street. She crossed the road and followed on, peering into the windows of the small shops along the street, in case he turned round and saw her.

Half way along the street, he took a sharp right down the pedestrian alleyway leading to the quay. She took the turn too, coming to an abrupt stop as he opened the side door to The Kings Arms and disappeared inside.

Esme stood for a moment, uncertain what to do next. Someone coughed behind her and she apologised and stepped out of the way. It spurred her and she went up to the pub door and peered in through the small window. The man stood at the bar, his back to her.

As she deliberated whether to pursue him inside and what to say to him if she did, she noticed two other people also at the bar, perched on stools, pints in hand. Drew and Alec Brannock.

She turned away and hurried back to the market. Another coincidence?

# 33

'OK, so it might be the Brannocks' local,' Maddy said, as they unloaded the market stock back at her workshop. 'But it's also a popular pub, especially being on the quay. People notice it. So why wouldn't your mystery man go in there?'

'So you're saying it's just a coincidence,' Esme said. 'Another one.'

Maddy gave Esme a wry smile. 'I'm never going to live that down, now, am I?' She sighed. 'OK. Tell you what. We'll keep an eye out for him next time and catch him in a pincer movement. You can approach him head on and I'll creep up on him from behind. He'll have no chance, then.'

Esme grinned. 'Don't think I won't take you up on that, Maddy Henderson. I don't like being watched. It makes me nervous.'

Maddy looked serious for a moment. 'Yes, I can imagine it does, Esme, after everything that's happened in your past. Sorry, didn't mean to be flippant.'

Esme flapped a hand in Maddy's direction. 'Don't be silly. I'm not that paranoid. Yet.' She looked around. 'Well, that's everything, I think. Oh, I thought I might drop in on that missing persons charity. They're only in here in town. A personal approach might get a better response than phoning.'

'Yeah, good idea.' Maddy rubbed her eyes and yawned. Esme raised an eyebrow. 'I hope you're not working too hard. Haven't you got a car boot sale tomorrow?'

Maddy nodded. 'But Harry's coming with me. That'll ease the pressure a bit.'

Esme nodded. 'That's good. Takes the pressure off me, too.'

'How's that?'

'Otherwise I'd feel I ought to come and give you a hand. But Ruth's invited me over for lunch.' She gave Maddy a wry grin. 'She's got a property she wants me to see.'

'Oh, house hunting,' Maddy said, sliding the campervan door closed. 'That's fun. I didn't realise you'd sold your cottage in Shropshire.'

'I haven't. Though if I give the word, it could happen. The tenant's keen to buy. I just wasn't ready to sell before.'

'That's handy. Saves on agent's fees.' Maddy snatched up her keys. 'Well, I'd better get going. I've promised to cook Harry a meal tonight. A sort of thanks for his help tomorrow. And I haven't decided what we're having yet.'

'Well, you'd better get to it, then,' Esme said, picking up her bag. 'I'll let you know how I get on at the charity.'

Maddy nodded. 'That'd be good. Drop me a text. See you Tuesday.'

*

The office of the missing persons organisation, LOST, was the same address as a charity shop along Mill Street, off the High Street. Esme found a plump young woman with blue hair, dressed in black leggings and a red T-shirt sporting the charity's logo, at the rear of the shop. She was sitting on a table staring at her iPhone. Leaflets similar to the one Maddy had were fanned out beside her, along with a collection box.

As Esme walked up to her, the girl jumped down from her perch and slipped her phone into her back pocket.

'Hi, I'm Baz,' she said, an infectious smile lighting up her face. 'How can I help?'

'It's a bit of a long shot, I'm afraid,' Esme said. 'It's about a woman who...' she pulled a face, 'it sounds a bit weird, I know...who *may* have gone missing in 1995.'

The girl's painted eyebrows shot up. '95? Wow.'

'Yes, I know. It's a long time ago. But I noticed your organisation has been around since the 70s so I wondered if it might have been a case the charity was aware of.'

'Was she a family member?'

Esme shook her head. 'No, I'm a researcher. I've been looking into the family history of the woman in question. Ellen Tucker was her name.' She looked at the girl, perhaps hoping for some recognition even though the charity worker wouldn't have even been born when Ellen was being taunted for being a witch. 'Or *is* her name, perhaps I should say,' she added. 'I'd imagine that your charity deals in hope much of the time.'

'You're right there. And we have our successes, too. Do you know that someone goes missing in the UK every 90 seconds?' Baz said.

'That's a shocking statistic,' Esme said, shaking her head.

'That's about 180,000 a year. Most people are found within 72 hours, but there are always those who aren't, and we won't stop searching until that person's found. That's been our policy since Penny first set up the charity in 1974 after her sister went missing.' Baz jerked a thumb towards the wall behind her where a series of photographs of smiling volunteers were pinned up between examples of charity paraphernalia - beermats, pens, keyrings and bookmarks. 'There's Penny, there, in the middle,' she said, 'being presented with a donation after last year's Fun Run.'

Esme looked at the central photo. A woman with long, frizzy hair was standing next to a tall man dressed in running gear. Both were smiling into the camera, each holding one end of an oversized cheque for £2,000.

'And did she find her sister?' Esme asked.

The girl shook her head. 'No trace of her ever found. She was walking back from her boyfriend's house one evening and never made it home. When another girl disappeared in similar circumstances, Penny got in touch with the family to offer her support. LOST grew from there, really.'

'Given the stats you quoted, it's obvious there's a need,' Esme said. 'You must be a comfort to anyone who finds themselves in such a nightmare situation.'

The girl smiled. 'We do what we can. This woman, Ellen Tucker. Was her disappearance reported to the police?' she asked.

'Ah, that I'm not sure.'

'We'll always give support and advice to worried family members and friends, of course, but we wouldn't have publicised her disappearance unless it had been made official.'

'I'm guessing that's so your services can't be misused.'

She nodded. 'You guess right. Don't need some unscrupulous sod using us to track down their ex-partner just so they can stalk them. Or worse.'

'Makes total sense,' Esme agreed. 'So, it's only if someone has been officially reported missing that you'd have any record yourselves?'

'You got it, yeah.'

'Would it be possible to check, d'you think?'

'Oh, I don't know. That'd be down to Penny. She does all the official stuff.' The girl grinned. 'I'm just a volunteer.'

'No one is *just* a volunteer,' Esme said, returning her grin. 'Where would the world be without people like you?'

Baz reached over the desk and slid a notepad and pen towards Esme. 'If you jot down your details here, I'll get Penny to call you, shall I?'

Esme filled in her contact information and handed it to Baz. 'Like I said, it's a long shot. But you never know.' She pulled her purse out of her bag and slipped a donation into the collecting tin. 'Thanks for your help.'

'No worries,' Baz said, glancing down at Esme's completed form. 'Penny will be in touch.' She looked up. 'And if you ever fancy volunteering, you know where we are.'

# 34

Ruth and Peter Gibson's farm, where Esme had once stayed during her sabbatical, was less than an hour's walking distance from her cottage. The day she'd been invited to lunch dawned bright and breezy, so she decided to take a chance and go on foot. She climbed the coast path up on to the clifftop towards Warren Quay, turning off across the fields to reach the farmhouse.

Ruth greeted Esme at the back door and took her into the warm kitchen, bidding her sit at the table while Pete poured her a glass of wine. Esme asked after the family and was assured all were well, including Ruth's mother, Bea, and told them about the photograph project she and Maddy had set up.

Ruth's cooking excelled as usual. Esme was treated to a delicious meal of roast beef and all the trimmings, and afterwards, her favourite: rhubarb crumble and custard.

'No, no, leave that,' Ruth said when Esme began clearing the table. 'Pete will do it. I'm dying to show you this property.' She snatched a set of keys off the hooks next to the dresser. 'If we go now, we'll have time for a walk down to the beach.'

They climbed into the farm Land Rover and headed out of the farmyard.

'So you know these people who are selling the cottage, then?' Esme said, as they rattled up the lane.

'Yes. Have done for years. They used to come to the farm for B&B, and then they bought this place as a holiday home. But they're getting a bit long in the tooth now, they don't get down as often these days.'

'They don't rent it out, then?'

'Oh, yes, they do that too. But I think it's all getting a bit of a hassle, so they've decided to sell up.' Ruth stopped at the junction to the main road and checked the traffic before pulling out and turning left, back towards Bideford. 'And when they told me, I immediately thought of you. It would be perfect.'

Esme laughed. 'You're rapidly become my official accommodation agent,' she said, watching the high Devon bank whizzing by as they trundled along. 'First letting me use your holiday cabin, then hearing on the grapevine about the cottage up for rent, and now this.'

'Oh, don't worry,' Ruth said, taking her eyes off the road fleetingly to give Esme a wink. 'My fees are quite affordable.'

After a few miles Ruth indicated left, driving down a steep hill into a wooded valley, passing a chapel on the left in amongst the trees, before turning into a car park on the right-hand side.

'We can walk the rest of the way,' Ruth said, turning off the engine and opening the door. 'Come on.'

They took a narrow path which joined the road on the bend as it turned seaward.

'It's down here on the right,' Ruth said, taking out a bunch of keys from her pocket.

'So it's not being rented out at the moment?'

'Oh, yes it is. Some Canadian chap is staying, over here seeing family. But I've got permission to show you around while he's out. It's all arranged.' She paused on the road and pointed down the hill. 'Look, the sea's only down there. There's a pebbly beach – perfect spot for blowing the cobwebs away. The local residents will be really pleased that someone's moving in on a permanent basis. Always good to get a better balance of residents and holidaymakers.'

'Ruth! I haven't even seen it yet.'

Ruth laughed. 'You'll love it. Trust me.'

They walked on, passing a row of cottages set right back from the road. A short way along, Ruth stopped.

'Here it is,' she said, turning right and climbing a set of steep stone steps between high hedges. Esme stood back and looked up. At the top of the steps stood a quaint stone cottage with whitewashed walls and a thatched roof. A scruffy climber, still clothed in the remains of its summer foliage, surrounded a central pale green door, and neat small-paned windows winked out at her on either side and from their counterparts above. She sighed, smiling to herself. Ruth was right. It was adorable.

She took a deep breath and caught up with Ruth, who was standing beside the front door. A flagstone path crossing the front of the cottage led to a gravelled parking space in one direction, and in the other, to an area of grass stretching out into the distance, parallel to the lane.

'First impressions?' Ruth said, a mischievous look in her eye.

'I'm reserving judgment,' Esme said, giving Ruth a guarded smile, 'lest I commit myself too readily.'

Ruth laughed. 'It's perfect, isn't it? Like a little house a child would draw.' She slid a key into the lock. 'Come and take a look inside.'

The whiff of woodsmoke hit Esme as Ruth opened the front door and they stepped into an open-plan ground floor. Esme was pleased to see a large inglenook fireplace, housing a wood-burning stove, in the end which served as a sitting room. At the opposite end was a good size kitchen. A large table stood in the centre, straddling the two areas. She looked up at the broad whitewashed beams a few inches above her head.

'Yes, it's low, isn't it?' Ruth said, reaching up to touch the ceiling. 'The chap staying at the moment's probably got a permanent stoop by now.' She strode over to the back wall and pulled open a latched wooden door. 'The stairs are up here. Two bedrooms and a bathroom. Same as your cottage in Shropshire, isn't it?'

Esme nodded and looked round, assessing the living space, before joining Ruth for the upstairs tour. The bedrooms weren't large, but adequate; the bathroom a little tired, but acceptable. The decoration, like downstairs, wasn't to her taste, but that was easy enough to remedy.

They returned to the ground floor. Esme stood in the middle of the room, aware of a growing sense of disappointment. She looked at Ruth and wrinkled her nose.

'It's gorgeous, Ruth, but I don't think it's going to be big enough.' She scanned around. 'Where would I put my desk, computer, printer, books? It's fine for a holiday home, but I need space to work.'

Ruth held up a finger. 'I've thought of that. Let me show you the garden.'

Esme followed Ruth outside and over to the grassy patch on the far side of the cottage. Ruth stopped at the end of the path and pointed to a low single-storey building, almost hidden in the undergrowth. Like the main cottage, it was built of stone, though it wasn't whitewashed. It had two windows to the front, one single casement and the other made up of three vertical small-paned units. There was a stable door in the middle, and under the mass of brambles, a roof of mostly broken slate.

'There you are,' Ruth said, extending her arm. 'Your future office. What do you think?'

Esme blinked. 'Are you kidding me? It's a hovel.'

'I thought you wanted a renovation project?' Ruth said, sorting through the bunch of keys in her hand. 'What could be better? Cottage cosy and ready to move into while you get this one done exactly the way you want it. You could set up your workspace in the spare bedroom temporarily while it's being done up.' She looked up. 'Don't think there's a key.' She went over to the window and looked in, shading her eyes with her hand. 'Being used for storage, by the looks of things.'

Esme joined Ruth and peered in through the grubby glass. There were piles of mismatched furniture, cardboard boxes and strange shapes draped in dust sheets.

173

Ruth stepped back. 'Doesn't look like anyone's been in there for years.' She looked at Esme. 'I could ask about a key if you want to see more?'

'Let me think about it,' Esme said, her mind a whirl of possibilities, but needing time and space to consider everything properly.

To her relief, Ruth nodded and after she'd lock up the cottage, they set off down the hill towards the beach.

'Great location, this,' Ruth said. 'As well as the beach, which I've already mentioned, there's easy access to the coast path. And it's a bit closer to Bideford, here, which is what you wanted, isn't it?'

'It's definitely got its plus points, I admit.' Esme said. 'Let me mull it over.'

*

They walked down through the rest of the village. Ruth pointed out which was holiday accommodation and which were full-time residential properties. The road opened out into a turning area, ahead of which it narrowed into a path, before turning sharply to the left and becoming steeper.

'That's The Cabin,' Ruth said, pointing ahead to a tiny narrow stone building on the right-hand side, built into the cliff edge. 'It used to be an artist studio years ago. The National Trust own it now and invite local artists to use it to promote their work. Nothing's been changed, so the previous owners' belongings are all still on display. It's like a time capsule.'

They passed and wound their way down the path to the pebble beach. An information panel told visitors there had been a quay on the spot since 1598, the remains of which could be seen at low tide. Under the text was an illustration of what the quay might have looked like, reminding Esme of the harbour at Warren Quay.

They stood for a few moments on the slipway, looking across the beach. A waterfall splashed on to the cobbles a little way along, and in the far distance, Esme could see the headland of Baggy Point. She gazed across the water, enjoying the pleasing rhythm of waves breaking on shingle.

As they climbed back up the hill, Esme slowed as they reached the stone steps to the entrance of the cottage. There was no doubt it had a certain something. It reminded her of somewhere, but she couldn't think where.

'Oh, that's a shame,' Ruth said.

'What is?'

'He's back'. Ruth nodded towards the gravelled area. A white Vauxhall Corsa was parked there, the hire-car's logo displayed on the passenger door. 'I was going to suggest we had another look inside before we go. Help you make a decision.'

Esme shook her head. 'Doesn't matter. I've seen enough for now.'

'Yeah, thought you might,' Ruth said, a knowing expression on her face.

Esme turned to Ruth and wagged her finger. 'Don't you say a word, Ruth Gibson,' she said, suppressing a smile. 'I shall decide in my own good time.'

Ruth linked her arm through Esme's and giggled. 'That'll be a yes, then.'

# 35

Morris Beveridge emailed to say he planned to call into Tuesday's market and collect the photographs he'd identified from the *Photos Reunited* website. Maddy spotted him across the hall, heading towards their stall.

'Your genealogist friend's on his way over,' she said. 'Don't forget to pick his brains about the Brannocks and the murder. If anyone's gonna know about it, he will.'

'Oh, I plan to, don't worry,' Esme said.

Maddy nodded and went over to talk to a customer who was deliberating over a wooden trinket box.

Morris shook Esme's hand and stood back to admire her photograph display. 'This is an admirable idea, Esme,' he said. 'I've mentioned your website to a number of people. They've been most taken with it.'

'Thanks, Morris. That's very much appreciated. We were quite busy on Saturday and I'm sure that's down to you.' She leaned over the stall and pulled out a padded envelope from the box behind the table. 'Here,' she said, 'your photographs. We're so pleased they'll be back with the family they belong to.'

Morris took the package and hugged it to him. 'Thank you. Have you had many successes?'

'One or two, but we've really only just started. I'm concentrating on getting Maddy's photo collection on to the website at the moment and trying to fit in the research when I can.' She indicated the display board. 'These were all taken by local photographers, so I thought I might as well show them off here. You never know, someone may recognise someone.'

Morris took a step closer, frowning at the photograph of a young man in World War One uniform, standing beside an ornate wooden table.

'Unless I'm very much mistaken, that's Seth Brannock.'

'Brannock?' Esme pulled out her reading glasses from her pocket and slipped them on to study the photo Morris had indicated.

'Yes, I was heavily involved in the research for the centenary commemoration. This young man was on the war memorial in the village on my patch.'

'As a survivor or a casualty?' Esme asked.

'Casualty. Died in the infamous Somme, I'm afraid. Left a widow and a 7-year-old son. Who, tragically, would grow up to die in World War Two while serving on HMS *Belmont*. Sunk by a U-boat in the Atlantic in 1942.'

Esme shook her head. 'Oh, what a tragic coincidence. And did he have a family, too?'

'Again, one son,' Morris said. He took off his wire-rimmed spectacles and polished them with a handkerchief from his jacket pocket. 'Aged 9 when his father was killed, I believe.' He slipped his spectacles back on and folded up his handkerchief before returning it to the pocket of his jacket. 'A tragic family history in many ways.' He nodded his head towards the image of the World War One soldier on Esme's display. 'Young Seth's father, Luke Brannock, survived a scarlet fever outbreak in 1871 when he was 5 years old. Both his parents died, along with Luke's five siblings.'

'Oh, poor little chap.' Esme felt an ache in her throat as she imagined the heartbreak of the little boy losing his entire family. 'All alone in the world at such a tender age. Old enough to feel his loss, but not really old enough to understand.'

'Indeed,' Morris said. 'Took a heavy toll on him over the years. He became convinced his family was cursed. Ended his days in an asylum, poor chap, when Seth was only a lad.'

'How awful,' Esme said. 'And upsetting for Seth and his mother.' She pictured a scene of a ranting husband, a distraught wife and a frightened child.

'Shall I give Iris Webb your phone number and ask her to get in touch?' Morris said. 'She's the one researching the Brannock family. She lives locally, so getting it to her won't be a problem.'

'Yes, of course. I can deliver the photograph, if she'd like me to.'

'Perfect. I'll let her know.'

'This isn't the Brannock line associated with Temperance Mill, is it?' Esme said. Although the names weren't familiar to her, there could still be a family connection. 'I've been doing some research on the mill's history.'

'Oh, have you? How interesting. The Brannock family owned a considerable amount of land at one time, including the mill. It wasn't always called Temperance Mill, you know.'

Esme nodded. 'So I discovered. It was Corvus Mill originally, wasn't it?'

'Indeed it was. The Latin for raven or crow.'

'Oh yes, of course it is.' It hadn't occurred to her before. 'I wonder why they changed it. Do you know?'

'It's believed that Silas Brannock renamed it after hearing an American temperance speaker in Bideford in 1854. And it's perfectly feasible. The Brannocks have always been staunch Methodists.'

'Silas?' Esme said, leaping on the name. 'Is that the Silas who was murdered by his daughter?'

Morris chuckled. 'Now why am I not surprised that you've come across that particular story? It's a strange one and no mistake.'

'So what do you know about it, Morris? And about the murder stone up at the mill?'

Morris raised his eyebrows. 'Murder stone? I wasn't aware there was one.'

'Well, perhaps not as you might imagine it. It certainly doesn't resemble a headstone like others I've seen. It's carved into bare rock. I could only make out the letter E and some dates. But although the timing's close enough, it doesn't fit Silas's murder because Joseph Brannock suggested the victim was a woman.'

Morris blinked. 'How extraordinary. Well, you must inform me of the finer details when you've solved the puzzle.' He smiled. 'Which I'm sure you will. Solve it, I mean. Now,' he checked his watch, 'I really must away, my dear.' He hugged the package of photos to him. 'I'm meeting the family to return this.'

He shook her hand once more and slipped away into the growing crowd, leaving Esme a little deflated. If Morris Beveridge's knowledge didn't stretch to the story behind the murder stone, she'd be lucky to find someone else whose did.

Maddy appeared at her elbow with two mugs of coffee. 'Anything?' she asked, handing Esme one.

'He didn't know about the stone.'

'Oh, that's a shame. I was counting on him.' She wrapped her hands around her mug and peered at Esme over the rim. 'He must know about Silas Brannock's murder, though?'

'Yes, he probably did, but I butted in about the stone and didn't get a chance to quiz him after that. He had to go. He was meeting the family to return the photos. I'll give him a call later, perhaps. And while we're waiting for Hope Brannock's birth certificate to arrive, I'll see if I can find time to do some more digging in the newspaper archives. I'd love to understand why Silas Brannock's daughter came to kill her father.'

She took a sip of the hot liquid, wondering what Morris meant about it being a strange story.

*

'Phew,' Maddy said, slumping against the stall table. 'That was a frenetic few minutes. Good, though. Did quite well there.'

'Yes,' Esme agreed. 'We could do with some more stock for next time, though. We're looking a bit thin.' She glanced around the market hall, assessing the numbers still left shopping. It usually began to quieten down about this time.

'I picked up one or two nice pieces on Sunday,' Maddy said. 'They just need a clean-up and a bit of polish, and I can bring them along. I've got a busy week coming up, but I should be able to find time before Saturday. It's the mill meeting this week, as well, isn't it?'

Esme nodded. 'Anna wants me to bring what I've found out about the mill's history with me. Though I thought this was the alternative energy expert coming to assess the practical feasibility of the scheme.'

'It is. I think Anna wants us there for moral support.'

'Yes, that makes sense. Well, let's hope this expert can convince Daniel and Drew to back Anna's scheme. She's pretty determined they're not going to stand in her way.'

Esme's phone buzzed. She took it out and looked at the screen. 'It's Morris,' she said. 'Probably about Seth Brannock's photograph. He was going to get in touch with the family doing the research.' She tapped to make the connection. 'Morris. Good to hear back from you so quickly.'

Morris confirmed he'd spoken to Iris Webb, who'd been thrilled about Seth Brannock's photograph, and would be in touch shortly.

'That's great, Morris, thanks,' Esme said. 'I'll wait to hear from her, then.'

'Perfect. Now, on another matter, I wondered, if you're not otherwise engaged tomorrow, whether you'd like to drop in on me at the Burton Art Gallery. I'm doing a book signing.'

'But I've got your book already, Morris. Remember? I came to your talk.'

He chuckled. 'Yes, I realise that. It's just I wanted to have a chat. I think I might have a theory about your murder stone.'

# 36

Esme left her Peugeot in the road which ran alongside Victoria Park and walked back up to the main road to the Burton Art Gallery, where she'd agreed to meet Morris Beveridge ahead of his book signing event. Children's voices echoed across the park from the play area, as they took advantage of the first dry day of the half-term holiday.

Esme climbed up the stairs to the museum section and found Morris reading the display board devoted to the story of the three Bideford Witches.

'You must know what's written up there by heart, I should think,' Esme said, as she approached.

Morris turned and peered at her over the top of his rimless spectacles. '*Ad verbatim*,' he said, his eyes twinkling.

Esme glanced at the image of the thatched cottage at the bottom of the board, alleged to be where at least one of the three witches had lived, noting the similarity of its small-paned windows to those of the cottage she'd viewed with Ruth a few days before. The witches' cottage, if that indeed was what it was, had burned down in 1894.

'Isn't there some superstition about thatch and witches?' Esme said.

'Ah, yes. Smoking out a witch. The theory being that if a handful of thatch was taken from the roof of a suspected witch and burned, she would come running, thereby implicating herself.'

Esme shuddered. 'Another absurd test,' she said. 'Along with the infamous sink or swim trial. Not much chance of being saved by being innocent. Damned if you floated and drowned if you sank.' She looked up at Morris. 'Anyway, I mustn't hold you up any longer than necessary. Your fans will be beating a path to your talk shortly, and I'm dying to hear your take on the mystery of the murder stone. You've obviously been doing some digging. You said you didn't know when I asked you yesterday.'

Morris gestured towards the double-doors through which Esme had just come through. 'Shall we take a pew in The Kingsley Room for a moment?'

Esme nodded. 'Yes, good idea.'

They went out on to the landing and through to the room beyond, which the gallery hired out for workshops and events. Chairs were set out in rows, and to one side stood a table displaying Morris's books.

'We've got a bit of time before people start arriving,' Morris said, taking his briefcase off a chair at the end of the row and inviting Esme to sit down. He took a seat in the adjoining row and swivelled round to face Esme.

'What have you learned so far about Silas Brannock's murder?' he asked, resting his arm on the back of the chair.

'Silas? But his murder doesn't fit. Unless you're saying that Joseph Brannock's wrong about the murder stone victim being a female?'

Morris shook his head. 'No, I don't think he's wrong. But the stone doesn't refer to Silas, although there is a connection.'

'OK,' Esme said, keen for him to share his story before the audience arrived and interrupted them. 'Well, I know that his daughter Sarah was charged for arson and murder. And that she was found guilty. But I'm intrigued as to why she was accused. I assume father and daughter had a major falling out?'

Morris chuckled. 'I think you could say that, yes.' He pushed his glasses further up his nose. 'It was the letter E that set me thinking.'

'The letter I thought was carved into the rock?'

'Yes. And then, of course, it made complete sense.' He shuffled in his chair. 'I'm sure it'll interest you to learn that Sarah was born a mere six months after her parents' wedding.'

'Oh, OK,' Esme said, nodding. 'So Sarah's mother was pregnant with Sarah when they married. Do we assume that Silas was the father?'

'That, it seems, was the crux of the matter. For some reason – and it's not clear what triggered it – Silas and his wife had an argument within Sarah's hearing. Silas was heard to declare that he had reason to believe Sarah wasn't his daughter and that Elizabeth, his wife – or Bessie, as she was more commonly known – had tricked him into marriage to cover up her predicament.'

'Do we know if he'd suspected this before?' Esme asked.

'I've no idea. He may have harboured the suspicion privately for years and something happened to bring matters to a head.'

'Maybe he'd recently found something out about Bessie's past?' Esme said, trying to envisage the scene: the confrontation between husband and wife, accuser and accused. Had someone told Silas something he'd been unaware of before? Had Bessie dismissed his charge? Admitted to it? 'So what happened next?'

'Silas became angry, struck his wife, and Sarah intervened in her defence. In the struggle, Bessie fell in the kitchen fire and died as a result of her burns.'

Esme winced at the memory of reading Bessie's death certificate, imagining the folds of her skirt catching alight from the kitchen fire.

'Which matches what was recorded as her cause of death.'

'Indeed it does,' Morris said. 'However, Sarah's version of events was quite different.'

'Really? In what way?'

Morris leaned forward and lowered his voice. 'According to Sarah, Silas didn't accuse her mother of *tricking* him, but of *bewitching* him. He then lunged at her and deliberately pushed her into the fire, saying she should burn for her wicked ways.'

'Bloody hell!' Esme's mouth fell open. 'And this all came out in court?'

Morris reached for his briefcase and pulled out a folder from which he took a bundle of papers. He read out loud from his notes. "*Sarah called upon her brother to summon the constable.*" Morris looked up. 'That's her younger brother, Isaac, who was only 11 years old at the time.'

Esme nodded. 'Yes, I remember seeing his name. He's the only one left at the mill by the 1871 census.'

'That's the chap. Meanwhile Sarah's sister, 13-year-old Susannah, goes to fetch the doctor, leaving Sarah to tend to their dying mother.' Morris continued reading. "*When Isaac returned with the officer*" – I think we have to assume by now that poor Bessie had passed away – "*Sarah pointed an angry finger towards her father and accused him of the murder of her mother.*"

'Wow.' Esme sat back in her chair to digest the information. 'Why is there such a misconception that witches were burned, Morris?' she asked. 'They were hanged, weren't they, like the Bideford Three?'

'In England, yes. Though, there was a time prior to the 16th century when they were burned in England, as in many European countries. I suspect the confusion is because burning is the church's punishment for heresy and witchcraft. Most witch trials in England were carried out by the state, not the church.'

Esme nodded. 'So was Silas charged with anything?' she asked, returning to the Brannock story.

Morris laid down the folder. 'It would be Silas's word against Sarah's. All too easy to dismiss Sarah's accusations as a reaction to her grief, having witnessed her mother's horrific death.'

'Yes,' Esme said, nodding. 'Hysterical young woman and all that. Very Victorian.'

'Bessie's family, on the other hand,' Morris continued, 'perhaps aware of relations between Bessie and her husband, were ready to believe Sarah's story.'

'Oh, I see now,' Esme said. 'It's Bessie's murder that's referred to on the outcrop of rock? The letter E is for Elizabeth?'

Morris nodded. 'I think that's a distinct possibility, don't you? Put there by the Meddon family, in protest of no action being taken against Silas.'

Esme thought of Joseph's comment. '*That wore no murder.*' An echo, presumably, of the view held by Silas's family, that Bessie's death was justifiable.

'So what about Silas?' she asked.

'Given relations between them, it was obvious Sarah couldn't stay with her father in the mill, so she went to live with her aunt, Bessie's sister, Martha. One day in town, she bumped into her father and they argued. She was heard to scream at him that he'd burn in hell for his crime.'

Esme put a hand to her mouth. 'Oh of course,' she said, nodding. 'So when he's found dead in the burned-out building, everyone assumes Sarah is to blame. That she's taken matters into her own hands.'

'Quite so.'

'I assume the verdict was a foregone conclusion?'

'You assume correctly. She was sentenced to death and was hanged in 1869.'

Voices floated up the stairs. People were beginning to arrive for Morris's event.

Esme stood up. 'Thanks, Morris. I really appreciate you sharing your research.'

'You're very welcome,' Morris said, getting to his feet. 'Pleased to be able to help.'

Esme hesitated. 'Do you think she was guilty?'

Morris smiled sadly. 'I guess we'll never know for certain. There were no witnesses to the crime and the evidence does seem to be pretty circumstantial.'

'It's ironic. If she'd been believed, the law was on her side.'

'Yes, indeed. In accusing his wife of witchcraft, Silas would have had to face the authorities. Where once those accused of witchcraft were the offenders, it was now their persecutors who were in the wrong.'

'She didn't stand a chance, did she?' Esme said, throwing her bag over her shoulder. 'She must have been convinced that everyone conspired against her.'

'Indeed,' Morris agreed. 'And in particular, the Brannock family.'

# 37

On the day of the meeting with the alternative energy expert, Esme parked her car in the reclamation yard and called in at the workshop for Maddy, her research file tucked under her arm. As they walked to the mill together, they talked over Sarah Brannock's story.

'You're telling me that people were still throwing witchcraft accusations about in the 19th century?' Maddy said, her eyes wide with astonishment. 'Even though the law was changed back in 1736?'

'Well, like Morris says in his book, it's all very well decreeing witchcraft is no longer a criminal act but you can't legislate against people's fervent beliefs. A fear of witches was embedded in the social psyche, whatever it said on the statute books. And sometimes people dealt out their own justice.'

'In what way?'

'Fifteen years after the act, a man and his wife in Hertfordshire were accused of causing the deaths of a farmer's cattle and a mob threw them in the village pond where the poor woman drowned. The ringleader was tried for murder and hanged, much to the disgust of the villagers, who thought he'd been very harshly treated when all he'd done was rid the village of a witch.'

'Well, I suppose fifteen years isn't so very long for people to get their heads round the new way of thinking.'

'No, but you'd have thought well over 100 years would be,' Esme said, as they passed through the gateway and turned left along the lane. 'A couple in Devon were brought to book in 1852 for attacking a woman they believed had harmed their daughter by witchcraft and scratching her face, due to a commonly held belief that it would break the spell.'

'Well, if you're thinking of passing on to Anna what you've learned from Morris about the murder,' Maddy said, nodding towards the mill ahead of them, 'today might not be the right time and place. You know what Daniel was like last time he got wind of it.'

Esme looked over and was surprised to see Daniel standing next to Anna, looking at what remained of the mill wheel. Beside them stood a tall man with blond hair and a ginger beard. A grey pick-up with *Eco-power South-West Ltd* written across the side was parked in the yard.

'I wasn't expecting him to be here,' Esme said, hoisting her research folder more securely under her arm. 'Do you think he's had a change of mind? He was pretty sceptical last time I saw him.'

'Maybe he's come to keep an eye on Anna,' Maddy said, opening the gate with a wry smile. 'Make sure she doesn't sign up to anything.'

Anna must have heard them coming, as she looked round and waved enthusiastically. She said something to her companions and came over to meet them.

'Esme's wondering whether you've converted your dad,' Maddy said.

Anna giggled. 'I told him he'd got to hear all the facts before he dismissed it out of hand,' she said, as they walked across yard. 'I'm sure Mike's input will convince him. He's advised on hundreds of mill conversions and we're very lucky to get him.'

Esme and Maddy nodded their acknowledgments to Daniel who did likewise and Anna introduced them to Mike Harrow.

'Hi, Esme, good to meet you,' Mike said, shaking her hand. 'You're the historian, I understand.'

Esme smiled. 'Yes, that's right. It's a fascinating project.'

Daniel made a guttural noise and looked away. Esme wondered whether it was due to his opinion of Anna's *pie in the sky* idea, or whether it was aimed at her and his disapproval over her resurrecting the story of the murder stone. Maddy's comment a moment ago suggested she was still smarting from his verbal assault on the subject. Perhaps the only reason Daniel had come was to make his feelings known to Esme, too. She'd not seen him since he'd taken Maddy to task.

'Maddy rents a workshop in our yard currently,' Anna was explaining to Mike. 'But she'll be the first in the queue if we can make a go of the mill.' She looked from Esme to Maddy, her eyes shining. 'Mike was just telling Dad that he thinks my idea is perfectly doable, don't you, Mike?'

Esme glanced at Daniel, but his face gave nothing away.

'In theory, yes,' Mike agreed. He nodded towards the dilapidated mill wheel. 'Lots of work to do, of course, but the central shaft's intact so it's only a case of replacing the damaged blades on the wheel. Naturally you'd have to clear away all the vegetation and clean it all out. But that's quite straightforward enough. If I could show you this?'

He led them through the undergrowth, pulling a large branch to one side so they could see the wheel more easily.

'You can't make it out at the moment,' he said, 'but underneath the wheel there's a sump which catches the water. It's silted up over the years, of course.' He turned, and they all trained their eyes to where he was pointing. 'The leat which feeds it is obviously completely overgrown, but I've walked alongside it and there's evidence of it all the way back to the stream beyond.' He looked round at their faces. 'Again, a matter of clearing it out.'

'But then what?' said Daniel. 'I mean, that's only the beginning, though, isn't it? There's the cost of the kit to set it up to generate electricity, not to mention the work to get the mill into a good state of repair before we start. What figures are we talking about?'

'I've got all the information in the pick-up if you'd care to come over.' Mike let go of the overhanging branch and they picked their way across to solid ground, where his truck was parked. He reached inside the back seat and pulled out a glossy folder.

'Everything you need to know is in there, and if you think of anything you want to ask, just give me a call. My mobile number's on the introductory letter.' He passed it to Daniel, but Anna intervened and took it.

'That's great, Mike. And your company will organise to do the work, will it, if we decide to go ahead?'

'Whoa, Anna,' said Daniel. 'One thing at a time.'

'I'm not engaging him, Dad, merely establishing the facts.'

Esme smiled to herself. Anna seemed pretty sure of her commitment. It would take some convincing to get her to drop the idea.

'Let's go inside, shall we?' Anna said.

As they walked, Anna talked to Mike about her plans for the mill's use. Esme found herself in step with Daniel.

'So, are you convinced?' she asked him, already anticipating his reply from the sour expression on his face.

'I don't want to pour cold water on Anna's enthusiasm,' he said, 'but I've said it before and I'll say it again: I think she's biting off more than she can chew. How's she going to run a building project at the same time as keeping the business going, *and* with a new family to deal with?' He turned to Esme, his eyes pleading. 'Can't you persuade her it's all too much?'

'Me?' Esme laughed. 'It's not my place to dissuade her, Daniel.' She looked up at Anna ahead of them, animated and excited, deep in conversation with Mike. 'Perhaps it's not so impossible if everyone gets behind it.'

Daniel scowled. 'Don't lay this at my door. Drew's not keen on the idea either.' He grunted. 'Maybe he can talk some sense into her.' He strode off ahead.

'Not sure Drew's keen on anything much,' Maddy muttered under her breath, 'particularly if it involves any effort on his part.'

They arrived at the large double doors to the mill and Anna took a key out of her pocket. She unlocked the padlock and pulled open the left-hand door. Daniel grabbed hold of it and opened it wide, back out of the way. Esme held it steady for him while he rolled a rock into position to act as a door stop.

Ahead of them, the others went inside.

'Bloody hell,' Maddy said.

'What's the matter?' Esme asked, hurrying across the threshold. She blinked, as her eyes adjusted to the light and allowed her to see what everyone else was staring at, open mouthed.

The walls of the ground floor had been daubed with blood-red paint.

# 38

For a moment, no one spoke.

'What a bloody mess,' Daniel said, eventually. He strode over to a discarded paint can lying on its side in the middle of the floor, still oozing red paint, and righted it. He looked around, running his fingers through his hair.

Esme took a step towards Anna, who was staring wide-eyed at the gaudy spectacle. 'Are you OK, Anna?' she said.

Anna flinched and turned to Esme. 'I'm fine. Thanks. Just amazed that someone would do this.' She shook her head. 'I mean, what's the point?'

Mike Harrow cleared his throat. 'Not everyone supports this sort of project, in my experience,' he said. 'Some of my clients have had quite a battle on their hands to convince the local community that...'

'But no one knows about it yet,' Anna snapped. 'And what the hell would it be to them anyway?' she added, anger now replacing shock. 'Who does it affect? Nobody. There's not another house for a mile! It's ridiculous.'

A shadow fell across the entrance and Esme turned to see Drew on his way inside. 'What's going on here?' he asked.

'See for yourself,' Anna said, gesturing with her arm. 'It'll take for ever to get it off.' She strode over to the closest patch of bright-red wall and touched it. 'Dry as a bone. God knows when it was done.'

'How did they get in?' Esme asked. 'The padlock was secure when we got here, wasn't it?'

'That doesn't mean anything,' Drew said, wandering over,

hands in his jeans pockets. 'Anna leaves the key hanging up in the office. Anyone could walk in and take it. I keep telling her.'

'What?' Anna said, a scowl of incredulity on her face. 'I don't recall you ever saying anything to me about the keys in the office.'

'Sure I have. You're far too lax.' He reached out and laid a hand on Anna's shoulder. 'You've got to take security more seriously, Anna, you really have.'

She turned and glared at Daniel. 'I'm not the only one with a key.'

'Hey, hang on a minute,' Daniel began.

'There's a difference,' Drew said, taking Anna's arm and turning her towards him. 'The yard is accessed by the public. Your dad's place isn't.'

'Are you suggesting it was one of our customers?'

Drew held up his hand. 'All I'm saying is that anyone could be in the yard, ostensibly there to buy something, but with another motive.'

Anna fished her phone out of her pocket and began tapping the screen. 'Well, we need to report it, whatever.'

'All in good time,' Drew said. 'But not right now, eh?' He took the phone out of Anna's hand. 'Let's go and check on a few things before we do. See if the insurance covers getting someone out here to clean this off.'

'If you claim on the insurance,' Esme said, 'you'll need to call it in to get a crime number.'

Drew glowered at Esme before adopting a more neutral expression. 'I do know that,' he said. 'But Anna's understandably upset.' He put an arm round his wife's shoulders. 'Let's just let the dust settle, shall we?' He steered her towards the door, glancing back over his shoulder. 'Oh, sorry,' he said, looking across to Mike. 'Meeting over. We'll be in touch if we decide to move things on.'

'We *do* want to move things on,' Anna said, pulling out of Drew's hold.

'Sure, whatever you say,' Drew said, taking her by the arm again. 'But not today, eh? You need a break. All this stress isn't good for you.'

Esme watched as Drew led Anna out of the mill and back towards the yard. She could see him with his arm around her, talking as they walked away.

She heard Daniel sigh. 'Well, mate. You heard the man.'

Mike flushed. 'Yes, of course. No probs. I'll get going then.' He gave Esme and Maddy a nod and hurried off to his pick-up.

Esme followed Maddy out of the door, her thoughts chasing around her head. Was this whole thing set up as an excuse to call the conversion off? By Drew? By Daniel? Everyone knew neither of them were supporters of the mill conversion. Would they be so brutal?

She paused and looked over her shoulder at Daniel as he came out of the building. Her suspicion must have shown in her face as he rounded on her.

'You laying this on me, Esme?'

But before she had time to respond, Maddy answered. 'Well it's no secret that you're not keen on the idea, is it?'

Daniel pressed his lips together and flicked his eyes from one to another. 'Only because I'm worried about Anna. The timing's all wrong. You have to admit that. But if you think I'd resort to these sort of shenanigans...' He cocked his head back at the mill behind, '...then forget it. Both of you.'

'So, who do you think is responsible?' Esme asked him.

'It's Halloween next week. Kids can take things a bit far, sometimes.'

'You really think this is kids?' Maddy said.

He shrugged. 'Maybe. Why not? Look, I'd better get on. I've the innards of a Massey Ferguson lying all over my barn. It's not going to rebuild itself.' He marched off back to his Land Rover parked on the lane.

Esme and Maddy stood for a moment and watched him go.

'So, do you seriously think it was Daniel?' Maddy asked. 'Don't forget about the stones being thrown on the roof, as well. And the funny phone calls.'

'Seems unlikely,' Esme said, with a sigh. 'It's rather childish. Doesn't seem to fit Daniel.'

'No, you're right. Drew, on the other hand...'

Esme looked at Maddy and raised an eyebrow. 'Mmm. Possibly. He seemed less shocked than the rest of us. Almost as though he expected it.'

Esme turned round and wandered back inside, scanning her eyes across the vandalised interior. She felt Maddy come up beside her.

'What's the point of it all?' Maddy said.

'That's exactly what Anna said,' Esme reminded her. 'Mike Harrow's comment implied it might be something she has to be prepared for, if people around here don't like her plans. Though she did point out that it was unlikely to impact on anyone, being where it is.'

'Some people make a fuss for the sake of it, though, don't they?' Maddy said, wandering into the middle of the space. She stood in the centre and made a slow 360 degree turn, taking in all the damage. About three quarters of the way round, she stopped, frowning.

'What?' Esme said, trying to identify what she was looking at.

'I'm not sure if it's just my imagination, but are those shapes of some sort?' Maddy pointed to a place on the wall above the door. 'I hadn't noticed them before. Don't think anyone else did, either.'

Esme walked a little closer. 'See what you mean. Less like it was thrown from the tin and more like something's been daubed on there.' She studied it for a moment. 'Can't make it out, though, can you?'

'I dunno. Perhaps it's...' Maddy shook her head. 'No. Ignore me. It's like looking at those ink blots and thinking you can see pictures.'

Esme wrinkled her nose and gave a half laugh. 'Shame. I thought for a minute maybe the perpetrator had signed his name.'

Maddy snorted. 'Well, he's got a way to go before he's any competition to Banksy, that's for sure. Come on, let's get out of here.'

They went outside and as Maddy locked up, Esme looked down at the folder still clutched under her arm. 'It's probably not the right time to show all this to Anna now.'

'No. And you might have to field Drew to get to her, anyway.'

Esme nodded. 'I'll arrange to see her another time.'

As they walked across the yard and out into the lane, Esme noticed a figure in the distance, watching.

'Isn't that Joseph Brannock?'

Maddy sighed. 'Not him again. Gives me the creeps. He's everywhere.'

'That might be to our advantage,' Esme said. She thrust her folder into Maddy's hands. 'Here, hang on to that. I'm going after him. Maybe he saw something.'

# 39

By the time Esme reached the bend at the top of the hill, Joseph Brannock was out of sight. She continued up the lane, expecting at every turn to see the old man ahead. But either he was travelling too quickly to catch, which was doubtful, or he'd taken a short cut she knew nothing about.

She carried on walking until the rear of the Brannocks' old farmhouse came into sight. It was a rambling old building, mostly Victorian, Esme saw as she got closer. A perimeter stone wall separated it from the lane, accessed by a central picket gate.

Someone was moving about on the other side of the wall, but when Esme reached it, she saw it wasn't Joseph, but Ria Brannock. She was raking up leaves on a wide area of grass bordered with apple trees which adjoined the concrete yard at the back of the house. Four rectangular garden beds had been cut out in the grass. One had been weeded recently, the soil moist and freshly turned. Rows of vegetables filled most of the others – kale, chard, cabbage, some scruffy lettuce plants and the feathery fronds of carrot tops – and in one, the dying remnants of a few annual flowers and some perennials, including a small patch of sedum, its florets still a glorious deep red.

'Hello,' Esme called out, leaning on the top of the wall. Ria turned in alarm and stared at Esme as though she was an alien from another planet.

'It's Ria, isn't it?' Esme said, smiling. 'We've not met before, though I saw you over at Temperance Cottage a couple of weeks ago. You were with Alec and Mr Brannock. My name's Esme. I'm a friend of Anna's.'

Ria pushed a limp strand of grey hair off her face and tucked it behind her ear, but said nothing.

'I was looking for Mr Brannock,' Esme went on. She pointed back in the direction from where she'd just walked. 'Some idiot has thrown paint all over the walls inside the mill. I know Mr Brannock often goes walking down there and I thought he might have seen someone hanging around.'

Ria looked anxiously around her and wiped her mouth with the back of her hand. 'He never said anything to me,' she said. Her eyes darted about, as though she expected Joseph to pop out from somewhere. Given Joseph's apparent ability to turn up anywhere at any time, Esme had some sympathy.

'Is he here?' Esme said.

Ria shook her head. 'Gone out.'

'Oh, I see.'

Ria returned to her raking. 'I can't be running after him all the time, can I?' she said, as though Esme had implied some criticism of her not knowing of Joseph's whereabouts.

'No, of course not.' The impression Esme had got that Joseph was kept under close scrutiny was clearly wrong.

'Doesn't listen to anything I say,' Ria continued, the raking becoming more vigorous. 'Only listens to Alec. Might as well talk to the wall.' She stopped to catch her breath, her face flushed.

'I don't suppose *you've* seen anything suspicious, by any chance, have you?' Esme asked.

'No.' Ria walked across the grass and propped the rake up against the wall.

'Well, when you see Mr Brannock, perhaps you'd say I called. I'll drop in another time.'

Ria gave a flick of a nod and walked over to the garden borders. A galvanised flower bucket of mixed blooms and foliage stood in the shade of the wall. Beside it, a wooden trug held a bunch of soil-covered carrots and some beetroots.

'Nice little productive plot you've got there,' Esme said. 'I love sedum, don't you? And bees and butterflies do, too.' She nodded towards the large clump of asters beside them. 'Looks like you have more luck than me with Michaelmas daisies. Mine always disappear. I never know if it's slugs or whether they just don't like my garden.'

A ghost of a smile appeared on Ria's face. 'I do like my flowers.' She nodded towards the farmhouse. 'They don't much care for them. Reckon I'm wasting my time and I'd be better off tilling vegetables.' She bent over and picked up the bucket, hugging it against her with one arm and fingering the feathered petals of the asters. 'But then men don't always appreciate the pretty things like us, do they?'

Esme smiled. 'No, they don't. And with sons and no daughters, you're in the minority.'

A shadow fell over Ria's face. 'No daughters, no. Not now.'

Esme bit her lip, conscious that her comment had exposed Ria's regret at not having had a daughter of her own. She wondered whether having a daughter-in-law went some way to easing that pain, and whether Ria and Anna were closer because of it.

'You must be excited at the idea of having a granddaughter shortly?' she said.

Ria nodded, a smile and a fleeting moment of joy appearing on her face, before being quickly replaced by another emotion which Esme couldn't determine.

Ria shifted the bucket on to her hip and reached down for the handle of the trug.

'Hey, hang on. Let me give you a hand with that.' Esme unlatched the gate in the wall and hurried into the yard.

'I can manage,' Ria said, struggling to keep the bucket upright so that the water didn't slop all over her.

'I'm sure you can,' Esme said, taking the trug from her other hand. 'But I might as well make myself useful as I'm here. Into the kitchen with these?'

Ria nodded. 'Thank you. That's very kind. It's this way.'

Esme followed Ria across the yard to the farmhouse, through a half-glazed door and into a long, narrow utility-cum-boot room. An ancient chest freezer, the enamel on its front flaking to rust, took up most of the space along one wall. Opposite was a row of hooks containing enough coats to clothe half of Bideford, below which lay an untidy heap of green and black wellington boots of all different sizes.

Ria led the way through a solid boarded door, crying out for a fresh coat of green paint, and into the kitchen. The room was spartan. Although clean and tidy, the cupboards were dated, of a style that Esme remembered her parents having when they had a new fitted-kitchen in the 1970s. The worktop was made of Formica, chipped in places on its square edges, and several of the doors drooped.

The door to the hall stood open and Esme noticed a mahogany long-case clock standing against one wall. 'Oh, how lovely,' she said, wandering over to the threshold to take a closer look. She turned to Ria. 'I love clocks, don't you? They're like old friends. I've got one similar and I really miss it at the moment.'

'Miss it?'

Esme nodded. 'It's in storage back in Shropshire with my other furniture. But it shouldn't be long now before it'll be back with me, if I can find myself a house to buy.' She cast her eye around the gloomy hall. The wall against which the clock stood had been decorated in navy-blue flock wallpaper and it had been many a year since the woodwork had seen a decorator's brush. A collection of small dark-framed pictures hung in the corner - a couple of faded watercolours and a quote by John Wesley, written in italic text, "*You have one business on earth – to save souls.*"

The door clattered open behind her and she spun round to see Joseph Brannock standing in the doorway, staring at her.

'Ah, Mr Brannock,' Esme said, walking back into the kitchen. 'I was hoping to see you.'

Joseph turned his glare on Ria. 'What's er doing here?' he barked.

Ria flinched. 'Oh she...' She ran her tongue over her lips. 'She, er...helped me bring some things indoors.' She gripped the handle of the trug and turned to Esme, her eyes anxious. 'There's been some trouble. You wanted to...' Her voice petered out.

Joseph said nothing, leaning on his stick and staring at Esme.

'I was admiring Ria's garden,' Esme said. 'It seems we have the same taste in flowers.' She gave Ria a smile, trying to put her at ease. 'Though, actually, it was you I came to find.'

Joseph jutted out his chin and regarded her darkly. 'And what you'm be wanting with me?'

'Someone broke into the mill and daubed the walls with red paint.'

He raised an eyebrow. 'Did they now? And what makes you'm think that's anything to do with me?'

Esme smiled. 'No, you misunderstand me. I just wondered if you'd noticed anyone hanging around, that's all.'

Joseph cocked his head towards Ria. 'And did her say her'd seen someone?'

'No,' Esme said. 'You hadn't, had you, Ria?'

Ria shook her head. She cleared her throat. 'No. Nobody.' She turned away. 'I need to get changed out of my dirty clothes.' She hurried out into the hall, closing the door behind her.

Esme turned her attention back to Joseph. 'Have you seen anyone hanging around, Mr Brannock? Someone acting suspiciously?'

'No, maid. I bain't seen no one.' He shuffled closer, his eyes still fixed on Esme. 'What's her been saying?' he demanded, poking out his chin again. 'Her talks nonsense sometimes.'

She frowned at him. 'What sort of nonsense? We talked about gardens, flowers in particular. Unless you class that as nonsense. No one else shares her interest in them, I understand.'

'You can't believe what her says, you know.' He tapped his temple with his forefinger. 'Her's not right in the head, see.'

Esme raised her eyebrows. He was a fine one to talk, given what she'd witnessed of his behaviour so far. As for Ria, living with two fractious sons and an overbearing father-in-law would be enough to drive anyone to distraction.

But she kept her thoughts to herself and moved towards the door. 'Well, I'd better leave you to it, then.'

For a moment he remained where he was, in front of the open door, blocking her way, glaring at her, his expression impossible to read.

'Yes, you do that, maid. And leave my family be. You'm hearing me? Us don't need your kind poking your nose in our affairs.'

Only then did he step aside and allow Esme to escape into the yard.

# 40

As Esme made her way back to the reclamation yard, she pondered on the relationship between Joseph and Ria. It was obvious that Ria was wary of him, but that was only to be expected, given his unpredictability. From the way he'd behaved towards Anna, it seemed she also had reason to be guarded. So perhaps it was no surprise that Daniel had reacted the way he had about her discovery of the murder stone, concerned that it would feed Joseph's irrational obsession with the historic feud between the Meddons and Brannock families, which seemed a greater reality for him than the present day truth. Was it what Daniel and Joseph had been arguing about the day she'd seen them together at the market? If it was, it suggested Daniel had known exactly what the faded red cross represented on the plan and had chosen to keep it to himself, hoping she'd not stumble across it.

As she walked past the mill, she noticed Maddy standing at the open door, her camera hanging around her neck, and headed over to speak to her.

'Learn anything?' Maddy asked, as Esme approached.

'Yes and no,' Esme said, and told her what had happened at the Brannocks' farmhouse. 'If he had seen anyone, I doubt he'd have let on.'

Maddy gave a sad shake of the head. 'Poor Ria, having to field that sort of behaviour all the time. No wonder she's a nervous wreck.'

'Yes, I had the same thought. Can't be much of a life, having Joseph Brannock for a father-in-law. What happened to his wife? Do you know?'

'Died when Scott was a kid, I think.'

'Who's Scott?'

'Alec and Drew's dad.'

'Oh, yes. I remember now. Drank himself to death, you said, when the boys were quite young.' Something else to add to Ria's fragile state of mind.

Esme nodded at Maddy's camera. 'Has Anna asked you to take photos for insurance purposes?

Maddy pursed her lips. 'They *are* for insurance purposes, but not the way you mean. Been thinking, I wouldn't put it past Drew to get it all cleaned off so Anna's got nothing to report.'

'You're pretty convinced he's behind it, aren't you?'

Maddy shrugged. 'Even if I'm wrong, there's no harm in being prepared, is there?'

'Guess not.'

'Anyway,' Maddy looked down at the screen on her camera, 'I've taken some shots of the damage, so if he ever did try and wriggle out of it, we have the evidence still intact.'

'Where's Anna now? Is she all right?'

Maddy shook her head. 'Don't know. Haven't seen her since Drew took her away.'

'Yes, he seemed extremely concerned about her.' Esme looked at Maddy. 'A bit OTT, didn't you think?'

'If I'm not very much mistaken, Mrs Quentin,' Maddy said, eyebrows raised, 'I detect some scepticism in your manner.'

Esme returned Maddy's look. 'Let's just say, I've never noticed Drew quite so attentive.'

Maddy shook her head. 'Me neither. Worrying, isn't it? And for all the wrong reasons.' She looked at her watch. 'Well, I'd better get a wiggle on. I still haven't polished up those bits and pieces I said I was going to for tomorrow's market.'

*

Maddy was in some kind of tunnel. In the distance, she could hear the sea and feared it would surge along the tunnel at any moment and engulf her. With leaden steps, as is so common in dreams, she forced her way along the tunnel, away from the threatening waters.

Then the tunnel mutated and became a room with a low ceiling. She could hear a dull, rhythmic thudding sound, but as she moved towards it, the ceiling of the room began descending, gradually, threatening to crush her against the earth floor. She staggered along the wall towards the sound, feeling the way with her hands, stooping lower and lower as the space between floor and ceiling steadily diminished. Long tendrils of cobwebs from above caught her hair and brushed against her face. She wiped them away but they stuck to her fingers. Soon there was a blanket of them covering her face. She cried out and thrust out her hands.

She woke up suddenly, breathing deeply and blinking into the darkness, adjusting to the unfamiliar surroundings of the workshop. The wood-burning stove was making tell-tale clicking noises that it was cooling down and she shivered. She must have fallen asleep in the chair. The last thing she remembered was congratulating herself for finishing polishing the boxes for tomorrow.

She stood up and stumbled over to the workbench, switching on the work-lamp and grabbing her phone to see the time, relieved that it wasn't as late as she feared. Even so, time she went home. As she picked her coat off the hook on the back of the door, she heard a scream from outside.

She rushed over to the door, yanked it open and ran outside.

For a moment, she thought the courtyard was empty. Then, on the edge of the beam of the yard's security light, the shadow of a figure sprinted away and melted into the dark.

Maddy stood for a moment, her heart pounding, trying to work out what was going on. The sound of muffled sobbing came from the direction of Anna's office. She ran across the yard, flicking the beam ahead of her

'Anna? Is that you? What's going on?'

Anna was standing outside her office, staring at something, her hand pressed over her mouth.

Maddy hurried towards her. 'What is it?' she said, putting an arm around Anna's shoulders. 'What's happened?'

Anna whimpered something and pointed to the office door, before jerking away and vomiting on the ground.

Maddy turned and looked to where Anna had pointed. Nailed to the door was the blood-covered body of a crow.

# 41

'I've got rid of it,' Maddy said, coming inside the office. Anna sat wide-eyed on a chair beside the computer, staring into the middle distance.

Maddy went over to the sink in the corner and vigorously washed her hands under the tap. She snatched a couple of paper towels from the dispenser to dry her hands, before going over to Anna.

'Are you OK?' she asked, crouching down in front of her.

'Who'd do such a revolting thing?' Anna said, her face grimacing with distaste. 'It's disgusting. I was on my way to go and feed Gypsy. I only came back because I heard the banging. Wish I'd ignored it now.'

'It's made a right mess of the door,' Maddy said, straightening up. 'I'll go and get a bucket of water and clean it up.'

Anna got up off the chair and grabbed Maddy's arm. 'No, I'll do that, Maddy. You've done enough disposing of the bloody thing.' She shivered and wrapped her arms around herself.

'No, it's fine. You stay just where you are.'

Anna sat back down. 'This is just kids, right?' she said, sliding her hands down between her knees. 'Same as the stones on the roof and the phone calls.'

The office door burst open and Drew appeared. 'What's going on? Granddad said you were screaming.'

'Trust him to be lurking around,' Maddy said, snorting.

Drew ignored Maddy and walked over to Anna. 'What now?' he demanded.

'Oh, for goodness' sake, Drew,' Maddy said. 'Show some sympathy. It was horrible.'

Anna jabbed a finger towards the door. 'Some maniac nailed a dead crow to my office door, that's what. Not a great way to end a day.'

'It's just someone's idea of a sick joke,' he said, dismissively. 'You're overreacting.'

'Overreacting?' Maddy said, taking a step towards him. 'She was terrified. We both were.' She narrowed her eyes. 'It wasn't you, was it? I saw someone leg it across the yard as I came out of the workshop.'

'Don't be stupid,' Drew said, throwing Maddy a contemptuous look. 'Do I look like I've just run a 100 metre sprint?'

Maddy scowled, but said nothing.

'In case it's escaped your notice,' Drew continued, 'it's Halloween in less than a week. Someone's just winding Anna up.' He reached out and took Anna's hand. 'Stop taking it so seriously. You're getting stressed again. Too much on your plate. I keep telling you. Ease off, why don't you?'

'She wouldn't have so much on her plate if you did more of your fair share,' Maddy said, unable to contain herself. 'You're supposed to be part of this business and you hardly lift a finger. What's going to happen when the baby comes?'

'Cut it out, the pair of you,' Anna said, standing up. 'This isn't helping.'

Maddy sighed and held up a hand. 'Sorry, Anna. Guess I'm a bit jumpy. I'd better go and lock up the workshop. I'll leave you to it.' She walked over to the door, pausing at the threshold as she saw the bloodied mess daubed all over it, and turned back. 'Are you sure you don't want me to clean this up before I go? I can easily get a bucket of hot water from the workshop.'

Drew strode towards her. 'I'll take it from here. You get off home. Thanks for your help.'

Maddy narrowed her eyes. If it was anyone other than Drew Brannock saying that, it would come across as sympathetic. As it was...

She shook her head and sighed. Perhaps she should cut him some slack.

'OK. If you're sure.' She glanced back at Anna. 'See you, then, Anna. I know it's gonna be hard, but try not to let it get to you, yeah?'

As she walked away, Maddy could hear the whining tone of Drew's voice and what sounded like Anna defending herself over something. Maddy shook her head again and headed over to her workshop.

She slipped on her coat and snatched up her keys. With one last scan around, she switched off the lights and went out into the yard. As she padlocked the workshop door, she sensed someone watching her. She dug into her coat pocket for her phone and flicked it on to flashlight mode.

'Who's that?' she yelled, pointing the light towards the path to the mill. A figure moved out of the shadows and began shuffling into the dark away from her, his stick tapping on the concrete.

Maddy closed her eyes and let out a shuddering sigh. Joseph Bloody Brannock. He was beginning to get on her nerves.

# 42

Saturday's market was bustling. The increase in footfall was likely due to the Halloween Painting Competition entries being on full display on one wall of the market hall. The winners were to be announced at noon.

Esme propped herself against the edge of their market stall and listened in horror to Maddy's report of Anna's unwelcome visitor.

'Oh, the poor girl,' Esme said, disturbing thoughts racing around her brain. 'Is she all right?'

'I think so. Bit of a shock - well, it was to me, too. But she'll be fine. She's tough, is Anna. Despite what Drew says.'

Esme frowned. 'Why? What's Drew saying?'

Maddy dismissed the comment with a shake of her head. 'Ah, I dunno. It's like he's feeding the fear. I was ready to clock him last night, I can tell you.'

'Perhaps with the baby coming, she's leaning on him a bit more than usual,' Esme said. 'And he's liking that.'

Maddy scowled. 'Mmm. That's a very charitable way of looking at it.'

Esme raised her eyebrows and gave Maddy a wry smile. 'So what's your take on it, then, Professor Henderson?'

'It feels more like controlling behaviour to me.'

An image of Ria flinching as Joseph arrived in the kitchen the day before flitted into Esme's head and she sighed. 'Well, if you're serious, it's worth us keeping an eye on her.' She looked round at Maddy. 'I trust she's going to report this, too? With the mill being vandalised, that's two incidents within a few hours of one another. The police have to take it seriously, surely?'

'I agree. But Drew's downplaying it.' Maddy folded her arms and propped herself next to Esme. 'Which he would, if he's behind it, of course.'

Esme gave Maddy a sceptical look. 'You don't really think he'd nail a dead crow to his wife's office door, do you? Surely even he isn't that callous?'

Maddy thought for a moment and sighed. 'Maybe not. I did accuse him, but he denied it.'

'So if it's not him, who?' Esme tapped her chin with her knuckles. 'And is there a particular reason why Anna's being targeted?'

'You think it's aimed at Anna personally?'

Esme sighed. 'It must have occurred to you that there are similarities between what's happening to Anna and what's happened in the past.'

'Ellen Tucker, you mean?' Maddy said, turning to Esme, her eyes wide. 'No, I can't believe that.' She bit her lower lip. 'Though you might be partly right. Someone could have got wind of the story.'

'Copycat, you mean? In which case, maybe Drew's right about it being kids.'

'About what being kids?' Cerys said, wandering over to join them.

'Crows and witches,' Maddy said.

'Ah, been looking at the Halloween painting competition entries, have you?' Cerys said.

Esme shook her head. 'Something rather more disturbing, unfortunately.'

'Oh?' Cerys glanced between them.

Maddy let out a long breath. 'A dead crow was nailed to the door of Anna Brannock's office last night.'

'Oh my. There's nasty,' Cerys said, her face sombre. 'And you think it's kids?'

'Drew does,' Maddy said, glancing at Esme. 'We're not so sure. It's not the only thing that's happened, either. Heavy breathing phone calls, stones thrown on the roof, and yesterday one of her outbuildings had been daubed with red paint.' Again she flicked an anxious look at Esme. 'We're trying to decide if it's a copycat of what happened to Ellen Tucker.'

Cerys looked at them both with troubled eyes. 'You're worried the history of twenty-odd years ago is repeating itself?'

'Except we don't know what did happen to Ellen Tucker,' Esme said. 'Not exactly, anyway. The newspaper report didn't go into any detail, so we don't know if Ellen's experience was the same as Anna's. All we know for certain is that Ellen was called a witch.'

'Then, there's your connection,' Maddy said, bobbing up and down. 'The message is symbolic. After all, crows are associated with witches, aren't they? Cerys, you know about these things.'

Cerys sighed. 'Well, you're right there. According to Scottish folklore, witches are said to be able to change into crows.'

'There you are, then,' Maddy said. 'I rest my case.'

'Crows are like ravens,' Cerys continued, clasping the talisman pendant she always wore around her neck. 'Both birds of prophecy and omen, their cawing call often interpreted as a warning. There's the association with death, of course, but then that's as much to do with the fact that they're carrion feeders as anything else.'

'Death?' Maddy said, turning to Esme. 'You don't think the message could be a death threat?'

'Hang on, Maddy,' Esme said, frowning. 'Careful you're not letting this get out of hand. There's a difference between wanting to scare someone, in some misguided sense of fun, and wanting to harm them.'

'Something you said earlier,' Maddy said, her expression solemn. '*We don't know what happened to Ellen Tucker.*'

'Which we don't.'

Maddy gave her head a shake of frustration. 'I'm not talking about whether she had phone calls, red walls and dead crows,' she said. 'I'm asking did something *happen* to Ellen Tucker? Maybe she never left Bideford after all. Maybe that's what Dad realised, and he was trying to find out the truth.'

# 43

Cerys was ecstatic. Her granddaughter's painting won first prize in her category.

'I told you, didn't I?' Cerys beamed. 'I knew if she entered, she'd win. She's so chuffed. You can see the confidence just oozing out of her. Perhaps now she'll believe me when I tell her she's got talent.'

Esme minded Cerys's stall while she went to watch her granddaughter's presentation at the far end of the hall. Later, as the crowd of customers began to thin ahead of the market closing, Esme and Maddy went across to view the winning artwork.

The categories were many, from the intriguing splodges by the under-fives to the careful detail of the older children's work. Various media were represented: water-colour and poster paint, chalk and pastel, collage and simple pencil crayon drawings.

The picture awarded third prize in the 5-7-year-old group caught Esme's attention. The subject was similar to many on display – a witch flying through the air on a broomstick. But it was the way the artist had depicted the witch's face, with an open mouth as though screaming, which she found herself drawn to. It reminded her of Edvard Munch's masterpiece, *The Scream*. Esme found herself troubled by the sight of it, though she couldn't put her finger on why. But then, Munch's painting was haunting and disturbing in itself. Perhaps it was just that.

She felt Maddy come up behind her. 'Why does that one look familiar?' she asked Maddy. 'It's giving me the heebie-jeebies.'

'Because it's the archetypal depiction of a witch?' Maddy suggested. 'And with all this talk of dead crows and what happened to poor Anna, it's probably playing on your mind.'

'Not to mention your grim speculation about Ellen Tucker,' Esme said, with a shudder.

'Sorry,' Maddy said. 'But we don't know, do we?'

Esme checked her watch. 'Come on. Time we got the stall packed up.'

\*

Esme glanced across the yard as they ferried the stock from the van to the workshop. Anna's office door was closed and there were no lights on.

'Looks like Anna's out,' she said. 'Not surprising after yesterday's fiasco, she probably decided to take the day off. I hope she's OK.'

'No, it's not that,' Maddy said, glancing back over her shoulder. 'Today's her birthday. She wasn't planning to come in anyway.'

Esme winced. 'Ouch. Last night was bad timing, then. Not much of a birthday present to find on your door, is it?'

Maddy plonked down the container she was carrying on the workbench and rested on it. 'I hope she liked her writing box,' she said, chewing her lip.

'Oh, of course. The renovation was a surprise present, wasn't it? Oh, I'm sure she did, Maddy. You made a fantastic job of it.'

They cleared the van and made some decisions on the stock for Tuesday's market.

'Well, I'll love you and leave you, then,' Esme said, slinging her bag over her shoulder. 'I'm seeing Iris Webb tomorrow morning to give her that World War One photograph. Shall I meet you at your dad's after? Say back end of the morning? Then we can load up what you want to bring back here.'

Maddy tugged her ponytail. 'You don't need to if you're busy, Esme,' she said. 'I'm sure I'll be fine.'

'I thought it was all the extra stuff you'd found in the loft you wanted to bring over?'

'It is.'

'Well, an extra pair of hands is on offer. I'm in Bideford anyway, so it's not a problem.'

Maddy smiled. 'Well, if you put it like that, then OK. Thanks. It'll make the job quicker, there's no doubt.'

'What sort of stuff is it?'

'Bit of a motley collection, if I'm honest. Might end up giving it all to a charity shop. There are a few nice picture frames worth cleaning up, though.'

Something stirred in Esme's head. 'Hey, talking of picture frames, I've just realised why that Halloween painting was familiar. It reminded me of the one you found inside the little secret drawer. Have you passed it on to Daniel, yet?'

'No, I've still got it. Hang on.' Maddy walked over to the desk and rummaged around in a drawer. 'Here it is,' she said, taking out a sheet of paper and studying it. 'I see what you mean about it being like the one in the market.' She held it out.

Esme crossed the room and took the drawing. The similarities were striking. A face, opened mouthed, long charcoal-black hair, though here the subject looked out from a window, not a broomstick. And a clue, perhaps, to the location. She turned the picture round and held it up for Maddy to see, pointing to the other building in it.

'Look. I thought it was a bush when I first saw it, as it's a bit difficult to tell through the scribble, but I reckon that's a mill wheel. I think this is supposed to be Temperance Mill.'

'Oh yes, so it is,' Maddy said, taking back the picture. 'I hadn't noticed that before.'

'So the cottage with the face at the window,' Esme continued, 'could that be Temperance Cottage, d'you think?'

Before Maddy could answer, the door of the workshop opened and Anna's face appeared.

'Not disturbing you, am I, Maddy? Oh, hi, Esme.'

'Happy birthday,' Esme said. 'Are you having a good day?'

Anna slipped inside, letting the workshop door close behind her. 'Yes, thank you,' she said, smiling. 'A very good day, so far.' Although her hair was in its usual plait, she was dressed in a pretty print tunic instead of her working clothes, and rather than brick dust on her face, she'd applied a touch of make-up, highlighting her delicate features.

'Sorry to hear about last night,' Esme said. 'Someone's got a very sick sense of humour.'

Anna rolled her eyes. 'Yeah, haven't they just. Be glad when Halloween's over and done with.' She turned to address Maddy, her face radiant. 'Actually, I only popped in to say thank you so, so much, Maddy, for renovating the box. It's absolutely beautiful.'

Maddy flushed. 'You're very welcome,' she said, with a shy smile. 'A special one for me, too. My first proper customer. I'm so pleased you like it.'

'It's amazing. Dad probably told you, it was my Granny Alice's. I hadn't seen it for years. Been packed away with all her stuff. I'm so glad Mum and Dad thought to dig it out.'

Maddy nodded. 'Perfect timing for me. It's been a pleasure to do.' She glanced at Esme. 'Actually, talking of timing, we were just looking at this.'

'What is it?' Anna said, coming over.

'I couldn't show you before or it would have given the game away.' Maddy handed the drawing to Anna. 'I found it in the little secret drawer. We assume it's yours. Your dad said you used to use your granny's slope occasionally.'

'Are we right in thinking it's Temperance Cottage?' Esme asked.

Anna peered down at the picture, frowning, before dropping it on the bench. 'Well, I didn't draw it,' she said, red blotches forming on her cheeks, her buoyant mood of earlier gone.

'Can you think of anyone else who might have?' Esme said.

Anna shook her head and looked away, avoiding Esme's gaze. 'I'd bin it, if I were you. It's not important.' She turned towards the door. 'Well, I'd better go. Drew will wonder where I've got to. See you later.'

She hurried out of the door, letting it slam behind her.

# 44

Iris Webb's house was part of a garden terrace, at the end of a side street in the older part of Bideford. There was no public vehicular access, so Esme parked in the street leading to the terrace and continued on foot.

She'd spent much of the previous evening reflecting on Anna's reaction to the drawing Maddy had found in the secret drawer. Clearly the sight of it had stirred something in Anna's head, something she'd not wanted to share. Or perhaps couldn't share because she couldn't remember. It was both baffling and concerning, given the distressed expression on Anna's face.

Esme walked along in front of the row of slim terraced houses until she found the number she'd been given and took the garden path up to the front door, where her knock was answered swiftly. She was greeted by a woman in pink-rimmed glasses, her short crimped hair held off her face by a flowery Alice band.

'Esme, I assume?' she said, with a broad smile. 'Spot on time. I'm Iris. Do come in.'

Esme stepped into a narrow entrance hall smelling of beeswax and fresh paint. It was carpeted in plain green, the staircase climbing away on the left, its banister rails painted to match the neutral off-white of the walls. The highly polished handrail ended in a decorative swirl at the bottom.

'I can't tell you how pleased I am that you got in touch,' Iris said, offering to take Esme's coat, which she hung on a set of iron hooks beside the front door. She chuckled. 'My husband will tell you that I've got more than enough photographs already, but as any family historian will tell him, there's no such thing as too many, is there?'

Esme smiled. 'And even better when you know who they are.'

'Amen to that.' Iris gestured towards the stairs. 'My family history den is upstairs. Shall I lead the way?'

Esme followed Iris up the stairs, turning right at the top, along the landing and into the bedroom which looked out to the front of the property. As she stepped into the room, she stopped, surprised. The decor was completely different in style to the simplicity of the hallway. Below a dark green painted picture rail, heavily patterned wallpaper adorned the walls, which were covered in old framed photographs. Several mahogany chests of drawers stood against the walls, more framed photographs arranged on top of each of them, with two tall filing cabinets in one corner. A large leather-bound desk sat in the centre of the room, on which stood a brass lamp along with a computer monitor and keyboard.

'Wow,' Esme said, looking around. 'This is amazing.'

'It's my time capsule,' Iris said, clasping her hands together against her chest. 'It was the desk that gave me the idea. It set the theme for the whole room. I couldn't live with the whole house as Victorian. Far too fussy. But here, it seems to work.'

Esme reached into her bag and pulled out the photograph that Morris had identified as Seth Brannock.

'Another one for your collection,' she said, handing it to Iris.

'Lovely, thank you so much.' Iris took it and walked over to the end wall, where Esme could see there were a number of photographs of World War One soldiers on display. 'I have one of him seated, you see. So to have this to add to it is marvellous.'

'Is Seth Brannock one of your ancestors?' Esme asked, looking around to take in the many faces which filled the walls. It was lucky that the house had high ceilings, allowing more pictures to be accommodated.

Iris shook her head. 'No, my husband's. Seth's wife was the sister of my husband's great-grandfather.'

'The family have a sad history, I understand,' Esme said.

'Indeed they do.' Iris went over to one of the mahogany chests and pulled open the top drawer. She took out a roll of paper and carried it over to the desk. 'I suppose it started with Seth's grandfather, Gideon, and Fanny, his wife, dying from scarlet fever, along with their children.' She pushed the keyboard out of the way and opened up the roll, holding the ends down with paperweights. 'And poor old Luke being the only survivor.'

Esme looked down at the printout of the family tree, homing in on the names of Luke's siblings, Harriet, Arthur, Jack and Kitty, their year of death, 1871, noted underneath each of their names.

'Being the only one left must have been so hard for Luke,' she said.

'Oh, yes, it must have been,' Iris agreed. 'Some might say he was the lucky one to have survived but the death of his family had its own impact and he lost his mind in the end, as Morris probably told you.'

'He said Luke was convinced his family was cursed.'

Iris slid her finger across the tree. 'You can probably lay the blame for that on this lot,' she said, tapping the table.

Esme peered at where Iris was pointing. 'Ah,' she said, spotting a name she recognised. 'Silas Brannock. Luke's great uncle. I've been researching Temperance Mill and came across Silas's murder by his daughter Sarah.'

'Yes, that's right. It was Sarah, apparently, who cursed the Brannock family.'

'Sarah?'

'Yes. From the dock when she was found guilty.'

Esme recalled Morris's comment when she'd suggested Sarah probably believed everyone conspired against her.

'*And in particular, the Brannock family*', Morris had said. He must have known about the curse.

'Would Luke have been aware of the curse?' Esme said. 'He'd have been only a baby when Sarah was convicted.'

Iris raised her eyebrows. 'And you don't think someone wasn't going to remember her words and remind everyone after every tragedy? I'm sure Luke would have grown up with it. And it would have gnawed away at him. Hardly surprising that it affected his mind the way it did.'

Esme nodded. 'He ended his days in an asylum, I understand?'

'Yes, for the criminally insane,' she said.

'Oh,' Esme said. 'I hadn't realised. What happened?'

Iris straightened up. 'He killed an old lady with a pitchfork.'

'Oh no, how terrible,' Esme said, wincing at the image that flashed in her mind.

'He was very disturbed,' Iris said, 'and under the impression he was doing the world a favour.' She slid the paperweights off the edges of the family tree and rolled it back up. 'He was adamant the poor woman was a witch.'

# 45

At Ted's house, Esme sat on a packing box and relayed Iris's story to Maddy, who was sitting on the floor.

'But why would Luke think she was a witch?' Maddy asked, her face puckered.

'Iris didn't know, specifically. But historically, anything bad that happened tended to get blamed on witches. Illness, poor harvest, a child having a fit. Which is why, if someone believed a neighbour had caused it and accused them of witchcraft, their chances of acquittal were pretty slim if others were willing to point the finger at them. That's all it took, usually.'

'But this happened in relatively modern times, I thought.'

'Yes, 1905. But the thing is, whatever his reasoning, Luke Brannock truly believed it. More to the point, he believed it was his duty to rid the world of witches and took it upon himself to do so. Iris blames the influence of Sarah Brannock's curse. He probably saw witches everywhere.'

Maddy hugged her knees. 'Ironic, isn't it, that if he'd lived a few hundred years before, he would have been the hero, rooting out witches for the benefit of the community. Devon's version of Matthew Hopkins, the Witchfinder General.'

Esme nodded. 'An interesting comparison. From everything I've read about Matthew Hopkins, he didn't come across as quite sane, either.'

They spent the next hour or so packing up boxes and ferrying them down from the attic room. From there, they carried them out to Maddy's van.

Esme loaded up the last few boxes while Maddy fetched her camera from the van to take photographs of the house for a potential buyer. Old friends of Harry's parents, currently living in Warwickshire, were looking to buy in the area. Maddy had promised to send a few interior shots, hoping that if they liked what they saw, they may arrange a viewing.

Having taken the last box, Esme returned to the house as Maddy emerged from the stairs, peering at the screen on her camera.

'What d'you think?' Maddy said, handing Esme the camera. 'Does it get enough across?'

Esme flicked through the images and nodded her approval. 'Yep. Looks good to me.' At the end of the house pictures, the photographs Maddy had taken of the daubed paint in the mill followed. Esme skimmed through these too, idly wondering if Anna had managed to report the incident or whether she'd been persuaded otherwise by Drew. As the pictures slid past, she slowed, stopping on one and zooming in on a particular smear of paint. She frowned.

'Interesting,' she said, as much to herself as to Maddy.

'What is?' Maddy asked.

'I was thinking about what you said the other day, about ink blots.' Esme turned the camera round so Maddy could see. 'Does that look like a letter to you?'

Maddy took the camera and peered at the small display. She stood up. 'We could do with seeing it on a bigger screen. Hang fire, I'll get my laptop from the van.'

Within moments, Maddy burst back into the house and sat down, setting up her laptop on the dining table. Esme stood beside her while Maddy uploaded the images and they both peered at the screen as the pictures slowly appeared to view.

'That the one you were looking at?' Maddy asked.

'Yes, that's it.' Esme pointed to a brush stroke. 'Ignore the drips for a minute and you can see what I mean. Could that be an X?'

'Yeah, you're right.'

'And that one before it,' Esme said, indicating, 'could be an E. So, EX something. To stand for what? Exeter?' She peered closer. 'What's after that?'

'It's numbers,' Maddy said, excitement in her voice. 'There, look, 2. And another 2.'

'EX22. A postcode? Is it a reference to a place? Where's EX22?'

'Holsworthy, isn't it? What's significant about Holsworthy?'

Esme shook her head. 'No idea.' Her mind went back to a comment Mike Harrow had made when they'd discovered the paint. 'Maybe it's another location where someone was trying to get planning permission to do something similar to Anna. Mike Harrow said he'd come across situations before with people causing problems.'

'Or is it Brannock related?'

'How do you mean?'

'Well,' Maddy said, perching on the edge of her chair, 'we both know what Joseph Brannock's like about land ownership. Maybe it's some sort of statement about land-grabbing. Historically, I mean. Perhaps some Holsworthy based Brannocks think they've a claim on Anna's mill. Have you come across any Brannocks with a Holsworthy connection?'

Esme shook her head. 'No, but that doesn't mean there aren't any. I've only concentrated on the one location, based on Anna's brief, so there could be...' She stopped, suddenly recalling Cerys's words. *Far-fetched, isn't it? Until you realise...*'

'Oh!' She put her hand across her mouth.

'What?' Maddy said, flicking her gaze between the screen and Esme. 'Have you worked it out? What does it say.'

Esme tapped the screen. 'There, look. That's 18 after it.'

'And?' Maddy said, impatiently. 'What's so significant about that?'

Esme swallowed. 'I think it means EX 22 18. As in Exodus, chapter 22, verse 18.'

Maddy's mouth dropped open. 'A bible quote?'

Esme nodded. She already had a pretty good idea what this was all about. She scanned around the room.

'Your dad had a bible lying around the other day,' she said. 'The one with the bookmark in you'd once bought him for his birthday. Where is it?'

Maddy darted across the room and knelt down by a box in the corner. She tore open the lid and rummaged around inside.

'Here,' she said, sitting back on her heels. She opened the bible, turning to look up at Esme, her eyes anxious. 'It's exactly where the bookmark was. Why would Dad have marked that page?'

'What does it say?' Esme said, her voice barely a whisper.

Maddy turned back to the bible and ran her finger down the page. She took a deep breath and read it out loud.

'"*Thou shalt not suffer a witch to live.*"'

# 46

Esme followed Maddy's van as they drove to the workshop, her head churning with unanswered questions, trying to put what they'd discovered into some sort of perspective. Surely this message was too sophisticated to be kids with a Halloween inspired agenda? Maddy still clung to her theory that Drew was behind it all, in an attempt to deter Anna from embarking on the mill project. But Esme wasn't convinced. Would he really be that smart? For Drew, the paint would have served on its own, wouldn't it? In fact it had, in a way. Everyone had seen it and assumed its message. So what was the point of the wording, which only she and Maddy had seen?

As they reached the outskirts of Bideford, two things occurred to Esme. The first was that the daubed message tied in even more closely with the dead crow and its witch association. The second strengthened her suspicion that what had been happening to Anna could also have been what Ellen Tucker had suffered. Were these the kind of things Ellen had meant when she'd complained of being labelled a witch?

But even if everything Ellen had suffered was what Anna was suffering too, it didn't explain *why* Anna was being targeted, as they'd discussed before. Could there be something that linked the two women? And if so, what could that link possibly be?

As Esme turned her car into the reclamation yard car park, another question slipped into her head. Should they tell Anna what they'd discovered? Surely forearmed was forewarned? Esme supposed it would be useful to add to what Anna planned to tell the police when she reported the incidents. That's if Drew didn't stop her.

Her mind was still sifting through everything as she got out of the car, thankful that it was Sunday and Anna wouldn't be at work. They needed to decide how much to tell her, without making it out to be more than it was. Anna was clearly already feeling vulnerable after everything else that had happened. Her reaction to the drawing was testimony to that.

Something fizzed in Esme's brain and she stood fixed to the spot, trying to pinpoint what it was.

'You OK?' Maddy said, sliding open the campervan door parked alongside.

Esme blinked. 'The drawing,' she said, stumbling over her words. 'Anna's drawing.'

Maddy frowned. 'What about it?'

'I need to see it.'

Maddy hesitated only briefly before hurrying across the yard to the workshop, Esme following behind. Neither spoke. Maddy unlocked the door and they went inside, Esme closing the door behind them while Maddy jogged across to find the drawing. She retrieved it from the desk drawer where she'd put it away after Anna had tossed it aside.

'So what are you thinking?' she said, thrusting it towards Esme.

'I was deliberating how much to say to Anna,' Esme said, taking the paper, 'in light of how she reacted to seeing this. It wasn't the response you'd expect from someone who claimed not to recognise it.'

'No,' Maddy agreed. 'You'd be intrigued, wouldn't you? Like we are. But something obviously touched a nerve.'

Esme gazed down at the picture, drawn to the image of the woman's face.

'So, what's your theory?' Maddy prompted.

'Just before Anna came in, we'd wondered whether this was Temperance Cottage.' She looked up at Maddy. 'Where Ellen Tucker lived.'

'And?'

'While I was driving over here, I kept thinking, what links Anna and Ellen Tucker? And when we arrived, I realised. This does.'

Maddy folded her arms and leaned against the workbench. 'Go on.'

Esme put her finger on the cottage in the picture. 'Look at the face at the window. Think how Cerys described Ellen. Long, dark, hair. This could be her.'

'Yeah, I can see that. Anna drew a picture of Ellen Tucker when she lived at the cottage. So what, though?'

'I keep coming back to what you said yesterday. And then I look at this.'

Maddy scratched her head and regarded Esme with bemusement. 'Remind me. What did I say yesterday?'

'You raised the question of what happened to Ellen Tucker. "*Maybe she never left*", you said.' Esme tapped on the drawing. 'What's this,' she said, taking a deep breath, 'if it's not a woman screaming?'

Maddy's bemused expression changed to alarm. 'You're suggesting that Anna saw Ellen Tucker screaming?'

'Yes, that's exactly what I'm suggesting. And maybe,' Esme took a moment to gather her thoughts, 'she saw more than that. Something no child should see.'

Maddy blinked. 'Oh my God.' She dropped down on to the stool beside the workbench. 'And she drew that picture, like some sort of child's witness statement.'

Esme returned her gaze to the picture. 'Perhaps that's why she scribbled all over it. As though she was trying to wipe the horror of it from her memory, to protect herself.'

Maddy let out a long sigh. 'So, did she manage it?' she said. 'Was she able to bury it, and forget about it for all these years?'

'If she was,' Esme said, closing her eyes as she recalled Anna's terrified expression, 'then we've just gone and forced her to remember.'

# 47

It was late by the time Esme got home. As she fell into bed, she wondered whether her active brain might prevent her sleeping, but the next thing she knew, it was morning. She woke suddenly, feeling she'd overslept, and was relieved to glance at the clock and find it was still only six-thirty. Not that it mattered too much, she reminded herself. No market today. She'd have plenty of time to reflect on her and Maddy's theories of yesterday. She only hoped it wouldn't prevent her brain from concentrating on her work.

After breakfast, she took her coffee into the sitting room and laid it on the coffee table, while she raked out the wood-burner and relaid it for later. She was tempted to light it straight away for the comfort of seeing the flames, but her musings were interrupted by the telephone ringing. She didn't recognise the number, but when she answered the call, the voice was familiar.

'Morning, Esme. James Willoughby, St Mary's, Bremleycott.'

'Morning, James. How are you?' Esme said, charged with surge of optimism. If he was phoning, surely he must have some new information. Perhaps he knew where Ellen had gone and they could dispel their disturbing hypothesis that she'd never left Bideford.

After they exchanged pleasantries, the vicar explained the reason for his call. 'You asked me whether we'd had a visit from a private detective,' he said.

'I did, yes. Sean Carlton. You didn't think so.'

'That's right. Apparently he did come to the village, but I was away at the time. He spoke to Mrs Stone at the shop.'

'And was Mrs Stone able to tell him anything?'

'Oh yes. Born and bred, she is. She knew both Ellen and Arabella. Though I doubt she and Arabella would have met at the local Women's Institute, if you know what I mean.'

Esme laughed. 'No, I imagine not, given what you told me about her. So did Mrs Stone have any idea where Ellen had gone? Perhaps she's the one who pointed Carlton in the direction of Bideford.'

'Well, if she did, she didn't say so specifically,' Willoughby said. 'But what she *did* tell him was she thought Ellen had left to get married.'

Esme's grip tightened around the phone. 'Married? Who to, did she know?'

'No, I'm afraid not. But I thought it might be useful to know to add to your family tree.'

'Yes, very useful. Thank you.'

After cutting the call, she reflected on Willoughby's information, curious that Carlton had made no mention of Ellen being married during his enquiries. *Miss* Ellen Tucker was how he'd referred to her the day he'd visited the yard. Was that because Mrs Stone hadn't told him of her theory, or had Carlton not followed it up? Maybe she should take a quick look.

Esme went over to her desk and booted her laptop. Given the number of Ellen Tuckers she'd encountered when she'd first searched for Ellen's birth record, she didn't hold out much hope of easily identifying a marriage. And that's assuming Mrs Stone was correct in her theory. There may be no marriage to find. Perhaps that was what Carlton had established. But it might be worth checking to make sure. And she'd found out a little more about Ellen since the last time she'd trawled the indexes.

She opened up her *Ancestry* account and filled in the information she knew for sure, not forgetting the crucial H for Hope as Ellen's middle initial. She was pleasantly surprised to find that the possibles weren't as many as she'd feared. Though even having several was a challenge. Any of them could be correct and she'd only be able to discern the finer details by getting copies of the marriage certificates. And then she might find that none of them were the correct Ellen Tucker. If Ellen *had* left to get married, she could have gone anywhere. Abroad even.

Esme clicked on the left-hand options and brought up the names under the category of England & Wales, Civil Registration Marriage Index, 1916-2005. The results now listed the spouses' names on the right-hand side, so easier to see.

Esme put her elbows on the desk either side of the keyboard and rested her chin in her hands as she scanned down the list. She sighed. Surely she was wasting her time, here.

Just as she'd reminded herself she'd other work she really ought to be doing instead of chasing her tail, a name leapt off the screen at her. She almost knocked the mouse off the desk as she grabbed it to bring up the details.

The record opened up in front of her and she stared at it, the implications swirling around in her head. In the March quarter of 1986, in Taunton, Somerset a marriage had been registered between Ellen H Tucker and Daniel Meddon.

# 48

There was a spit of rain in the wind, but not enough to deter Esme from slipping on her coat and wellies and going out for a walk. She pulled the hood up over her head and made her way across the gravel to the grassy area overlooking the beach, pausing to look down into the cove.

The tide was out, exposing a wide expanse of battle-grey rocks in their familiar knobbly line formation beyond the soft grey cobbles below. She made her way over to the steep rock-formed steps and climbed down on to the beach, slithering a little over the boulders to reach the shingle and sand, where it was easier to walk.

What can of worms had she opened? And what could she, *should she*, do with the information? But perhaps this wasn't what it seemed. Maybe, as she'd cautioned Maddy about in the past, the names were a coincidence. Another couple called Ellen H Tucker and Daniel Meddon could have married. Though, given it had taken place in Somerset, where Ellen had been born, what were the chances of that? No, it had to be the same pair.

It seemed obvious now that the reason for Daniel being less than candid about knowing Ellen was because he was embarrassed by his past. People didn't like to admit to their mistakes. A foolish teenage decision, regretted almost as soon as the ink was dry on the certificate, one that Daniel didn't wish to revisit. James Willoughby had mentioned Arabella's opposition to the relationship, which suggested the pair had sneaked off and engineered the event without her knowledge. Perhaps that had compounded Daniel's discomfort.

But this wasn't simply a matter of a bad decision made in an age of innocence, to be dismissed and forgotten. There was the question of Daniel's marriage to Marianne, the year before Anna was born. If Daniel and Ellen had divorced by mutual consent, they would have had to wait two years, or if on the grounds of adultery or unreasonable behaviour, a year. Neither scenario would have freed Daniel in time to legally marry Marianne.

Who was it who said, once something is known, it can never be unknown? And didn't they also say it was a burden which couldn't be given away?

Esme sighed and wandered over to one end of the beach to a large pool at the bottom of the cliff. At least her discovery answered one question. It seemed likely that Ellen had come to Bideford to find Daniel. Why then, eight years after they'd married? Had something happened to prompt her search?

Esme peered into the rock pool, unable to assess its depth due to the blackness of the water. As clear as her next move, she thought, wistfully. She was as stuck as that sea-beaten driftwood caught between the rock and a large boulder. She could tell no one. Except, she realised, Daniel himself. She might at least put her mind at rest. Maybe there had been some sort of technicality and the marriage had been annulled? What reason would she give for looking into his private affairs, though? But she'd not been looking into Daniel's private affairs, had she? She'd been researching Ellen.

Esme turned away from the pool and made her way back towards the stone steps, thinking over the conversations she'd had with Daniel in the past couple of weeks. He'd been cagey about her research, implying his motive was concern over Anna's mill conversion project. But perhaps he'd simply been nervous at what she'd turn up. Though why would he think she might stumble upon his marriage to Ellen, when her research had been about the mill?

The distant sound of a car engine carried over the ground above her and she climbed the steps from the beach to see a

Torridge Reclamation pick-up turn into the parking space by the cottage and come to a halt on the asphalt. As the engine died, Esme suppressed a surge of panic when the passenger door opened and Anna climbed out.

Her immediate thought was her laptop screen, still open in the sitting room, declaring the damning information about Anna's father.

She hurried over to meet her. 'Anna, good to see you. Another delivery out this way?'

'Something like that,' Anna said with a tired smile. 'Hope you don't mind me dropping in on you like this.'

'Of course not. Any time.'

Anna stared out towards the sea and took a deep breath. 'You're so lucky to have this place, away from everything. From the rest of the world.'

'That sounds like someone feeling the pressure.'

Anna sighed and forced a half-laugh. 'Sorry. Didn't mean that to come out so morose.'

Esme cocked her head towards the sea. 'Come and sit on the bench over here for a moment,' she said, 'if it's not too damp. If I need a break, I sit here and watch the sea. It's very therapeutic.'

Anna followed and they perched on the narrow rustic seat overlooking the bay. Anna rested her chin on her hands, elbows on her knees, leaning forward.

They sat for a while, absorbed by the waves running along the lines of rocks on the beach below.

'You know your dad worries you're taking on too much,' Esme said, after a while.

Anna rolled her eyes. 'Don't you start, Esme. It's bad enough with Dad and Drew ganging up against me.'

'Do they have a point, though?'

Anna gave Esme a sceptical frown. 'You think I'd be frightened off by a sick individual with a macabre sense of humour?'

'Ah, yes. The dead crow. It can't be easy trying to forget about it. Did you report it to the police? And the vandalism in the mill?' Esme studied Anna's face. Her mouth was working, as though she was debating something.

Anna looked down at her hands. 'Drew doesn't think there's any point. It's not like it was our pristine living room, is it? It's just a building site. No harm done, really. Nothing that a few coats of whitewash won't sort out.'

Esme thought it would take more than a few coats of whitewash to cover the depth of colour, but she didn't say anything. 'But it all adds up, doesn't it - the crow, the phone calls? And someone had been throwing stones on the roof, too, Maddy said.' No one else, it seemed, had realised there was a deeper message in the daubed paint. Perhaps it was best kept that way. Let whoever put it there fail in their efforts to intimidate Anna further.

'So what do you make of it?' Anna said, turning to Esme. 'What does it all mean?'

Esme hesitated. 'Why are you the target of someone's perverted Halloween fun, you mean?'

'That'd be a start.'

'There's a chance that someone's got wind of your plan for the mill and doesn't approve, as Mike Harrow suggested. And if it *is* just high jinks, it's unlikely to be personal. Though, if it continues after Halloween, you might have to take it more seriously. It would perhaps suggest then that it isn't just kids.'

'Drew says it'll go away after Halloween.' Anna shuffled on the bench, sliding her hands under her thighs. 'He's convinced it's just antisocial behaviour.'

'No *just* about it if you're on the receiving end.'

Ann shrugged. 'True enough. Drew says I should toughen up. He says everyone's done stuff like that when they were kids. That I should forget it.'

Esme's mind drifted again to Ellen Tucker and the strange parallels of Anna and Ellen's experiences. Would it help for Anna to know this sort of thing had happened before? But how could it help, given Anna's reaction to seeing the drawing?

'Are you OK, Esme?' Anna asked.

'What? Yes, fine.'

'Something's the matter, isn't it? What have I said?'

'Nothing. You've not said anything.'

Anna frowned. 'Is there something you're not telling me?'

Esme shook her head. 'I'm just trying to fathom something out, that's all,' she said, forcing a smile. She went to stand up, but Anna grabbed her hand.

'You know something, don't you? You know what this is all about?'

'No, I don't *know* anything,' Esme sat back down. 'If I did and I could help by telling you, then I would.'

Anna narrowed her eyes, holding herself stiffly. 'So tell me what it is you're trying to fathom out,' she said.

Again the image of Anna's horrified face swam into Esme's mind. She gave a half laugh. 'You trying to bully me, Anna Brannock?'

Anna continued staring, her face flushed. 'I'm waiting, Esme. Stop treating me like a child. You're as bad as Drew.'

Esme let out an exasperated sigh. 'Yes, you're right. I'm sorry.' She cleared her throat. 'It seems you're not the first person to suffer the sort of harassment that's been going on of late. Your parents' former tenant, Ellen Tucker had the exact same problem while she was living in Temperance Cottage.'

'The woman that private investigator was asking about?'

Esme nodded.

Anna said nothing for a moment. 'So why didn't you tell me before?' she said, her voice strained.

'I suppose because the connection was a bit tenuous at first, but then when...' Esme's voice petered out.

'When what?'

Esme looked up at her. 'When Maddy showed you the drawing she'd found hidden in you gran's writing slope, it seemed to upset you. Did you draw it?'

Anna looked away, but not before Esme detected anxiety in her eyes.

'Well, so what if I did?' she said, with a shrug. 'I don't remember. Why is it even relevant?'

'Because,' Esme said, treading carefully, 'it appears that no one knows where Ellen Tucker is. Which is why that private detective was looking for her. Do you know what happened to her, Anna?'

'Me? Why should I know anything?' Anna got up off the bench and strode away, coming to a standstill at the top of the steps down to the beach. Esme watched her for a few moments, frustrated with herself for allowing Anna to goad her into speaking out, when she'd intended to say nothing. She got up and wandered over to stand next to Anna.

'I'm sorry. I should have kept my thoughts to myself. When we found that drawing…well, it seemed as though it might be significant in some way, that's all. But if you can't remember, don't worry.'

Anna shook her head. When she spoke, her voice was barely audible. 'I wasn't out here delivering anything,' she said, blinking rapidly, her gaze still fixed on the horizon. 'I came because I wanted to own up.'

'Own up? To what?'

Anna's head whipped round and she stared at Esme, tears filling her eyes. 'You're right about the picture, Esme. It is mine. And I do remember drawing it.' She blinked her tears away. 'I only wish I didn't.'

# 49

Esme suggested they retreat inside the cottage. Her laptop would have slipped into hibernation by now, blanking out the screen showing the incriminating marriage records. But Anna said she'd rather be outside. So instead, they took the track across the stream and climbed up on to the clifftop.

'I was telling the truth the other day,' Anna said, 'when you showed me the drawing in the workshop.' By now they'd reached level ground and had joined the coastal path towards Warren Quay. 'I honestly didn't recognise the drawing at first.'

'But you did later?'

Anna thrust her hands into the pocket of her fleece. 'It wasn't as simple as that. I couldn't understand why the sight of it filled me with terror. Then you asked me about it and I didn't know what to say.'

'You poor thing. It was obviously a shock, seeing it after all these years,' Esme said. 'Do you remember hiding it?'

Anna pursed her lips. 'Not exactly. But I knew about the secret drawer. Granny showed me. Clearly something compelled me to put it in there. I must have drawn it at Granny's house, mustn't I? She used to live where me and Drew live now.'

'Yes,' Esme said, 'I remember you telling me. Did you go there a lot?'

Anna nodded. 'Yes, I suppose I did, thinking back.' She stopped on the path and turned towards Esme, the wind catching the loose hair from her plait and flicking it across her face. 'I don't have all the answers, Esme, but I can tell you what I remember.'

Esme smiled and nodded. 'I'm listening.'

They continued along the well-trodden path. Sheep peppered the clifftop around them, too busy munching the grass to pay them any attention.

'I wasn't in a happy place, when I drew that picture,' Anna said. 'Of course I was too young to understand at the time, to realise what was going on. All I knew was that there was something amiss between Mum and Dad, and the woman staying in the cottage was somehow the reason they argued.'

'Did you recognise the name, Ellen Tucker, when Sean Carlton came round asking questions?'

'No, I didn't. I'd probably never known it, even back then.'

'Did something particular happen to prompt the drawing?'

Anna said nothing for a few moments, as though working out where to begin her story. 'It was Halloween,' she said, after a while. 'I was supposed to be going to a party after tea. I was so excited. I had a witch outfit and everything. The day before Mum and I had made a pumpkin lantern, ready to put a candle in. But it all went wrong.'

'In what way?'

'Mum and Dad had a row. I could hear them in the kitchen as I was upstairs getting dressed up, ready to go out. I waited for them to shut up, for Dad to storm out and slam the door, like he'd been doing so often recently. But they just went on and on. Eventually I went downstairs and walked into the kitchen and told Mum it was time to go. She looked at me for a moment, as though she didn't know who I was. When I repeated it was time for her to take me to Alison's house, she said she'd changed her mind, that I couldn't go. She said we'd do some apple bobbing instead in the morning. I think I must have said something unforgivable to her at that point. Well, I was so upset. I'd been so looking forward to it. Whatever I said, it was bad enough for her to pack me off to bed early.' Anna gave a short snort at the memory. 'I remember sitting in my bedroom, fuming.'

A couple of hikers came along towards them, each carrying walking poles, swaying rhythmically as they strode along. Esme nodded an acknowledgment, but Anna was lost in her thoughts.

When they'd gone past, Anna continued. 'I didn't change into my pyjamas, though. I sat on the edge of the bed in my witch's garb, waiting for her to come upstairs. It was some sort of defiance, I guess.'

'What did she say when she came up?'

Anna shook her head. 'She didn't. Her and Dad just kept on arguing. I realised they'd forgotten all about me, and it suddenly occurred to me that if they were so wrapped up in one another, they'd not notice if I went to the party on my own.'

'Was it far, the party?'

'Only at the end of the lane. I'd been down to Alison's loads of times, though not on my own at night, as you might guess. I crept downstairs, out of the front door and into the yard. It looked scarily dark out in the lane and I almost got cold feet. But then I thought how cross I was with Mum and Dad, and if I got lost in the dark, Mum'd be really sorry she'd been so mean, so I forced myself to keep going.

I was half way across the yard when I heard the back door open and realised Mum was on her way out.'

'What did you do?'

'I ducked down behind the Land Rover, but then I realised she was heading straight for it. So if I didn't want her to see me, I only had once choice. I climbed under the canvas at the back.'

'And she didn't see you?'

Anna gave a sad smile. 'She was completely oblivious, her mind on where she was headed, I guess. She started the engine and sped out of the yard. I don't think I've ever known her drive so fast. I curled up in the back and kept my head down.'

'And she drove down to Temperance Cottage?'

Anna gave a brief nod. 'When I heard her get out and slam the door, I looked out and saw her march across towards the front door. I didn't get it. What was she doing at that woman's house? She didn't like her, so why would she go there?'

'You already knew your mum didn't like her?'

'Oh, yes. I couldn't tell you how I knew, but I did.'

Esme guessed that, as children often do, Anna had sensed Marianne's animosity towards Ellen, rather than knowing because of anything done or words she'd overheard.

'Did Ellen come to the door?' Esme asked, thinking of Anna's drawing, showing Ellen at a window.

Anna paused for a moment. 'I think so. She must have, mustn't she, to open the door?'

'Yes, I suppose she must have. Go on.'

Anna frowned, her focus distant but concentrated as she dug up the images in her childhood memory.

'I climbed down from the back. There were lights on inside the cottage...no, not lights. Candles. Yes, that's right. It must have been candles because the light was flickering.' She slapped her hand across her mouth and stifled a sob.

Esme put an arm around Anna's shoulders. 'I'm so sorry, Anna. That drawing's clearly stirred up a lot of bad memories for you.'

Anna nodded. Tears squeezed out of her closed eyes and ran down her cheeks. She wiped the back of her hand across the end of her nose and sniffed.

'The next thing I remember is Mum coming back out.'

'Didn't she see you?'

'No. She was crying. She probably couldn't see much at all. And I was in the shadow between the Land Rover and the cottage. It was easy to climb back in without her seeing.'

'She didn't hear you then?'

'She was sobbing by now. I'd never, ever seen her cry before. Tears over a soppy film, but not like that. Huge racking sobs.' Anna lifted her head, letting the wind blow away her own tears. She let out a shivering sigh. 'I wanted to go to her, give her a hug, but I daren't. She'd have been horrified that I'd been hiding in the Land Rover, that I'd defied her by not going to bed as I'd been told.' She looked at Esme. 'And that I'd seen her so distraught.'

'I'm guessing you've never told her about that night?' Esme said.

Anna shook her head, vigorously. 'I wouldn't have wanted her to know I'd been there or I'd have got into serious trouble, and then...'

'Over time, you forgot about it. Buried it, even.'

Anna nodded.

'And then,' Esme sighed, 'Maddy and I dragged you back there by showing you the drawing.'

Anna shook her head. 'You weren't to know, Esme. You can't blame yourself.' She forced a smile. 'It's probably good to get it out in the open, isn't it?'

They walked along in silence, the old ruined folly coming into view. Esme suggested they retrace their steps and they turned back towards the cottage.

'Do you think Mum knows about the harassment Ellen Tucker was getting?'

The question jolted Esme. If Marianne was so desperate for Ellen to leave, had she been the culprit, trying to force her out? She dragged herself out of her reflection, realising Anna was speaking to her.

'Sorry. Miles away. What were you saying?'

'No, it's OK,' Anna said. 'I was just wondering what Mum told that private detective.'

'I don't think he got to speak to your parents,' Esme said. 'Your mum said she'd not seen him.'

Anna stopped and turned to Esme, a puzzled expression on her face. 'He had a yellow car, right?'

'Yes, that's the one.'

'I saw it. In the yard at the farm. That day Maddy said she'd sent him up there.' She frowned. 'So why would Mum lie about him not been there?'

# 50

By the time Esme followed Anna across the yard at Hill Farm, she was already regretting her decision. She should never have allowed Anna to persuade her to come with her to see Marianne. Anna needed to talk this through with her mother alone.

But Anna had been insistent. 'Please, Esme,' she'd begged, her face crumpling. 'I know Mum. I won't get anything out of her if I tackle her on my own. She'll take it more seriously if you're there.'

Any resolve Esme might have had to stay away had been undermined by Anna's final comment. 'And we both have questions, don't we?'

But now, she was trailing after Anna into the kitchen, the smell of freshly baked bread emphasising the cruel contrast between the very essence of homeliness and comfort, and the disturbing truths that might be disclosed in the conversation to come.

Marianne stood at one end of the long kitchen table, her hands in a bowl of flour, rubbing fat into pastry. She looked up as they came in.

'Hello. This is a surprise,' she said, smiling. She looked at Esme, her eyebrows raised. 'Something about the mill history, is it?' She laughed, compounding Esme's guilt by adding, 'I hope it's something good. Apparently you're supposed to have nice thoughts while you make pastry.' Her smile faded. 'Everything all right, darling?' she said, looking at Anna. 'You look a bit washed out.'

'Mum, I need to talk to you,' Anna said. She pulled out a chair and sat down facing Marianne.

Esme remained standing. She gripped the back of the chair closest to the door.

Marianne paused, her floury hands held in the air above the bowl. She must have sensed the tension; anxiety was imprinted on her face.

'Talk to me about what?' she said, flicking a wary glance at Esme and back to Anna.

Anna clasped her hands together and laid them in her lap. 'You remember that private detective, Mum? He was asking about Ellen Tucker.'

'Can't say I do,' Marianne said, her tone brusque. She brushed off her hands and picked up a jug beside her and dribbled some water into the mixing bowl, before picking up a knife and stirring the contents of the bowl with a brisk motion.

Anna looked round at Esme, her expression pained, as though saying, '*You see what I mean? I told you she'd be like this.*'

Esme cleared her throat. 'Maddy sent him up here to talk to you. Did you speak to him?'

'His car was here,' Anna said, turning back to her mother. 'I saw it in the yard.'

'Is that so? Well, I don't remember. I must have been out.' Marianne put down the knife and began gathering up the pastry dough in her hands, pressing it together to make a ball.

'You weren't out,' Anna said. 'I'd called in for a coffee. I saw it parked there when I left to go home.'

Marianne threw down the ball of pastry into the bowl. 'Would you like to explain why, exactly, this is so important all of a sudden?'

Anna leaned forward. 'Do you remember Halloween night, when I was 8?'

'What?' Marianne stared at her daughter with incredulity.

'You banned me from going to Alison's party because you and Dad had a row.'

245

'Did I.' It was a bored statement, rather than a question.

'You know what I'm going to say, don't you?' Anna said.

'No, I do not know what you're going to say, Anna. And I can't for the life of me work out why you want to know about a child's party all those years ago.'

'The point is, Mum, that I didn't go to the party. You sent me to bed.'

'Is that so? Well, poor old Anna. Deprived of a fun night out.' She took a roll of greaseproof paper from a drawer under the kitchen worktop, tearing off a piece and wrapping it around the dough. 'I take it there's a point to this discussion?'

'But I didn't stay in bed,' Anna continued. 'I came downstairs and sneaked out of the house while you and Dad were yelling hammer and tongs at one another.' Anna's eyes followed her mother as she put the pastry dough in the fridge and took the bowl over to the sink. 'My plan was to walk to the party,' she said to her mother's back, 'but you came out of the back door. So I hid in the back of the Land Rover.'

Marianne spun round, her eyes wide with alarm.

Anna nodded, slowly. 'So, you *do* remember?'

Marianne gawped at Anna, colour draining from her face. 'You did what?' she said, eventually.

'I hid in the back and you never saw me.' Anna looked back at her mother, her eyes pleading. 'I saw you go to the cottage, Mum. And I saw you come out. Crying.' Her voice cracked a little. 'What happened, Mum? Why were you crying?'

Marianne shot a look at Esme. 'This has got nothing to do with Esme,' she said. 'I don't understand why she's here.'

Esme floundered around in her head for the best way to answer, but Anna spoke before she could marshal her thoughts.

'What happened to Ellen Tucker, Mum? You know, don't you?'

Marianne pressed her lips together and pulled herself up to her full height. 'I don't know what you're talking about, Anna. Ellen Tucker left. That's all there is to it.'

'So what happened when you went to her cottage?' Anna said. 'Why were you crying? What happened between you?'

'Nothing happened between us,' Marianne said, her tone angry now. 'The woman left. Her bags were all packed. I saw them.' She looked away. 'And I was crying...' she swallowed, 'because your father and I had argued. I was upset. That's all.'

'Argued about what?' Anna said. 'About her?'

Marianne cocked her chin. 'Yes, if you must know.' She twisted her hands together. 'But it was nothing. Just a silly misunderstanding.'

The room fell silent. From outside came the approaching growl of a tractor as it was driven into the yard.

Anna turned to Esme, her expression wounded and confused, as though looking for guidance. Esme looked at Marianne.

'Do you have any idea why Ellen left, Marianne?'

Marianne shrugged dismissively. 'Why would I know? She decided to go. Fine by me. She was causing enough friction as it was.'

'Friction? In what way?'

The back door opened behind them and they all looked towards it. Daniel hesitated, his hand still on the door handle. He grinned.

'What's all this, then?' he said. 'Mothers' meeting?' The grin vanished. He stepped inside and closed the door. 'What's happened? Anna? You all right?'

'It's about that tenant we had,' Marianne said, glaring at Daniel, her mouth turned down at the corners. 'You remember? Miss Tucker?'

Daniel's colour deepened. 'Yes, I think so. What about her?'

'Dad,' Anna said, standing up, 'do you know what happened to her? Ellen Tucker, I mean. The woman the private investigator was looking for. Did you speak to him?'

Daniel half opened his mouth. He looked at Marianne again. 'I... She left, didn't she?' he said, eventually.

Marianne nodded. 'Yes, I've told Anna. I saw her cases. No doubt at all that she was planning to leave.'

Daniel nodded. 'Well then.' He glared at Esme and she braced herself for an onslaught. Clearly he blamed her for Anna's unwelcome questions. But it was as though he couldn't put his anger into words.

'And that's what you told Sean Carlton?' Esme dared to say.

'That's exactly what I told him.' He forced a laugh. 'Well, I don't know, do you, Marianne? Can't a man come in for a cup of tea without having to suffer the Spanish Inquisition?' He turned. 'I'll come back later, when you ladies have finished gossiping.' He yanked the door open and disappeared back into the yard, slamming the door behind him.

'Dad, please,' Anna said, heading for the door. 'It's not a joke.'

'Leave it, Anna,' Marianne said, hurrying over to her. 'Come and sit down. I'll talk to him later.' She took Anna's arm and guided her back to the table. 'He's just embarrassed. He made a fool of himself with that woman, that's all it is.'

Esme let go of the back of the chair and stretched out her fingers. She hadn't realised how tightly she'd been clenching her knuckles.

'I'd better get on my way. Sorry to have disturbed you, Marianne.'

Marianne's look was hostile. It was clear that in her eyes, Esme should have left a long time ago.

'See you later, Anna,' Esme said.

'Yes. Thanks, Esme,' Anna said, her voice small and subdued. She looked shattered. Hardly surprising, given the emotional toll it must have taken to confront Marianne with such harrowing memories.

Esme slipped outside and closed the door behind her, pausing on the step to take a deep breath. She hoped Anna had found some solace in learning the truth, but there was still so much left to resolve about Ellen Tucker, she couldn't help feeling that so far, all they'd done was expose the tip of a hornets' nest.

She walked across the yard to her car, speculating whether Marianne was aware of the former relationship between Ellen and Daniel. Perhaps that had been at the core of their quarrel. It would explain Marianne's bitterness towards Daniel's first wife arriving on their doorstep. She wondered whether Daniel knew where Ellen had gone. If he did, it was unlikely he'd have admitted it in front of Marianne. Should she seek him out and ask him?

But she recalled the way he'd glared at her, too furious to speak, and dismissed the idea. He was far too volatile to approach at the moment.

She pulled out her car keys from her pocket and pressed the button to unlock the car. But as she went to open the driver's door, a hand seized hers. She cried out and recoiled, stumbling back into whoever had come up behind her.

'And just what the hell d'you think you're you playing at?' Daniel snarled in her ear.

# 51

Esme jabbed Daniel with her elbow and pulled away. 'I might say the same to you,' she said, turning to glare at him. 'Do you usually treat your visitors like that?'

Daniel backed off, raising his hands in surrender. 'Sorry, sorry, I didn't mean to be so...'

'Aggressive?' Esme snapped. She felt herself shaking, annoyed as much with herself for getting drawn into the family's internal dispute, as with Daniel for his inappropriate behaviour.

'Yeah, well,' he said, sulkily. 'It's hardly surprising, is it? Dragging Anna into something that doesn't concern her.'

'Doesn't concern her?' Esme said, staring at him. 'Of course it concerns her. She remembers Ellen, not least because of the way you and Marianne argued about her. That investigator's search has reignited the trauma she suffered all those years ago.'

Daniel rubbed his hand across his face, his fingers stained from engine oil. He leaned his back against Esme's car and sighed.

'I didn't realise. She never said.'

'Well, she wouldn't have. She'd buried it all. Until...' She hesitated. 'Until recently.' It was Anna's place to tell him about the drawing, if she chose to.

'What did Marianne tell you?' Daniel said, calmer now.

'Tell me? About what?'

'Ellen.' He shuffled, looking down at the ground. 'It was just a silly infatuation. Marianne knows that. We sorted it out between us years ago.' He glanced at her out of the corner of his eye.

Esme frowned. Was he trying to look coy? 'You and Ellen have history, I understand?'

'So she did say something.' He scraped the toe of his boot in an arc on the concrete. 'We'd known each other when we were teenagers. I was over on Exmoor working on the farms one summer. Ellen was serving in the pub where we used to go of an evening. We hung around together for a while.'

Esme waited for him to go on, but he didn't elaborate. 'So just a holiday romance, then?'

'Yeah, that's right.'

'Did you know Ellen was related to the Brannock family?'

His head turned sharply. 'What?'

'You didn't know?'

'No, I didn't.' He looked up at her, seemingly confused.

'I thought it might have been her reason for coming to Bideford,' Esme said. 'To find her family. Until I realised it was probably to look for you.' Daniel didn't seem to have heard. 'Something the matter?'

He gave a brief shake of his head. 'She despised the Brannocks. Ellen's mother, I mean.'

Esme recalled Willoughby's comment, that Arabella had been against the relationship between Ellen and her boyfriend.

'Perhaps Arabella thought Ellen was too young to be tied down.'

He snorted. 'She hated me. She came between us, convinced Ellen that I was no good. She was almost,' he rubbed his chin, 'obsessive in her dislike of me. Once she found out my mother was a Brannock, anyway. She'd been fine before that.'

'Is that why you ran off to get married?'

His head shot round, the shock evident on his face. 'How dare you spy on me,' he said, glaring at her. 'You had no right.'

'I wasn't spying on you, Daniel. I was trying to find out about this mysterious woman who no one has seen for 24 years and who...' She stopped before she inadvertently dragged Maddy's interest into the conversation. 'Well, let's say I didn't expect your name to come up.'

Daniel stared down at his hands. 'I thought once we were married, her mother would drop her stupid ideas. It would be too late to do anything about it. She'd leave us be. But she didn't.'

'So what happened?' Esme asked. 'Ellen couldn't have agreed with her mother or she wouldn't have gone ahead with the wedding.'

'No, you're right. She didn't. Ellen thought as I did, that her mother was being ridiculous to lay some unknown family feud at my door, as though somehow it was my fault.'

'So what changed?'

Daniel shook his head. 'At the time, I had no idea. Suddenly Ellen wouldn't talk to me, even refused to see me. Arabella said Ellen had realised her mistake and threw me out. Well,' he gave a humourless half-laugh, 'got a couple of her admirer thugs to do it for her. I limped back home.'

'And into Marianne's arms.' He flashed her an uneasy glance. 'Had you known Marianne before?'

Daniel pushed his hands into the pockets of his overall. 'We'd been going out for a few weeks earlier that year. Nothing serious.' His eyes darted towards the farmhouse.

'I haven't told her, if that's what you're worried about.'

He sighed and nodded, before looking away across the yard. 'Thanks. She wouldn't understand.'

'I bet she wouldn't. Bigamy's still a crime, you know.' Esme turned towards him with a hard stare. 'So what did happen to Ellen, Daniel? You must know something.'

He turned away, pulling himself upright so he was no longer leaning against the car. 'Marianne's told you what we know. Ellen's bags were packed. She wanted to leave.' He glanced back at Esme. He looked weary, as though weighed down by the past with no way to shed his load. 'And, for the record, I didn't want her to go.'

Esme saw moisture in his eyes and understood the hurt

that Arabella's intervention had caused. He'd come home to Marianne and taken up with her on the rebound. She tried to imagine his reaction when Ellen walked back into his life. So why had he stayed? For Marianne? For Anna?

'Ellen'd had enough of this place,' Daniel was saying. 'Can't say I blame her, the way people were towards her. Narrow-minded bigots. They made her life a misery.'

He closed his eyes and took a deep breath.

'I should get some work done.'

Esme nodded. 'Yes, of course. Thanks for telling me about Ellen.' She opened the car door and paused. 'You said you had no idea *at the time* what Arabella had said to Ellen which turned her against you. Ellen must have told you when you met up again?'

Daniel looked down and kicked the ground with his boot. 'She told Ellen lies about me,' he said. 'Said I'd tried it on with her and that I'd made out it was her coming on to me.' He looked up at Esme, his eyes beseeching. 'There's been enough damage done here, Esme. Isn't it time we left it alone?'

'Can we, though? After everything you've told me about the way Ellen was hounded?'

He scowled. 'What are you getting at?'

'Hasn't it occurred to you that Anna's being targeted in exactly the same way? Don't you want to find out if there's a connection?'

'There is no connection.'

'You know that for certain, do you?'

He hesitated, as though he was about to say something else, but instead he shook his head and walked away across the yard.

Esme watched him go, something he'd said echoing in her head. *Narrow-minded bigots. They made her life a misery.* But who were *they*? People like Marianne, other wives and girlfriends who resented Ellen's good looks? Kids and their taunting?

Something slipped into her mind, something that Anna had mentioned Drew saying, how she mustn't let the intimidation get to her. *Everyone's done stuff like that when they were kids.* Had he been talking about himself? What was it that Maddy had called Drew's mates when she'd pointed them out in the school photograph? *Drew's little bunch of low-life vermin.* The sort of group whose agenda might include winding up a woman living on her own?

She pulled out her phone and found Maddy's number. She had an idea.

# 52

'Wouldn't surprise me in the slightest that Drew was behind Ellen Tucker's trouble,' Maddy said, as they stood in her living room. She was holding Ginger in her arms, peering at Esme over the curve of his furry body. 'You know I've always had him down for all this hassle of Anna's. It probably gave him the idea.'

Maddy dropped down on to the edge of the sofa and Esme took the armchair opposite. 'I don't think it was just him,' Esme said. 'But his little gang of cronies, too.' She told Maddy about Drew's comment to Anna, implying inappropriate behaviour was a normal part of growing up. 'Remember the newspaper report about Ellen's harassment? It mentioned a group of youths. Then I remembered that you'd not been very complimentary about Drew's friends when you pointed them out on the school photo.'

'No, I wasn't. That sort of harassment would have been right up their street.'

'And we reckoned they'd have been about fifteen.'

Maddy nodded. 'I think I see where you're going with this. Lads and testosterone. Old enough to be getting the hots for an attractive woman like Ellen Tucker, but too young to be on her radar.'

'Exactly. So instead, they got a kick out of tormenting her.'

Maddy leaned back in her seat, stroking Ginger on her lap. 'So what's your idea? Ask Drew? He's not gonna admit to anything, is he, despite his chilled *"doesn't everyone do it?"* attitude.'

'No, but I wondered about the others. You know what it's like when you're young. You might have got tangled up in something a bit unsavoury when you were caught in the moment, and later felt ashamed of what you'd got yourself into. They'd all have families of their own by now. Upstanding citizens.'

Maddy gave a bemused half-grin. 'I wouldn't go that far. I knew them, remember.'

'Yes, but could we track them down? Speak to them. See what they know about Ellen. Even if they won't admit to being involved, they might have something to say. Do they still live in the area?'

'OK. Let me take a look.' Maddy stood up and placed Ginger down in her place on the sofa. 'Where did I put that school photo?' She disappeared out of the room and reappeared moments later with the photograph roll in her hand. She put it on the table and unrolled it, using coasters to hold down the corners. 'Right,' she said, grabbing a notepad and pen and pulling out a chair. 'Let's make a list of these guys.'

Esme grabbed her coat and slipped it on. 'I'll let you get on with that, then, shall I?'

Maddy nodded. 'OK. I'll fill you in at tomorrow's market, unless I come across anything mind-blowing in the meantime.'

Esme slipped her bag over her shoulder and left Maddy to her investigation.

*

Tuesday's market was quiet. Only the hardy punters were out and about in the pouring rain. Esme wished she'd worn an extra layer. Wind whirled in through the large opening to the market, sucking any ambient heat out of the hall. She paced up and down in front of their stall, scanning for custom, which was thin on the ground.

Maddy's search for Drew's old cronies had come up short. 'Of the four of them that used to knock around with him,'

Maddy told Esme, 'one died in a car crash not long after we left school, one emigrated to the States, one's the CEO of some global financial institution in the City and one joined the police force and has since moved to Liverpool.'

'Any of them contactable?' Esme asked, hopefully.

Maddy shrugged. 'None of my old mates who I spoke to were in touch with them. And why would they be? We moved in different circles. I did bang off an email to the CEO guy, through his company website, but even if it gets past his admin staff and lands in his personal inbox, he may not remember who the hell I am. So don't hold your breath.'

'So much for that idea, then,' Esme said, folding her arms and leaning against their stall.

'Nothing from the missing persons charity, I assume?' Maddy asked.

'No,' Esme said. 'And the longer it goes on, the more I don't hold out much hope, to be honest. I thought Penny – that's the woman who founded the charity – might remember Ellen if there'd been any sort of campaign at the time. But if there had, I'm sure other people would have remembered. Cerys actually knew her and she couldn't recall anything along those lines. So if Penny does get in touch eventually, I'm sure it'll only be to confirm Ellen was never on their books.'

By midday, the small number of tenacious shoppers had dwindled to nil and they decided to pack up early. Loading up Maddy's van in the persistent rain did nothing to lift their despondency and they drove back to the workshop in a silent, subdued mood.

*

They unloaded the stock and Maddy filled the kettle.

'I've got a sachet of cup-a-soup somewhere in here, if you want to take a risk,' she said, rummaging around in the cupboard under the sink. 'Not *MasterChef* standard, but it might warm us up.'

'Oh, why not,' Esme said, sitting down at Maddy's workbench. 'I like to live dangerously.'

Maddy grinned and pulled out two packets. 'Limited choice, I'm afraid,' she said, holding them up. 'Leek and Potato or Potato and Leek?'

'Mmm, that's a tough one,' Esme said, leaning her elbow on the bench. 'I'll try Leek and Potato.'

'Leek and Potato it is. Coming right up.' Maddy tore a corner of each of the packets and tapped the powder into two mugs.

'I wonder if Daniel's spoken to Anna about Ellen,' Esme said, watching Maddy prepare their modest lunch. Perhaps Marianne's reassurance had been enough, that her father had made a fool of himself.

'Too embarrassed, probably,' Maddy said. 'Funny how we guessed he'd been one of Ellen's conquests right from the get-go, when he'd reddened up on hearing her name that day at the market.'

Esme said nothing. She'd not shared with Maddy about finding the marriage record. While the information was in the public domain, she didn't feel it was her place to mention it. Besides, it didn't change the key facts. Ellen and Daniel had a relationship, official or otherwise.

'We were so convinced Anna's drawing held the key to Ellen's mystery,' she said. 'Instead it exposed an unrelated trauma for Anna, poor thing. The law of unintended consequences.'

The kettle clicked off and Maddy poured the boiling water into the mugs. 'We don't know it *is* unrelated,' she said.

Esme sat up. 'How do you mean?'

'Don't look so expectant,' Maddy said, handing Esme her soup. 'I only meant, until we get to the truth, we don't know what's connected and what isn't.'

Esme blew on the hot soup and took a sip of the creamy liquid. It was surprisingly tasty.

'I suppose Anna ought to have her drawing back.'

'She said to bin it.'

'I know that's what she said, but I think *she* needs to do that. It might be quite cathartic for her.'

Maddy put down her mug and reached over to the desk. She took Anna's picture from where it lay on the top and dropped it on to the workbench.

Esme pulled it towards her. It was hard not to keep studying it. The familiarity of the buildings. The furious mass of scribble in one corner, stretching out across the page, now explained and understood. She was again drawn to the face of Ellen at the window, her mouth open as though screaming.

'I suppose, knowing what we know, this could be Ellen yelling at Marianne,' she said.

'Did she leave, d'you think?' Maddy said, sipping her soup.

'Marianne and Daniel seem to think so. As does Cerys.'

'Pity you've heard nothing back from Penny whats-her-name at the charity. Then we'd know if Ellen had been registered as a missing person, whether that's what the empty file was all about at Dad's.'

Esme nodded. 'Perhaps I'll chase them up. Though I think if they had something, they'd have got back to me by now.'

Maddy sighed. 'Perhaps we should hire our own private detective. Get him to establish that Ellen Tucker did leave of her own accord and is out there somewhere having a happy life. We might get some sleep, then.'

Esme studied Maddy's face, noticing the dark shadows under her eyes. 'You don't need all this, do you, Madds? Not now, not dealing with the aftermath of your dad and everything.'

Maddy stood up. 'Well there's no use in feeling sorry for myself. I've got a busy day tomorrow with that auction in Surrey. Harry said I should do a bit less and stop trying to run before I can walk.'

Esme smiled. 'It might be sensible to ease up. Just till things have settled a bit. It's a lot to keep all your dad's network intact as well as clear his house and everything that goes with it. Something has to give.'

'Yes, I know. I do need to downscale a bit. At least until Dad's place is sorted. Talking of which, are you still OK for Thursday? Don't worry if you can't. You've done more than enough already.'

'You keep saying that, but it's no bother, really. I won't abandon you till everything's done and dusted, don't worry.'

Esme's phone pinged. 'Hey, she said, putting the mug down on the bench. 'Maybe that's Penny now.' She reached for her bag and pulled out her phone, scrolling down her email list with a mixture of hope and anticipation.

'Well? Is it from Penny?'

'No. It's an email from the General Register Office. Hope Brannock's birth certificate's available to view.' Esme looked up. 'Can I borrow your laptop to get into my account? So much easier to see properly than on a phone screen.'

'Sure,' Maddy said. She fetched her laptop and booted the machine, before swivelling the screen round towards Esme.

Esme slipped on her reading glasses and sat down. She navigated her way to her account and found the recent order she'd placed for a PDF copy of the certificate. Maddy took up her soup and came around the bench to stand beside her as the screen refreshed.

They both stared as the image of the certificate appeared before them.

Maddy gasped. 'What? She was born in gaol?'

'And look,' Esme said, tapping the screen. 'Look who her mother was.' She took off her glasses and blinked up at Maddy. 'The woman convicted of Silas Brannock's murder. His daughter, Sarah.'

# 53

Esme chewed the arm of her glasses as she considered the implications of what they'd discovered.

'So Sarah was already pregnant when she stood trial,' Maddy said. 'And that's why she had Hope in prison?'

Esme nodded. 'The death sentence on a pregnant woman would have been deferred until she'd given birth.'

'Oh how very considerate of them,' Maddy said. She dragged a stool closer to Esme and sat down. 'It explains why Hope ended up in the workhouse, until she was rescued by her adoptive parents.'

'That's right. Obviously, Sarah would have been held in custody once she was charged and stayed there until her execution.' An idea flitted into Esme's head and she sat upright, before turning back to the laptop and tapping the keys.

'What?' Maddy said.

'Just had a hunch who Hope's adoptive parents might have been,' Esme said, clicking around the website for the birth indexes.

'Susan and Thomas Moss, wasn't it?'

'Yes, but I think there's a family connection. Let me check it out.' Below Hope's entry in the 1881 census, where she appeared as an adopted daughter, three other half-siblings had been listed. If Esme could locate their records, it would confirm her theory. She filled in the relevant boxes with Moss as the surname and approximate dates. The screen refreshed and she scanned it eagerly. 'Yes, I was right. Look. There are the three Moss children, their mother's maiden name was Brannock.'

'Susan Brannock?'

'Or Susannah, to use her full name. She was Sarah's younger sister.'

'So she took Hope on?' Maddy sighed, slowly shaking her head. 'Quite a commitment. But didn't you said she was only 14 when Hope was born?'

'Yes, that's right,' Esme said, nodding. 'She'd be far too young for the responsibility to begin with and we know Hope was in the workhouse for at least a couple of years, so clearly no one else in the family took her in.'

'Wasn't able to? Or wasn't prepared to?' Maddy said.

'Good question.' Esme imagined a conversation between the sisters before Sarah's execution. Had Susannah made a promise to Sarah to take care of her baby? Had the family resisted, with Susannah deciding that she would herself give Hope a home, once she was able?

'I wonder how far through her pregnancy Sarah was when she was convicted,' Maddy said.

'Yes, I'd wondered that.' Esme rubbed her scar, recalling her conversation with Morris about the background to the murder trial. 'Morris said there'd been an argument at home, remember, between her parents? Silas alleged that Sarah wasn't his daughter. Things escalated, ending in the tragic death of Bessie in the fire.'

'Which Silas said was an accident and Sarah said had been deliberate.'

Esme swivelled round to face Maddy. 'Perhaps that argument was sparked when Bessie told Silas about Sarah's condition.'

'Makes sense,' Maddy agreed. 'The Brannocks were of the fire and brimstone fraternity, weren't they? Silas was gonna be no happy bunny that his daughter's fallen pregnant.'

'But more than that, according to Morris, the dates suggest Bessie had been pregnant when she and Silas married. If Silas had been harbouring suspicions from the start that Sarah wasn't his daughter, hearing the news could well have been the trigger for all that pent-up anger to come out.'

Maddy gave a slow shake of the head. 'Can't believe why his action was so extreme. I mean, accuse her of witchcraft? It's bizarre.'

'It's a common theme. Morris's book includes several accounts where men blamed women for bewitching them. Henry VIII said it of Anne Boleyn. She lost her head over it. Poor Bessie Brannock burned for it and her daughter hanged for it.'

'Not for being a witch, though,' Maddy protested.

'Not directly, no. But by accusing her father so publicly and cursing the Brannock family at the trial, Sarah sealed her own fate.'

Maddy stood up and wandered over to the window.

Esme sat back, thinking over the connections. 'You do realise what this means?' she said to Maddy's back. 'Both Ellen and Anna are related to Sarah Brannock. And, therefore, to Bessie, the victim who's remembered on the murder stone. That's a connection we'd not known about before.' Could it have been Susannah who'd arranged for the erection of the stone? She was at home when her mother had fallen in the fire because Morris said she'd been dispatched to fetch the doctor. She may have even witnessed the event.

Maddy folded her arms and turned round to face Esme. 'Are you saying the family connection to Bessie explains why Anna's being targeted, and why Ellen was? I can't see how.'

'No, neither can I.' Esme thought of Daniel and his annoyance at the murder being discussed. Surely this wasn't why he was so sensitive about it? 'I asked Daniel if he wasn't interested in finding the link between Ellen's harassment and Anna's. He said there was no connection.'

Maddy scratched her head. 'Well, he could be right. It's a bit tentative, isn't it? I mean, no one can accuse Anna of being a wanton woman bewitching Drew and tricking him into marriage to cover up her pregnancy. They've been married for years. Neither is she in the *femme fatale* category, like her distant cousin Ellen Tucker.'

'So it would seem,' Esme said. 'So what *is* the common factor?'

'Perhaps there isn't one.'

'You might have a point. It wouldn't get us any closer to understanding why your dad got involved, because Anna's problems only started recently. Which brings us back to Ellen herself, doesn't it?'

Maddy pressed her lips together. 'There has to have been something significant Dad knew, or found out, for him to get sucked into this. And I don't mean just Carlton searching him out. If Ellen Tucker had moved on and was out there somewhere, they'd know, wouldn't they? Both of them had the necessary contacts to find out that sort of information, surely?'

'Not yelling, but screaming?' Esme said.

'What? Oh, you mean the drawing.' She nodded. 'If Anna hadn't explained everything, I'd be with you on Ellen's face. She looks scared to me, not hacked off.'

Maddy collected up the soup mugs and took them to the sink to swill out. Esme wondered what was going through Maddy's mind. Should they resign themselves to never discovering the truth about Ellen Tucker? Or was there another avenue they'd not yet explored?

'I'll chase that charity, if you like,' Esme said, getting to her feet. 'I don't hold out much hope, but you never know.'

Maddy grabbed a tea towel and turned round, drying her hands. 'D'you think this is going to stop after Halloween, like Drew and Daniel seem to think?'

'Guess we'll have to wait and see. I'd like to think so, for Anna's sake.' She picked up her coat off the hook on the door and slipped it on. 'Well, I'll love you and leave you. I need to do a food shop or I'll waste away. Will you give Anna back her drawing?'

'She's not in today. Delivering in South Devon, or something.'

'Glad she's back at work. I was a bit worried about her after yesterday. Oh, well. You can give it her in the morning.'

'I won't be here, remember?' Maddy said. 'I'm away at that auction.'

'Of course, yes. I'd forgotten. Shall I take it, then? I could call in tomorrow. I'd like to see how she is, you know?'

'Yes, do that. You could tell her about Hope. She'd be interested. Though you might leave out the bit about witches burning on the fire.'

Esme hesitated, Maddy's words connecting with something. 'Odd you should say that,' she said. 'Reminds me of what James Willoughby told me. Ellen's mother had a lifelong fear of being burned. That's why Ellen arranged for her to buried in Bremleycott churchyard and not cremated.'

'Sounds like she was well aware of her family history,' Maddy said, returning to her workbench.

Esme nodded, thinking of Arabella's resentment towards Daniel for being a Brannock. Now she'd be able to tell him why.

She looked over at Maddy, her eyebrows raised. 'Now,' she said, slipping Anna's drawing into her bag, 'don't work too hard. Make sure you have a good rest before your early start tomorrow.'

Maddy gave her a mock salute and Esme left her to her work.

# 54

Esme pushed her trolley away from the supermarket checkout and out towards the exit. A woman, dressed in a long black coat, her frizzy grey hair pulled back into a clasp at her neck, stood in the entrance lobby, holding a charity collection box and in earnest conversation with a uniformed supermarket employee. Esme hesitated as she went past, trying to think why the woman's face looked familiar. It wasn't until she'd gone through the automatic doors that she realised why. The charity she was collecting for was LOST - Esme recognised the logo on the box - and she'd seen the woman holding it in the photograph in the charity shop. It was Penny Collins, the charity's founder.

Esme wheeled her shopping over to her car and unloaded the bags into the boot. She returned her trolley to the undercover trolley park and headed back into the supermarket's entrance lobby.

Penny was talking to an elderly couple. As Esme approached, the man pushed a note into the box before the pair turned and walked away.

Esme stepped forward and posted a few coins into the box.

'What's going to happen to these charity box collections if we become a cashless society like banks keep telling us?' she said.

'Yes, someone else said that earlier,' Penny said. 'We have loads of events where I live - fundraisers of one kind or another - and cash is king. I mean, where would the village fete be without it?'

'True enough,' Esme said. She held out her hand. 'I really ought to introduce myself. Esme Quentin. I called in the shop the other day and spoke to Baz.'

Penny shook Esme's hand. 'Oh, yes,' she said. 'It's good to meet you. I'm sorry I've not got back to you. I intended to email you, but we've been so busy, I'm all behind myself.' She indicated the collecting box. 'I shouldn't really be here now, but the guy who was supposed to do it went down with flu.' A little boy came over to her clutching something in his hand and she bent down so he could reach to put his coins in the slot. She thanked him with a smile and he skipped back to his mother waiting with a pushchair next to a depleted pile of orange pumpkins on special offer for Halloween.

Penny returned her attention to Esme. 'Ordinarily, I'd not share information due to data protection and confidentiality, as I'm sure Baz would have explained. But it's not really relevant in your case, as I'm afraid I didn't turn up anything in our files about your Ellen Tucker.'

'I'm not surprised, to be honest,' Esme said. 'As I told Baz, I'm not sure that she was ever a missing person or wether she just left the area without leaving a forwarding address. She certainly wasn't happy here so it could be that she chose deliberately not to keep in touch with anyone.'

'It happens,' Penny said, nodding.

'I understand there was no happy outcome for you,' Esme said. 'I'm so sorry. It must be hard never to know the truth of what happened.'

'It is. Never goes away. In a way, setting up the charity saved my sanity.'

'Prompted by someone else in a similar situation, Baz said?'

'Different circumstances, same angst,' Penny said, with a sad smile. 'And very little in the way of clues, too. Just like in my sister's case. Debbie had gone to meet her boyfriend. Never arrived. Never came home. Other than the confusion over whether he'd been expecting her, nothing seemed out of the ordinary.'

'Confusion?'

'They'd only been going out a few weeks,' Penny said, her voice almost monotone. Esme guessed she must have told the story hundreds of times. There was a sad resignation about her delivery. 'Scott was going off to university so perhaps he didn't see it as a serious relationship. Maybe Debbie had felt the opposite, I don't really know. If she had, I'm sure she'd have made it clear to him. She wasn't backward in coming forward, was Debbie. Anyway, whatever she'd said or not said, he wasn't expecting her to visit that day, so didn't realise she hadn't arrived. Perhaps that lost time might have made a difference to us finding her.'

Esme gave a slow nod in acknowledgment. She was no stranger to the negative impact of *if only* and the toxic effect it could have on one's state of mind over time.

'So,' Penny said, taking a breath and forcing a smile, 'what will you do next? She isn't a family member, I gather. It's a part of some genealogical research?'

'Yes, that's right. I have no emotional ties with her. It all started because a private investigator came asking questions about her. It was only later I discovered she was tied in to some family history I was researching.'

'A private investigator?'

'Yes, that's right. Sean Carlton. Perhaps he approached you too?'

Penny pursed her lips. 'I don't remember him saying he was a private investigator.'

Esme's stomach gave a lurch. 'So he did approach you, then?'

Penny flushed and gave an embarrassed laugh. 'Walked into that one, didn't I? Perhaps I shouldn't have said that.'

'About three weeks ago, it would have been,' Esme continued, hoping Penny wouldn't clam up. 'He was the poor guy who drowned in his car when it went off the quay.'

'Oh, God, yes. That was horrible, wasn't it?' Penny said, grimacing. 'Was it really three weeks ago? Time whizzes past so quickly, doesn't it? I lose track.'

'So you do recall him?' Esme said. 'Tall and thin, smartly dressed. Cropped blond hair.'

'No, couldn't have been him,' Penny said, shaking her head. 'This guy had dark hair with a beard. Wearing a brown leather jacket.'

Esme flinched. The man who'd been watching their stall in the market.

'Oh yes,' Penny added, holding out the collection box to a shopper dipping into her purse. 'He was Canadian.'

*

Esme walked back to her car, sifting everything Penny had said around in her head. She'd been unable to squeeze anything further from the charity's founder. Clearly Penny felt she'd said more than enough already.

So who was the mystery man? Another private investigator, hired by whoever had hired Sean Carlton, to pick up the case following Carlton's demise? It would make perfect sense.

To begin with, the thought comforted her. Until she realised that any private eye would have made the nature of his business known – which he'd clearly not done so with Penny – and he'd approach people who he considered had useful information, not scurry away if he was challenged. So who was he?

She sighed and clicked the key fob to unlock the car. Pity she'd not acted quicker when she'd spied him at the market. Now it was going to be pure luck if she saw him again, unless she wanted to hang around in The Kings Arms on the off chance that he'd turn up. And given the likelihood that she'd bump into Drew and Alec, the idea didn't appeal. Maybe Harry could put the word out? She must mention it to Maddy. Or perhaps the bearded man would turn up at the market on

Saturday. If he did, she thought, climbing into the driver's seat, she'd be ready for him.

*

Back at the cottage, she unpacked her groceries and lit a fire. By the time she'd eaten, she'd forced her concerns over the mystery man to the back of her mind. The sight of the flickering flames through the glass of the wood-burning stove added to her sense of comfort, the smell of the woodsmoke creating its own quality of reassurance.

Until, with a jerk, Morris's story of Bessie Brannock being shoved into the kitchen fire thrust its way into Esme's consciousness and she flinched. She snatched up a cushion and hugged it to herself as Maddy might cuddle one of her cats. Perhaps, if she decided to take on the cottage Ruth was so keen for her to buy, she should consider having a pet of her own. Another living soul to share the ups and downs of life.

# 55

Anna was hunched over a pile of papers at her desk when Esme arrived at her office the following morning. She looked up as Esme peered round the door, and smiled.

'Not disturbing you, am I?' Esme said, noticing the dark shadows under Anna's eyes. She closed the door and wrapped her coat around her, against the damp chill of the office. It was flimsy in construction, little more than a shed, gaps in the feather-edge boarding walls that were slowly rotting away, letting in the cold outside air. The portable gas heater in the corner threw out little warmth, despite the optimism of its orange glow. It was obvious why Anna was so determined to press ahead with the refurbishment of the mill and invest in the more substantial stone building.

'If you are, it's because I need disturbing,' Anna said. 'I'm getting nowhere with these invoices. I can't concentrate.'

Esme frowned. 'Can't you employ someone else to do that sort of thing?'

'I do, as a rule. But she's on maternity leave, so needs must.' She tapped her bump and smiled. 'Timing, eh? It must be something in the air. Even Gypsy's getting in on it. She's expecting kittens.'

'Oh, how lovely,' Esme said, smiling. 'Congratulations!'

'Thank you. I think. Let's hope I can find them all homes when the time comes.' Anna closed the file and sat back in her chair. 'So what can I do for you? Any new stories about the mill?' She indicated a well-worn office chair on the other side of the desk.

Esme sat down, dropping her bag on to the floor. 'Yes, I do have some, actually. Though primarily, I wanted to see if you were OK.'

Anna sighed. 'Yes, it wasn't very edifying, was it? Sorry.'

'No,' Esme said, shaking her head, 'you don't need to apologise. It must have been horrible for you.'

Anna stood up. 'I need a cup of tea. I'm gasping. You?'

Esme nodded and smiled. 'Where would we be without tea?' she said.

Anna filled the kettle from the tatty stainless steel sink in the corner of the room and plugged it in. 'I think all this poking around in the past is getting to Mum,' she said, dropping two teabags into mugs.

'Oh?' Esme said, turning round in her seat and looking over at Anna.

'She's been a bit fractious. With Dad, especially. I expect hearing that name again has raked up old wounds for both of them.'

'Oh, I'm sorry.' Esme felt her cheeks burning. She wondered if Daniel had confessed to Marianne about his teenage wedding.

'It's not your fault, Esme,' Anna said, folding her arms. 'This all started because that private investigator came asking questions.'

'Yes, but I can't help feeling that what I've uncovered has only fanned the flames.'

'You weren't to know that. You were just doing some family history.'

Esme looked away, brushing a mark off her jeans and recalling what she'd said to Maddy the day before about unintended consequences.

The kettle boiled and Anna filled the mugs, dunking the teabags and discarding them in the bin. She brought over the mugs and put them on the desk.

'Thanks,' Esme said, picking up a mug. 'Talking of private

detectives, no one else has been around asking questions, have they? About Ellen Tucker, I mean.'

Anna stirred her tea and peered at Esme over the rim of the mug. 'No,' she said, her tone wary. She put down the mug. 'Why are you asking?'

'Oh, nothing specific,' Esme said, trying to make light of it. 'There's a charity in town, supports families whose loved ones have gone missing. Apparently, Ellen Tucker's name had been mentioned to one of their staff.'

'And this wasn't by the person you saw?'

'Not Sean Carlton, no. This was more recently. A Canadian, so I was told.'

Anna stared for a moment before giving Esme a cross between a shrug and a shake of the head. 'So,' she said, flipping her plait over her shoulder, 'what's new on the mill history?'

'It's about Sarah Brannock, actually.'

Anna inclined her head. 'The woman who murdered her father?'

'Yes, that's her. It turns out she was pregnant when she was convicted. She gave birth to her baby in prison and called her Hope.'

Anna's brow furrowed. 'Oh bless. If that doesn't express her despair, I don't know what could.'

'No, it's quite poignant, isn't it? It seems from then on, the name Hope was passed down through the generations.' Esme hesitated and sipped her tea. In any other circumstances, she'd explain how Anna shared her ancestry with Ellen Tucker. But it wouldn't be appropriate. The association with Ellen was still too raw. She should, though, fulfil her promise to Maddy.

'Before I forget,' she said, putting down her mug and reaching into her bag, 'I also came to give you back this.' She took out Anna's drawing and laid it down on the desk between them. 'I know you told Maddy to throw it away, but we felt it was best that you do that, if that's what you want.'

Anna stared down at the picture. Esme wondered what was going through her head. Was she reliving that night? Deciding whether to dispose of the offending drawing?

Esme picked up her tea and sipped it. 'How are the baby preparations coming along?' she said, determined to turn the conversation on to a more positive subject.

For the first time since Esme had arrived, Anna's face brightened. 'Good thanks. We've started a list.' She counted off the items on her fingers, explaining which things they'd already bought and which she intended borrowing from friends and family. 'Oh, and I've decided how we're going to decorate the bedroom. Nursery. I must remember to call it the nursery.' She wagged a finger. 'And I've told Mum, it's not going to be pink. I'm not succumbing to the advertising industry's hype. We're going neutral.'

Esme laughed. 'Good for you,' she said. 'I thought we'd done away with all that rigid pink-blue stuff, but it seems worse than ever. It's as if there are no other colours.'

'Exactly what I said.' Anna stood up, looping the handles of the empty mugs together and carrying them over to the draining board. 'I know there's still plenty of time before she arrives,' she said, turning on the taps, 'but it's fun thinking of things.'

Esme twisted round in her chair. 'The time will go quicker than you think,' she said. 'Might as well get ahead.'

Anna looked at Esme over her shoulder. 'I have this idea of painting a huge mural on one wall,' she said, sweeping her arm through the air in an arc. Her hand caught one of the mugs and sent it crashing into the sink. 'Oh, God. Stupid me. How did I manage to do that?' She reached into the sink and shrieked.

'Oh, no! What have you done?' Esme said, getting up out of her chair and hurrying over to Anna. The mug lay in shards in the sink and Anna's hand was bleeding into the swirling water. 'Where's your First Aid kit?' Esme said, reaching over to turn off the tap before scanning round the room. She noticed a dark green plastic box on top of the filing cabinet, a white cross on its lid. 'Well, that was clever, I must say,' she teased, fetching the case and laying it on the draining board. 'Let's stem the flow, first,' she said, pulling out two paper towels from the dispenser above the sink. 'Then I'll see what I can do about a plaster. Do you want to give me your hand?'

But Anna didn't move. She remained fixed, staring down into the sink, as though she hadn't heard Esme speak. Esme took hold of Anna's wrist, gently pulling it closer so she could wrap the towels around her hand.

'Come on, Anna,' she said, quietly. 'Let's get you cleaned up.'

Suddenly Anna went rigid and gave out a long, shuddering sob. 'I saw,' she whispered. 'I saw the blood through the window.'

Esme blinked, unable to speak as Anna's red blotchy face morphed into the image of Ellen Tucker, staring out of the cottage window. Screaming, not yelling.

Anna turned and gripped Esme's arm. 'Oh my God,' she said, her body shaking and her mouth agape. 'Did Mum kill her, Esme? Is that why she was in such a state?'

They both looked round as the door opened and Marianne stepped into the office.

# 56

For a moment, the three of them stood, motionless – Esme and Anna at the sink, Marianne on the threshold of the office door.

'What's happened?' Marianne said.

'Anna cut herself on a broken mug,' Esme said. 'I was about to bandage her up. Perhaps you'd give me a hand.'

'Oh, poor girl,' Marianne said, pulling the door closed behind her. 'Of course.'

'No,' Anna said, backing away and holding her damaged hand protectively against her chest. She sniffed. 'It'll be fine. Just a simple plaster will do.'

Esme frowned. 'I'm not sure it will,' she said. 'It's quite a gash.'

'Perhaps I should take you up to the hospital, darling,' Marianne said.

'No,' Anna repeated with a vigorous shake of her head. 'I'm not spending hours in A&E for a silly cut on my hand.'

Esme turned and delved around in the First Aid box. 'Maybe there are some steri-strips in here. That'll make a better job of it. Ah, here we are.' She guided Anna to the office chair at the desk. 'You sit there a moment.'

Marianne stood behind Anna with a troubled expression, watching Esme apply the dressings. Surely she must have sensed an atmosphere, but perhaps she didn't know how to address it. She slid round to the other side of the desk and sat down on the office chair.

'Are you sure you're all right?' she said, frowning at Anna. 'You do look a bit strained. Aren't you sleeping?' She reached out across the desk, but Anna pulled back.

'Hey, careful,' Esme said. 'I can't do this if you're wriggling.' She glanced up and saw Marianne's eyes settle on Anna's drawing, still lying on the desk.

Marianne pulled it towards her. 'What's this?' She picked it up and studied it.

Anna fixed her gaze on the picture, but didn't respond.

'It's a drawing Anna did years ago,' Esme said. 'Maddy found it while she was restoring the writing box.' So Anna hadn't mentioned the drawing to her mother.

Esme secured a piece of gauze over the steri-strips and patted Anna on the shoulder. 'There, all done.' She closed the First Aid box and returned it to the top of the filing cabinet before going over to the sink to wash her hands.

'I drew it after that night,' Anna said. Her voice was cold, and having avoided eye contact with her mother before, she was now watching Marianne intently. 'Seeing that started me into remembering.'

Marianne stared at Anna for a moment, her face pale and taut. 'Well, it's all over now,' she said, dropping the drawing back on the desk.

'Except it isn't, Mum.' Anna leaned towards Marianne. 'I've remembered something else.'

Esme detected a fleeting moment of alarm in Marianne's expression before she composed herself.

'Anna,' Marianne said, with a tired smile, 'aren't you getting this a little bit out of proportion? It was all a long time ago. I know it was a difficult time, I understand that.' She pushed the drawing away with one finger, as though it was contaminated. 'But it's not healthy to dwell on it, it really isn't.'

'I looked in at the window,' Anna said in a small voice.

Marianne's smile wavered a little. 'You're imagining things, Anna. It's perfectly obvious that by looking at that picture,' she flicked her hand at it, 'you've conjured up all sorts of horrible...'

'Was she dead?' Anna said. 'You were standing over her. There was blood on the floor.' She swallowed. 'Did you kill her?'

Marianne's head shot up and she glared at Esme, her face distorted with anger. 'Have you put this despicable idea in her head?'

'Of course she didn't,' Anna snapped, anger giving her strength now. She thrust out her chin. 'What am I supposed to think when you're standing over her, looking down...' She buried her head in her hands and began to shake.

Esme put her arms around Anna's shoulders, her eyes drawn to the picture. Not yelling, not even screaming. Ellen was already dead. She looked up as Marianne reached across the table and laid a hand on Anna's arm.

'Oh, Anna,' Marianne said. 'How could you think such a thing? Of course I didn't kill her. That's how I found her.' Tears were falling down Marianne's cheeks now. 'I'm as horrified by what happened as you, I can promise you.'

'So why didn't you report it?' Esme asked, striving to keep the accusation out of her voice, concerned Marianne might clam up. 'Everyone's under the impression Ellen left. That's what you told us before, even though you knew it wasn't true.'

Marianne bowed her head. 'I didn't know what to do. I was in shock.'

Esme took a breath and slowly released it, as she tried to keep control of her emotions. There was something more here. She could sense it. She cleared her throat.

'So you came away, drove back to the farm, and then what? Did you tell Daniel?'

Marianne turned away. 'I don't remember.'

Esme frowned and shook her head. 'Come on, Marianne. You've just found a woman lying in a pool of blood in your cottage. Why didn't you pick up the phone and call an ambulance?'

'It was obvious she was dead. What was the point?'

'The police, then?'

Marianne looked away. 'I wasn't thinking straight.'

Esme let her arms drop to her sides and stood upright. 'Or you *were* thinking straight. And decided it would be so much better if everyone thought she'd moved out. Why was that, Marianne? Is that because you know who killed her?'

Another sob escaped from Anna and she turned to look at Esme with terrified eyes. 'There was someone else there,' she murmured.

Esme met Anna's gaze. 'What?'

Anna grabbed the drawing and dragged it towards her. She pointed to the darkened, intense scribbles on the edge of her picture.

'There, outside,' she said, with a shuddering breath. 'There was someone outside. Who was it, Mum?'

Marianne scoffed. 'I'm supposed to identify who that is from a child's drawing? Are you mad?'

'That's not what Anna's asking,' Esme said, indicating the picture. 'That's Anna's record that she saw *someone*. Who was it, Marianne?' And as a sudden realisation came into her head, 'Who are you trying to protect?'

'Mum!' Anna implored, her face streaked with tears. 'Was it Dad? Did Dad kill Ellen Tucker? Is that why you won't tell me?'

Marianne said nothing at first, her lips pressed together as she stared defiantly at her daughter. But it seemed Anna's distress was too much for her. She bowed her head and began silently sobbing.

# 57

The office felt oppressive suddenly, a complete contrast to the chill Esme had felt when she'd walked in a while ago. When was that? It felt like hours.

Esme dropped on to a stool beside the shredder, struggling to absorb the implication of Marianne's silent confession. The only sounds came from the passing cars on the road outside and the clicking of the portable heater as the metal expanded and contracted.

'I should never have gone down there,' Marianne said, eventually. She stared down at the desk, her tone flat. 'Daniel told me not to. I should have listened to him. He knew what I'd find.'

'He told you what he'd done?' Esme said, shocked. She glanced round at Anna, who seemed lost in her thoughts, detached.

Marianne's head snapped up. 'No, of course not.' She glared at Esme, her eyes shining. 'What do you take me for? Some sort of sadistic voyeur? I just thought he was trying to stop me turning her out of the cottage. That he believed he'd be able to convince me that she could stay. But I'd had enough. I wasn't going to turn a blind eye any longer.'

'What happened?' Esme asked. She spoke quietly, as though any louder and the spell of uncovering the truth might be broken.

Marianne shrugged. 'He'd walked out in the middle of a row earlier. I guessed then that he'd gone to her. I even accused him of it when he got back.'

'And did he admit he'd been to see her?'

Marianne tossed her head, her lips pinched. 'Oh, yes. He felt sorry for her. He was always pointing out how bad people treated her. But he was talking to the wrong person if he thought I'd be sympathetic.'

'So when you got back from the cottage, after finding Ellen, was Daniel there?'

Marianne looked down at her hands. 'Tinkering in the barn. He could hardly have left, could he? Anna was upstairs in bed. He wouldn't have left her on her own.'

Esme again glanced at Anna. 'Except now you know she wasn't. She'd been with you.'

Marianne blinked away tears. 'Yes,' she said, sniffing. She reached across the table and took Anna's hand. 'Poor darling.'

Anna pulled her hand away and recoiled back into her chair. She narrowed her eyes at Marianne.

'I can't believe what you did,' she said, her voice hoarse and her face blotchy. 'How could you bring me up championing honesty and integrity when all the time...' her voice cracked.

'I was thinking of you!' Marianne cried. 'How would life have been for you with a father arrested for murder, the police prying into our private affairs? We would have had to move away to somewhere no one knew us, lose our home, lose everything that's been in my family for generations.'

Anna stared down into her lap and said nothing.

'So when Daniel came in from the barn...' Esme began.

'Oh, he didn't,' Marianne said, shaking her head. 'He went out again. And when he came back...hours later, it was... I was sitting at the kitchen table. The Rayburn had gone out. It was cold, but I hadn't noticed. When the door rattled, it was as though I'd come out of a trance.' She pressed her fingers against her lips and stared into the middle distance, as though reliving the image. 'He faltered when he saw me. Then he said, "You don't have to worry any longer, she's gone." I just stared at him. Then he said, "We don't need to say anything about it again."

'And you never discussed it? Ever?' Esme asked.

Marianne shook her head.

Anna's phone buzzed on the desk and the screen lit up. Esme saw Drew's name on the screen. Anna snatched the phone and stood up, wiping her nose with the back of her hand.

'Drew? Where are you?' She walked across the room, the phone to her ear, listening. 'I'm on my way,' she said, after a moment. She cut the call and slipped the phone into her back pocket. 'I'm going home to Drew,' she said, her lip quivering.

'Anna, please,' began Marianne, as Anna walked towards the door. 'You won't say anything to him, will you?'

Anna's only answer was a glare before she walked out of the office, letting the door close behind her with a bang.

Esme and Marianne sat without moving, listening to the engine of Anna's pick-up as she started it up and drove out of the yard.

Esme looked across the desk at Marianne, wondering what she was thinking. She must be asking herself whether anything would ever be the same again between her and Anna. But how could it? How did anyone cope with the discovery that their mother was guilty of covering up a violent crime? And worse, that the crime had been carried out by their father. And what would Anna say to Daniel? What would his reaction be to Marianne's confession? No wonder they'd never rented out the cottage again. Perhaps that was part of the psychology in dealing with the aftermath. Shut the place up and pretend it had never happened.

'So what will you do now?' Esme said, breaking the silence.

Marianne took a deep breath. 'Do?'

'Will you go to the police yourself or try and persuade Daniel to?'

'I don't plan to do either,' Marianne said, standing up. 'Nothing's changed. Ellen Tucker left Bideford 24 years ago of her own free will. That's what everyone believes and that's what they'll continue to believe.'

'But you've just told me and Anna something completely different,' Esme said, getting to her feet. 'You can't, surely, believe we're going to say nothing about it?'

'I really don't know what you're talking about. And I'd warn you against upsetting Anna at the moment. She's under enough stress as it is. You don't want to be responsible for her losing the baby, do you?' Marianne wheeled the office chair under the desk. 'And now I think it's time you left. I need to lock up.'

Esme stared in disbelief, as though she'd just woken from a disturbing dream. She stumbled out of the office and across the yard to the car park. Was Marianne really that naive? Did she imagine Esme would simply shrug and forget everything she had just confessed?

By the time Esme reached her car, she was furious with herself. Why hadn't she stood up to Marianne? Why hadn't she pointed out that the police would be very interested in what she'd have to say in light of Sean Carlton's investigation into Ellen Tucker's whereabouts?

But if Marianne had maintained for this long that Ellen had left of her own accord, she would just play her part as she'd done before. And ironically, if Carlton had spoken to Daniel at the farm, as Daniel had alleged, and had been convinced the Meddons knew nothing, any case notes he'd left behind would confirm Marianne's claim.

And what about Anna? Would she back Esme? Despite the friction between mother and daughter, might Marianne yet persuade Anna that it was in everyone's best interests to say nothing, exactly as she'd decided in 1995? What incentive did Anna have to destroy her family?

Esme unlocked the car and climbed inside. She fished out her phone and put it in her lap, dropping her bag down in the passenger footwell. She closed her eyes with a sigh and leaned back against the headrest. What would happen if she went to the police? How would they respond? Would they believe her insistence, that there was more to Ellen's story which needed investigation? Should she share what she and Maddy had found at Ted's? She clicked her tongue. If only they knew who'd sent Ted that file, they could speak to him or her, use them as an ally.

But they didn't know. Which meant she had to act alone. Would the police believe her if she told them what Marianne had told her? Or would it, in the end, come down to a simple case of Marianne's word against Esme's?

She picked up her phone, scrolled to Maddy's number and made the call. But it switched immediately to voicemail. Maddy must be driving, on her way back from the auction. Esme disconnected. This wasn't something to leave in a message. She'd call her in the morning. They were meeting up in the afternoon. Plenty of time to talk it over and decide what to do.

She started the car and pulled out of the car park. From the corner of her eye, she saw Marianne standing outside Anna's office, watching her drive away.

# 58

Esme wasn't surprised at her sleepless night. She dragged herself out of bed when it was clear her overactive mind wasn't going to allow her the respite of sleeping in late. After forcing herself to eat breakfast, she clambered up the steep cliff path overlooking the cottage and stood on the headland, staring out to sea and allowing the gusts of wind to penetrate her numb state. Only when she felt the chill through her jacket, did she climb back down the path and return to her cottage. She picked up her phone and with a deep breath, dialled Maddy's number.

*

Later, in Ted's living room, Esme perched on the sofa and, with Maddy sitting cross-legged on the edge of the hearth, they talked through what had taken place the day before.

'Marianne's living on a different planet,' Maddy said, shaking her head. 'And Anna, poor little Anna. No wonder she'd buried the secret so deeply.'

'It seems to have been a pact between Marianne and Daniel,' Esme said, 'that they'd never talk about it again.'

'And neither of them had any idea that Anna had witnessed everything?'

'Well, not everything, thank God,' Esme said. 'At least she hadn't seen the actual murder. Can you imagine what damage that would have done? It was bad enough as it was.' Something else flitted into her head, but evaporated before she could fix on it.

Maddy shifted position, hugging her knees. 'And of course it's that – your empathy towards Anna – that Marianne's using to emotionally blackmail you into keeping quiet.'

Esme nodded. 'So what do I do? In theory, by not speaking to the police, I'm withholding information about a crime. But in reality, I have no evidence a crime was committed. Only Anna's drawing, which doesn't really count for anything, and hearsay - what Marianne told me, which she'll deny anyway.'

Maddy's phone rang out from the dining room table and she jumped up to go into the next room to answer it.

'Harry. Hi. How's things?'

Esme stood up and looked around. The room was relatively clear, other than the actual furniture. Shelves were empty and packed boxes were stacked in the corner. Maddy had said something about starting on the bedrooms next. She walked through into the dining room, heading for the stairs.

'I've just said, I can't,' Maddy was saying, a note of agitation in her voice. Her eyes locked on Esme's.

Esme paused. 'Problem?' she mouthed.

Maddy shrugged and rolled her eyes. 'So why can't you just tell me?... Look, Esme's here and we're in the middle... Jeez, Harry, cut it out, you're scaring me.' An impatient sigh. 'OK, OK. You win. See you in a minute.' She cut the call.

'What was all that about?' Esme asked.

'Dunno,' Maddy said, walking over to the hall and snatching her jacket off a coat hook. 'He wants me to meet him at the lifeboat station. ASAP.'

'I'm guessing from the bit of conversation I overhead, he wouldn't say why?'

'You guessed right.'

Esme nodded. 'OK, well, I'll stay here and start...'

'No,' Maddy said. 'He said you should come too.' She looked anxious, her eyebrows drawn together.

'Me?'

*"You both need to hear this"*, is what he said.'

*

Esme and Maddy left Ted's house on foot and headed down Appledore's narrow streets to the lifeboat station, the wind spitting with rain and buffeting them as they walked. As they emerged on to the quay from the shelter of the buildings, Esme had to hang on to her hood to stop it from being whipped off her head.

She glanced round at Maddy. 'You OK?' she said, seeing Maddy's worried expression.

'Yeah, fine,' Maddy said, striding a little faster. 'I have a hunch I know what this is about.'

'Yeah?' Esme said, increasing her speed to keep up. 'What?'

'Some guy tried to talk to me as I came out of Dad's the other week.'

'What did he want?'

'Ah well, that's just it. It was getting dark and he stepped out of the shadows. I nearly had heart failure and he apologised for freaking me out, basically, then walked off.' Maddy glanced round at Esme. 'He said something about speaking to me another time. I got the impression it was about Dad.'

'Perhaps he just wanted to pass on his condolences?'

'Yeah, that's what I assumed afterwards. He was wearing a baseball cap with an RNLI logo on, so he could be a volunteer and knew Dad. But I wasn't in the best of moods at the time so I wasn't exactly very welcoming.'

'Hardly surprising, in the circumstances. So why do you think this is about him?'

'Because Harry said it was about Dad and we're meeting at the lifeboat station.' Maddy glanced at Esme. 'Just a coincidence? You know what I think about coincidences.'

'Well,' Esme said as they rounded the corner by the pub, 'you'll find out in a minute.'

As they approached the lifeboat station, Esme could see Harry on the slipway talking to someone. He saw them and waved.

'Looks like your hunch was right,' Esme said. The stranger was wearing a baseball cap and Harry's introduction confirmed it. Jamie was an RNLI volunteer.

'Sorry about the other week,' Jamie said, shaking Maddy's hand. 'My mistake. I shouldn't have assumed you'd recognise me. I've seen you with your dad at some of our fundraising events.'

Maddy nodded. 'Yes, your face is familiar now I can see you properly. Sorry for the brush-off.'

He flapped a hand. 'No worries.'

Maddy turned to Harry. 'So what's with all the cloak-and-dagger?' she said.

Harry nodded at Jamie. 'You'd better tell her what you told me.'

Jamie hesitated, chewing his lip and throwing Harry a nervous glance.

'It's all going to come out at the inquest, anyway,' Harry said. 'But Maddy shouldn't have to wait until then to hear it.'

'The inquest?' Maddy said. She looked at Harry. 'But that's just a formality, right? What more is there to know?'

Jamie hesitated, shifting his weight from one foot to the other. Esme sensed Maddy stiffen beside her.

'So will someone tell me what the hell this is all about?' Maddy said. She looked pointedly at Jamie and waited.

'This isn't easy for me,' Jamie said, his eyes skimming the three of them. 'I knew Ted. He was like family. All our volunteers are.'

'All the more reason, then,' said Harry.

'I honestly didn't give it any thought at the time or I would have said something.' He nodded at Harry. 'But when Harry started asking questions about your dad's accident...'

'What questions?' Maddy said, glaring at Harry.

'Jamie...' said Harry, avoiding her gaze. 'I want Maddy to hear what you've got to tell her first.'

Maddy held up her hand. 'Hey, hang on a minute. Questions

about Dad's accident?' She turned to Harry. 'Why would you be asking about Dad's accident?'

'Just let Jamie tell you...'

'No, I want to know why you were asking questions.'

Harry shook his head. 'I just had an idea, that's all.'

She continued to glare at him. 'Go on.'

'It was something I'd been thinking about...well, to come to the point, I wondered whether your dad's accident wasn't an accident at all.'

'You what?' Maddy stood open mouthed.

Esme watched the confrontation, a nervousness creeping into her body.

'But how could you come to a conclusion like that and not say anything?' Maddy was saying. 'You should have discussed it with me.'

'How could I?' Harry threw back. 'I might have been way off the mark. Then I would have worried you for nothing. I'm sorry. Perhaps I should have warned you.' He looked at Jamie. 'But I wanted Jamie to tell you what he saw and let you decide whether there was anything in it. I didn't want to prejudice your take on it. I might be completely wrong.'

'Even more reason to talk to me about...'

'Come on, you two,' Esme said. 'Perhaps if we hear what Jamie's got to say and then argue about it afterwards?'

Maddy sighed and rubbed her forehead. 'Yes, yes, you're right, Esme.' She turned to Jamie. 'Go on. What is it that I need to know.'

'Look, sorry, I didn't mean to stir things up...' protested Jamie, glancing between Maddy and Harry.

Maddy shook her head. 'Just say it, OK?'

Jamie cleared his throat. 'We found your dad's tender, floating in the estuary, as you know.'

She nodded. 'Yes, and we'd assumed he'd fallen out of it.'

'And that's maybe what happened,' Jamie said.

'Except...' prompted Harry.

'Except that I remember seeing his tender earlier on that evening.'

'He'd gone out more than once?'

Jamie shook his head. 'No, I didn't see him. I saw someone else getting out of it just down there.' He indicated a flight of steps which led down to the water. Esme looked over to where he was pointing, trying to read some significance into his words. 'I only saw him briefly,' Jamie went on, 'but I'm sure it was your dad's tender.'

'How sure?' Maddy said.

'One hundred and one per cent,' Jamie said. 'Bit hard to miss. Bright red with a blue stripe. No one else has got one like it round here.'

Esme was struggling with the significance of his information. Was Jamie saying Ted's tender had been stolen?

'I'm sorry, but I don't understand,' she said, appealing for someone to enlighten her. 'Why does this have a bearing on Maddy's dad's accident?'

'Because when we found his tender floating in the estuary,' Harry explained, 'we thought it must have come loose from his boat when it capsized and floated away.'

'Yes, I know that,' Maddy said, looking between Harry and Jamie. 'Or he might have been untying it when the wave hit. So what's changed?'

'You're missing the point, Madds,' Harry said. 'The tender was *brought* back here, to the quay, by someone, who then let it go again.'

'But who would do that?' Maddy said, staring at him with wide eyes. She turned sharply to Jamie. 'You said you saw them. Who was it? Who did you see in my dad's tender?'

# 59

Back at Ted's house, Esme made tea for them all. She could hear Harry's voice, calmly talking to Maddy, doing his best to convince her that racing back to Bideford to confront Drew Brannock about what he was doing in her dad's tender might be one sure way of ending up the same way as Ted.

As Esme came into the living room, Maddy was perched on the end of the sofa, Harry crouched down in front of her. When he saw Esme with the tray, he stood up and fetched a small table from the back of the room, before dropping down in the armchair beside the fire.

'Nature's shock remedy,' Esme said, putting down the tray. 'Super-sweet tea. Thanks, Harry.'

'I'd rather have gin,' Maddy grumbled.

'There isn't any,' Esme said, sitting down next to her. 'So this'll have to do.' She picked up a mug and handed it over to Maddy, before looking up at Harry. 'I didn't sugar yours,' she said, with a half-smile. 'You're quite safe.'

Maddy gripped the mug. 'I know I've said some pretty derogatory things about Drew Brannock over the years but to think that he would...' She sniffed and took a shuddering breath. 'And all because of some antisocial behaviour he did years ago as a kid. I don't get it.'

'You think it was cos of that?' Harry said.

'What else would it be?' Maddy looked up at him, her face puckered. 'And tell me again what you meant about *asking questions*. Since when?'

'Since I found out that Drew and Alec were drinking together with your private-eye buddy that night. Though it was just a vague idea at the time.'

Maddy's jaw dropped and Esme looked at him in alarm.

'You think Drew was involved in Carlton's drowning, too?' Esme said.

'Why not? If he thought Carlton was close to finding out the truth about what happened to Ellen Tucker.' He frowned. 'You do suspect something did happen to her, right? Isn't that what this has all been about?'

'Yes,' Esme said, glancing at Maddy. 'Though, until yesterday, we were never sure she didn't just walk away.'

'Yesterday?' Harry said, inclining his head quizzically. 'Not because of this?'

'No.' Esme told Harry what she'd learned about how Daniel had killed Ellen and how he and Marianne had covered it up.

'Daniel? Why? How?'

Esme shook her head. 'I don't know how it happened.' She hesitated before saying, 'Daniel and Ellen knew each other before, in their teens. I think she came looking for him, causing friction between him and Marianne.' She recalled wondering about the choice Daniel had made. Had Ellen expected him to leave Marianne and go with her? Did they argue and things got out of hand?

'So Drew didn't play a part in Ellen's murder?'

'We don't know that,' Maddy said, suddenly alert. 'What if Drew was there that night, playing silly buggers with his mates, with cat calls and witch taunts? Maybe he saw Daniel kill her. Maybe he's held it over Daniel all these years, their dirty little secret.' Her gaze dropped down and she stared again into her mug. 'And then Dad found out.'

'We don't know he *did* find out,' Esme said. 'Only that he was trying to. And as such, he was a threat to uncovering something.' She looked at Maddy. 'Do you remember, the other day when we were talking about your dad being right

292

in the middle of it, in the very place where the Ellen Tucker mystery originated?' She looked over to Harry. 'We can't be sure whether it was Carlton who set him thinking or whether he'd recalled the case himself, but it would've been natural for him to start asking questions.'

'And so alerting Drew Brannock to the fact that he was interested in what happened,' Harry said, nodding. He got up from the chair and again crouched down in front of Maddy. 'So, have you got it yet, why you can't go storming up to Moody-Boy and shout your mouth off? We have to go at this another way.' He stood up and downed the last of his tea, before replacing the mug on the tray and checking his watch. 'Now, I'm gonna catch up with Jamie and make sure he tells his story to the right authority before close of play.'

'Which is?' Esme asked.

Harry rubbed his chin. 'Not sure. The police is the obvious one, but with there being an accident inquiry imminent, we might get more traction going down that route. I'm going to ask a mate who knows about these things. Don't forget - seeing Drew with your dad's tender is only circumstantial. I'm pretty sure the police wouldn't give it a second glance without something more to go on. Same for the car dunking in the Torridge.' He bent over and kissed the top of Maddy's head. 'See you tomorrow. Don't forget I'm working late tonight.'

'Don't worry, I'll look after her,' Esme said. He nodded and left the house.

For a while, neither of them spoke, Maddy sitting with her head down, staring at the floor, Esme silently sifting through questions in her mind. How long would they have to wait to hear back from Harry and Jamie? And if Jamie's account was taken seriously, would that be the time to pass on her conversation with Marianne?

But then the image of Anna's distraught face came into her mind, along with another question. How was Anna going to react to the suggestion that Drew was implicated in Ted's death? Esme closed her eyes and took a deep breath. It was all such a mess.

She looked round at Maddy, who was still staring at the floor. 'What are you thinking?' she asked.

Maddy took a sip of tea, grimaced and put the mug back on the tray. 'Exactly what it is I'm going to say to Drew Brannock in the moments before I throttle him.'

'I have to admit, I'm a bit lost as to Drew's motive, here,' Esme said. 'I can see Daniel panicking if your Dad started asking questions. But on your own assessment of Drew, can you seriously see him putting himself out to do something so… abhorrent for Daniel's benefit?'

Maddy stood up. 'Like I said before, we don't know what part Drew played. He could be more implicated than we think. He could have been covering his own back, not Daniel's.'

'Covering his own back for what?'

'Well, I don't know, do I?'

Esme sighed. 'Well, there's little we can do about it now,' she said. 'We have to wait for Harry's feedback from Jamie reporting to the coroner or police or whoever. Look, what about carrying on here? Might take your mind off things.'

Maddy's mouth was fixed in a thin line, lips pressed tightly together. 'I suppose,' she said. 'How long d'you think they'll be?'

'No idea. Why don't you give Harry a call in an hour, say, and get an update? He should know more by then. Now,' she said, getting to her feet, 'if I remember rightly, you'd planned to start on the bedrooms next. You up for it?'

'Yeah, give me a minute. I'll just clear this lot.' Maddy picked up the tray of mugs and disappeared into the kitchen. Esme grabbed a couple of cardboard boxes from the supply behind the sofa and took them upstairs. She wondered what had gone on between Marianne and Anna since yesterday's revelation. Was it only yesterday? It seemed much longer. The thought reminded her of her disturbed night and she felt her energy sap. As she went into the first bedroom, she was tempted to collapse on to the bed and catch up on her sleep, salve her frazzled brain and escape from the frantic theories exhausting her.

She squeezed her eyes shut and opened them again, before giving her head a shake and wandering over to the window. She peered out across the garden to the narrow track beyond. The rain of earlier had eased, but it had morphed into a heavy mist, muting what daylight remained so that the outdoor lamp had come on prematurely. A group of children came giggling down the track, returning from school, she assumed. One of them carried a stick with something hanging on it, flickering. As they went past, Esme saw it was a small pumpkin, a grotesque face carved out of the flesh and a light within. She'd forgotten it was Halloween. Did this mean that tomorrow Anna's tormentors would cease their campaign? Or was she being naive in hoping it was that simple?

She turned back into the room. This wasn't getting anything done. She marched over to the bed for a box, scanning around to decide where to begin. What was Maddy doing? Was she OK? She cocked an ear. It had gone very quiet down there. She stepped out on to the landing and called Maddy's name as she heard footsteps in the dining room below. Sounded like she was on her way up.

Esme turned back towards the bedroom just as the front door slammed, echoing up the stairs and leaving a tell-tale silence. She retraced her steps and hurried down the staircase.

'Maddy? Are you there?'

Downstairs was empty. Maddy's jacket was gone, as was her phone and the keys to her van. And Esme had a pretty good idea where she was heading. To the reclamation yard to tackle Drew Brannock.

# 60

Maddy knew she didn't have long before Esme worked out where she was going. She hurried down the alley and out into the street to her campervan, hunkering down against the intermittent rain. A white Vauxhall Corsa was parked in tightly behind her – a hire car, judging by the logo on the side door – and for a moment she panicked that it'd boxed her in. But she managed to manoeuvre out of the space without too much difficulty before speeding off up the hill out of Appledore.

As she reached the bend at the top, her phone started ringing on the seat next to her, making her jump. She usually set it to silent when she was driving. But she ignored it anyway. She guessed it would be Esme, trying to get hold of her to convince her that tackling Drew on her own was a bad idea. Well, that was easy for her to say. And for Harry, for that matter. It wasn't their dad who'd died, leaving a big question mark hanging as to how. And it wasn't good enough what Harry said, that the evidence was all circumstantial. That was just a different way of viewing coincidences. And there'd been far too many of those.

She pulled out on to the main road between Westward Ho! and Bideford into a stream of vehicles queuing to get on to the roundabout at the end of the new Bideford bridge. As they crawled along, she checked her rear view mirror for any sign of Esme. She couldn't see her Peugeot, but the badly parked white Vauxhall was in the queue behind her, a few cars back. Slowly she moved closer to the end of the left-hand lane and spent a frustrating few minutes waiting for a gap in the traffic.

Eventually she entered the roundabout and took the exit down into town.

As she drove along the quay and passed The Kings Arms, she thought of Harry and wondered if Esme would try and get hold of him to tell him what she was up to. But even if Esme had his number, which she doubted, Harry was likely to be incommunicado in some solicitor's office somewhere, if he and Jamie had decided to report what Jamie had witnessed to the coroner. After that, he'd be heading off to the pub, working late at the Halloween themed evening. It wouldn't be until tomorrow that she'd have to deal with his disapproval, and by then, she wouldn't care. She'd have told Drew Brannock just what she thought of him.

Despite the inclement weather, a few Trick or Treaters were already out and about. She had to stop at the crossing for two child-sized zombies and a skeleton, huddled under their mother's misshapen umbrella. The dull glow of the street lamps lit up the luminous bone-work on the skeleton's outfit. The three of them made ghoulish gestures at the vehicles at the traffic lights as they went, receiving a scolding from the adult for messing about while crossing the road.

The lights changed and Maddy pulled away. She glanced in her mirror and noticed the white Vauxhall was still behind her, its headlights on full beam. Something about the way it closed in on her made her nervous. She pressed her foot down and accelerated away, slipping neatly between a bus and a pick-up as she crossed the mini-roundabout at the end of the Old Bridge. She sped along the quay and took the turn to Torrington before she dared look back. The road was clear. Whoever it was had either been left behind at the roundabout or had gone another way. She took a deep breath, slowed down and told herself to relax.

The gloom of the approaching dusk swallowed up the van as she passed the no-limits signs. The windscreen wipers droned back and forth and she sensed, rather than saw, the choppy waters of the River Torridge churning in turbulent currents in the shadows on her left-hand side.

She reached the reclamation yard and slowed to negotiate the entrance. She pulled into the car park and got out of the van, thinking what she'd say to Anna if she encountered her before Drew. Probably not a great idea to mention anything yet. She hesitated beside the van and, for the first time, questioned her impulsive decision. Perhaps she should have thought this through before she set off.

The roar of an engine startled her. Maddy turned, expecting to see Esme's car coming through the gate. But it wasn't Esme. It was the white Vauxhall hire car.

The vehicle screeched to a halt alongside her and the driver climbed out, looking across at her over the car roof. He was dark, bearded and wearing a brown leather jacket. Maddy stood rigid beside her van, staring as the man slammed the driver's door and strode towards her.

# 61

Esme turned into the gateway of the reclamation yard, relieved to see Maddy's van in the car park. She pulled up alongside and turned off the engine, peering out through the windscreen across the yard. So where was Maddy? The workshop looked deserted, as did Anna's office. She hoped Maddy hadn't run into Anna while she searching for Drew. The last thing Anna needed was being forced into a corner to defend Drew against Maddy's allegations. Which she would, of course. Maddy's opinion of Drew was bad enough as it was. And no secret to Anna, either. So anything Maddy said against Drew would be dismissed as her personal prejudice. Esme shook her head. Why couldn't Maddy have waited for Harry and Jamie to report back?

Esme unclipped her seat belt and got out of the car, grabbing her duffel coat from the back seat and slipping it on before locking the car. The rain had eased, but there was a dank chill in the air which perhaps explained why there were no customers in the yard. Esme glanced across to the other vehicle parked next to Maddy's campervan as she headed towards the office, faltering as she registered something familiar about it. A regular customer, perhaps? Though a regular customer wouldn't generally drive around in a hire car. Where had she seen that logo recently?

She gave her head a shake and turned away. Perhaps one of Anna's usual vehicles was in for service or repair and she was using a courtesy car.

Esme stopped by at Anna's office but, as anticipated, it was empty, Maddy's workshop the same. Maybe Anna had shut up early. In fact, given the traumas of the past few days, it was possible she'd not opened up today at all.

Esme stood for a moment, deciding what to do next, then an idea slipped into her head. Wasn't this the time of day when Anna went down to the cottage to feed Gypsy? Perhaps she could catch her. She had no idea what she'd say to her, but she'd think about that when the time came.

She left the office and hurried down the path which led out on to the lane beyond, pausing at the gate to scan the lane across the bridge and towards the mill for any sign of movement. But nothing. There was no one. Not even the omnipresent Joseph Brannock.

She turned her head to peer down the lane in the other direction, towards Temperance Cottage. If she were going to look for Anna, she'd better get on with it. Dusk was closing in.

Opening the gate, she turned right and hurried along the road to the cottage.

*

As she walked, Esme tried again to reach Maddy on her phone. Still no response. Still straight to voice-mail. She left another message, this time telling Maddy where she was, in case she thought better of her actions and switched her phone back on.

When Esme arrived at the cottage, she paused in the yard where Marianne had parked the Land Rover, with Anna hidden inside, all those years ago on Halloween night: the night Ellen had died. As she stood, Anna's tearful voice echoed in her head, describing how she'd peered in through the window and the nightmare had begun. There had been candles alight in the cottage that night. Anna had seen them flickering from inside, and for a moment, Esme imagined she could see them too, their flames dancing behind the grimy glass of the sitting room window.

She saw a movement at the cottage door and Gypsy emerged through the cat-flap. She bent down as the black cat padded across the concrete towards her.

'Hello, puss,' she said, tickling the cat under the chin. 'Where's your mistress? Is she inside?' She wondered if Anna would still feel able to use the cottage, now that she'd remembered what had happened here.

Gypsy rubbed herself against Esme's legs, purring loudly, until the clatter of the cottage door opening spooked her and she shot off, trotting away down the lane. Esme straightened up, relieved to have found Anna.

But it wasn't Anna who emerged but Drew's mother, Ria.

Esme called out her name and walked across the yard towards her. Ria's head jerked round and she stared at Esme in alarm.

'Sorry, didn't mean to startle you,' Esme said. 'I thought you were Anna for a minute. She's not in there, I assume?'

Ria twitched and pulled her shapeless cardigan around herself. 'Is she safe? Where is she?'

Did Ria know something of Anna's traumas? 'I'm not sure where she is, actually,' Esme said. 'I thought she might be down here feeding Gypsy.'

Ria gazed out across the lane, in the direction the cat had gone. 'I've done what I can.'

'Oh, OK. Well, if I find Anna I'll tell her you've fed Gypsy shall I?' Anna hadn't mentioned that Ria helped out caring for Gypsy, but Ria would be well aware of Joseph's spiteful behaviour towards cats and probably looked out for her.

Ria turned back to look at Esme, put out her hand and gripped her arm. 'She's not safe,' Ria said, her eyes wide. 'Tell her, will you, when you find her? I've done what I can, but she's not safe.' And turning on her heel, she hurried away down the lane.

*

Esme watched Ria's departure in confusion. What was she talking about? Of course, Esme realised with a shudder. She must mean Gypsy's kittens. If Joseph had his way, they'd be thrown in a sack and drowned in a water butt.

She sighed as the thought brought an unwelcome memory of the mummified cat Anna had unearthed in a building the same day that Carlton had come to the yard looking for Ellen Tucker. Esme turned and looked back at the cottage which had seen so much sorrow.

As she gazed across the yard, she again got the impression of flickering candles in one of the cottage windows. It was just her imagination, wasn't it? She wandered a little closer. Maybe. She couldn't be sure. Perhaps she should take a look inside. Ria may have left a light on.

She walked over to the front door and turned the door knob. The latch released and she pushed open the door, pausing at the threshold to take out her phone. She switched on the flashlight, held it out in front of her and stepped inside.

The harsh blue light picked out a dilapidated Rayburn cooker housed in a large inglenook fireplace. Its once cream enamel was grimy and disfigured. The door to the lower oven was missing completely. Piles of leaves, blown in from outside, gathered in heaps in the corners of the room. On the floor beside the Rayburn was a neat rectangle of vinyl cloth, on which stood a bowl of fresh water and an automatic pet feeding station. Beside that, a furry igloo which must be Gypsy's bed.

A door in the far right corner stood ajar. Sweeping the light ahead of her, she crossed the kitchen and went through into a small hall at the bottom of a steep staircase. Black staining on the treads suggested rotting timber. The cottage, it seemed, was in the same poor state as the mill.

Across the hall was another door, partially open. She hesitated. This must be the sitting room where Marianne had found Ellen Tucker; where Anna had seen her mother standing over the poor woman's body.

Esme shuddered. She didn't need to look in there. But what was the light, the soft glow coming from inside? Wasn't that why she'd come here, to find out?

She took a deep breath and, reaching out with one finger, pushed at the door. It swung open with the characteristic creak of grime-encrusted hinges.

In the centre of the room was a circle of black lighted candles, their flames quivering in the draught from the open door. Esme stared spellbound, blinking at the bizarre sight, trying to make sense of it, striving to push away the disquiet the scene provoked.

Something lay in the middle of the candle ring. She took a few steps closer and flooded the floor with her flashlight. It was a small doll, wrapped in a piece of red cloth. The doll's hair was braided in one long plait. Anna. It was meant to be Anna.

Esme staggered backwards, panicking as she knocked into the door behind her, slamming it shut. She yanked it open, stumbling back into the hall and into the kitchen beyond, where she slumped against the wall to catch her breath.

Had Ria done this? Was she trying to harm Anna? But why? Was Ria responsible for the stones on the roof, the phone calls when no one was there, the daubed paint and the dead crow? It seemed inconceivable, and yet what was this? What did it mean?

Esme squeezed her eyes shut and gave her head a shake. For goodness sake, she scolded. Listen to yourself. This is not the 17th century.

And another thing. Hadn't Ria, not a few moments ago, told Esme that Anna needed to stay safe? Why would she say that if she was behind Anna's intimidation?

Esme sighed. If only Cerys was here to make sense of it all. Cerys, yes. Something tumbled into Esme's head. Something Cerys had said. What? When? Esme rubbed her forehead and tried to remember.

She retraced her steps back into the sitting room and stared down at the tableau. It was at the market. The day she'd seen Ria hurrying away from Cerys's stall. Cerys had been tidying her stall. Crystals, Tarot cards, smudge sticks and candles. Candles. Cerys had spoken about candles. White ones for healing, green for prosperity, red for vitality. And black for protection.

Ria wasn't trying to harm Anna. She believed what she was doing would keep Anna safe. But safe from what? From whom?

Esme bent down and blew out the flames, offering a silent apology to Ria for ruining her spell. But leaving them alight risked the cottage catching fire.

Now she must find Anna, make sure she was OK and try to work out why she was in danger.

As she stood up, the front door slammed shut. Who was that? Had Maddy read her text message and come to find her? Had Anna come to feed the cat?

Esme hurried through into the kitchen. And straight into a blinding beam of light. She turned her head away, screwing up her eyes.

'What the hell...?' she said, holding up her arm against the light.

'"What the hell?"' is a very good question,' Daniel said.

# 62

Daniel flicked a switch and the fluorescent tube on the ceiling clicked and burst into life, bathing them both in a jarring white light. Esme winced. It hadn't occurred to her that the power might be still connected.

For a few moments, they stood, eyes fixed on one another as questions piled into Esme's head. What did Daniel know? Had he spoken to Anna? Had Marianne told him about their conversation? Or had Marianne held with their pact of silence on the matter over the last 24 years and said nothing?

'Daniel,' she said, forcing a smile. She glanced at the door behind him, her escape route. 'I was looking for Anna. Thought she might be here feeding Gypsy.' She wondered whether she should mention what she'd discovered in the other room, until a terrifying thought threatened to wreck her fragile self-control. Did Ria know the truth about Ellen Tucker? Was it Daniel who Ria believed posed a danger to Anna? But how could that be? Not Anna's own father, surely?

Daniel's expression darkened and he took a step towards her. 'What have you told Marianne?' he said, scowling.

For a moment, Esme was disoriented. '*I've* told her? I don't understand. About what?'

'You know bloody well about what. Changed your mind, did you? I should've known. *I haven't told Marianne, if that's what you think,* didn't mean that you wouldn't tell her if it suited you.'

It took Esme a few seconds to work out what he was talking about. 'You mean that you and Ellen were married?' she said. 'No, I haven't told her. Why?'

He peered at her, as though he didn't believe her. 'She's acting odd. Something's going on. But she won't tell me what.' He cocked his head, concern on his face. 'Hang on a minute. You said you were looking for Anna? Is this something to do with her? What's happened? Is she OK?'

Esme cleared her throat. 'Ria was here earlier,' she said. 'She seems worried about her.'

Daniel pursed his lips. 'Ria's not been right in the head for years. Wouldn't pay much store to what she says. I thought you'd have realised that by now.'

Esme recalled Joseph saying something similar. And Marianne implying the same about Joseph. It was impossible to know who to believe any more.

'Well, I'll be on my way,' she said, making a move towards the door.

Daniel stepped in front of her, barring her way. 'Not yet, you don't. I want some answers.'

'Answers about what, Daniel? I've already told you I've said nothing to Marianne.' She made another attempt at getting past him, but he grabbed her arm. She yanked it out of his grasp and pulled away. An image flashed into her head of Daniel grabbing her arm that day at the farm, as she'd gone to get into her car. Had his temper got the better of him when he'd argued with Ellen? Is that how it had happened?

'Whatever your problem is, Daniel,' she said, backing away, 'I don't appreciate you taking it out on me. OK?'

'What puzzles me, Esme,' he said, ignoring her, 'is why you're here, poking about in this cottage. Though, thinking about it, perhaps I shouldn't be. Is this about Ellen again? Because, let's face it, we all know you've been hung up on her since…'

'Since Sean Carlton came looking for her, yes.' Esme glared at him. 'And given that you knew her as well as you did, I could never understand why you weren't that interested in finding out what happened to her.'

He frowned. 'Meaning, you do now?'

'What?'

'You said, you *could never understand*. Does that mean you understand now?'

Esme flushed. She shouldn't have let him goad her. Now she'd said too much.

'You need to talk to Marianne,' she said, turning away. 'Now, if you'll excuse me, I really must go. Maddy will wonder where I've got to.'

'Talk to Marianne? Why? What's she said?'

Esme made another bid to reach the door. But Daniel wasn't ready to give up.

'My God. She's told you, hasn't she?' he said, his voice barely a whisper. 'She told you what happened on that night.'

Esme froze. What should she say? What would he do if she admitted the truth?

'You really need to talk to Marianne,' she said again, taking another step towards freedom.

'I don't need to talk to Marianne,' he said, his voice rising. 'I'm talking to you. Did she tell you what happened on that night?'

Esme felt her chest tightening. 'I need to go,' she said. Her voice sounded strange and distant.

'She did, didn't she?' Daniel said, staring at her. 'I can tell.' He let out a long sigh, slowly shaking his head. He was calmer now. 'I can't believe it, that she'd do that, after all those years keeping it to herself. Perhaps she finally needed to tell someone, and with you asking questions...' He sighed and shook his head again. 'And now you're worried, aren't you? Scared I'll be shocked. But you don't have to protect me, Esme.'

For a moment, his words stumped her. 'Shocked?' she said, eventually. 'Why would *you* be shocked?'

'Because you'd assume I didn't know.' Daniel wandered over to the window and looked out into the gloom of the yard, his arms folded. 'But I do know. I knew from the start. I had to protect her, you see.' He turned back into the room. 'Do you blame me for that? But what else could I do? It was an accident, Esme. She didn't mean it.'

Esme blinked, a knot of alarm forming deep in her stomach. 'What do you think Marianne told me, Daniel?'

He gaped at her. She saw the fear in his face as he knew he'd said too much and didn't know how to retract it.

Esme swallowed, drawing the only conclusion possible. 'Are you saying you didn't kill Ellen?' she said.

'Me? Of course I didn't!' He peered at her, his expression a mix of anger and confusion. 'Why would you think that, you of all people, who knows more about me and Ellen than anyone?' He scoffed. 'Only a few seconds ago, you were accusing me of...' He faltered and Esme knew he'd finally grasped the implications of her question. 'Marianne told you *I* killed her?' he said, thrusting a thumb into his chest.

Esme gave the briefest of nods.

Daniel shook his head. 'You have to believe me, Esme,' he said. 'It wasn't me. It was Marianne.'

# 63

Esme pushed past Daniel and out into the yard. The sky had darkened since she'd entered the cottage and rain was falling again, the drops running into her eyes and against her face. She stumbled across the concrete apron and leaned on the gate, her mind in turmoil over the conflicting so-called truths of Ellen Tucker's death.

She sensed Daniel behind her and she moved away, grappling to open the gate.

'No, don't go,' Daniel said. 'We need to get things straight.'

'No, I've heard enough,' Esme said, her voice shaking. 'You need to talk to Marianne.' She unlatched the gate and hurried out into the lane, back towards the reclamation yard.

But Daniel wasn't deterred. He came after her and caught her up.

'How do I know you're telling me the truth?' he said, marching along with her.

Esme shot him a sideways glare. 'How do I know *you* are?' she countered, increasing her pace.

'Because there was a witness. Oh, give me a break, Esme. Talk to me. I want to know what Marianne's been saying.'

Esme stopped, breathing heavily. She turned towards him.

'Go home, Daniel. Go home to your wife and ask her. And leave me alone.' She broke into a run, some of the tension leaving her body as she realised Daniel was no longer behind her.

When she reached the gate to the path to the reclamation yard, she paused to catch her breath. Where was Anna? She needed to know the truth. But what *was* the truth? Who was covering for whom? Marianne said she and Daniel had never spoken of Ellen's death after that night, when Daniel had come home saying Ellen had gone, that Marianne need not worry any more. Was that something Marianne had made up to cover her own culpability? Or did she genuinely believe her husband to be guilty? *I had to protect her,* Daniel had said. What did he mean?

Esme sighed. It would be for the police to sort out now. She must report her conversations with the Meddons, despite the hurt it would cause Anna.

The thought of Anna forced Ria's warning back into her head. Was there any credibility to what she'd said? Or was it, as Daniel suggested, merely the rantings of a disturbed woman? After all, who could possibly be a danger to Anna, anyway? Her mind shot back to why she was here in the first place, to stop Maddy confronting Drew about Ted's death, and she felt a jolt of panic go through her. Where did Drew fit into all of this? What if Marianne and Daniel were both telling the truth, and neither of them had killed Ellen? Then, who did?

She opened the gate and hurried down the path to the yard. She must find Maddy.

As she came down towards Maddy's workshop, she saw the lights were on. She burst in through the door, overwhelmed with relief when she saw Maddy sitting at the workbench with a rag in her hand.

Maddy looked up in alarm. 'Where the hell have you been?' she said, standing up. 'I saw your car, but I couldn't work out where you'd gone.'

'I could say the same about you,' Esme said. She flopped down in the old leather chair beside the stove, sorry that the stove was unlit. She could have done with its heat right now.

'Are you all right?' Maddy said, coming over to her. 'You look terrible.'

'Did you find Drew?'

Maddy pulled a face. 'No, sadly. The bugger wasn't home.'

Esme threw her head against the back of the chair. 'Ah, didn't think of you going there. Why was your van here, then?'

'Tried the yard first. Then when I got no joy, I jogged up to the bungalow. Thought the run might do me good. Put things into perspective.'

'And did it?'

'If you mean by that, have I decided against speaking to Drew, the answer is no.'

Esme knew when Maddy heard what she had to say, she'd be even keener to challenge him.

'Was Anna there?'

'No. Haven't seen her.' Maddy pulled out a stool from underneath the bench and dragged it over to Esme. 'So, what happened to you?' she said, sitting down. 'Oh God. *You* didn't find Drew, did you?'

Esme shook her head. 'No, nothing like that.' She told Maddy what she'd learned from Daniel.

'Bloody hell,' Maddy said. 'Do you believe him?'

Esme closed her eyes and sighed. 'I don't know what to think. Either could be lying. Or they could both be telling the truth, unaware of the part the other had played.'

'The toxicity of secrets, eh?' Maddy said, staring unfocused at the wall. 'Well, I'm inclined to believe them. That neither of them killed Ellen.' She turned to Esme. 'But we know who did, don't we? Drew. The cat calls, the harassment. It might have started off with antisocial behaviour, but then things spiralled out of control.' She swallowed. 'And Dad found out,' she added, in a whisper.

Esme didn't know what to say that would be any comfort to Maddy. Hadn't she all but come to the same conclusion herself? She sat up straight in her seat.

'Look, I know it's starting to look that way, but perhaps we should keep our powder dry for a bit longer. Have you heard anything about how Jamie and Harry got on?'

'No. I've left messages, but he's not got back to me yet.'

'Perhaps it would be better to wait until he does before we tackle Drew. Until we know where we stand, because...' She stopped, the strange encounter with Ria thrusting itself into her head.

'What's the matter?' Maddy said.

Esme pinched the bridge of her nose. 'There's something else you should know. I saw Ria down at the cottage. She was in a right state. Particularly about Anna. She seemed genuinely frightened for her safety.'

'Why?'

'She wasn't specific and I didn't realise what she meant until she'd run off. It was bizarre, Maddy. She'd put a poppet looking like Anna in a ring of candles in the middle of the sitting room.'

'A poppet?'

'A little doll used in witchcraft spells. Cerys sells them on her market stall.'

'Don't people usually stick pins in them?'

'No, not necessarily.' Esme leaned on the arm of the chair. 'Ria said she'd done what she could. She was trying to protect Anna, I think. Though from what or who, I've no idea.'

Maddy shrugged. 'I'm not sure you can take Ria's thinking seriously, Esme. She's been living on the edge for years. I didn't realise she'd got this bad, though.'

'I don't think Cerys would thank you for that assessment,' Esme said, with a wry smile. 'Ria's a regular customer of hers.'

'Oh God, that reminds me. That creepy guy we'd seen on the market followed me here earlier.'

'What?' Esme's mouth dropped open.

'Yeah. Gave me the fright of my life when he got out of his car, I can tell you.'

'Who is he? What did he want?'

Before Maddy could reply, the door flew open and Drew marched inside. He scanned the workshop.

'Where's Anna?' he said.

# 64

'You bastard,' Maddy said, standing up and taking a step towards Drew.

Esme scrambled to her feet and grabbed Maddy's arm. 'Hang on, Madds.' She turned to Drew, Ria's bizarre warning ringing in her ears. 'What's this about Anna?'

'No, I won't hang on,' Maddy said, pulling away. 'What were you doing on my dad's tender the night he died?'

'What?' Drew's scowl was scathing.

'You heard. And don't say you weren't there. I've got a witness. Dad found out, didn't he, about what happened to Ellen Tucker? And you had to get rid of him.' She ended on a sob.

Esme pushed between them. 'Look, let's all calm down, shall we? Drew, I met your mum earlier. She seemed really worried about Anna. Do you know why?'

Drew dragged his scowl away from Maddy and aimed it at Esme. 'It's all complete shit. Mum's ill. She doesn't know what she's saying.'

'But what about these nuisance phone calls, vandalism and dead crows nailed to Anna's door?' Esme said. She studied his face, looking for a clue as to what was going on in his head. 'Aren't you concerned?'

'No, of course he isn't,' Maddy said, her voice still unsteady. 'He knows who's behind it.'

'What? You accusing me?'

'If the cap fits.'

Drew scowled. 'Well, for your information, it wasn't me. Just some...'

'Kids having a laugh, yeah,' Maddy said, prodding him in the shoulder. 'Not unlike yourself in your time, eh?'

He jerked his chin at her. 'You know nothing.'

'Look, can we get back to Anna, please?' Esme said. 'You seemed to think she was in here, Drew. Why?'

Drew shrugged. 'Cos she's not in the office.'

'So?' Maddy said. 'She could be anywhere. Maybe she's out on a job.'

'Nah, she can't be.' Drew jerked his thumb back towards Anna's office. 'Door's open. Lights are on. Her stuff's there. Thought she'd be in here gossiping.' He sneered at Maddy. 'Only came in to check. Didn't expect to get my ear bent.' He turned and went out of the workshop, the door banging behind him.

Esme glanced at Maddy before going after him, Maddy in her wake. They followed Drew across the yard and into the office. The door stood open, lights ablaze and the computer switched on, a white geometric design morphing into multiple patterns back and forth across the screen.

'Maybe she's gone to the loo?' Maddy suggested.

Drew shook his head. 'Checked.'

'Have you tried calling her?'

'I already did on my way over. She wasn't picking up.'

'Try again,' Esme suggested. She couldn't get Ria's warning out of her head. Something wasn't right.

He grabbed his phone out of his back pocket and tapped the screen. Esme and Maddy stood, watching, waiting for Drew to speak. Anna's ringtone sounded from somewhere on the desk. Esme reached over and lifted up a pale blue folder. The volume of ringing grew as she exposed the phone underneath.

'She must have gone out in a hurry,' Esme said. 'An emergency.'

Drew picked up Anna's phone. 'Someone called her?' he said, tapping and scrolling.

'Anything?' Maddy said.

'Nah. My call was the last one. Nothing recent before that.'

'The landline,' Esme said. 'Maybe it was on the landline?'

Drew grabbed the handset and dialled 1471. Again they stood, watching, eyes fixed on his face. He severed the call.

'Last call an hour ago.'

'She could have been gone that long,' Esme said.

Maddy shook her head. 'No, she wasn't in when I got here. She must have come back in the last twenty minutes or so. Someone could have called in. We wouldn't necessarily have seen them.'

Esme scanned the office, looking desperately for clues. 'Perhaps she got a message,' she said, pointing to the answerphone's red indicator light on the base unit.

'Good shout,' Drew said, stabbing the playback button. *'No new messages'*, announced the robotic voice, before running through the previous recordings.

A familiar, if tinny, disembodied voice reverberated around the room. *'Uz've told ye before about letting your vermin in my mill. You'm better get up 'ere befur 'er and 'er kittens meets a watery death.'*

'Oh, no!' Maddy said, her hand over her mouth. 'Anna said Gypsy was looking for somewhere to make a nest to have her kittens. Typical she chose the mill. It's like it was deliberate, to wind up old Joseph Brannock.' She turned on Drew. 'Well, don't just stand there. Your bloody granddad's about to drown Anna's cat. Go and help her, for God's sake.'

'I'm allergic,' he complained. 'Cats make me sneeze.'

'You can't just abandon her,' Esme said. 'And you might be able to make your granddad see sense.'

Drew let out an exasperated sigh but, surprisingly, turned on his heel and headed for the door. He paused when he reached it and looked back, glaring at Maddy.

'And for your information, I haven't been anywhere near your dad's precious tender. Me and Anna were away on holiday the week he died, as you bloody well know.'

He stormed out of the office, leaving Maddy gaping wide-eyed at his disappearing back.

Esme touched Maddy's arm. 'Is that true?' she said.

Maddy blinked and wrapped her arms around herself. 'I can't remember,' she said in a small voice. 'They might have, I suppose. But Jamie saw him, didn't he? So they couldn't have been.'

'What's that?' Esme said, listening. 'Someone's shouting.' They hurried outside and Esme looked across the yard, to where Drew was running down the path to the mill, his phone clamped to his ear.

'What the hell -?' Maddy said, coming up beside her.

Esme stared across the valley as the pungent smell of smoke invaded her nostrils and a flickering orange glow lit up the darkening sky. The mill was on fire.

# 65

Drew had almost reached the gate by now. Esme and Maddy hurried after him. The glow from the fire threw distorted shafts of light on to the lane as they jogged along. They caught up with Drew on the bridge opposite the mill, all three of them standing in the lane, gazing up helplessly at the burning building. Flames had taken a hold of the lower floor, engulfing the panelling along one side.

'Where the hell is the fire service?' Maddy wailed, looking around as though she might conjure them up.

'Give them a chance, Madds,' Esme said. 'Drew's only just called them.'

Drew paced back and forth like a caged animal. 'Where's Anna?' he yelled, scanning around. 'Where the hell is she?'

Maddy stared up at the flames. 'She can't be still inside looking for Gypsy, can she?' she said, her hands gripping the scarf wrapped around her neck.

'But she'd have come out, wouldn't she,' Drew said, 'before the bloody place went up? I mean, how long does it take to pick up a cat?'

A spasm of terror tightened in Esme's stomach. 'I don't think Gypsy was in there in the first place,' she said. 'I saw her earlier down by the cottage. She was headed in the opposite direction.' She looked round at Maddy, with a rising sense of panic. 'And that phone message was logged at around the same time.'

'You saying it was all lies?' Maddy said, her face convulsed in alarm. 'That Anna was lured there? But why?'

'Ria knew,' Esme said, her voice unsteady. 'Ria knew she was in danger. But nobody would listen.'

Drew shouted Anna's name and ran into the yard.

'Drew, for God's sake,' Esme yelled after him. 'Don't get any closer, it's too dangerous.'

And then they saw what he had. Scraps of wood were tumbling from a small half-boarded opening, high up under the eaves of the roof, and landing on the concrete below. As they watched, the opening grew bigger until finally a face appeared in the gap. Anna's face.

*

Drew ran back across the yard towards the mill's entrance. But flames were already licking at the thick wooden door.

'There's no way you can get in there,' Esme shouted.

Drew staggered backwards, shying away from the heat.

'But I have to get her out.'

'Is there another way in?' Esme said, glancing from one to the other.

'Top floor,' Drew said. 'I can get to her from the gantry.'

'But it's wrecked,' Maddy said. 'It'll never take your weight.'

But Drew was already on his way. He darted off to the left, running across the rough grass to the uneven rock face which formed the mill's boundary, and began to scramble up between the scrub, the glow of the fire illuminating his way.

Esme grabbed her phone from her pocket. 'We're going to need an ambulance,' she said, tapping the screen and putting it to her ear.

'I'm going round the other side,' Maddy said, turning on her heel and heading in the same direction as Drew. For a moment Esme thought she was planning to scale the bank after him, until she remembered the day Joseph had mysteriously got away from her by taking another route when she'd gone after him and met Ria in the garden.

Esme hurried after Maddy, her phone to her ear. She heard a click on the line followed by the voice of a call handler.

'Ambulance Service. Is the patient breathing?'

Esme explained the urgency and, despite the call handler's request for her to stay on the line, she insisted it wasn't possible and disconnected, once she'd been assured an ambulance had been dispatched. As she returned her phone to her pocket, Esme hoped the call handler didn't think the whole thing was a hoax, that she was someone trying to inject some drama into the Halloween revelries.

She jogged after Maddy, who was already some distance ahead of her up the hill. At the first bend, Maddy stepped off the tarmac on to an overgrown footpath and Esme followed, climbing the path which led up to the field above the mill.

Drew had already reached the broken gantry. He had one hand on what was left of the handrail and was calling Anna's name.

Esme and Maddy ran across the wet grass towards him, past a rusting sheep's trough half full of rainwater and through the smoke which swirled around them, stinging Esme's eyes. She couldn't imagine what it must be like for Anna inside and felt a jab of alarm. In most fires, smoke inhalation was the killer, not the flames themselves.

The gantry, what there was left of it, linked the rocky outcrop on the field's edge to a boarded panel in the top of the back wall of the mill. The opening would have once served to load and unload goods at the higher level. The one and only advantage of the mill's fragile state was that the panel itself should easily give under pressure, if Drew could get across and kick it in. But the downside was that the poor state of repair extended to the gantry, Drew's only access. Would it hold him? And if he did make it across, would it hold both him and Anna on the return journey?

Esme peered down into the black void between the walls of the mill and the rock face, to the remnants of the old water wheel below and the unyielding concrete yard beyond.

She pulled back and turned her attention to Drew, who was taking his first tentative step on the decaying wooden gantry. She held her breath as the flimsy structure creaked beneath him.

'Wait,' she shouted. He stopped and turned. 'You need something to protect you from the smoke,' she said, casting around for something she was wearing that he could use.

'Here,' Maddy said, slipping off her scarf.

Esme pointed to the sheep trough behind her. 'Wet it,' she said. Maddy ran over and soaked the scarf in the water, before running back and handing it to Drew, who tied it around his head, covering his mouth and nose. Then he restarted his attempt.

'We should have some rope to tie round him,' Maddy whimpered. 'Why didn't we think of rope?'

Esme grabbed her hand and squeezed it. 'No time,' she said. 'Even if you'd suggested it, Drew wouldn't have waited any longer. And where would we have got it from?'

Drew took two more steps, keeping to the runner along the edge rather than the weaker planks in the centre. Every couple of steps, he paused and shifted his balance.

Esme turned away and squeezed her eyes shut, as another cloud of smoke engulfed them. When she looked again, Drew had reached a little under half way, but there were missing panels in the next section, allowing a taunting glimpse of the horror awaiting him below if the gantry gave way. Drew hesitated for a moment before stretching out his foot across the gap, and landing securely on the other side.

Esme let out a long sigh. But he wasn't there yet. She took deep breath and prepared herself for another few moments of trauma.

Maddy looped her arm through Esme's. 'I take it all back,' she sniffed. 'The Drew I thought I knew would never have done this.' Esme patted her hand and they gripped one another as Drew moved to his next position.

But this time the wood under him crumbled, sending a piece of rotten timber crashing into the chasm below. He grabbed the handrail and managed to regain his footing further along.

'I don't know if I can take any more of this,' Maddy said.

'Nearly there,' Esme said, trying to ignore the building smoke and the growing intensity of the fire.

Drew leapt the last two steps, landing on the threshold of the opening. From inside, a section of wooden panel was wrenched aside and the top of Anna's head appeared, along with the distressing sound of her coughing. Drew shouted for her to stand back and he kicked in the remaining pieces, tumbling inside after them.

Esme and Maddy stood transfixed, eyes focused on the yawning aperture, willing Drew and Anna to reappear, as the distant cry of sirens cut through the dank low cloud. Esme tried to home in on the sound, assessing how far away the emergency services were, silently urging them to hurry and reach the mill to rescue Drew and Anna before the fire destroyed it, and them.

Esme sensed someone behind them and turned to see a dark figure emerging from the gloom. As he got closer, she thought for a moment that her eyes were playing tricks on her until she realised it was Alec Brannock.

Maddy pulled away from Esme and strode over to meet him. 'This down to you?' she shouted. 'Arson was a hobby of yours once upon a time, if I remember.'

He sneered at her and folded his arms with a shrug. 'The place's a wreck. Probably the electrics. Accident waiting to happen, if you ask me.'

Maddy thrust her arm out behind her. 'But Anna's trapped in there,' she yelled, her voice breaking. 'And Drew. He went in to get her.'

'And they can't get out,' Esme said, running over. 'The gantry's about to give way.'

'What?' The cocky attitude vanished. 'Anna? What was she doing in there?'

'You did it, didn't you?' Maddy screamed. 'You started the bloody fire.' She rushed at him, pummelling him in the chest.

Alec grabbed her by the wrists and shoved her aside. 'You mad bitch. You think I'd hurt Anna? She...'

'Wasn't meant to be in there?' Maddy said. 'Not part of the plan, eh?'

Alec turned and ran off into the mist and gloom.

'Bastard,' Maddy said, sniffing and wiping her nose with the back of her hand.

Esme turned back to look for any sign of Drew and Anna. 'Where the hell are they?' She took a few paces closer and shouted. 'Are you all right? What's going on in there?' A sudden thought. Maybe Anna was still looking for her cat. 'Gypsy's safe, Anna. I've seen her.'

The siren was closer now, but not close enough. Esme peered down the valley, desperate to see the reassuring sight of a red fire appliance hurtling along the lane.

Something moved, deep in the darkness of the tree canopy beyond the gantry, and she turned her head to look. Smoke swirled down and it was gone. No, there it was again. She squinted into the shadow. Someone was there, watching the drama unfold. And she had no doubt who that person was.

Thundering steps of someone running across the field distracted her and Alec reappeared, a long scaffold plank under his arm. He took it over to the gantry and yelled for Drew. For a moment nothing, then Drew appeared, coughing. And beside him, Anna, her face wrapped in Maddy's scarf.

Alec slid the plank across the gantry and Drew caught hold of the other end, resting it on the opening's stone sill. He coaxed Anna out on to the plank, and with everyone urging her on, she crossed the makeshift bridge and escaped into the field. Drew followed, as the sound of falling masonry exploded from deep inside the mill behind him, sending dust billowing into the air to merge with the suffocating smoke.

Everyone staggered back out of the way, cheering and hugging one another in celebration.

Esme turned to see Ria standing a short way off, staring ahead, her hands over her mouth, her thin body shivering. She hurried over to her.

'It's OK, Ria,' she said, her eyes smarting and her face stinging from the heat of the fire. 'Everyone's safe. Anna's safe.' She put her arm around Ria's shoulders and guided her back to the others.

As they reached the group, the figure Esme had seen in the shadows emerged. She'd been right. Joseph Brannock. True to form. Spying on them all from the sidelines.

He stood in front of the gantry and let out a roar which defied his age and frailty.

'No!' he yelled, spittle spewing from his mouth. He lifted a bony finger and jabbed it at Anna. 'Her should've perished.'

# 66

For a moment, no one spoke. The fire snarled behind them and, down below, sirens wailed, before ceasing abruptly, replaced by the slamming of doors and shouts of the firefighters.

Esme felt Ria tense beside her as Anna's words reverberated around her head. *I don't think Joseph likes me.* But this was not a simple matter of like or dislike. This went deeper. Much deeper.

Joseph lunged at Anna. But Drew intervened and pulled her away.

'You leave her be, Granddad.'

'You stupid bay,' Joseph said. 'Her's evil. Her's bewitched you with her fancy ways. Us have to stop it. Afore there's another born.'

Maddy gasped, her hand across her mouth, and Ria whimpered. A sudden coldness spread through Esme's body as she remembered what else Anna had told her that day, that Joseph had scratched her and called her a bitch. But Joseph hadn't called her a bitch. He'd called a witch and scratched her, believing that drawing blood would diminish her power.

Drew gaped at his grandfather, then began to laugh. He turned to Alec.

'He's mad. I always told you he was.'

'He dun't know what he's saying,' Alec said, going over to Joseph. 'It's the dementia talking. Come on, Granddad, let's get you home.'

He went to take Joseph's arm, but Joseph pulled away and waved his stick at his grandson. 'You let me be, Alec Brannock,' he growled. 'Don't you dare treat me like I've lost my marbles. I knows things about you, don't forget. Things you'z done. And I bain't afraid to share 'em if it suits me. So think on that.'

Maddy glanced fearfully at Esme as they shared a silent acknowledgment. It hadn't been Drew on Ted's tender. It was Alec. Easy to understand how Jamie had mistaken one brother for the other.

Alec backed off, glancing around at the wide-eyed group as if unsure whether to protest his innocence or follow his brother's cue and laugh it off. He did neither. He turned on his heel and hurried away.

Anna started coughing again and Esme winced at the sound of it. 'Drew, you must take Anna down to the ambulance,' she said. 'Both of you need checking out.'

Drew put his arm around Anna and began steering her away, but the action roused Joseph and he thrust out his stick once more.

But Drew was ready for him. He grabbed the shaft of the offending stick and shoved it to one side, causing Joseph to stumble to his knees.

'You leave my wife and my baby alone, you evil old man,' he shouted. 'You need locking up.' He gathered up Anna again and hurried off across the field towards two paramedics, dressed in high visibility coats, on their way over to meet them.

Joseph staggered to his feet. 'You'm cursed,' he shouted after Drew. 'Us have to kill her to stop the curse.'

Beside Esme, Ria let out a piercing moan. She ran over to Joseph and thrust her face close to his.

'You wicked, wicked man,' she screamed. 'You killed my baby. You killed my baby girl.'

Maddy uttered an oath under her breath and Esme felt a sob rise in her throat. Baby girl? Ria'd had a little girl? A sister for Drew and Alec? Did they even know?

Joseph backed away. 'Get away from me, woman. Twas meant to be. Us don't need no more witches.'

'It's all in your head,' Ria said, tapping her forehead. 'Don't you see? You're not right up here. You're as crazy as your mad ancestor. My baby wasn't evil. No more than the rest of them were.' She gulped, gasping for a breath. 'It finished Scott, that did, when he heard what you'd done. It was the last straw, killing his little girl.' Her voice broke, her face smeared with tears and mucus.

She lunged forward. She put her hands on Joseph's shoulders and thrust him away with a force which seemed to come from deep within, her fury unleashed after decades of suppression.

Joseph stumbled and toppled backwards. He grabbed at the handrail to save himself, but missed it. He landed heavily on the gantry, which shattered under his weight and sent him crashing down on to the decaying mill wheel in the void below.

Ria let out a howl and covered her face in her hands. 'No, no,' she wailed.

Esme ran over and pulled her back from the edge, guiding her on to safer ground. 'It's all right,' she said. 'It was an accident. You didn't mean to push him over.'

Ria turned to Esme, her reddened eyes wild and angry. 'Oh, but I did! But he was meant to fall in the fire. That should have been his punishment. It's what that evil man deserves. And if you knew everything he'd done, you'd think so too.'

# 67

A young female paramedic, with a warm smile and an efficient manner, met them half way along the path from the field and Esme passed the distressed Ria into her care. The paramedic took Ria's arm and guided her towards an ambulance parked in the lane to join her colleagues accompanying Drew and Anna.

'What'll happen to her, d'you think?' Maddy said, as they watched Ria and the paramedic negotiating the path ahead of them. 'When the police arrive, I mean.'

'I don't know,' Esme said, pulling her coat around her. 'But they'll surely take into account the way Joseph's controlled her all these years, won't they?' Ria's words kept repeating over and over in her head. *And if you knew everything he'd done.* There was something else troubling Ria had said, too, but Esme couldn't bring it to mind.

Maddy sighed. 'You were right, what you said earlier, about Ria knowing what a threat Joseph was to Anna and her baby. She'd seen it happen before.'

Esme nodded. 'She must have been terrified of history repeating itself.' She sighed. 'Poor woman. She must have been at a loss as to how to tell anyone. That's if she could even put it into words.'

'And let's face it, who'd believe her?'

'Well, she tried telling me, didn't she?' Esme said. 'But I couldn't grasp it. Even Drew dismissed her concerns.'

Maddy pulled out her phone and switched on the flashlight, to make it easier for them to see the path ahead of them as they followed Ria and the paramedic.

'D'you think she knew about Ellen, too?' Maddy said. 'Because it was Joseph who killed Ellen, wasn't it?'

'It's got to be, hasn't it?' Esme said. 'His motivation for targeting Anna matched exactly. In his eyes, Ellen was a witch and he was duty bound to get rid of her.' Esme's thoughts drifted back to the time she'd helped Ria indoors with her garden produce. There'd been a framed quote on the wall in the hall, attributed to John Wesley. "*You have one business on earth – to save souls.*" Morris had told her that Wesley had been vehemently opposed to the 18th century change in the law, effectively denying the existence of witches. Joseph Brannock, it seemed, had taken such a stance and reinterpreted it to fit with his own distorted view of the world.

They came to the end of the narrow path and turned out on to the road, the headlights of the ambulances reflecting on the tarmac, wet from the earlier rain. It was easier to see where they were walking now and Maddy slipped her phone back in her pocket.

They passed the ambulance as its patients were ushered inside. Esme wondered if Drew and Anna would be taken off to hospital immediately or whether the crew had the necessary equipment to deal with the situation. She was concerned about Anna and the baby. She gritted her teeth.

Please don't let Joseph Brannock's malicious scheme succeed.

As she and Maddy reached the bend in the road, they stood for a moment, looking across to the mill where two fire appliances stood in the yard. They watched as the firefighters, half-kneeling and with hoses cradled under their arms, aimed arcs of water at the burning building, shouted instructions drowned out by the drone of the heavy-duty pumps.

'So where does Alec fit in?' Maddy said, as they stood on the edge of the lane. 'Why did he target my dad? And Carlton, for that matter, cos I'm putting that down to him, too. Would he really do that to cover up for his granddad?' She nodded towards the burning building. 'And that's got to be his doing, too, hasn't it? He didn't seem too surprised when he saw it.'

'Not until you told him Anna was in there. Then he panicked. Which suggests killing Anna wasn't on his agenda, whatever his reason for starting the fire.'

'And Ellen?' Maddy said. 'Whose agenda was she on?'

'Joseph's, surely?' Esme frowned. 'Though, you have a point. Was Alec involved in some way? Is that what Joseph meant by knowing things about what Alec had done which he wasn't afraid to share if he needed to? Though he had plenty else to choose from.'

Maddy pulled a face. 'I wonder what Drew knows about it?'

'Good question.' Hearing Drew's name triggered something in Esme's head. She looked round at Maddy. 'When we speculated about Drew and his mates being behind Ellen's harassment, you said they were old enough to get the hots for her, but too young to be on her radar. Alec's two years older. He'd have been 17.'

'He might have fancied his chances, you mean?'

'Exactly that. And it could have gone either way. If she reciprocated, Joseph would see it as his grandson being corrupted.'

'Bewitched, you mean,' Maddy added, a hint of bitterness in her voice.

Esme acknowledged her comment with a nod of the head. 'And if Ellen rejected him...'

'And with anger management not being Alec's most accomplished skill,' Maddy said, latching on, 'he loses it. And Ellen ends up dead.'

The whine of a distant siren echoed up the valley, becoming louder as it closed in. As the police car appeared, Esme realised with alarm that there could be another more disturbing scenario. After her first encounter with Joseph Brannock, Maddy had explained how Joseph had taken on the two boys after their father died, when Ria was too distraught to function properly. '*Ruled with an iron fist*', Maddy had said. What toxic dogma had Joseph fed into his grandsons' heads over the years? And what control did he still have over them? For all his faults, Drew seemed less under his power than his brother. Perhaps Anna was the reason for that. And maybe it was why Joseph wanted rid of her, because it was she who now had a greater influence on Drew than he did.

But what about Alec? What twisted plans had Joseph had for his dysfunctional loner grandson? To pick up the baton of his distorted campaign? Esme shuddered.

The police car turned into the yard of the mill, its siren cutting off abruptly as the vehicle came to a halt and the driver got out. As she and Maddy walked across the lane towards the police officer, Esme took comfort in the thought that Joseph may have been deluded – if Alec felt the same way about 'witches' as his grandfather, surely Anna would never have survived.

# 68

The plethora of pulsating lights from ambulance, fire and police vehicles doused the mill in stark electric blue, the sky's orange glow fading, now that the two fire crews had brought the blaze under control.

Esme sat beside Maddy on the low boundary wall on the far side of the mill, a blanket draped around her shoulders, issued by one of the paramedics. They'd declined the offer to sit in a police car while waiting to speak to detectives. Esme knew outside was preferable to the claustrophobia of being confined inside a vehicle, even with the oppressive smell of charred wood in the air.

She tugged the blanket a little tighter as she gazed out on the surreal sight in front of her. Hoses lay like spaghetti across the yard, attached to the back of the fire tender in a row of giant optics. The crew's work was almost done, now. Reels were being wound in and disconnected, leaving just one hose in situ, to damp down the structure and ensure no flames reignited.

Blue and white tape stretched in a cordon around the black hole into which Joseph had fallen, deployed by the officer who'd arrived first on the scene. His patrol car had been promptly joined by a second, and it was in this vehicle where Ria now sat, waiting for the detective team to finish their deliberations. Esme watched them, wondering what they were discussing, willing them to get on with it so they were free to come over and talk to her and Maddy. Although they'd told the uniformed officer what they'd witnessed, he'd informed them a senior officer would want to speak to them before they went home.

Esme wondered if they were waiting for an initial assessment of the crime scene from the forensic team. Not for the first time, she thought of Joseph's broken body at the base of the mill wheel and shuddered.

The ambulance which had arrived in response to Esme's initial 999 call was still parked in the lane, with Drew and Anna inside. She'd taken it as a good sign that they'd not raced away to hospital with sirens blaring, though she was sure the couple might yet need to be admitted.

She looked down the dark lane towards Daniel and Marianne's Land Rover parked beyond the mill on the grass verge, its headlights on. The couple had turned up a short while ago. Either Anna had phoned them or they'd been alerted by the sirens and traffic rushing past their farm.

When they'd first arrived, Marianne had come running up the lane, only to be intercepted by a police officer. Almost immediately, she pushed past him, hurrying over to the ambulance with her daughter inside and hammering on the back door. The door opened marginally, but after a few moments, Marianne withdrew and the door was closed once more.

Daniel had been some way behind her and was stopped by the same policeman. He'd gesticulated towards the ambulance before following after Marianne. But by then, she was on her way back and they clashed in the lane, Daniel reaching out to grab Marianne's arm. Marianne was clearly not interested in dialogue and, after a brief exchange, she pulled away and returned to the Land Rover. Although she climbed back inside, she made no attempt to drive off.

Daniel now stood on the tarmac beside the Land Rover, his eyes fixed on the activities of the fire fighters.

'I bet theirs was an interesting conversation earlier,' Esme said, recalling her exasperated command to Daniel to go home and talk to his wife.

'Yeah,' Maddy said. 'Love to have been a fly on the wall.'

Esme rearranged the blanket around herself. 'What did

he mean by protecting Marianne, d'you think?'

'By saying nothing? Keeping up the pretence that Ellen had left?'

Esme stared out into the melee of lights. 'When Marianne admitted to me and Anna that she'd found Ellen in the cottage, I asked her why she'd not phoned the police or an ambulance. We now know it was because she believed Daniel had killed her. Daniel's reaction was the same. He was convinced that Marianne had done it.'

Maddy grunted. 'Nice to have so much faith in your partner's integrity.'

'Exactly. So why was he so ready to believe she was responsible?' She turned to Maddy, pieces slotting into place as quickly as she could gather them together. 'Daniel said there was a witness. I didn't register it at the time. Too busy trying to get away from him. That's why he was so convinced. Someone told him they'd seen Marianne do it.'

Maddy's head shot round. 'Joseph.'

'Who else?' Esme said. 'Not the witness, though. The killer.'

'If he *was* the killer. It could have been Alec?'

Esme shook her head. 'Even if Alec struck the final blow, Joseph was the driving force. It was Joseph who wanted rid of Anna, remember, but it was Alec who set the fire.'

'He was set up. He didn't know Anna was going to be inside. It was Joseph who lured her there.'

'As for his influence over Daniel,' Esme continued, 'don't forget, Joseph would only have been in his fifties 24 years ago and pretty dominating. Daniel would've been quite intimidated by him.' She thought for a while, imagining how it might have happened. 'Marianne must have turned up just at the right moment. Joseph hid out of the sight - we know how deft he is at doing that - and she came in and saw Ellen's body.'

'He must have thought all his Christmases had come at once when Daniel arrived,' Maddy said. 'Not difficult to convince him Marianne was responsible. Joseph would know full well the aggro Ellen was stirring up between the two of them and used it to full advantage to shift the blame off himself.'

'Or Alec.'

Maddy shrugged. 'Same difference.'

Esme remembered Daniel's attitude at the farm when she'd let him know she'd found the record of his marriage to Ellen. He'd almost been coy about Ellen searching him out. Did that show a certain arrogance? That he was worth killing for? Is that why he'd been so ready to be persuaded?

'Joseph also gained a powerful hold over the Meddons from that point on,' she said. 'No wonder Daniel didn't back the mill conversion. Joseph didn't want it, so Daniel was forced to take the same line.' What other liberties had Joseph been granted under this arrangement? Was money involved?

She looked back towards Daniel. He'd wandered along the road towards them on this side of the mill, and now stood peering into the cluster of police vehicles in the yard, as though trying to work out what was going on. She wondered if he'd noticed Ria in the police car. As she watched, Daniel marched over to the police officer standing in the lane and began remonstrating with him.

'Will Daniel and Marianne know everything that's happened, d'you think?' Maddy said.

'I was just thinking the same,' Esme said, turning to Maddy. 'He'll know about Anna being caught up in the mill fire, but I'm not sure what she knows about what happened after Drew led her away. And I'd imagine the police being a bit cagey at this stage.' She glanced back at Daniel, alarmed to see he was staring their way.

Maddy had seen him too. 'Oh God, he's coming over. What do we say? Do we tell him?'

'He'll find out sooner or later, won't he?' Esme said. She watched him stride across the concrete towards them.

He jerked a thumb over his shoulder. 'What's going on? No one will tell me anything. And what's it got to do with Ria Brannock?'

So he had noticed Ria in the car. Esme gripped the edge of her blanket and looked up at him, but it was Maddy who answered.

'Joseph lost it,' she said. 'He was ranting all sorts of crap about witches and Ria shoved him off the edge of the field.'

'Bloody hell.'

Esme looked out across the yard, flinching as she saw two people with a stretcher carrying a black body bag manoeuvring between the vehicles.

'Look,' she said. 'They've got him.' They all watched in silence as the remains of Joseph Brannock were loaded into the back of the black van.

Esme stared up at Daniel. 'It was Joseph, wasn't it, who told you Marianne had killed Ellen?' she said. 'He was the witness you told me about.'

Daniel turned to Esme, flicking a wary glance at Maddy. 'What's that got to do with anything?'

'Don't you get it?' Maddy said, scowling at him. 'Joseph tried to kill your daughter. For the same reason he killed Ellen Tucker.'

Daniel's face drained of all colour and Esme realised that, even now, he still believed Marianne had killed her. His eyes shot between the two women as the chilling truth seeped into his conscious brain of how he'd been duped by Joseph Brannock for the past 24 years.

From across the yard, they heard a shout from behind the police cordon. A figure dressed in a white protective suit and mask waving his arm in the air, beckoning towards the police detectives huddled together beside a patrol car.

Maddy stood up. 'Looks like they've found something else.'

Esme heard Daniel mutter something under his breath and she turned towards him. His face was drained of all colour, his fists clenched by his sides.

'*What did he mean by protecting Marianne, d'you think?*' she'd asked Maddy a few moments ago. Now she knew. Joseph's manipulation had been even greater than they'd first realised.

'They're going to find Ellen down there, aren't they, Daniel?' she said. He turned to face her, his eyes wild and filled with terror. For a moment she thought he was going to say something, but in the end, he backed away and hurried down the lane towards Marianne.

# 69

A light dusting of snow over Bremleycott churchyard glistened in the sunshine of the bright winter's morning.

Esme pushed open the wooden gate and walked up the flagstone path to the porch where Reverend James Willoughby was waiting. As she stepped inside the porch, she turned to the man accompanying her. Dark haired with a beard. Today he wore a parka over his brown leather jacket.

'James,' she said. 'This is Cody Tremblay.'

'Hey, how ya doing?' the Canadian said, with a wide grin as the two men shook hands.

'I'm doing fine, thank you,' James said. 'It's good to meet you.'

Cody scratched his cheek. 'Esme will have filled you in with my story.' He pronounced her name Es-may with equal emphasis on the two syllables.

'Indeed she has. You were born Dean Tucker, I understand, and adopted as a baby.'

'Yeah, you got it. My adoptive parents emigrated to Canada when I was a few months old. Dad's from Toronto.'

'That's Deene, spelled D, double-E, N, E, James,' Esme said. 'It means hope.'

James smiled. 'Ah, carrying on the family tradition.'

Cody nodded. 'So I've discovered.' He glanced at Esme. 'There's quite a heap of stuff I'm discovering about my birth family.' He turned back to Willoughby. 'Esme here tells me you knew my mother?'

'That's right. For a short time, anyway.' The vicar gestured towards the door of the church. 'Shall we go and sit down inside?'

Esme glanced at her watch. 'I'll leave you two to have a chat, then, shall I?' she said.

'No problem, Esme,' Willoughby said. 'We've plenty of time before the service.'

Esme nodded and pulled on a pair of black leather gloves before stepping out into the sunshine. The tranquillity of the churchyard was the antithesis to the turmoil of the mill scene she and Maddy had witnessed those many weeks before, and she welcomed its restful effect on her state of mind. She turned right out of the porch and strolled down to the old gravestones she'd studied on her last visit.

A small headstone between two taller ones mourned the loss of a child less than a year old, steering Esme's thoughts to Ria's lost baby girl. She'd since learned that the baby had been barely a month old when she'd died after suffering from a respiratory illness. It was rumoured that Ria had come across Joseph standing over the baby's cot, and when paramedics arrived she'd accused him of smothering her little girl. At the time, it was disregarded as the irrational outburst of a grief-stricken mother.

But, as Ria had laid bare moments before she'd pushed him to his death, she held Joseph responsible for much more than the murder of her own baby, blaming him for pushing her husband Scott to his limits, for being the reason Scott had turned to the numbing oblivion of alcohol, until the truth of his father's abhorrent crime finally drove him to suicide.

When the second body had been discovered in the sump beneath the decaying mill wheel, Daniel's horrified reaction confirmed to Esme he'd known it was there. In hiding Ellen's body and concealing the murder, he'd protected not Marianne, but the real killer. But Daniel had said nothing on the matter and, as Esme had only suspicions and no proof, neither had she.

It was when the crime scene investigators stumbled upon further remains, that Esme had finally recalled Ria's earlier words and realised why they'd troubled her. '*My baby wasn't evil*', Ria had yelled in defence of her child. '*No more than the rest of them*.' Who, Esme had wondered, were *the rest of them*?

Part of the answer had come a few days after the fire when Esme got a call from Penny Collins, the founder of the LOST charity. 'The police have been in touch,' she said. 'They're talking of a possible lead on Debbie's disappearance. It seems to be all tied up with the woman you were looking for.'

'Debbie's boyfriend was Scott Brannock, wasn't it?' Esme said. 'It was him she'd gone to see.'

'Yes,' Penny said. 'How did you know?'

Esme had wondered what Ria had known about her husband's former girlfriend. But perhaps the police had made the connection because of where Debbie's body was found.

What more did Ria know? What else had she shared with the police? Would the accidental death of Joseph's wife, Agnes, when Scott was a boy, be re-examined? Though, whether it had been Joseph who'd caused Agnes's fatal fall down the stairs and on to the stone floor below must surely be all but impossible to prove.

Agnes, Debbie, Ellen and Anna. Were there others who Joseph believed fitted his criteria? And why had Ria not been in danger? Esme thought of Anna, a strong, determined woman who knew her own mind. Penny had spoken about her sister in a similar light. Everyone knew how Ellen had been perceived. So what about Agnes? What had she been like? Had she been confident and self-assured too? Joseph had perhaps seen them all as a threat in one way or the other, to himself and to his son and even his grandsons. Perhaps Ria had quickly realised after her husband's death that to survive in the Brannock household, she must adopt a conciliatory tone, become subservient. And while she took on the role of domestic skivvy, she was both useful and safe. It was why she'd never dared challenge Joseph about what he'd done.

Had Joseph's knowledge of his ancestral link to Luke Brannock, who'd murdered a woman with a pitchfork in 1905 in the belief she was a witch, been the driving force behind his distorted views? Maddy had likened Luke Brannock to a 20th century version of The Witchfinder General. Joseph seemed to have taken on the mantle of his *mad ancestor*, as Ria had called him, when he'd tried to justify his murderous actions as stopping the curse. How ironic, Esme thought as she wandered around the back of the church, that it was Joseph's own death that had done that, breaking a feud between the Brannocks and the Meddons, which only existed in his own mind, and preventing the poison seeping into the next generation. She pushed thoughts of Alec Brannock out of her mind. Whatever his misdemeanours, and there were plenty still under investigation by the police, she was certain they were driven by something other than the ideology of a misguided ancestor.

Esme reached the end of the church, having come almost full circle. She looked back towards the wooden entrance gate. A hearse was waiting in the lane and James was standing on the path, talking to the funeral director. Her long brown hair was tied back neatly in a low ponytail and she was dressed in a dark grey suit with a cravat, over which she wore a heavy black coat. She held a top hat in her hand.

Cody stood by the porch and Esme went to join him. 'OK?' she asked.

He nodded. 'Sure.'

It had been Cody who'd hired Sean Carlton to track down his birth mother. In an early report to his client, Carlton, it seemed, had implied he'd uncovered something dubious, promising to be in touch when he'd learned more. When the follow-up never came, and Cody discovered what had happened, he'd come over to the UK to investigate in person.

Conscious of the menace Carlton had stirred up, Cody had given little away until he'd established who he could trust.

Esme looked out across the hedge for any sign of further mourners. She'd told Daniel the time and place. But he'd not given her any indication that he'd be coming. Cody knew nothing of his father. When he was born, Ellen had been under the influence of Arabella's anti-Brannock prejudices. His birth had been registered in Ellen's maiden name, with no father recorded. Daniel had admitted to Esme that Ellen had told him of her pregnancy and the baby's subsequent adoption when she'd come to Bideford in 1995. But, of course, she had no knowledge of the whereabouts of their child.

Daniel had to decide whether he risked damaging further what must already be his fragile relationship with Marianne by telling her that he had a son, and telling Anna that she had a half-brother. While he might point to his willingness to cover up a murder as proof she was more important to him than Ellen, Marianne must always wonder whether, had Ellen not died, Daniel would have chosen her. And then there was the crucial issue of how readily he'd believed Marianne capable of such a crime and her apparent inability to convince him otherwise. Esme guessed that despite the distraction of the arrival of their first grandchild, Alice, there was plenty between them yet left to resolve.

The modest funeral cortege made its way up the stone path, turning right on to the grass and over to the graves in the corner of the churchyard for the simple burial service. The plot beside Arabella had been prepared in readiness and soon mother and daughter would be reunited.

*

As the small gathering sauntered away from the graveside, Esme looked out towards the gate into the road beyond. There was a Land Rover parked against the hedge and a stocky man, wearing a badly fitting suit which looked out of place on his large frame, stood beside it. Daniel. He'd come. She swallowed and turned to Cody.

'There's someone else I'd like to introduce you to, Cody,' she said, damping down a flutter of emotion in her voice. 'He knew Ellen too.'

'That's great,' Cody said, looking around.

'I'll make the introductions, and then I'll be on my way,' Esme said. 'But give me a call later, if you like. Or drop in, if you want to. You know where I live.'

'Sure.' He grinned. 'Cute little place, that. Quite a coincidence that you bought it after I'd stayed there.'

Esme smiled, thinking of Maddy's opinions on coincidences. 'Yes, wasn't it?'

'You sure you don't want to stay and chat?' Cody said. 'You're more than welcome.'

Esme shook her head. 'Thanks, but no. I must get back. It's amazing what damage two kittens can do if you leave them on their own for too long. Now,' she said, pulling on her gloves, 'come and meet Daniel.'

And they turned to walk down the stone path as Daniel came through the gate.

# A Message from the Author

Thank you for reading *The Fear of Ravens*. If you enjoyed the book and have a moment to spare, writing a short review on Amazon or Goodreads (or your favourite site) would be greatly appreciated. Authors rely on the kindness of readers to share their experiences and spread the word.

# Join Us!

To keep updated on giveaways, special promotions and new releases, and to receive my quarterly newsletter, join the Readers Group mailing list.

You can sign up on my website www.wendypercival.co.uk

Subscribers also receive a FREE copy of the Esme Quentin prequel novella:

*Legacy of Guilt*

*The shocking death of a young mother in 1835 holds the key to Esme Quentin's search for truth and justice for her cousin.*

With the tragedy of her past behind her, Esme Quentin has quit her former career, along with its potential dangers, and is looking to the future.

But when she stumbles upon her cousin in traumatic circumstances, Esme realises that her compulsion to uncover the truth, irrespective of the consequences, remains as strong as ever.

You can also visit me on:
Facebook: www.facebook.com/wendypercivalauthor
Twitter: @wendy_percival

I look forward to hearing from you.

Printed in Great Britain
by Amazon

41852376R00199